H🧭RIZON

ARIA WYATT

Cover design by Lori Jackson Design
Photographer: Wander Aguiar
Editing by Silvia's Reading Corner, Eve Arroyo Editing, and The Picky Bitch Editing
Proofreading by My Brother's Editor, Proofingstyle, Inc., and Alexa Gregory
Formatting: Champagne Book Design

ISBN: 978-1-7359505-6-3

When hemispheres collide . . .

It started out innocent.

He was my older brother's best friend. The teen who built sandcastles and splashed in the waves with me when I was a little girl. We'd collect seashells and build moats around our castles to protect the imaginary princess within. He was my Jake. I was his princess.

His summer visits to Australia became less frequent after scoring his first record deal, but I never forgot him. While the multiplatinum singer-songwriter traveled the world, melting hearts and panties with his lyrics, I filled a notebook with his name.

Everything changed when Jake flew in for my brother's thirtieth birthday party. At eighteen, I'd come a long way from the girl he remembered. One lingering touch was all it took to ignite us. I kissed him, but he walked away. He was still on tour, I was about to start college, and let's not forget my hotheaded brother.

But after graduation, when a New York internship opportunity lands me in the Brooklyn brownstone across from his, the ocean between us is replaced with a street.

Jake thinks he can't have me—we're different as earth and sky—but I'll prove him wrong. Those five years of distance only deepened my ache. His demons don't scare me. He's everything I've ever wanted, and I know I can make him happy if he'll let me.
I'm determined to try. After all, his old sweatshirt is not the only thing I've held on to for him . . .

When earth meets sky on the horizon, Jake Bennett,
the King of Ballads, will be mine.

HORIZON

To my cherished friend Melissa,
I admire your ferocity and resilience. I adore you, and I'm beyond thankful
for our years of friendship. Fuck lupus. This book is for you.

Cassandra (and all the other lupus warriors out there), keep fighting.
You rock, lady!

Ho · ri · zon (noun)

Definition of horizon:

The line where the earth seems to meet the sky; the apparent junction of earth and sky.
—Merriam Webster

CONTENT WARNING

This novel explores mental health topics, including depression, anxiety, and obsessive-compulsive disorder. There is extensive discussion about lupus erythematosus, kidney transplants, and cancer. Please read with caution.

IF WE'RE RELATED OR WORK TOGETHER:
Skip the sex scenes. Please & thank you.

PROLOGUE

Isla Rose Emerson, age 18

(Pronounced: EYE-la)
Internal playlist: "Waiting in Vain" by Annie Lennox

Five years ago

It's no secret that tightly woven fabrics excite me. Bonus points awarded if they're stretchy. Today, as I scan the packed private beach, my love affair with spandex and neoprene has never been more relevant. In fact, I'm considering a ménage à trois with nylon and polyester. Maybe even Lycra. If anyone needs me, I'm building a mental shrine for the people who design men's bathing suits.

All around me, blokes wearing boardies, rashies, and wetsuits pulled down to their waists parade their sculpted bodies across the sand. As a girl who grew up toddling in Australia's Bass Strait and Tasman Sea, one would think I'd be used to seeing so many muscles in one place. Nope. Still gets me.

A salty breeze ruffles my hair as the sunset paints streaks of color over the crashing waves. Music is blasting. People are laughing, drinking, and surfing. Someone built a huge bonfire. The crackle of burning wood is barely audible over the surf. Leaping orange flames mesmerize me almost as much as the abundance of rippling abdomens and toned arses . . . *almost.*

I sip my watered-down wine cooler and smile. My oldest brother's birthday bash is the last place I expected to find myself tonight, mainly because I wasn't invited to the bloody thing. That is, according to Reed, middle child, and resident party planner. His decree didn't sit well, so I went over his head and asked Wes. It's *his* birthday, after all.

As the youngest, and the only girl in the family, I'm used to getting what I want—especially from Wes. This time is no exception. So here I sit, feasting my eyes on a delicious buffet of scantily clad musculature.

Across the fire, Reed's still glowering at me. Nothing new. I get it, we're ten years apart and he can't stand me, but that's his problem. Our relationship has never been a close one. Truth be told, it bothers me sometimes. As far as I know, my greatest offense to him was being born. You know, something I had zero control over. I blow him a kiss, and his lip curls.

My gaze drifts to Wes, who's standing near a shed that houses surf equipment, waxing his surfboard. I still can't believe he's thirty. The scar from five years ago contrasts with the bronze of his skin. My fingers instinctively trace along my matching scar—the one that represents our bond and my freedom from dialysis.

It doesn't seem possible I've had his kidney for half a decade. It took years for the doctors to come up with a diagnosis. When they finally did, it was too late. Lupus nephritis landed me in renal failure at age twelve. My health has been a rough ride, but I finally have a handle on my illness. I'm nothing if not resilient, and I'd like to think posttransplant Isla is much stronger. Wiser. More refined and in control.

Mostly.

Movement in the parking area draws my attention. The party has been going since noon, and everyone who was supposed to come is here. A Jeep rolls to a stop, and the driver's door pops open. A man emerges, silhouetted by the glare off the car's windscreen. He walks across the sand, approaching Wes from behind.

Who's this?

I squint and blink a few times, holding up a hand to shield my watery eyes. *Where the hell are my sunglasses?* Lupus makes me extremely photosensitive, which is why I chose to arrive closer to sundown. This time of year, the sun doesn't set until after eight, which means I missed most of the party. Sadly, I didn't have a choice. Even with ample protection, my skin and eyes can't handle sunlight for more than a couple hours.

I blink to clear my vision as mystery man claps my brother's shoulder, causing him to spin around.

"Bennett!" Wes's surfboard and wax hit the sand as he throws his arms around his best mate.

Jake Bennett.

I stare openmouthed at the man I've loved since he built sandcastles and splashed in the waves with me when I was a child. We collected seashells, played Barbies, and he endured endless games of hide and seek. I taught "my Jake" everything I knew about hopscotch.

Now, my Jake is a multiplatinum singer-songwriter with the sexiest voice I've ever heard. I have the audio file for every song he's put out, and I adore listening to his smooth, deep baritone on repeat. I especially love falling asleep to the ballads. Thanks to his touring schedule, I haven't seen him in person in almost three years.

Jake is here.

My.

Jake.

Is.

Here.

Aviator sunglasses obscure his eyes, but I can picture those warm chocolaty irises like I saw them yesterday. Dressed in a plain, gray T-shirt and khaki shorts, with a charcoal hoodie draped over his arm, his muscled physique heats my insides. Forget the blokes in boardies, my reaction to him surpasses sparks, bordering on a bushfire. Factor in his tousled chestnut waves and stubbled jawline, and I'm done for. I've crushed on Jake my whole life, but nothing could've prepared me for this tidal wave of longing.

He doesn't see me yet. Just as well—I need a few minutes to cool down. I duck behind the surf shed. Careful to stay hidden, I peek around the corner to where the men are standing.

Wes grins. "Holy fuck, mate, I didn't think you could make it. I thought you were still on tour."

"I am. Got another six months for this leg, but I had a few days off between shows, so I hopped on a plane." Jake glances at his watch. "I can hang for a couple of hours, but I need to fly out in the morning."

I spy like the quintessential little sister that I am. Perhaps it has something to do with Jake being the speaker, but their conversation is perfectly audible from my vantage point.

Austin "Memphis" Pines, pop star and tonight's chef, jogs over to Jake and Wes. Austin is their other best mate, and the one who brought all the guys together as kids. "Bennett, you made it." He turns to Wes and grins. "Surprise!"

Jake hugs Austin. "What's up, Memphis? You save me any food?"

"Yeah, man. The ribs are almost done, and I made my famous honey-bourbon wings. Saved you some bourbon too."

"Sweet. Thanks." Jake runs a hand through his waves. "I could use a drink after that flight."

"Screaming babies?" Wes asks.

Jake nods. "Triplets."

Wes chuckles. "Ah, the Three Musketeers like us."

Jake, Austin, and Wes are affectionately known in the entertainment industry as the Three Musketeers. Instead of swashbuckling swordsmen, two singers and an actor comprise this inseparable trio, brought together as kids by an international youth talent competition. With Austin hailing from Tennessee, and Jake being a Brooklyn, New York native, their globe-spanning friendship has been going strong for two decades.

My family resides on the Mornington Peninsula, in Victoria, Australia. We're not too far from Melbourne, where our mum works. Wes's acting career has taken him all over the world. He's climbed the ranks and is now a bona fide Hollywood A-lister. Since details about the party were kept under wraps, the paparazzi haven't shown up.

Yet.

Wes's fame is still weird for me—especially the way women throw themselves at him since his lead role in the Olympus Fire franchise. To the rest of the world, Wes is Ares, the Greek god of war. The bikini-clad group of giggling women following him around are clearly enthralled by the Ares persona. To me, he's just my big brother.

"The flight was awful." Jake shakes his head, then massages the back of his neck, making me ache to touch him. "The babies were in the row in front of me. At one time or another, they were barfing, shitting, and screaming."

Wes cocks his head to the side. "You didn't fly first class?"

"Nah, it was booked."

"Thanks for suffering to come to my party."

Jake claps his shoulder. "Of course, man. Happy dirty thirty." He flashes a wicked grin. "I spent the flight thinking up ways to harass your old ass, so you don't miss me too much when I leave."

Wes's booming laugh makes me jump. I'll need to dial back my jitters if I have any hope of interacting with Jake.

"I'd expect nothing less from you, Bennett. And don't worry, I'll be sure to return the favor for your thirtieth."

Austin chuckles and points to the eskies. "Bennett, I'll grab you a drink. Be back in a min."

Reed makes his way over to them and gives Jake a fist bump. "Glad you could make it, mate."

I edge my body away from the shed's corner and peer through a crack instead. If Reed sees me, he'll gladly blow my cover. He fucked up every game of hide and seek we played.

Austin returns, handing Jake a shot of bourbon. "Bottoms up, brotha."

Jake smoothly knocks it back. His throat moves on a swallow, making me jealous of the amber liquid. I glance at the diluted piña colada wine cooler I'm holding like the shitty excuse for a beverage insulted me. Watching everyone party, the subtle lupus reminder may as well be a gut punch. I can't drink hard liquor but wish I could do shots with the guys. I'm so bloody tired of having limitations.

"What's new? How's the family?" Jake asks Wes and Reed.

"Everyone's good, mate. Mum and Dad are on a trip, and Isla's here somewhere," Wes answers, gesturing to the partygoers.

"Really?" Jake scans the beach, his smile doing something to my insides. "I haven't seen Sprite in years. Where is she? I can't wait to catch up."

Oh my God, he wants to talk.

To me.

Sprite is the nickname he gave me when I was a kid because I'd flit around like a bird or a fairy. It's one of my more endearing pet names.

"Yeah, Bird Brain's crashing the party like always," Reed grumbles, ever the sullen fucker.

Wes shakes his head. "Don't call her that. I said Imp could come. Besides, she's not bothering anyone." He smirks and lightly punches Reed's shoulder. "Other than *you*, obviously."

Austin chuckles. "Yeah, be nice to Flight Risk. She brought that mango dessert I can't wait to get my hands on."

Bird Brain, Flight Risk, and Imp. Talk about a shitty nickname trifecta. It's not that they're wrong—I am flighty—but if dialysis taught me anything about myself, it's that I hate being caged. Why stick to the ground when the open sky awaits?

Jake nudges Reed. "I see nothing's changed in the Emerson family."

"Don't remind me," Reed mutters. He shields his eyes, scanning the beach once more. "I swear, she was just here."

I press my body to the weathered building, praying no one spots me. Given my penchant for eavesdropping, I should probably pursue a career in espionage instead of fashion design.

Down the beach, someone calls Wes to help with their surfboard.

"Be right back. Reed, come with me. I want you to meet this bloke." He jogs across the sand.

Reed limps after him. The familiar wave of sadness crests as I watch him move. It's no wonder he's miserable. A drunk driver shattered his acting career, along with his leg and vertebrae when he was my age. He hasn't been the same since. The only positive to come of it was Cora Priest, his physical therapist girlfriend. Only Cora sees Reed's soft side. Much as his distance hurts me, I'm grateful he has her to turn to.

Austin laughs, bringing my focus back to him and Jake. They discuss some music industry stuff, and I continue to listen, hanging on every word that leaves Jake's lush lips.

Cora catches sight of me after retrieving a dry towel from her car. She cocks her head at my position behind the shed.

I hold a finger to my lips and wave her over.

"Why're ya hidin' out here, love?" she whispers.

"Oh, uh . . . well, I—"

Her knowing smirk stops me as heat floods my face. "He's only gonna be here a few hours, so you'd better make it count."

"Please don't tell my brothers," I whisper.

She wraps her little finger around mine and tightly squeezes. "Pinky promise."

Cora is the big sister I've always wanted, and our bond makes up for what I lack with Reed. We've been sharing secrets for years, sealed with our signature promise.

"Thank you." I meet her emerald gaze before gesturing to my bikini. I'm also wearing a floral sarong since I'm more than a little body conscious. "Do I look all right?" I smooth my hair and show my teeth. "Any lettuce?"

Cora giggles. "No herbs or other greenery. You look stunning, as always. Are they new bathers?"

"Yeah."

"Well, I approve. Yellow's your color." She motions to my chest. "The halter makes your boobs look bigger *and* shows off your new ink."

"Good. That's what I was hoping for."

Despite my nicknames, I like birds. So much, that I got a huge phoenix tattoo on my eighteenth birthday to symbolize my freedom from dialysis. Situated on my upper back, the colorful bird's wings stretch across my shoulders. Wes has a much smaller one on the inside of his left wrist. Matching scars, tattoos, and eye color are only a few things I have in common with my favorite brother.

I touch my transplant scar. "Does this look bad?" Cora cocks a brow, and I backpedal. "Yeah, yeah, I know. Battle scars and all."

"Your beauty's soul deep, Little Bird. Now, get your arse over there before your brothers cockblock ya."

I snort. "I don't think Moody Melvin would give a shit either way, but Wes may be an issue."

"That's an understatement, love." She grips my shoulders. "You know damn well he's fierce about you."

I sigh. "Yeah, well, at least one of them is."

Cora bites her lip. "Reed loves you. He's just—"

"Reed."

"Right. Where is he, anyway?"

I pick up a conch shell near my feet and turn it over in my hands, admiring the smooth, pink inside. "He's up the beach helping Wes with somebody's board."

"Still pouting?" she asks.

"Of course."

"I can't do anything about keeping Wes occupied, but I'll try to keep Reed out of your hair tonight." She squeezes my shoulder. "Call me tomorrow with details."

"I will." I watch Cora leave before making my way toward Jake.

In my hurry to hide, I left my thongs by the bonfire. I slide the yellow shoes back on and summon my inner wild child.

Pretransplant Isla didn't take risks. I followed the rules and did what was expected of me. My reward? I was chained to dialysis for over a year. Now, I live my life by my rules. I follow my heart, and my dreams, like they could be shattered at any moment. Should I do more looking and less leaping? Probably.

But being careful didn't save my kidneys.

Austin's at the grill, brushing more sauce onto his famous chicken wings. Jake stands near the coolers, tapping out a text on his phone.

Now or never.

Suppressing the little voice telling me he might be texting a woman, I stop beside Jake and touch his arm. "Hey, you."

He turns to face me, and his brow furrows, his gaze searching my face. "Hey . . ." He slides his phone into a pocket.

My innards shrivel at the realization he doesn't recognize me. It hurts more than a little. Yeah, maybe I have come a long way from the dorky, awkward version of myself he'd last seen. I'm taller. My skin's clear. Teeth are straight, and I finally have boobs—sort of. Wes does his best to shield me from the spotlight, and social media isn't my thing, so I haven't posted a picture in ages. But still . . . It can't be possible he doesn't know it's me.

I hand Jake the shell. "It's been a while."

His frown deepens as his fingers close around it. "Uh, thanks."

"Put it with Malibu Stacy." I give him an exaggerated wink. Years back, I'd given him one of my Barbies. According to Wes, he'd kept her. "I hear she's still in existence."

His brows shoot upward. "Holy shit." His jaw drops open, and he blinks a few times before shaking his head. "Isla?" My name leaves his lips on a husky whisper, and everything inside me catches fire.

"Was starting to think you'd forgotten me."

"No, I . . . uh—" Jake clears his throat and looks me over, his attention like a physical touch. "I'm sorry for swearing, but I didn't recognize you." His gaze snaps to mine, and redness creeps across his cheeks, spreading to his neck and ears. "You've grown up."

My gaze sweeps over him, mirroring his eyeball caress. "You too." I realize how lame I sound but being this close to him makes me incapable of a better reply. "I mean, obviously you've *been* an adult—"

He motions to my wine cooler. "You're drinking?"

"Good observation."

Jake rubs the back of his neck. "Let me rephrase. *Why* are you drinking?"

"You sound like my brothers. I'm of age, ya know."

Pocketing the conch shell, he steps closer to me. "Seems that way."

"Which means a wine cooler's a perfectly acceptable refreshment."

His gaze wanders to my scar and lingers, making me feel more exposed than if I'd skipped the bathers entirely. "It's acceptable for someone other than you."

"It's my first one. Besides, my liver's fine." I lift the bottle to my lips. "One wine cooler won't kill me."

In a lightning bolt move, he snatches the bottle before I realize what's happening and tilts it on end. "I'd rather not take that chance."

Cool liquid spatters my ankles and soaks into the sand at my feet.

My hands fly to my hips. "Uh, excuse me, do ya mind?"

"Actually, I do. You need to take care of yourself. Don't be reckless with your health, Sprite."

I cross my arms over my chest. "I'm *not* reckless."

He lifts a brow and holds up the empty. "Fine. We'll call it nonchalance."

I clench my jaw and stare at the waves. I'm not some foolish ankle-biter in need of a scolding. And while I take some risks, I'm not irresponsible. The last thing I'd do is jeopardize my transplanted kidney. I endured dialysis for over a year while my family went through a battery of compatibility tests. Wes was the only match, and our surgeries were the day after his twenty-fifth birthday. He gave me a new life like it was as simple as sharing chips with me. I'm forever grateful for his sacrifice and furious Jake thinks I'd take it lightly.

Jake tilts my chin to face him. "Don't be mad, Sprite. I'm only looking out for you."

That's the problem. Everyone's always looking out for me. People treat me like a bloody fuckwit hanging out at the edge of a cliff, incapable of self-preservation. I'm not some fragile little girl who can't hold her own—I'm a fucking survivor.

"Who said I'm mad?"

His plush lips quirk into a smile. "Just a hunch."

"I wanted the freedom to celebrate my brother's birthday like a normal person. For the record, my doctor said it was fine." I point to the empty bottle. "I chose a wine cooler with the lowest possible alcohol content, poured out half, and refilled it with water. That diluted monstrosity is the only one I've had, and I nursed it for over an hour."

Then you show up and have the balls to dump it in the fucking sand.

He holds his hands up in surrender. "Okay, I'm sorry. Didn't mean to upset you."

"I'm not upset." At his raised eyebrow, I stiffen my spine. "And I'm not reckless *or* nonchalant. I can look out for myself."

"Hey." He sets down the empty and grips my shoulders. "No one's questioning that."

"You're insinuating I'm a birdbrained lush."

He tightens his grip, fury flashing in his gaze. Framed by thick, dark lashes, the chocolaty depths unravel me. "You know damn well that's not what I meant." My lungs hold oxygen captive as he steps closer. "No one's questioning your ability to look out for yourself, Isla Rose Emerson. Especially, not me."

I nearly moan when his deep voice rumbles my full name. The air between us crackles. His pupils dilate, telling me he feels it too.

Jake consumes my senses—every sight, every sound, every scent. Crashing waves fade into the background, replaced by our breaths. The bonfire's smoke dissipates, and I savor his clean, woodsy scent. As I stand before the boy who I've known my whole life, I drink in his muscles, his stubbled jaw, his heated gaze. My eyes flick to his dimples—visible even when he's not smiling. Thick waves fall over his forehead. I want to thread my fingers through them, pull his face to mine, and kiss him with everything I've got.

He releases my shoulders and clears his throat, taking a step back. "Let's start over. How have you been?"

His sudden distance brings me back to reality. I'm his best mate's little sister—not one of the beautiful women ogling him from across the fire. So help me God, if they start following him like they've been doing to Wes, I'll lose my shit.

I draw a calming breath and come back to center. "Great. I signed up for uni next year."

"You still interested in fashion design?"

"Yes." I cock my head to the side. "I'm surprised you remember."

"I remember everything," he murmurs, casting a glance at his feet. "It's a gift and a curse."

"There's my favorite imp!" Wes bounds over, stopping beside Jake, who takes another step back and stuffs his hands inside his pockets. Wes ruffles my hair with one of his massive paws and flashes me a grin. "Thought you went home already."

I strike a pose. "Nope. I'm still here in all my glory."

Something flares in Jake's gaze, and he looks out at the ocean.

"Good. I was worried Reed made you leave." Wes glances at Jake. "You eat yet, mate?"

"Nah, I'm good. Thanks." He uses the tip of his foot to line up some shells. "I, uh, grabbed a panini at the airport."

Funny, he was just asking Austin if he saved him something to eat.

"All right, well, don't be shy. Memphis made more food than we know what to do with."

Jake nods, plopping onto a log near the fire.

Needing some distance between us before I combust, I settle across the way and peer at him through the flames. His molten gaze never leaves mine, even as people gather around the fire, laughing, singing, and sharing memories. Jake watches me with an intensity that defies his laid-back demeanor—elbows resting on bent knees, fingers steepled in front of his lips. No one has ever looked at me like this. He's certainly never looked at me this way before.

I shift on the log and brush sand off my ankles. My skin's gritty, yet sticky from my spilled drink. I rub particles between my fingers, picturing the sandcastles of my youth. We didn't have much growing up, but our family spent a lot of time at the beach, especially when Austin and Jake visited from the States. Before his motorcycle accident, Reed was an avid surfer. He and Wes spent hours riding waves and even attempted to teach Austin. Jake was never interested in surfing—content to watch from a distance and build castles with Mum and me.

Jake let me use the shovel to dig, while he used his hands as spades. Our castles were never sprawling structures, instead, they were tall. He showed me how to use wet sand as plaster to make them structurally sound, but ours still teetered precariously. That was part of the excitement.

We loved seeing how tall we could make them before they fell. Then we'd start again with a new one rising from the ruins of the last.

I remember sloshing back and forth with buckets of seawater to fill the moat. We always had a moat—a requirement of mine. Once the foamy moat water was deep enough, we'd set sail a fleet of boats. I called them guard boats, for the purpose of protecting the princess, of course. He'd laugh when I insisted we decorate the castle with seaweed and shells, but he let me do it. We'd stroll along the beach collecting shells, bits of urchin cases, and sea glass. He'd carry the bucket when it got too heavy for me.

The boy in the red swim trunks had messy chestnut waves. I peer across the fire into the eyes of the man he's become.

The man I want.

He stares, gaze swirling with unnamed emotions. *What's on his mind?* Is his head taking him on a trip down memory lane too? Does he feel this magnetism, this inexplicable pull between us? Does he sense this attraction that started long before either of us understood what it was? Warmed by memories and the heat in his expression, I smile.

He returns the smile, stealing my breath. My sanity. My heart. My hand instinctively flies to my chest.

He's mine. He's always been mine.

The soul-deep realization floors me. Veins thrum with knowledge. My heart hammers against my ribcage. As each shaky inhale expands my lungs, I fight the urge to throw myself in his lap.

The breeze picks up, and I shiver. I should've brought something to change into, but I was excited to come and forgot. I briskly rub the goose bumps on my arms, willing them away.

Jake frowns and climbs to his feet, walking over to me. He shrugs out of his hoodie and holds it out. "Put this on, Sprite."

I pull it over my head. "Thank you."

He nods and returns to his spot, hard nipples visible beneath his thin T-shirt as he lines up bits of sea glass by his feet.

Cloaked in his warmth, my body relaxes, and the chills stop. I glance down at the maroon block lettering spelling out Brooklyn and slide my hands into the pockets. They close around something metal—his keys. I make a mental note to tell him before he heads out. Another thought punches my gut.

He's on tour for six more months.

The pain surprises me. I burrow deeper into the heavy sweatshirt and breathe in his scent, my eyes fluttering closed. It's decided—he's not getting it back. I'll wear it until it's threadbare.

Three hours later, Jake glances at his watch and stands to hug my brother. "Happy birthday, Wes. I'm gonna head back to my hotel."

My heart sinks, the ache in my chest making it hard to breathe. I've been dreading this moment since he arrived.

"Thanks for making the trip, mate. Means a lot."

"Anytime, man."

Jake bids everyone goodbye and makes his way to me. His eyes capture mine. "It was really good seeing you, Sprite."

"You too," I whisper. "Good luck on the rest of your tour. Be safe out there."

"Will do, thanks. Good luck with college. Make us proud."

"I will." *Please tell me I'll see you before then.* "Wait, don't forget your hoodie." I tug at the hem.

"Keep it." He stops me with a hand on my shoulder and a devastating smile. "It looks much better on you."

"Thanks." My throat is thick with emotion. I want to say more, but words won't come.

Jake squeezes my shoulder, his warmth radiating through the sweatshirt. "Promise you'll take care of yourself, Isla Rose."

I clench my jaw and nod. He gives everyone a wave and trudges across the beach toward the parking area.

I meet Cora's gaze across the fire. Her compassion-filled smile is enough to make my tears well. Thank God, my brothers are oblivious. I stare at my feet and shove shaking hands inside my pockets.

His keys.

"Shit." I leap to my feet and hold them up. "He needs these."

I sprint after Jake, my bare soles sliding in the cooling sand. Thanks to my achy joints and wobbly ankles, beach jogs are no picnic. Too bad I have a habit of chasing after things I shouldn't catch.

Standing in the dark lot near the Jeep he rented, Jake tries the door handles and searches his pockets.

"Wait!" I catch up and wave the keys. "You forgot—" My foot snags on a rock, launching me into him. Our collision sends him stumbling backward against the car.

"Whoa. Easy, Sprite." He holds me to his warm, hard chest.

"Sorry." I clutch his shoulders. "Didn't see that rock."

"You need to be more careful. You'll break an ankle if you keep running in the dark. This isn't what I meant when I told you to take care of yourself."

I grip the front of his shirt, desperate to keep him here. "I don't want you to leave."

"Isla, I—"

Our eyes meet. Once again, the rest of the world disappears. We're alone in this perfect, electrifying moment. I feel him from my scalp to my toes—a bone-deep awareness that leaves me breathless.

"Don't go." I lick my lips, and his eyes track the movement. "Please."

His gaze flickers to mine and darkens, pupils dilating. "Why?"

Now or never.

I grip the sides of his face, pull his lips to mine, and kiss him like my life depends on it. Every breath, every heartbeat begins and ends with him. I want to spend the rest of my life kissing him.

Only him.

A groan escapes his chest. His thick, strong arms tighten around me. He deepens the kiss, sweeping his tongue into my mouth.

I clasp the back of his neck and pull him closer. He groans again and spins us, pressing me against the vehicle. He leans into the kiss, and his muscular thigh wedges between my legs, the friction making me moan. The rock-hard length of him presses into the side of my belly. Fire spreads through my veins, burning a path from my head to my heart and beyond.

Jake weaves his hands into my hair, fingers tugging the strands. Our tongues stroke and slide against each other with a desperation that surpasses anything I've felt. This isn't my first kiss, but so help me God, I wish it were. Now I *know* what I've been missing. I know beyond a shadow of a doubt nothing will ever compare to this.

He's mine. He'll be my first.

The thought unleashes a flood of heat between my thighs. I've had plenty of boyfriends, but I've never had sex—never really wanted to. Now, with my knees weak and palms sweating, I want nothing more than to feel

Jake inside me. Holding me. Loving me. Whispering my name in the darkness. The thought consumes me until he's all I know. His masculine scent. His warmth. His kiss, with the brush of lips and scrape of stubble. The weight and heat of his body pressed against mine. His fingers tugging my hair, pulling me closer, deeper.

Jake jerks his lips from mine and jumps back like I'm a leper. Eyes wild and chest heaving, his expression's a mix of shock and horror that rips my heart in two.

"What's wrong?" I gasp.

"I have to go."

"Let me come with you."

He squeezes his eyes shut. "No."

"Jake, please—"

"I've gotta go." His voice is cold and distant, like we're strangers. Like he didn't kiss me into oblivion. "I'm sorry."

I watch in bewilderment as he unlocks and yanks the door open, hops inside, and guns the engine.

He rolls down his window. "Please take care of yourself, Isla."

"Jake—" My voice breaks on the sob lodged in my throat. "Don't leave."

"I'm sorry, Sprite." He speeds away, taking my heart with him.

CHAPTER 1

Jake Bennett

Mood: "Speechless" by Dan + Shay
Present day

She's here.

I've traveled the world, witnessed some truly breathtaking vistas, but none compare to this. My heart catapults into my throat, watching Isla descend the escalator to the waiting area near the gate.

The lack of clothing on her willowy frame doesn't surprise me—she's never been one to cover up—not that I'm complaining. My gaze journeys along the expanse of flawless skin like she's a desert oasis.

And I'm fucking parched.

My body temperature ratchets up a few degrees, but it's still bitter cold outside. Gladiator sandals and a floral bohemian sundress, with its thigh-skimming hemline, is hardly November attire. Not in New York, anyway. I didn't check the weather in Melbourne. I didn't check much of anything other than my zipper, stove knobs, and door locks. The hours since I received her call are a blur, and I'm surprised I made it to the right airport, let alone the correct terminal.

JFK is a mob scene, courtesy of the upcoming holiday. I can't accuse her of poor planning. Australians don't celebrate American Thanksgiving.

Surprising her brother for his belated birthday bash next weekend is reason enough for the trip.

I squeeze my phone. "I gotta go. She's here."

Jesse chuckles in my ear. "Oh, so I'm dismissed?"

"For now."

"Do yourself a favor and pick your jaw up off the floor."

My childhood best friend is the only person who understands the approaching woman's impact on my being. Jesse Quinn knows absolutely everything about me, which is how he can tell I'm gaping without laying eyes on my stupid slack jaw.

I snort and close my mouth. "Thanks."

He laughs. "Remember what I said . . . I know it's hard but try not to act like a bumbling idiot."

"No guarantees," I mutter. "Catch you later."

"Good luck, man." He hangs up.

As Isla steps off the escalator, wheeled carry-on in tow, I linger to the side, ever the dumbstruck fool. I need a few moments to take her in before I attempt interacting. *Who am I kidding?* Like Jesse said, even after days of preparation, I'd still be a bumbling idiot.

With her dewy, porcelain skin, golden-brown waves, and cobalt-colored eyes, Isla Rose Emerson is a goddess. She's an ethereal, beachy vision with a heart of gold and legs that go on for days. She's also the much younger sister of Wes Emerson, my hotheaded best friend of too many years to count. Isla is forbidden in every sense of the word. Yet I've wanted her for longer than I have a right to.

I'll never forget that weekend in Australia five years ago when I flew in for Wes's birthday. She sidled up to me in her yellow string bikini, handed me a seashell, and smiled. The little girl who tagged along—the one I collected shells and built sandcastles with—had become a woman. She was gorgeous. Flirty, yet sweet, she looked at me like I was her hero. She kissed me, and at barely eighteen, ruined me for all other women. We've crossed paths a few times since then, but I've kept my distance. There's no sense torturing myself when I can't have her.

Now, she's twenty-three and hotter than lava. I'm thirty-three and ready to erupt. If Wes knew the thoughts running through my head, I have no doubt he'd castrate me—and feed me my own balls. My hands instinctively brush my zipper, checking my fly for the sixty-fifth time since I got here.

It's zipped. Just like it was three minutes ago.

Isla spots me and smiles. I stop breathing.

Me thinks barbeque will be the best dipping sauce for my family jewels.

She glides through the crowd, closing the distance between us. Fresh faced and makeup free, you'd never know she spent more than twenty hours in the air.

She throws her arms around my neck and kisses my cheek. "Jake, it's so great to see ya."

I've always enjoyed listening to Wes and Reed talk. Their accents and lingo amuse me. Wes has come out with some hilarious sayings that have kept me on my toes over the years, and I've incorporated a few into my day-to-day speech. But with Isla, it's different. She makes the Australian accent sound fluid and sexy as hell. It's no exaggeration to call her voice an aphrodisiac—especially the way she says my name.

My arms find her waist and pull her close. "Great seeing you too, Sprite."

Her hair tickles my nose as I breathe in her scent. *Dessert.* Warm coconut with a hint of mango. I've never smelled anything more enticing.

"Thanks for coming for me. Sorry for the short notice. Lena had something pop up at the last minute."

Lena Hamilton, aka matchmaker extraordinaire. I chuckle because I know damn well Wes's girlfriend has nothing going on today. She told me so herself. This is all part of Lena's elaborate scheme—a ploy that I am *not* buying in to.

I close my eyes, trying to memorize how it feels to hold Isla. *Perfection.* She's everything soft and fragrant, just like I remember from five years ago. This hug is all I'll allow myself, so I savor the fuck out of it. And God, does the embrace do something to me on a fundamental level. I should let go of her, take a few steps back, place as much distance as humanly possible between us. No, what I should really do is bury this desire before it destroys us both. I refuse to smother her with my pathology. Bottom line, I'm a needy motherfucker and she can't give me what I need.

Isla melts into my hug. "You're nice and warm."

"Where's your coat?" I tighten my arms around her. "Please tell me you brought one."

"I did."

I pull back slightly to meet her gaze. I'm six foot one and we're damn near eye to eye. "Then, why aren't you wearing it?"

"Well . . ." She gnaws her lower lip and something inside my chest tightens. I love how her Amazonian height brings her plush, beautiful lips closer to mine. "I packed it in my suitcase."

I release her—not because I want to stop hugging her, but because my cock is stirring. Pretty much the last thing I need right now.

She's off-limits.

"Your suitcase? That's a good place for it." I lift her carry-on and nudge her along. "C'mon, let's find the baggage claim so you can put on some clothes."

She laughs. "I'm wearing clothes."

"Maybe something a bit more weather appropriate?"

"It was warm when I left home." She spins dramatically. "And I wanted to show you my dress."

The lavender frock, with its little white flowers and off-the-shoulder neckline, showcases her curves. Since she's not overly busty, Isla can get away with not wearing a bra—when it isn't freezing cold. Now? Not so much. Perky breasts tease me from beneath the material. Images of her in that yellow bikini come to mind. How I wanted to untie it with my teeth, kiss and lick her until she moaned my name. My cock stands at attention.

Please tell me my fly is zipped.

"Beautiful." I force my gaze from her body, but I'm too late. She caught me staring. *Fuck.*

A sultry smile curves her lips. "Thanks. It's one of my own creations."

She majored in fashion design, but this is the first I've seen of her work. The woman clearly knows her way around a sewing machine.

Wes mentioned a few months ago his sister was looking at internships, but I never imagined she'd choose one in Manhattan. Last week, when Lena let it slip Isla was moving to Brooklyn, I nearly choked to death on a mouthful of wine.

Oh, but it got even better.

Since Wes didn't want Isla living alone in the big city, he purchased the newly listed brownstone across the street from mine. No biggie.

"I hear we're gonna be neighbors," I say.

It's a reality that entices and terrifies me, since I can better handle my attraction with an ocean between us. I'm not on tour right now, so I spend most of my time at home or in my studio.

"I know!" she squeals, hugging me. "I'm so excited to move in."

"When's that happening?"

"Wes said probably late December."

"Nice. Let me know how I can help." We silently shift out of the way of oncoming travelers and stand in comfortable silence for a beat or two. Desperate to hear her voice again, I smile and gesture to her dress. "I see purple's still your favorite color."

Her brows pop. "You remembered?"

"Yeah." *I remember everything about you.*

"I have a ton of pictures on my phone. I'll show ya the whole collection." She giggles. "And yes, there's heaps of purple."

"I've yet to master an iron and you're actually making clothes. I'm impressed."

She laughs. "You can't iron?"

"Nope. That's what dryers are for," I tell her with a wink. "The baggage claim's over here." We stop at the carousel with her flight number listed. "What does your suitcase look like?"

"It's a shiny blue one with a yellow ribbon." She stands beside me, scanning the bags. "They were unloading the plane when I got off. I figured it would be here by now."

"Oh my God!" A woman approaches to our left, an awestruck expression on her face. "Jake Bennett, is it really you?"

"Yeah."

"I'm so sorry to be annoying, but could I please have a picture with you? I'm a huge fan."

"Sure." I set the carry-on down and lean in for an awkward, outstretched-arm selfie.

Fan encounters come with the territory, and I always make time for my fans. I wouldn't be where I am without them. I have no problem posing for pictures or signing autographs, as long as they're not too pushy.

Fame is something I have in common with my other two best friends, but Jesse is a regular dude. I'm somewhere in between. The level of attention I receive is manageable. What they deal with is downright stifling. Fortunately, they're both taken. Austin's engaged and Wes is likely heading there. Me? Not so much. I'm unlucky in love, and I've been the odd man out for longer than I care to remember.

Isla moves her carry-on out of the way and touches the woman's shoulder. "Let me see your phone. I'll take a picture for ya."

"Thank you so much." The woman glances up at me. "I loved your last album. I can't wait to hear what's in store for the new one—especially your collaborations with Austin Pines."

"Thank you. We're still working on it, but this album's been a lot of fun to make."

"Do you think you'll do a tour after it releases?"

It's not official yet, but Austin and I are discussing the possibility of a dual-headliner tour when our collaboration album comes out. In the past, we've both done extended world tours that last for a year or two. *If* we make this one happen, it will be *much* shorter.

I can't suppress my Cheshire cat grin. "Maybe."

Her eyes light up. "Oh my God! I'm *beyond* stoked. I'll buy tickets the second they go on sale. Seeing my two favorite singers on stage together would be a dream come true."

My heart swells with her enthusiasm. "Thank you so much. Austin and I appreciate your support. What's your name?"

"Julie."

"Nice to meet you, Julie."

"All right, gimme a big smile," Isla commands, holding up the phone. I loop an arm over Julie's shoulder and do as instructed.

"I never noticed your dimples in pictures," Julie says, pointing to my face.

"He's had them forever," Isla informs her. "But he's certainly been hitting the gym." She flashes her breath-stealing smile and heat spreads from my cheeks to my neck and ears.

"Thanks for noticing."

I admit, I'm pleased she noticed. I've been busting my ass at the gym ever since my trip to Alaska, where it became abundantly clear I needed to lift some weights. Nothing highlights one's weaknesses like having their ass handed to them by Mother Nature. Isla knows all about the guys' trip Wes, Austin, and I went on. Courtesy of the media, so does the rest of the world. We spent three weeks stranded in the wilderness. Three weeks wondering if we'd make it out alive. After suffering a brutal fall and subsequent near drowning, Wes almost didn't. It pays to have a trauma nurse in your circle, and I hate to think what would've happened if Lena hadn't been there.

"Duh. Of *course*, I noticed. I felt your muscles when you hugged me," Isla explains.

I release a rough exhale. *I hope my muscles are the only thing she felt when we hugged.*

Julie grins. "Just keep singing. Your voice is phenomenal. Honestly, you're like a fine wine. You keep getting better."

"Wow, Julie. You're making me blush." Ears burning with her praise, I smile and squeeze her shoulders. "That means a lot. Thank you so much for listening."

"Thank *you* for making music. And for everything you do for the community." She accepts her phone from Isla and flashes a huge grin. "Nice meeting you, Jake. I hope to see you and Austin at Madison Square Garden. Hint, hint."

I laugh. "Don't worry. We'd never skip the Garden."

She rubs her hands together with excitement. "Can't wait."

"Take care, Julie. And thanks again."

Isla watches Julie leave and turns to face me. "That was sweet. Your fans are polite and appreciative. I *hate* the shit Wes deals with."

"Yeah, well, unlike your brother, I'm not seen as a sex object."

"You should be."

Wait, what? I open and close my mouth, but words won't come.

Isla squeezes my biceps. "You were in sex object territory *long* before these got so big." She meets my gaze. "For me, anyway."

My mind takes me back to our kiss, like it's done every goddamn day since it happened. She kissed me like she was starved for me, like she only had eyes for me. It was nothing short of earth shattering. It broke my heart to walk away from her, but I had to.

For the past five years, I've pined from a distance, kicking myself for walking away. I've dreamed of her. Burned and ached for her. I've even written several songs about Isla—some more obvious than others—which is how Lena knew of my predicament in the first place. No one does blunt better than Lena, and I'll never forget the way she called me out in Alaska.

Yes, I'm in love with Isla Rose Emerson, but it's a love I can't act on. I respect her brothers too much to jeopardize our friendship, and I respect her too much to threaten her bond with Wes.

If I'm being honest, Wes is only the tip of the iceberg. Even if Isla weren't his sister, it could never work between us. She's only moving to New York for one year. Then she'll be gone, off to pursue bigger and better things. I'm at the point in my life where I need someone who will stick around. Isla doesn't keep men in her orbit for more than a few months. Every time I adjust to the idea of her seeing someone new, she kicks him to the curb. Her revolving-door love life has always baffled me, but it's not like I can ask Wes about it. He'd get suspicious and kick my ass. Not to mention, her choices are none of my business.

While we shared the best kiss of my life, for her it was just that—a kiss. I'm a pair of lips among the many dudes she's kissed. No matter how much she flirts, I won't delude myself into thinking she's interested. Besides, my baggage is far heavier than anything I'd shoulder her with.

She's off-limits. Off. Limits.

"Thanks," I mumble, reciting the mantra in my head.

Isla returns her attention to the baggage carousel. "I wonder what's taking so long."

I point to the far side of the belt. "I think I see it."

"Yes, that's the one." She rushes over.

I follow a few steps behind, stopping her when she reaches for the luggage. "Let me carry it."

"Careful. It's really heavy."

"Pretty sure I can manage, Sprite." I lift her suitcase from the belt and extend the handle. "You want to dig out that coat of yours now?"

She grimaces. "It's stuffed in there. I don't want my shit falling out in the middle of the airport."

"Well, you're not going outside like that. C'mon." I guide her to an airport gift shop and motion to a rack of sweatshirts. "Pick one."

She touches my arm. "I'm fine, Jake. Really."

"It's cold out. Pick one, or I'll pick it for you."

She smirks, jabbing a finger in the middle of my chest. "Getting mighty bossy, Jake Bennett. Sounds like you've been spending too much time with Wes."

I snort. "We can revisit that statement when I start banging my chest and stomping around here like a caveman." I head for the rack and select a purple "I love New York" hoodie. "This work for you?"

"Is it a medium?"

I find the tag. "Yep."

"Then, yes."

Some heathen messed with the hangers, so I put the shirts in size order before making my way to the register to pay the cashier. When he hands me my change, I take a moment to fix the bills so they're all facing the same direction, arranging them from smallest denomination to largest. *There. Much better.* I can't have a haphazard wallet.

I hold the hoodie out to Isla. "Put this on."

An unnamed emotion flares in her gaze, and I can't tell whether it's pain or something else. "Thank you," she murmurs, pulling it over her head.

"Better?"

"Yes."

"Next item on the docket is food. What do you feel like having?"

She gives me a sheepish smile. "I was hoping we could stop at a grocery store on the way to your flat. I'm on a strict diet."

"Diet?" I balk at her statement. "Why the fuck do you need to diet? You're perfect."

I have a handful of close friends with eating disorders, so society's toxic relationship with body image—especially for women—hurts my soul. The idea of anyone projecting that negativity onto Isla, or insinuating her body needs changing, *infuriates* me.

"Well, thanks." She flushes and toys with the clasp on her necklace. "But it's an anti-inflammatory diet that's supposed to help with my lupus."

"Right. Sorry. I thought you were referring to weight loss." I hold up my hands in surrender. "I mean, I'm *not* implying you need to lose weight. Or that you're too skinny. Your body is perfect. Not that body type has anything to do with anything. Because it doesn't." I rub my jaw, pondering my statement's inaccuracy. "Well, it *shouldn't*—fuck society's idealism—but that's another story."

She blinks. "Huh?"

"What I mean is, you're perfectly fine the way you are. Not *just* fine though. I mean, you're way better than fine. You're perfect. Besides, what matters is you're healthy. Obviously."

Shut the fuck up, Jake. I pinch the bridge of my nose, wondering when I'll stop vomiting words. *Why do I always make an ass of myself?*

"Okay . . ." She lifts an eyebrow as if waiting for my tirade to continue, but I'm all done now.

Feeling a wee bit foolish for getting unnecessarily amped up, I clear my throat. "You know what? Never mind. Ignore me."

Amusement dances in her eyes. "So . . . can we go to the grocery store?"

"Of course we can. Or, if you'd prefer, I can drop you off at home and then I'll go. I'm sure you're jet-lagged—you should probably rest."

Her face lights up like I offered her a million dollars. "Oh, I'd *love* a nap."

"Then that's what we'll do. Make me a shopping list, and I'll take care of everything."

"Are ya sure? It's pretty specific."

"Whatever you need."

I'll take care of you, sweetheart. My hand clenches on the suitcase handle. *No, you won't. She's too young, you stupid fuck.*

She clasps my wrist with cool fingertips. "Thank you."

"My pleasure, Sprite." I meet her gaze. "I'm serious. You let me know what you need, and I'll make it happen."

Traffic was a bitch today. A trip that should've taken a half hour at most, was twice that. To my delight, there's close parking for once, so I stop the car in front of my brownstone.

Isla dozes in the passenger seat wearing the sweatshirt I bought her, dark sunglasses resting atop her head. Beautiful and peaceful in slumber, her gorgeous eyes are hidden behind her lids. I love her eyes—they knock me senseless and move me in ways I don't fully understand.

But life can be cruel sometimes. Case in point, Isla and Wes share the same eye color. For the past five years, every time I looked at him, I saw *her*. The constant reminder fucks me up. Same with the guilt. He's my best friend and I want his little sister—it's like I'm betraying him.

I gently nudge her shoulder. "Wake up, sleepyhead. We're here."

Those eyes flutter open and pierce my soul like always. She takes a moment to get her bearings before pointing to the brownstones across the street. "Which one's mine?"

"The one with the blue front door."

She nods. "Would it piss you off if I painted it purple?"

I laugh. "Of course not. Do whatever you like. Purple, lime green, I don't care. Just keep it locked."

"Why? Is this a dangerous neighborhood?"

"No, but it's not like your parents' place, either." Brooklyn and Australia are worlds apart—figuratively and literally.

"Are there trains near here? Or should I get a car?"

I shake my head. "You don't need a car. You've got plenty of mass transit options. There are buses, taxis, the subway, and Ubers."

"I'm a little nervous about being in New York City for my internship." She bites her lower lip. And fuck, does it make me want to tug it between my teeth and kiss her senseless.

I shift in my seat. "I'll show you around, and once you've been here for a while, you'll get used to it."

She squeezes my arm. "Thanks for reassuring me. I think what freaks me out most is the subway."

"My studio's in Manhattan. I go there most days, so I'll drive you if that makes you feel better."

Her eyes widen. "You'd do that?"

I'd do anything for you.

"I'll take you anywhere you want to go, Sprite."

Her gaze, full of need, lingers on mine. I feel her pull—magnetic, electric, and fucking soul deep. I want to cradle her face and kiss her again, feel those soft lips on mine. I want to hold her close and make love to her. And I almost tell her. Luckily, the rational side of my brain kicks in.

She's forbidden.

I unfasten my seat belt. "Let's go inside."

She nods, climbs from the car, and meets me around the back. I unload her stuff and carry it up the stoop, pausing to press the button on my keys. My car beeps, but I press it two more times.

Just in case.

Unlocking my front door, I hold it open and follow her inside. My home suddenly feels smaller.

Isla's decadent perfume floats to my nostrils—sweet coconut and mango. Her shoulders rise and fall with her breaths. I can't help but imagine her in my bed beneath me, breathless and spent. I clench my fists and shove them into my pockets to keep from touching her.

"Wow, your flat is immaculate."

"Thanks." I smooth the wrinkled doormat with my foot. The fringy pieces on the end always curl under and it drives me fucking crazy.

"Do ya hire a cleaning service?"

"Nope. It's all me."

"I'm impressed."

"Don't be."

Even though I clearly recall locking my car three damn times, I quickly press the button on my keys once more and listen for the responding beep outside. Then I press it again for good measure.

It's locked, Jake.

I jiggle the doorknob and slide the deadbolt before hanging up my keys. "It's an anxiety thing . . . one of the only plus sides to my OCD."

That is, when my rituals don't occupy the precious hours I could spend in my studio writing songs. Or the time better spent accomplishing something, period. Gotta love those days when they make me late to appointments. Better yet, my own fucking concerts. Yeah, OCD has a lot of benefits where my shitstorm brain is concerned.

She touches my shoulder. "I never knew that about you."

"Not too many people do."

And that's how I like it. It's easier to hide my struggles than talk about them. Unfortunately, my close-lipped default mode hasn't served me well on the relationship front.

Isla follows me into the kitchen and plops onto a stool at the island. "What makes you anxious?"

A dark laugh bursts from my lips. "Honestly?"

"Yeah, tell me."

"Almost everything, Isla."

Her eyes widen, and she touches me again. "Does Wes know you have anxiety?"

"Yeah, but that's a recent development," I explain, pouring her a glass of water. "He only knows because he saw the effects of it in Alaska."

"Whaddya mean?" Her tone is soft and full of concern.

I focus on filling my glass instead of answering. My mental health is not something I'm open about. I struggle—daily—even after years of therapy. Not only with the depression and anxiety that plague me, but the sense that I'm somehow less of a man. I know it's ridiculous. I certainly don't judge anyone else, but when it comes to me, there's a certain level of shame involved. It's a vulnerability I don't feel like exposing to her right now.

I swallow a gulp of water and meet her gaze. "Near-death experiences have a funny way of putting one's weaknesses on display."

"Weaknesses?"

"Yep. Factor in a few weeks of being unmedicated and I was a regular shitshow." I shrug. "But I'm back to normal now."

Until I found out you were moving across the street.

"I'm glad to hear it."

"Thanks." I hand her a pen and paper. "Make your shopping list so you can go nap." While adjusting to a new time zone is important, Isla's lupus requires her to rest more often than most.

"I feel rude going to sleep right now."

I cock an eyebrow at her. "Don't be ridiculous. You were stuck on a plane for twenty hours. Don't pretend that little car nap was enough."

She squeezes my hand, and it radiates down to my toes. "Thanks for opening your home to me on such short notice."

No amount of notice could've prepared me. After she called earlier, I threw clean sheets on the guest bed and straightened the room a bit. I checked the ceiling fans and beneath the furniture for dust bunnies. That turned into a two-hour steam mop fest. Then I got crazy in the bathroom with the bleach spray. Granted, I'd cleaned it the other day, but I didn't want her to think I was a slob.

"Like I told you, your family's always welcome to stay with me." I return the hand squeeze. *Why are her fingers so fucking cold?*

"I know you said that, but I mean *me*, specifically." Her gaze burns into me.

The air between us crackles, sizzling with a chemistry I'd give anything to explore. It's not fair she can do this to me.

I force a swallow. "I'm happy to have you here."

"Do I make you nervous?"

Absofuckinglutely. "Of course not."

"Good." She licks her lips, and for a moment, I think she might kiss me. She sips her water instead, and I make a mental note to add filters to my shopping list.

I turn my focus to her suitcase. "I'm gonna take this upstairs to your room."

"Thanks." She scans the kitchen and furrows her brow. "I think we left my carry-on in the car."

I shake my head. "The trunk's empty."

Her spine turns to steel. She clutches the countertop and stares at me with wide eyes. "Are you sure?"

"Yes, but I'll double-check."

I bound down the stoop and check my car twice, even though I know for a fact the trunk and back seat are empty. *Nope. Nothing.* When I go back inside, I find her pacing the kitchen.

"Did ya find it?"

"No. The car's empty."

"Oh, no," she whispers, her eyes welling with tears.

I walk over and grip her shoulders to stop her from pacing. "Talk to me."

"I think I left my carry-on at the airport."

I mentally retrace our steps. "When was the last time you saw it?"

"By the baggage carousel before I took your picture with Julie." Her lower lip quivers. "I moved it out of the way and never got it afterward."

I distinctly remember seeing it there and could kick myself for not grabbing it. I yank my phone from a pocket. "Don't get upset. I'll call the airport to see if anyone turned it in. Worst-case scenario, you can add stuff to your shopping list. I have shampoo, conditioner, and all that jazz. I'm sure I've got an extra toothbrush too. If you need anything else, I'll pick it up for you when I go out."

She grabs my hand, her tears spilling over. "Jake, you don't understand. My *medicine's* in there."

Ice fills my chest. "*What?*"

Without the lifelong anti-rejection drugs she takes to protect her transplanted kidney, Isla's body could attack Wes's gifted organ.

"I kept some in my handbag, since I take them so many times during the day, but I've only got two days' worth in there. The rest are in my carry-on. Mum told me not to pack them in my luggage in case the airline lost it." A tear rolls down her cheek. "Then *I* lost my carry-on. I'm *such* a fuckwit."

My scalp prickles, but I force a confident tone. "Take a deep breath. We'll figure this out."

I remember when she was first diagnosed with lupus nephritis. How her family learned of the autoimmune disease after months of searching for answers, only to discover they were too late.

Renal failure.

Those two words held more weight than any of us imagined. I'll never forget how Wes cried when he found out she needed dialysis. The anguish on his face when he described her hooked up to those machines will haunt me for the rest of my life. My touring schedule was insane, so I never made it to the dialysis center for a visit. Correction, I *avoided* visiting Isla while she was on dialysis. I couldn't bear to see her that way—the bright, spirited girl I built sandcastles with, attacked by her own body. It infuriated me. I kept tabs on her though. My regular check-ins with Wes were as much for my benefit as his.

Finally, after she endured over a year of dialysis, Wes's tissue samples came back as compatible. I'll never forget my relief at the news. When I saw Wes before his surgery, he beamed with a sense of purpose, a deep-seated pride in his ability to help her. Part of me was jealous, which didn't make sense at the time. I would've gladly donated a kidney. I never told Wes I'd made an appointment for compatibility testing. I didn't need to—he was a match, Isla was getting a kidney, and that's all that mattered.

On the day of their surgeries, I flew in for a surprise visit and stopped by the hospital gift shop first. Isla loves koalas and everything purple. As luck would have it, the shop had a purple koala on display. I grabbed the stuffed animal and a massive bag of candy for Wes. They were lying there, hospital beds side by side. Matching eyes, matching bandages, matching smiles. Her face lit up at the sight of it. "Koalas are my favorite! And it's purple!" You would've thought I'd given her the keys to a Mercedes. Wes ate all the candy in one sitting. Isla said something that day that has stuck with me for ten years now. "When life gives you a second chance, you take it."

Life gave her a second chance. Wes gave her a second chance. I don't know how, but come hell or high water, she'll get her medicine—even if I need to storm every goddamn pharmacy in the tri-state area to get it for her.

CHAPTER 2

Jake

Mood: "Waving Through a Window" by Ben Platt

Frustrated and anxious as fuck, I plop onto the couch beside Isla. "The airport gave me the runaround, but no one's turned it in. I gave them both of our contact information, just in case."

She chews on her nails, hugging her bent knees to her chest. "Maybe I can get my parents to refill my meds and ship them here."

I shake my head. "You're looking at over a week's turnaround. You can't be without them that long."

"I can't be without them *period*." She buries her face in her hands. "I can't believe I lost my fucking carry-on."

I shake my head. "No, *I* was the one carrying it in the first place. I let us get distracted. I should've refused Julie."

"What am I gonna do, Jake?"

I straighten and reach for my phone. "I'll call my friend Maura. She's a friend from elementary school and one of the pharmacists who owns Compass Rose Apothecary. Maybe she'll have some insight." I dial the pharmacy and ask the technician to transfer the call.

Maura picks up. "Jake, how's it going?"

"Hey, Mo, I have a little predicament I need your help with."

"What's up?"

"I have a friend visiting from Australia who lost her medication."

"Ugh, that sucks. What kind of meds are we talking about?"

"Immunosuppressants for a kidney transplant."

"Oh, boy. That's not good. Does she have a doctor in New York?"

"Not yet. Can you fill a prescription from an Australian doctor?"

"No, we can't. Here's what I suggest. Take her to an urgent care clinic and see if they'll write the prescriptions for her."

"Do you think an urgent care doc would be willing to write for heavy-hitting drugs like that?" I rub at my temples. "I mean, without knowing her history?"

Maura sighs. "I don't know, but unless you have a doctor friend, that may be her only option. The other issue she's gonna face is cost. We can't process foreign insurance claims. Without insurance, those types of drugs will cost a small fortune."

I clench the phone. "I'll pay for them. I don't care what they cost."

"What medications are they? I want to make sure we have them in stock."

"I'm gonna give the phone to her. Hang on." I hand my cell to Isla and pace the room while she talks.

I need to figure something out. Plain and simple. She can't go without her meds.

Isla hangs up with Maura after a few minutes. "I guess I need to go to urgent care."

"There's a health center uptown. Let's get something to eat and then we'll make a trip over there."

"I'm sorry," she mutters miserably.

I pause in front of her. "Isla, please don't apologize. Shit happens. We'll figure it out."

"What if they won't do it? Then what'll I do?"

Lena.

I perk up. "I can't believe I didn't think of this earlier. I'm going to call Lena. She's a nurse . . . maybe she has a doctor friend who can help."

I dial Lena's number, and she picks up on the second ring. "Hey, you."

"Lena-Bean, we've got a problem."

"What's up?"

I explain the situation, including Maura's suggestion. "Do you have any kidney doctor friends?"

"No, but I know an orthopedic surgeon who owes me big time."

I frown. "An orthopedic surgeon?"

"Marc."

Her ex-fiancé.

"He'd prescribe them even though it's not his specialty?"

"He's a doctor first, and therefore, he'd never let a transplant patient go without their meds."

"But she's Wes's sister."

"Yeah, and he'd do it for Wes if *I* asked him to."

"The guy's still in love with you, isn't he?"

"He had his chance," she declares with her typical bluntness. "Let me talk to Isla to get the specifics."

I hand over the phone once more, and Isla lists out the names and dosages of her medications. My heart clenches at the sheer number of pills she must remember to take on a daily basis. As she recites the directions to Lena, I discover she takes some of them multiple times per day. How the hell does she keep track of everything? I have enough difficulty remembering to take two meds each morning, and she's already listed at least seven.

She hangs up. "Okay, so now what?"

"Well, we wait and see what Lena can do. If anyone can solve this mess, it's Lena-Bean. I'm sure she'll call us back soon."

"True." She rolls her head from side to side, loudly cracking her neck.

My stomach turns. I can't explain it, but something about the sound of cracking joints makes me want to hurl.

Isla lifts a brow. "Why're ya making that face?"

"Please don't crack your neck—or anything else. It freaks me out."

"Sorry. It's a habit of mine. I'll try to remember not to do it."

"Thank you."

"No problem." She lifts an eyebrow. "I thought you helped Lena put Wes's shoulder back into place."

I shudder at the memory. "No, that was all Austin. I supported his torso while they did it, but I don't think I was much help. Nearly puked on your brother's head."

She giggles. "Too bad it wasn't Reed."

"How's he doing, by the way?"

Reed and I are friendly, but he's much closer with Austin, which makes sense since he's the one who brought everyone together. They met as contestants in a youth talent competition set in Australia. Reed introduced him to Wes, and the three became inseparable. I joined the party a few years later, like always. Austin and I shared a vocal coach and became close during our preteens. The summer after my parents' divorce, he brought me along on his month-long trip to Australia to visit the Emerson boys. Wes and I hit it off immediately, but Reed has always been a little standoffish toward me—even before the accident. While I understand his circumstances and feel terrible about them, the way he treats his sister has never sat well with me.

Isla shrugs. "Reed's the same."

"How's married life treating him?"

"I dunno how Cora deals with his shit."

"Austin said he's different with her."

"Thank God for that," she mutters, crossing her arms over her chest.

"What's his issue with you?"

Her gaze snaps to mine. "Oh, so you've noticed?"

"Yeah."

Her posture softens like she knows she's found an ally in me. "I honestly don't know what I did to him . . . other than being born." She picks at her cuticles. "I mean, I'm sure I was annoying as a kid."

"I never found you annoying."

"You're also not one of my brothers," she reminds me with a smirk.

"True." *Thank fuck for that.* I'd be in the market for a whole different kind of psychiatric help. "But, even so, it's not like you were overly bratty or whiny."

She fans herself with a throw pillow. "Christ, you're killing me with the compliments over here."

I laugh. "Well, it's true. The kid I remember did way more smiling and giggling than pouting."

"You had something to do with that." She touches my arm. "You were always so sweet to me, Jake. Some of my fondest childhood memories are building sandcastles with you."

My chest tightens. I'd give *anything* to pull her into my arms and kiss her. Run my fingers through her hair, feel her soft skin. Hold her while she sleeps. Laugh with her. Dry her tears.

I clear my throat. "Likewise." It's not much of a response, but it's all I can muster. I change the topic before I lose my resolve not to touch her. "Did you ever ask Reed what his problem is?"

"No. I'm not sure it would matter."

"Maybe if he knew his behavior was hurtful to you, he'd change."

"You clearly have more faith in him than I do." She gnaws her lower lip.

"This is going to sound terrible . . ." She shakes her head. "You know what? Forget I said anything."

"Can't do that. Tell me what's on your mind, Sprite." I rest my hand on her knee, unable to stop myself from brushing my thumb over her silken kneecap. "You know you can always talk to me."

"It's just . . ." She stares out the window for a moment. "I can't believe I'm saying this out loud." Her body deflates on a sigh. "Don't get me wrong, I love both of my brothers—"

"No one's questioning that."

Her big, blue eyes find mine. "But when you guys were lost in Alaska, a huge part of me wished Reed had gone on the trip."

"You mean, instead of Wes?"

"Yeah." She looks away. "I felt so cruel, ya know?"

"What do you mean?"

"I mean with how readily I would've traded one for the other." She squeezes her eyes shut. "Family shouldn't be like that. I shouldn't have felt that way."

"Don't beat yourself up. Reed's given you more than enough reasons to justify your feelings. I've seen it firsthand, which is why he and I aren't close. I've never liked how he treated you—even before the accident made him . . ." I pause, searching for the right word.

"Miserable?"

I chuckle. "I was gonna call him a dick, but miserable works too."

"He's both." She crosses her arms and rubs at them. "Yet he's perfectly fine toward Wes. Reed was devastated when he went missing. Absolutely inconsolable. I try not to vent to Wes about it—or my parents—because I don't want to put them in the middle. I wish I knew what I did to him, ya know?"

I nod. "Feel free to vent to me anytime. I don't have a problem taking sides."

"Wow, all this time I worried he'd convinced you I was a birdbrain too."

"Well, he didn't. Because you're not. You shouldn't worry about what I think."

"I *do* worry about what you think. And for the record, it would've killed me if I lost Wes *and* you in Alaska." Her gaze burns into mine. "I would've traded Reed ten times over if it meant I could save you both."

"Isla," I whisper.

She shifts on the sofa, bringing her knees closer to mine. Her warmth seeps through my jeans. She hasn't changed since we got home, so her legs are bare. Visions of them wrapped around my waist make my throat go dry.

I want her so badly, I can fucking taste it. My gaze drifts to her lips. I want to kiss them and tug that plush lower lip between my teeth.

My phone rings, snapping me out of the trance she's got me in. I yank it from my pocket. "Hello?"

"Jake, it's Mo. You must have friends in high places."

"Huh?" At this point, Isla's got me bewildered as fuck.

"Dr. Marc Donnelly phoned in all your friend's prescriptions with *five* refills. So, she's good to go for the next six months."

"Excellent. How long do you need to get them filled?"

"My tech's on lunch. Can you give me an hour?"

"Absolutely. Take your time. I have other errands to run first."

"I'm curious how you got an orthopedic surgeon to cover meds for a renal patient."

"He's a friend of a friend."

"A good friend to have, apparently. Oh, but I need to warn you . . . you're looking at over two thousand bucks."

"Doesn't matter. Fill them."

"All right, see you in a bit."

I hang up and turn to Isla. "Crisis averted. Your meds will be ready for pickup in an hour."

Her jaw drops and fresh tears well in her eyes. "Really?"

"Yup. All taken care of."

She throws her arms around my neck, startling me. "Thank you for figuring this mess out for me. You're a lifesaver."

The fact that there's truth in her words is a punch to my gut. I wrap her in a tight hug and take a moment to breathe in her scent before releasing her. "I'm happy to help. Did you finish your list?"

"Yes." She releases me and stands. "Hang on, let me grab my handbag."

"What for?"

"I hit up the currency exchange after I went through customs in Los Angeles."

I wave her off. "Don't worry about it."

"You picked me up from the airport at the last minute, opened your home to me, saved my kidney, *and* you're running errands for me so I can nap."

I smirk. "Your point?"

"I'm paying for my shit."

I shake my head. "Doesn't work like that with me. You're my guest—you're not paying for a damn thing. Consider it my welcome to the neighborhood gift."

Let me take care of you, honey.

She props her hands on her hips. "Jacob Warren Bennett, you *will* let me reimburse you."

I cringe at her use of my middle name. While I can appreciate the meaning behind it—my mother's maiden name—I've never been a fan. I'm also mildly surprised Isla knows it. "We're gonna have to agree to disagree on that one, Sprite." I reach for the sheet of paper in her hand. "Give me your list."

Isla

Internal playlist: "Sledgehammer" by Fifth Harmony

I press a finger to the middle of Jake's chest, holding my list behind my back. "Only if you promise to let me reimburse you for my medicine."

"Sorry." His lips twitch into a smile. "Not gonna happen."

The breath leaves my chest in a huff. "Why not?"

"Because I don't make promises I can't keep."

Realizing I'm not going to win this row, I roll my eyes at him. "Fine. I'll find some other way to pay you back." I let him think he's won and turn my focus to my list. I run through the items once more, but it still feels like I'm forgetting something. My brain's fried from the missing meds fiasco, so I can't think straight. I hand over the page with a sigh. "I hope everything's on here."

He pockets my list, then shrugs on a wool coat and grabs his keys. "Text or call if you think of anything else you need. In the meantime, make yourself at home." He smiles that sexy smile of his, dimples in full force, and I melt on the spot.

"Okay, thanks." My reply is more breathless than I intended.

He waves and disappears through the front door.

I flit around the living room, studying the artwork on his walls. Most of it's related to music or theater—Jake's specialty. My favorite piece is a large painting of a grand piano. I've always loved the piano, but I have zero musical ability. Jake, on the other hand, could put Beethoven to shame. Mum had a rickety old keyboard she kept in the den when we were growing up. I think she always hoped one of us would take lessons, but we wanted no part of it. Wes and I aren't musical, and Reed's a drummer. The only time our poor old piano got any use was when Jake came to visit. He'd make our house sound like a concert hall. It surprises me not to find a piano in his living room.

I yawn and make my way into the kitchen. I should nap, but I'd rather familiarize myself with Jake's home—especially since I'm going to be in New York for about a week. After my visit, I'll return to Australia to pack up my flat. While it would've made more sense to wait until closer to my move to make *one* trip across the ocean, I have a compelling reason to be here.

Lena planned a big party for the Saturday after Thanksgiving. She's calling it "Friendsgiving" and it's doubling as a belated thirty-fifth birthday bash for Wes. They didn't get the chance to celebrate on Halloween—his actual birthday—because he was traveling. The press tour for his most recent film release ended only a few weeks ago.

Lena asked me to make a surprise appearance, and I jumped at the opportunity. Obviously, I love spending time with Wes, but I've never been part of an American Thanksgiving celebration and I'm excited to try some of the different foods. I'm also looking forward to spending time with Lena. I'd be hard pressed to find a better woman for my brother than if I designed her myself. She's smart, sassy, caring, and she doesn't take any of his shit. She fights fire with fire, and to say I adore her would be an understatement. Between Lena and Cora, I wonder what my brothers did to deserve such amazing women.

I originally planned to stay in a hotel, but Lena suggested I call Jake instead. A couple of months ago, Jake made a passing offer to show me around New York if I ever came to visit. I decided to take him up on his invitation when I accepted the internship in Manhattan. Never, in a million years, did I expect my lunatic brother to buy me a house—across the street from Jake's, no less. While I'm exhilarated by the prospect of being close to him, I want him closer.

I made the first move and kissed him five years ago, confirming what I knew in my heart. It crushed me when he walked away, but I get it—I was barely eighteen and we lived an ocean apart. I didn't chase after him because I still had some growing up to do. Now, at twenty-three, I'm in grown woman territory. I want him, more now than ever before. In December, when the ocean between us is replaced with a street, he'll be mine. But this time around, *he's* going to make the first move.

CHAPTER 3

Isla

Internal playlist: "Changing Colours" by Josh Groban

So, this is what his lair looks like.

At some point, my self-guided tour of Jake's place leads me to his bedroom. I briefly consider climbing into his bed for the nap that's not going to happen but decide against it. It's better if I ride out the jet lag and force myself to stay awake.

I make my way along the room's perimeter, thrilled to glimpse his private space. His tidy dresser boasts a cactus arrangement and several framed pictures. I trace my fingertips along a gorgeous silver frame. Inside is a photo of Jake holding up his first Grammy award, flanked by Wes and Austin. There's also a carved wooden frame featuring Jake with a suited dark-haired man and a pretty blonde in a wedding dress. I pick up a different photograph. A woman with warm brown eyes and graying waves peers back at me with a familiar smile. *Must be his mum.* I return the frame to its rightful position and mosey over to peek at his nightstand.

My breath catches when I spot the conch shell I'd given him atop a stack of spiral-bound notebooks. I can't believe he kept it all these years. Heart racing, I ponder the significance of its bedside placement. Does he think about me during his dark, lonely nights? Or am I the only one still pining? I feather my fingertips over the notebooks. *Hmm, song lyrics?* Resisting the urge to snoop, I instead press the shell to my ear and listen to the ocean. Images of our sandcastle days flutter through my mind, making my heart clench with soul-permeating wistfulness.

Eventually, I make my way into his massive walk-in. I probably shouldn't be nosing through Jake's clothes—or his bedroom, for that matter—but I can't help it. My love of closets goes hand in hand with my fashion background.

I flick a light on and take a minute to survey his wardrobe. My first observation is the abundance of gray: charcoal, heather, platinum, ash, and gunmetal. Maybe he really likes gray, or maybe he's sad. Either way, the man seriously needs some fucking color in his life.

I study the neatly hung garments, struck by the organization. It's sheer perfection. I know he mentioned having OCD, but to see the manifestation of it is really something. His shirts are arranged by style, from short sleeved to long, casual to collared. He's grouped them by shades within each section—from light to dark. Jake has hidden his anxiety among crisp lines, straight hangers, and a truly dismal color palette.

My heart aches at the sight. Part of me wants to rearrange them, shake things up a little and get him to loosen up, but I realize the cruelty in that. This is his control, how he copes with the unknown. Who am I to take that away from him? I turn off the light and head back to my room.

I plop onto the bed and rummage through my suitcase, shoving underwear and socks aside. I packed a ton of underwear in case—

Shit.

I suddenly remember what I needed to add to my list. *Maxi pads.* My fucking period is overdue. Panic creeps into my gut. All my supplies were in the carry-on with the bulk of my meds. I rush into the bathroom and search the cabinets and drawers, thinking maybe he's got something in there from a past girlfriend. No such luck. I do a quick check of my panties, and sure enough, I'm spotting.

Fuck.

I stuff a wad of toilet paper in my undies and quickly wash my hands. What the hell am I going to do? The last thing I need is to bleed all over Jake's perfect heather-gray sheets. I hurry back to my room. Eyeing the phone on my nightstand, I shake my head.

No way.

I am not asking Jake to buy feminine products for me. My lower belly cramps in protest, telling me I don't have a choice. My periods are extremely heavy and painful courtesy of lupus.

Swallowing my pride, I reach for the phone.

He answers on the first ring. "Hey, Sprite. Why aren't you napping?"

"I . . . uh, I thought of something else I need."

"Food-wise? I'm at the pharmacy now, but I can go back to the grocery store if you need me to."

"No. Not food." I squeeze my eyes shut. "I need pads."

"Like maxi pads?"

"Yes," I croak. "And a big bottle of paracetamol."

"I'm not sure what that is."

"It's for pain. Do you have a heating pad?"

"No, but I'll grab one. Okay, I'm in the pain aisle and I don't see anything called paracetamol. There's ibuprofen, aspirin, naproxen, acetaminophen—"

"That's it. Sorry. I forgot it's called acetaminophen in the States. Please grab the biggest bottle they have."

"Tablets or gel caps?"

"Doesn't matter. Whatever they've got that's five hundred milligrams."

Thanks to my transplanted kidney, I'm limited with what I can use for pain. Since most of the over-the-counter analgesic drugs are processed through the kidneys, they're a no-go. Paracetamol—aka acetaminophen—is metabolized through the liver, so that's my only safe option. Oh, the many things to consider on a borrowed organ.

"Got your Tylenol. All right, I'm in the tampon aisle. Tell me what you need, Sprite."

Why is this happening to me?

Why did I have to lose my carry-on with my arsenal of meds and toiletries?

Better yet, why in God's name do I have to ask Jake to buy me pads?

Why can't I bleed like a stuck pig in private?

"Hello?" he says. "Are you there?"

I cover my face, not wanting to have this conversation. "Yes."

"Good. Thought I lost you for a minute. Okay, what do you need? Super? Gentle glide? Multipack?"

I think of the time I had to send Wes on this errand for me. He didn't even blink, thanks to his years of being with Rachel. He simply asked me what I needed and made it happen. Now, I *know* Jake is more mature than my brother—and he's had long-term girlfriends, so he likely has experience with this—but I'd rather run naked through the streets than spell it out for him.

"There's a lot to choose from, and I'm no tampon expert. You've gotta help me out here, Sprite."

I clear my throat. "Not tampons . . . they freak me out." As someone who's considered immunosuppressed, I'm at an elevated risk for toxic shock syndrome, so I'm a strictly no-tampons girl. The way I see it, after surviving renal failure, I'm not about to chance my health over a wad of cotton fiber. Convenience be damned.

"Okay, tampons are a hard pass." He chuckles. "Now we're getting somewhere. I'm looking at six shelves of maxi pads. They have regular, long, extra-long, overnights . . . sport. Huh. That must be a new thing. I wonder what makes them qualify as sport. Maybe they're thinner?"

Mother.

Of.

God.

"Oh! Look at that, they even have organic ones with aloe . . ."

"Please get me the biggest bag of ultrathin, heavy flow pads you can find," I blurt.

"You got it, Sprite. With or without wings?"

Oh, sweet baby Jesus. Why?

"With." The word leaves my lips on a sigh of mortified defeat.

"Do you want the organic ones? They sound sooth—"

"Don't care."

He chuckles. "Okay, got 'em. Any other requests?"

Yeah, let me wake up from this nightmare. "Nope."

"All right, see you in a bit."

Unless I die of embarrassment first. "Mm-kay." I hang up and bury my face in my hands.

I guess it could be worse. Jake could've been a dick and refused to buy them or made me feel gross about having a uterus, but it didn't seem to faze him. *I'm* the one who got all worked up over it, feeling icky and shy and embarrassed.

Get over it.

Returning to my suitcase, I withdraw what I originally went in there for—my crocheting supplies. When I packed, I stuffed a bunch of yarn along the bag's perimeter, so I'd have something to do in my downtime.

Jake wasn't wearing a scarf when he went out. I'm going to make him one since I hate the idea of him being cold. After seeing his closet, one thing's for certain—it won't be gray. Picturing his chestnut waves with their auburn undertones, and the warm brown of his eyes, I decide to use green. I pick through the skeins of yarn, select my colors, and head for the living room.

Sunlight's streaming through a beautiful bay window illuminating one end of the couch. I settle in that spot, reveling in the cushion's warmth. I pull a luxe silver blanket over my goose-bumped legs. I probably should've changed out of my dress when I was upstairs, but the pad fiasco distracted me. Now that I'm feeling cozy in the sunshine, the thought of moving makes me groan. Plus, my ankles are a little swollen and I don't feel like climbing the stairs again.

I close my eyes and let the sun's rays warm my face. The light filtering through the window doesn't hurt my eyes as much as direct sunlight, but I'll need to move to a shaded spot soon. Since lupus makes me photosensitive, I don't get to spend much time in the sun. Pure torture for a girl who grew up on the beach. I often look back on the days of tanned skin with a soul-deep wistfulness. I've traded sun-kissed for porcelain, but I guess it could be worse. I make a mental note to keep my sunglasses downstairs in case I make this spot a habit.

The front door squeaks open, and Jake wipes his feet on the mat. "I'm gonna go out on a limb and assume you're still not napping."

"You picked a sturdy limb. I'm in here."

He chuckles, and the sound warms me better than his blanket. "Lemme put the groceries in the kitchen, and I'll be right there."

Glass bottles jostle as the fridge door opens and closes. Moments later, he appears in the living room archway.

"Okay, the only thing I didn't grab was fennel because I've got some here."

"Thank you so much for shopping for me."

"Anytime, Sprite." Grinning, he points at the crochet hook and yarn. "Look at you over there knitting."

"Crocheting," I correct him.

"Same thing."

"Actually, they're not. Knitting uses two needles, while crocheting uses a hook. Among other differences."

"Whatever. It's cute either way." He hands me a white paper bag. "Here're your meds. Maura said that depending on what manufacturers your pharmacy at home stocks, the pills may look different than what you're used to."

"I'll keep that in mind, thanks."

He hands me another bag. "Here's your heating pad, acetaminophen, and lady stuff."

I flush. "Thank you. I wish I didn't have to ask you to do that."

He waves me off. "Don't be ridiculous. Despite how it may have sounded, it's not my first rodeo with that type of thing. I'm sorry for all the questions, but I didn't wanna get the wrong ones."

I peek inside the bag. "These are perfect, thank you."

"Good. I'll add 'perfect pad picker-outer' to my résumé."

I burst into laughter, complete with tears. "Dare I ask what else is on there?"

His smile widens. "Maybe I'll let you read it sometime." He holds up a hand. "Hang on, I forgot a bag in the kitchen. Be right back."

I wipe my watery eyes. His one-liner made me laugh *and* squashed the awkwardness, and I love him for it.

He returns a minute later with a paper bag and places it in my lap.

"What's this?"

"A little something from me."

"What for?"

"It'll make sense when you open it."

I reach inside and pull out the first item, a box of piña colada Italian ices. "Oh, I love piña coladas!"

"Yes, I remember. I know women often crave ice cream when they have their period, but I noticed you're not doing the dairy thing, so I thought you might enjoy these instead."

"Jake, you are beyond sweet. Thank you."

"My pleasure, Sprite." He points to the bag. "There's more."

I withdraw the other items—coconut-mango tea, dried pineapple, macaroons, and a giant bar of dark chocolate—some of my favorite treats on the planet. He also grabbed the newest issues of *Vogue*, *In-Style*, *Harper's Bazaar*, and *Elle*.

"Thought I'd make you a care package," he says sheepishly.

I leap to my feet and hug him. "Thank you. No one's ever done anything like this for me." I close my eyes against the tears pricking at them.

"You're welcome," he tightens his arms around me, "and I'm sorry that's the case."

I want to cup his face and kiss him, show him how deeply his gesture affects me. Instead, I cling to him, even though I know I shouldn't. Even though it goes against my plan. I'm not making the first move, but damn, do I want to.

My heart's racing, and with his chest pressed to mine, I can feel his pounding too. His shoulders move faster with each jerky, shuddered inhalation and rough exhalation that follows.

Kiss me.

I nearly say it aloud. I want his lips on me, his tongue moving with mine, possessive and intense. More than that, I want him to carry me upstairs and make love to me. In his gray room, beneath his silver comforter, on his charcoal sheets.

I want to brighten his monochromatic world with my body, heart, and soul. I don't need to *see* the colors around us because I *feel* them. I always have.

From the time we were kids, we've burned yellow—warm and buttery soft like friendship and rays of sunlight filtering through the clouds. The longer we stand here, bodies pressed together, the faster our colors deepen. From the attraction burning between, around, and through us, engulfing us in flames of red and orange, to our inevitable passion and pleasure—a rich, decadent purple. Blues and greens for the tranquility we'll feel when we're finished, sated, and spent, panting in each other's arms.

I want to feel Jake in every hue, shade, tone, and tint. I need him in color, gray scale, and black and white. I want the full spectrum with him.

And I'm tired of waiting.

Without thinking, I press a tender kiss to the side of his neck. His breath catches, and I feel him harden.

"We need to put the ices in the freezer." He pulls away from me, snatching the box from the couch cushion, then steps back. Chest heaving, he runs a hand over his face. "Before they melt."

Or we do.

I nod, breathing just as heavily. How the hell am I supposed to keep my resolve to let Jake make the first move when his care package already put my heart in checkmate?

CHAPTER 4

Jake

Mood: "I Want You" by Third Eye Blind

That was fucking close. *Too close.* I make my way to the sink and splash cool water on my face. I still feel her lips on my neck. Her breasts pressed to my chest. Her hair tickling my nose. Her arms around me, clinging to me like I'm the savior she's waited for her whole life.

Isla follows me into the kitchen and starts emptying grocery bags like nothing just happened between us. "Oh, cool. You found the ginger tea."

Ginger tea? She's thinking about ginger tea while my cock is ready to bust through my zipper and my balls feel like lead. *Anyone want a crumpet with their ginger tea?*

I laugh one of those maniacal laughs steeped in frustration, because that's what I am. Frustrated with myself, the situation, the fact I can't have her . . . plastic wrap sticking to itself, mismatched socks, one-way streets, the Department of Motor Vehicles, parking tickets, you name it. If it's frustration worthy, I'm feeling it. Right here, right now.

Isla tilts her head to the side. "What's so funny?"

I hold up a jar. "The pickles are expired." I laugh harder and she looks at me like I have six heads.

"Okay . . ." She takes the jar and heaves it into the trash. "Did ya have your heart set on pickles?"

I run my hands through my hair and over my face. "No. I hate pickles. How about you?"

"I mean, I like them with a sanga, but I think I'll survive without them," she says cautiously.

"What's a sanga?"

She giggles. "A sandwich, silly."

"Ah, makes sense." I pull some boxed items out of the freezer because everything needs to be reorganized to make room for the Italian ices. I quickly categorize what is now on the counter, make sense of the boxes, and restack, placing the ices inside the freezer. I spin back around to find her leaning against the island, arms crossed over her chest.

Shit. Did she see that?

I thought I was quick enough where it wouldn't look weird, but not too quick where I seemed manic.

She raises a brow.

Oh, God. Did I forget to zip my fly? I glance down at myself. My hard-on is more than a little obvious. *Fuck.*

"What?" I ask, feigning normalcy.

"You tell me, Jacob."

"There's nothing to tell," I mumble, retreating from the kitchen. I need to place some distance between us. I need a second to think. I need—

A cold shower.

"I'll be back in a bit." I take the steps two at a time, rush down the hall to my bedroom, and barge into the attached bathroom. Closing the door behind me, I sag against the solid oak and glance at my crotch.

Yep, still rock-hard.

"Fuck this." I shed my clothes and turn on the faucet, adjusting the water to lukewarm. Let's be real, who the fuck can handle a legit cold shower?

I step inside and close the curtain. The stream pummels my back, cooling my skin, but it does nothing for the situation down yonder. It looks like I'm going to have to take matters into my own hands—something I seldom do.

Facing the wall, I use one hand to brace myself and palm my cock with the other. I close my eyes, lean my forehead against the cool tile, and start to move. I envision Isla—her lips, her long legs, the curve of her breasts, the way she held on to me. A groan rumbles in my chest. It feels *so* fucking good. I tighten my grip and imagine clutching her hips and pumping inside her, making her moan my name. The gasps come freely as I tug my cock harder and faster. I'm close.

Really fucking close.

My balls tighten. I lean against the wall so I can use both hands, one cupping them while the other strokes my shaft. I pick up the pace, roughly yanking now, groaning with each stroke. Desperate for the release building inside me, I imagine how sexy Isla would look in my bed. Digging her nails in my back. Her body squeezing me as she comes. The visual takes me over the edge.

"*Isla.*" I groan her name, both hands still moving. "*Fuck.*" My cock jerks, spurting my release, taking my tension along as it washes down the drain. Chest heaving, I finish my shower and turn off the water.

I dry off and rub a towel over my hair before heading to my room to dress. I select a gray T-shirt and charcoal plaid pajama pants, because now I'm relaxed as fuck and feel the need to dress the part. I head downstairs after dousing my shower with bleach spray.

Isla's in front of the stove stirring something. She glances over her shoulder. "Feel better?"

I pull a beer from the fridge, crack it open, and swallow a huge gulp. "Yeah." I nod to the saucepan. "What are you making?"

"Dinner for us."

I come up beside her. "Smells good."

"It's pesto risotto. Do ya want chicken in yours?"

"Are you having chicken?"

"I wasn't planning on it, but I figured you'd need some protein," she says, adding more basil.

"I'm happy with whatever you're making. You don't need to do anything special for me."

"I appreciate everything you've done for me today. Cooking you a meal is the least I can do. And you didn't answer my question."

"And that was?"

"Do you *want* chicken?"

"No, thank you." I point to the prescription vials on the counter. "Did you take your medicine?"

"Yup." She nods and looks me over. "We really need to do something about your wardrobe." Her subject change tells me the meds are a sensitive topic, so I make a mental note not to hound her about them.

I look down at myself. "What's wrong with my clothes?"

She gestures to my pants. "Your outfit is all wrong."

I bark out a laugh. "I'm sorry, are you the fashion police? They're pajamas, Sprite."

"I'm talking about all the gray."

"What's wrong with gray?"

"Nothing," she stirs the risotto, "when it's not your sole color choice."

"Too bad I don't know an extremely talented designer. Oh, wait . . . I do!" I give her a smile. "Maybe you'll have to make me something colorful."

Her eyes light up. "Will ya wear it if I do?"

"Depends what it is. I'm kinda plain. I don't think I could handle it if you came at me with a lime green romper."

She laughs. "I hate rompers, so you don't need to worry about that. Maybe after dinner I'll show you some of the pieces in my collection?"

"I'd love that."

"I brought a few of the dresses I've made—I'll model them for ya."

My cock twitches, and I regret my choice of pants. Hell, she probably already knows I want her, so I chug the remainder of my beer and decide not to worry about my anatomy.

"I'd love to see them." I grab bowls from a cabinet and set them on the counter beside her. "I'm curious what colors you want to see me in."

"All kinds of colors, but I think I'd start with green." She reaches up and ruffles my still-damp hair. "With your hair and eye color, green would look amazing on you."

"You mean as a complement to my boring-ass brown?"

"Nothing about you is boring, and you can't say *brown*. That implies something flat and lifeless."

I snort. "Like mud."

She shakes her head. "Your hair is chestnut with auburn undertones. Your eyes are warm and inviting like melted chocolate—definitely *not* mud." She peers into them. "I've always loved your eyes." I stop breathing and stare into wide pools of swirling cobalt as she continues, "It's been that way for as long as I can remember."

She's off-limits.

You're too complicated.

No one wants to deal with you long-term.

"Don't tell me things like that, Isla," I say on a sigh.

She shrugs and turns back to the risotto. "I'm simply stating a fact."

"But you're slowly killing me."

"Gimme your bowl." I hand it over and she scoops some risotto into it. "That enough, or do ya want more?"

I know she's referring to the food, but it feels like a loaded question, so I answer it as such. "I'll *always* want more."

That's the reason I can't let myself have her—aside from Wes, of course. Because I know that once I have a taste of her, I could *never* get enough. She ruined me five years ago with a simple kiss. If I ever took her to my bed, I'd be fucking *insatiable*. And she deserves better than that.

She deserves better than me.

She adds another spoonful to my bowl. "Tell me when."

"That's good, thanks," I say, grateful she didn't read into my statement. Isla fills her bowl and settles beside me at the island. "Dig in."

I take a bite and moan. "This is incredible."

"Thanks. I'm glad you like it. There's plenty *more* . . . if you want it."

Her eyes burn into me in a way that tells me she's not talking about food. Maybe she *did* read into my statement. I swallow a gulp of water and turn my attention to the risotto.

I lounge on the couch and wait for Isla's fashion show with a pillow strategically placed in my lap. I try to appear relaxed, when in reality, I have zero chill. It doesn't help that my body and mind thrum with a hyperawareness of her.

My phone chimes with a text.

> **Jesse: How's it going?**

I quickly type my reply.

> **Me: She's so fucking perfect. Beautiful and funny. I want her more now than EVER before. I'm so fucked, dude.**

> **Jesse: I say go for it. You deserve to get what you want for once. Besides, she's not eighteen anymore.**

I roll my eyes.

> **Me: Uh, did you forget about big brother????**

> **Jesse: He's not her father.**

Me: Yeah, but he'd kill me just the same.

Jesse: He might surprise you.

I scoff at my phone.

Me: Doubtful.

"Ready for me?" Isla calls.

Oh, fuck yeah. My cock twitches in agreement.

"Yeah," I say with forced neutrality, pressing on the pillow to stifle my anatomy. I text Jesse that I'll catch up with him later.

I toss my phone aside as Isla sashays into my living room wearing a pale yellow, fitted pantsuit with a lavender camisole. The ensemble accentuates her lithe figure, putting her curves on display. She reminds me of sunshine, warmth, and blooming flowers. A sexy Easter daffodil. A goddamn buttercup goddess. A fairy queen.

"Wow," I murmur, my mouth going dry. "You look like springtime."

She grins. "That's exactly what I was going for! Attire to brighten up the office."

"You brighten up every room you enter." The words leave my lips before I can stop them.

Looks like my filter's on sabbatical again.

Isla flushes. "Thank you, Jacob."

I clear my throat. "You designed that?"

"Yes."

"I'm beyond impressed, Sprite."

"Wait until you see the pretty dresses," she squeals.

"Let's see them."

"Be right back." She rushes to her room to change.

Isla returns a few minutes later, and my mouth drops open. Her royal blue sheath dress matches the color of her eyes. The hemline reaches mid-thigh, showing off those gorgeous legs I want wrapped around me. My gaze drifts to the low-cut neckline and the way the material clings to her breasts.

I force a swallow. "That's for the office?"

She giggles. "No, silly. This is for Friday night happy hour or a company party or something."

"Oh." It's all I can muster.

She bites her lower lip, unsure. "Does it look all right?"

"Uh-huh." *It would look better on my bedroom floor.* I shake my head to clear more inappropriate thoughts before they completely dismantle my filter. "It's beautiful."

She slowly turns in a circle. "Do you think women would want to wear it?"

"I want to wear it," I blurt.

Wait, what? Way to give her the wrong impression, asshole.

Fuck.

Think, Jake. THINK.

I clear my throat. "I mean, if I was a woman, I'd wear it." What I really mean is that I want to wear *her*. Thankfully, my backup filter kicked in for that one before I sounded like fucking Hannibal Lecter.

She smiles and points to the bejeweled belt cinching her waistline. "I made this belt because the dress needed something to liven it up."

"It's sparkly."

"I love sparkle. Since this collection is supposed to be somewhat office geared, I had to rein in my sparkle side. I'd love nothing more than to throw some sequins on the bodice." She cups her breasts. "I mean, I could totally jazz this up as a New Year's Eve outfit." As if suddenly realizing where her hands are, she jerks them away and flushes.

"Or a cocktail party," I offer. *Speaking of cocks, mine is totally game for a party with you.* Shuffling in my seat, I press against the pillow in my lap.

"Right. Any fancy dinner party, actually." She smiles. "Do ya wanna see one more?"

I'll watch you all night, sweetheart. "Yes."

She retreats, moving slowly this time, and I catch the hint of a falter in her gait. It takes her longer to return and she reenters the room wearing a lilac-colored dress. She approaches me with a definite limp.

"Are you all right?" I ask, frowning.

"Yeah, my ankles are getting sore from all the walking I did today. The one buckled a bit on the stairs before, but I'm okay." She points to the long, flowy sundress. "Do ya like it?"

"It's beautiful." I pat the couch cushion beside me. "Sit."

Settling in, she gives me a pouty lip. "But I'm not done modeling."

"Yeah, you are. I don't need you falling down the stairs."

She rolls her eyes. "Relax, Jake. I'm not gonna sue ya."

"That possibility didn't even find its way onto my long list of concerns." I study her face. "You know, like, what if you trip going up the stairs? Or what if you tumble, break your nose or something, and need to go to the doctor?" *Or what if she slips, breaks her nose, and drowns in her own blood before I can get to her?* That would certainly ruin the surprise of being in town for Wes. "I don't want to see you get hurt, Sprite."

"I'm fine, Jacob. This is a normal lupus thing for me."

"Well, seeing you in pain is not a normal thing for me, so I'm sure you can understand why it bothers me." I point to the couch. "If you want, we can set you up down here, so you don't have to go up and down the stairs all day."

She shakes her head. "Then lupus wins."

"Huh?"

"I can do the stairs—I just need to watch my footing and move more slowly. If I allow lupus to defeat me, it wins, and I can't let that happen." She stiffens her spine. "I mean, I *won't* let that happen." Her lips quirk into a smile. "In case you've forgotten, the Emersons are sore losers."

CHAPTER 5

Isla

Internal playlist: "Adore You" by Miley Cyrus

Like some sort of soulmate homing beacon, I *feel* Jake coming long before I see or hear him. I attempt a nonchalant glance over my shoulder as he enters the kitchen. "Good morning, sleepyhead."

Even with messy waves falling into his face, his smile makes my knees go weak. "Morning, Sprite. What are you making?"

"It's a green smoothie. The anti-inflammatory properties help with my symptoms. I hope you like kale and spinach."

He curls his lip. "Wait . . . as a *beverage?*"

"Yeah, most people drink their smoothies, but I can getcha a spoon if ya want." He stares at me in disbelief, so I laugh. "Trust me, it's not as bad as it sounds. You can't even taste the kale over all the apple and blueberries."

"I'll take your word for it." He rearranges the dishes in the dish drainer, turning the spoons so they all face the same direction.

"Nope. You're gonna try it, Jacob." I hand him a glass and wait.

Jake takes a miniscule sip and grimaces. "It's . . . interesting."

I pat his shoulder. "Drink up. It's good for ya."

He points to my feet. "How's your ankle?"

"Much better, thanks. Doesn't hurt yet today."

"Yet?"

I shrug. "It's a fluid situation."

And it's true. One minute I can feel fine, and the next, the pain or exhaustion takes over. I've learned not to have high comfort or productivity expectations—it's better to go with the flow.

He frowns. "Please let me know if there's anything I can do to help."

I point to the coffee maker. "You can start the coffee. I wasn't sure how strong you like yours, so I figured I'd let you do it."

"You're my guest. I'll drink it however you like it," he says, scooping some dark grounds into the filter. "But for future reference, I like my coffee strong."

"Yeah, Wes likes jet fuel too."

"I enjoy more bang for my buck. I'm all about efficiency, Sprite."

I point to his spice rack. "And organization."

He grins. "You gotta admit, alphabetizing them makes sense. I mean, where's the coriander? Oh look, it's between the cinnamon and cumin. Where it *should* be."

I snort. "Do ya even use coriander?"

"No. I have no fucking clue what it's for," he admits with an embarrassed smile. "I included it for completeness sake."

I hold up a bottle and arch a brow. "You use a lot of saffron?"

He chuckles. "Nope. I've never used it once."

"Are you sure these aren't expired?"

"No way," he scoffs. "I routinely check expiration dates on everything in my house. I can assure you, nothing in my kitchen or medicine cabinet is past its prime."

"Except the pickles . . ." I laugh, and without thinking, reach up and ruffle his hair. "Your hair's so soft." I brush the satiny strands back from his face.

His breath catches, and he clears his throat. "Uh, thanks."

I jerk my hand away. "Sorry."

"No need to be sorry." His gaze drifts to my lips and for a moment, it seems like he might kiss me. My heart hammers in my chest as I await his next move. Then he straightens and walks to a stool at the kitchen island.

I quickly turn my attention to my smoothie. "What're you doing today?" I ask with forced nonchalance.

Jake rubs his jaw. "I dunno. Was there something specific you'd like to see in Manhattan?"

"Well, we're kinda limited for the time being."

He tilts his head. "How so?"

"Lena doesn't want Wes to know I'm in town, so if we're out and about, and we happen to be photographed, it'll ruin the surprise."

"Good point. Although, the paparazzi don't really bother with me much. Nowhere near the scale of what Wes and Memphis deal with. I could always wear a hat and sunglasses if necessary." The coffee pot beeps, and he makes his way over to it. "Last night you mentioned wanting to see a Broadway show. Maybe I can snag tickets to something." He pours us each a mug of coffee and adds creamer to his. He pauses with the carton hovering over my cup. "Shit. This creamer isn't dairy free."

"No worries, I can drink my coffee without. I'm also a fan of getting a bang for my buck."

"I'll keep that in mind." He points to the colorful capsules on the counter beside my smoothie. "Did you touch base with the airport to see if they found your carry-on?"

"Yeah, I called them earlier. No one's turned it in, but they promised to call me if anything changes." I pop the meds into my mouth and swallow them down with a gulp of smoothie. "I'm not overly concerned about it now that I've got my meds. Although, I'll probably leave some with you when I go back home to pack up my flat. No sense in declaring bulk overseas meds in customs if I'm coming right back to the States."

He nods. "You can leave anything you want here for safekeeping. So, listen, I know Dr. Donnelly phoned in a bunch of refills for you, but you should still look into getting established with some doctors around here. You know, for monitoring and whatnot."

"I will." My stomach flip-flops because I hate how vulnerable the whole situation makes me. Determined to squash my anxiety, I opt for a subject change. "Have you ever seen *Wicked*?"

He blinks a few times, no doubt registering my abrupt transition. "Yes, but I wouldn't mind seeing it again." He sips his coffee. "A good friend of mine plays backup Glinda when the lead is out. I'll call her to see if she can get us box seats."

Grinning, I rub my hands together excitedly. "Thank you so much."

"My pleasure, Sprite." He cocks his head. "Now that I'm thinking about it, I thought you didn't like the *Wizard of Oz*?"

I flush. "Well, as a kid I was afraid of the flying monkeys."

"Makes sense. So was I."

"Yeah, but *you* didn't have Reed making monkey screeches and flinging himself atcha in the middle of the night."

Jake chuckles. "He did that?"

I nod. "Yep. He was a real dick."

"Yeah, it sounds like it." He glances at the clock and reaches for his phone. "I'll text Kelly right now and see if she can get us seats for the matinee." He taps on his screen.

My phone chimes with a text. "Must be the hour for technology. I wonder who this is." I glance at the screen and curl my lip. "Ugh. Speak of the Devil, he is *such* a dick."

Jake raises a brow. "What did Reed do now?"

I show him the family group text. "Mum and Dad are in France for a month. Anyway, one of them sent us a picture of the Eiffel Tower. Wes replied with some cheeky 'ooh-la-la' comment, so I told them to ask someone to take their picture in front of it. Maybe Dad can give Mum a kiss or something."

"That's a great idea. Paris *is* the city of love after all." He sips his coffee and smiles.

"Yeah, well, Reed thought it was lame."

Jake rolls his eyes. "He would."

"That's fine if he thinks it, but he went out of his way to call it another birdbrained idea of mine."

Jake scowls. "Ignore him. He's a dick."

The final curtain falls, and I join in the standing ovation for the cast of *Wicked*. To call me awestruck would be an understatement.

Jake wraps an arm around me, sending tingles down my spine. "So, what did you think?"

"I'm blown away right now," I gush, hugging him. "Thank you so much for bringing me."

"You're welcome." He tightens our embrace. "I'm glad you enjoyed it."

I hold on to him for a little longer than I should, but I love hugs. I pull back slightly and peer up at his face. "Let me make you dinner."

"But you made me dinner last night. *And* breakfast."

"Yeah, and your point? *Someone* needs to put the spice rack to use."

Jake laughs. "You gonna use up my saffron?"

I arch a brow, accepting the challenge. "Maybe I'll use the coriander too. I've got plenty of tricks up my sleeve. You'll have to wait and see, Jacob."

We file out of the theater and head for the lot where we parked Jake's car. It had gotten quite windy while we were inside. Dark clouds loom overhead.

"We're supposed to get freezing rain today," he announces, opening his car door for me. "Good thing we hit the matinee."

"Ugh, I've heard about how shitty it is to drive in sleet."

"Yeah, it is, but sleet's different from freezing rain," Jake informs me with a wink. He closes the door and makes his way around to the driver's side.

I watch him as he settles. "Are you a meteorologist now?"

"A Jake of all trades, if you will." He squeezes my knee, his warm palm lingering for a moment. Then he tenses and pulls it away. He starts the car and pulls into traffic.

My skin, bereft of his touch, still tingles. I ache to feel his warm hands all over me, stroking my body and holding me tightly. I want to be close to him in every way possible. I study his jawline. Stubbled and sexy, his dimples still hint at their presence even though his expression is neutral. His gaze is fixed to the road ahead, so I admire my view of his long eyelashes.

The corner of his mouth lifts in a smirk. "What?"

"Huh?"

"I feel your eyes on me, Sprite. Do I have something on my face?"

"No, I'd tell you if you did. I was just, uh . . . well . . ." I clear my throat and focus on my hands. "Never mind."

We stop at a traffic light, and he looks over at me. "You all right?"

"Yeah. I forgot what I was gonna say." Since I suddenly don't know what to do with my hands, I crack my knuckles. My joints are swollen and inflamed, so it's not the wisest idea, but the numbness is driving me crazy.

Jake snatches the hand closest to him. "Please don't do that."

"Shit. Sorry," I mumble, feeling like an arse for not remembering his aversion to cracking joints.

He doesn't answer. Nor does he release my hand. Before I realize what I'm doing, I interlace my fingers with his and squeeze. Jake returns the squeeze and surprisingly, doesn't pull away.

"Your hands are cold," he points out.

"They always are. Shitty circulation."

Jake mumbles something and squeezes tighter, his heat infusing my skin.

We belong like this—connected and close, our hands intertwined. His breath catches when I brush my thumb over his knuckles. Neither of us speaks. We don't have to—our bodies speak volumes. The invisible current flowing between us electrifies me like a lightning bolt. My thundering heart beats harder with each passing moment. The rapid rise and fall of his shoulders tells me he feels it too.

Our perfect storm.

CHAPTER 6

Jake

Mood: "Wicked Game" by Chris Isaak

My life is full of *shoulds*. I should pull back, but I can't bring myself to let go. The more time I spend with Isla, the more I want her. Her soft little hand fits in mine perfectly. It takes every ounce of my self-control not to lift it to my lips and kiss each knuckle.

Images of our kiss flood my memory. It feels like yesterday, not five years ago. Though our embrace was brief, I loved having her in my arms. Her lips made time stand still. I remember the sweet coconut scent of her and the whimper she made when I pressed her up against the Jeep. I'd give anything to hear her moan again. Hell, I'd give my soul to be with her. But it's not just about me.

It's about Wes too.

If I don't get my shit together, I face the possibility of losing one of my best friends. The pain of that thought is enough to make me release Isla's hand. She and I can't be together. It would infuriate Wes and jeopardize her relationship with him. I can't put them in that position. I wasn't blessed enough to have a sibling, and I'll be damned if I come between a pair so close. I clench the steering wheel and try to focus on the reasons I can't have her.

We arrive outside my brownstone, and I glance over at Isla as I put the car in park. "Wait for me to come around to your side. It's slippery, and I don't want you to fall."

She nods and chews on her lip. That perfect bottom lip I want to kiss until—

She's off-limits.

I roughly unbuckle my seat belt and fling open the door. Forcing myself to breathe, I make my way to her side of the car and help her out. The sidewalk is slick, so I'll need to throw some salt down later.

I guide Isla up the stoop with a hand on the small of her back. Once inside, we remove our coats and shoes, and head for the kitchen.

"Do you want some tea?" I offer.

"Yes, please." She points to the fridge. "I'll get our dinner started. Does chicken work for you?"

"Whatever you feel like making is fine." I fill the kettle and place it on the stove. "Let me know how I can help."

"You relax, Jacob." She starts pulling ingredients out of the fridge and cabinets. "I never get to cook for anyone, so let me do my thing."

I retrieve a mug, grab the tea I'd purchased for her, and hold up the box. "Coconut-mango sound good?"

She smiles and nods. "That's a given. Thank you."

I lean against the counter and watch her flit around my kitchen like she's been cooking in it for years. I pour some water in her cup when the kettle whistles. "You want honey?"

She looks over her shoulder at me. "Yes, please."

God, she's beautiful. Kind and thoughtful. Funny. Enticing. Everything I've ever wanted. I stir honey into her tea like it's the world's most important task. Because in this moment, it is. I want to make her happy, please her in every way possible.

She walks over and wraps her arms around me. "I can't thank you enough for opening your home to me. I really enjoyed the play too."

I hug her tightly. "It's my pleasure, Sprite. I'm happy to have you here." Closing my eyes, I breathe in her scent and hold her close. I love the way she feels in my arms. My cock stirs, and I know I should let go, but I don't want to.

A soft sigh reaches my ears, and I imagine her beneath me, sighing and gasping in pleasure. The visual makes me rock-hard in an instant. I jump back, hoping she didn't feel it, but the expression on her face tells me she did.

Her eyes flick from mine to the sizable bulge in my jeans, then back again. Her gaze darkens despite the flush creeping over her skin. "What're we gonna do about this?" she asks, gesturing to the space between us.

"Nothing," I mutter. "Because we *can't.*"

A slow smile crosses her face, and my cock grows impossibly harder. "I can do whatever I want."

"Well, I don't have that luxury."

"You don't *have* the luxury or don't *want* to have it?"

"I think you know the answer to that one." My gaze darts to my crotch. "And if you don't, you're not paying attention." In desperate need of some space to cool down, I make my retreat, slowly backing away from her.

She props her hands on her hips. "I have more questions."

I pause in the doorway. "You've reached today's quota for questions."

Forty minutes later, after a lukewarm shower and *another* self-induced orgasm, I head back downstairs.

Isla looks up as I enter the kitchen. "Perfect timing. The chicken's almost ready."

"Smells great in here. What is that?"

She grins. "You're smelling the saffron I used in our rice."

"Did you know saffron is the world's most expensive spice?"

Her face falls. "Are ya mad I used it?"

"Of course not. I'm spewing random pearls of trivia at you, Sprite."

She laughs. "Your brain amazes me. I'm not sure if you're trying to impress me, but it's working."

"Yeah, I'm full of useless information." I snort. "Don't even get me started on pianos."

Isla holds up a hand. "Uh, that's *not* useless. You are a piano god."

Flushing, I settle on a stool. "I'm hardly a god. But thank you."

"I've been meaning to ask. How come you don't have one here?"

I tilt my head. "What? A piano?"

She gestures to the living room. "Yeah. I was surprised when I didn't see one out there."

"My favorite piano is in my studio, but I have a keyboard upstairs. Maybe I'll play something for you later."

Her eyes light up. "Oh my God, I'd love that." She places some chicken and rice on a plate and sets it in front of me. "Your talent has always amazed me."

"You're making me blush."

She shrugs. "Well, it's true. I remember when you'd play that rickety old one at my parents' place."

"It wasn't exactly rickety, just needed some TLC."

Isla settles beside me with her plate. "Are you gonna have lots of pianos at your community center?"

I nod. "I want as many instruments as possible."

As a testament to our hunger, we eat our food in relative silence. She's an amazing cook—melding flavors and textures I've never experienced before.

"This is so good, Isla."

She flushes. "Thank you. I'm glad you like it."

"Who taught you how to cook?"

"Mum, mainly. But I learned the more adventurous stuff on my own."

"You're gonna have to give me lessons."

She raises her eyebrows. "Really? You wanna learn to cook?"

"Yeah. I know the basics, but I need all the help I can get."

"I'll keep that in mind." After a moment, her hand closes around my wrist. "Oh, and by the way . . . I would've been happy to help you with that."

I frown. "Huh?"

"You know," her gaze darts to the ceiling, and it dawns on me that we're directly beneath the bathroom, "up there."

Oh, no . . .

She fucking heard me.

My fork hits the floor along with my jaw. Blood rushes to my face with such force, my capillaries might burst. Unable to breathe, I clutch the edge of the countertop with both hands until my knuckles turn white.

"Don't get your jocks in a twist. I'm simply putting it out there for next time."

"Were you spying on me?"

"Of course not." She points to her yoga pants. "I was cold, so I went upstairs to put these on. I went to your room to let you know dinner was almost ready. Your door was open, so . . ."

I squeeze my eyes shut. "Fuck."

She smirks. "Heard *that* too."

I can't make eye contact with her. I've never been this mortified in my entire life—not even when my pants got caught on the chain-link fence by the playground in sixth grade. I remember how they fell to my ankles, bringing my boxers with them. Mrs. Thompson's fourth period class saw my ass cheeks. I'd rather relive that moment *twice* than live with the fact that Isla heard me jerking off in the shower—saying her fucking name, no less. *Why the fuck didn't I close my bedroom door?*

I stand and put my plate in the fridge.

She eyes me. "What're you doing?"

"I can't eat right now."

"Oh, would ya please relax?"

"I'm going to bed. I'll see you tomorrow." I leave the room before she can answer and rush upstairs once more.

Locking my bedroom door, I send a quick text to Jesse.

> **Me: Dude, she fucking heard me moan her name when I jerked off in the shower!!!!!!! SHE HEARD ME!!!!!!!!!! FUUUUUUUCCCCCKKKKKK.**

I toss my phone on the bed and flop facedown. Hopefully, I'll smother myself in the process.

Maybe I'll become a monk and move to some distant mountaintop so I can jerk off in peace. Yeah, that's what I'll do—get me some gray robes and live out my days alone. Me and my lonesome cock. Like old buddies, we'll watch the sunset together. Drink beer and play cards. Maybe get a dog or something.

I would've helped you with that.

Since my traitorous brain decides now would be a good time to explore the fantasy, I close my eyes and imagine Isla in the shower with me. Water running over her curves, soaking her hair. I picture her eyes with droplets on her lashes as she peers up at me. I envision her hands, graceful and delicate, fingers wrapping around my cock like they gripped my wrist in the kitchen. I know it would feel ten times better if she stroked me. I groan into my comforter at the thought. I can't fucking imagine her mouth on me. My hands fist the fluffy goose-down bedding, like it's the only thing keeping me from burning alive. I'm hard again. I've been at least semihard since I picked her up at the airport, but I'll suffer through it this time. I can't risk her hearing me *again*.

I want all of her—body, mind, heart, and soul. I want her so fucking badly it's going to kill me. Exploring my desire is not an option. Indulging is out of the question. All I have is the fantasy of her. This bittersweet fucking torture that's ripping me apart. She's closer than ever before, but I still have an ocean of reasons not to touch her. No matter how deep the ache, I can't wade into these waters.

She's off-limits.

My phone chimes with a text, as if confirming my thoughts.

> **Wes: It's about bloody time you're getting laid, mate! Who's the lucky lady? More importantly, when can I meet her? You gonna bring her home to your mum?**

Wait, what? I narrow my eyes on the phone.

Oh.

My.

Fucking.

God.

I texted Wes instead of Jesse.

My cock and balls shrivel up, then climb through my pelvis to hide out in my abdomen somewhere near my spleen. My lungs refuse to take in air and my pulse sounds like a jackhammer in my head. I'm such a fucking idiot. I cringe at the thought of how much worse it could've been if I'd mentioned her name.

I think about Wes—all six foot five of him. He's two hundred and forty pounds of solid muscle with a hairpin trigger. I'm not wimpy, but I'm no fighter either, and I'd never be stupid enough to fight him. I respect him. He's always been there for me—even when the women in my life weren't.

I'll never forget how he dropped everything to come to my dad's funeral. He was filming the second Olympus Fire movie in Greece. I called to let him know about my father's heart attack, and the next thing I knew, he hopped a plane to New York. He blew off his priorities to be there for me, staying two days after the funeral to make sure I was all right. Jesse and Austin came too. Those guys have always had my back. They've always been there when it mattered.

I think about Nadia, my past girlfriend of almost three years, a Russian model with platinum hair, steel-blue eyes, and a gunmetal heart. Beautiful. Smart. Ice cold. She was in Paris when my dad died, strutting along some fancy runway. I asked her to come to New York to be at my side. She didn't. Apparently, modeling was more important. That was it for me. A few weeks later, when she had time off and wanted to visit, I told her not to bother. That was almost two years ago, and there hasn't been anyone since.

If I'm being honest, I never loved Nadia. I went through the motions of a relationship to take my mind off Isla. It didn't work.

Not even a little.

The thing is, I have a long history with her. As Wes and Reed's kid sister, Isla was always sort of underfoot. Yeah, Wes *sometimes* tried to include her, but Reed was dismissive at best. I felt bad when she'd pout because her brothers "were meanies." Raw and sad from my own parents' divorce, I couldn't bring myself to be anything but kind to the chubby-cheeked little girl who followed us around. It didn't kill me to throw a ball for her, or build a goddamn sandcastle, so I never understood why my friends didn't want her around.

I remember visiting one day after her appointment with the orthodontist. She proudly flashed her rainbow smile, showcasing a different color rubber band on each bracket. Instead of sharing in her excitement, Reed called her "Crayon Head." Another unnecessary dig. As tears welled in her eyes, I molded my green chewing gum to my teeth and gave her a dopey grin. She laughed and ran off to do her homework.

It takes zero effort to be nice. I wish more people would figure that shit out.

Isla got sick during one of my world tours, but Wes's updates made it feel like I was there at each specialist's appointment, each dialysis treatment. After her and Wes's surgeries, the relief of knowing she was going to be okay was bone deep.

I was in Melbourne for a visit about a month after Wes broke up with Rachel. He was still depressed over it, but knew their split was long overdue. I swung by his parents' place to say hello. I asked Isla what she thought about the breakup. She said, "If Rachel put as much energy into loving my brother as she exerted trying to control him, they'd still be together. Wes needs someone's ultimate support, not ultimatums. One day he'll find a woman who sees him and loves him for who he is, not who she wants him to be." I thought it was poignant for a fourteen-year-old. Sometimes I wonder if she had a crystal ball. Did she see Lena in her brother's future, or did she simply hope for someone like her?

Fast-forward to Wes's thirtieth birthday. I hadn't seen Isla in a few years, and I won't say I *forgot* about her, but life got busy. Other than checking on her health now and then, I didn't give her much thought, so I was fucking *blindsided* when she approached me on the beach.

When it finally clicked that the beauty standing in front of me with the shell was Isla, my attraction hit me so hard I stopped breathing. The fucking air sizzled around us, and I was drawn to her with a force that defied logic, gravity, science, and every philosophical and metaphysical truth that had ever existed. There was a disconnect between the part of my brain that remembered her as a kid and the part that recognized her as a woman. It didn't seem possible they were one and the same.

It. Fucking. Floored. Me.

And then, she pulled the rug out from under me. To call her kiss a shock would be like calling a blue whale a big fish. I reacted on instinct, and my body took over. I kissed her back with a ferocity that still scares me.

What terrifies me even more is that I haven't gotten over it.

Every part of me pulsed with the need to claim her, but Isla was only eighteen and I was twenty-eight. When my brain finally woke the fuck up, I pulled back. I stayed as far away as I could for five years.

And to be honest, I'm not sure it helped. Even with minimal contact, my feelings have been . . . confusing. My desire consumes me, swallowing me whole. I never knew it was possible to crave anyone—or anything—the way I crave Isla. And I didn't think I could possibly want her more than I have during the years since our kiss.

Until she got off the plane yesterday.

Now she's here, in my home, driving me crazy with heated glances and suggestive comments.

A soft knock sounds on my door. "Jake?"

"Yeah?"

"I wanted to apologize for upsetting you."

"It's fine, Sprite. I'll see you in the morning."

"Thank you for the care package and for taking me to the show. It means a lot to me. *You* mean a lot to me." My heart cracks wide open at the emotion in her muffled voice.

"You mean a lot to me too," my voice is thick and gravelly, "more than you know."

"Can I please come in?" she asks.

I'd give anything to fling the goddamn door open and pull her into my arms.

But I can't.

I clear my throat. "No. That's not a good idea."

"Fine, then I'll tell ya through the door. A car service is picking me up at eleven tomorrow morning to take me to a hotel."

I launch myself off the bed, stalk to the door, and yank it open. "Cancel it."

"I can't. It's nonrefundable."

"I don't care." I grip the doorframe, white-knuckling it. "You're not leaving."

Wide eyed, she searches my face but doesn't say anything.

"Cancel it," I repeat, tightening my grip. "Right now."

Isla takes a step back and crosses her arms over her chest. "*Now* you're saying you want me here?"

"I never said I didn't."

"No, but you implied it when you skipped dinner, stormed away from me, and locked yourself in your bedroom."

"Gee, I dunno, Isla. Maybe I was a little embarrassed?"

"Why?"

I release the doorframe and knot my fingers in my hair. "Seriously?"

"Yeah, seriously. I wanna know why having feelings for me embarrasses you."

I shake my head in disbelief. "Isla, you heard—" I squeeze my eyes shut and suck in a shallow breath. "You fucking heard me, okay?"

"Jake, if you had any idea how many times I've moaned *your* name during an orgasm, I guarantee you wouldn't be embarrassed right now."

CHAPTER 7

Isla

Internal playlist: "Power Over Me" by Dermot Kennedy

Jake grips the doorframe and stares at me like I told him I was carrying his child. Shoulders and chest heaving, mouth opening and closing on words I can't hear, the utter bewilderment in his gaze makes me smile. Maybe it's cruel, but I like this feeling of power over him, knowing he wants me as much as I want him. Knowing my words alone can tilt his world on its axis makes me feel like maybe these past five years haven't been in vain. Maybe my decision to wait for him wasn't some futile, misguided romanticism.

Regardless, I'm tired of waiting. Twenty-three years is a long time to hold on to something. I think my past boyfriends would agree, given the sheer number of them I shut down when things got to that level. Most of my relationships clocked in at three months or less—about the length of time it would take until they'd start pressuring me to put out. That's not to say I was a prude. I got *them* off plenty and let them kiss and touch me—from the waist up.

I had one long-term boyfriend at sixteen. Lucas Dawson was a star cricket player. Tall. Athletic. Gorgeous. At nearly nineteen, he'd been a gentleman for months. One day, he decided blowies weren't enough for him anymore and pushed me to go further. I'll never forget how dirty I felt when he pressured me for sex. Turns out, he had a bet going with his friends that he'd get me to give it up on his birthday. His plan backfired when I found out and dumped him that afternoon. I never looked back.

Lucas called me a dick tease, but he was wrong. Just because I wouldn't let him ram his dick into me, didn't mean I teased him. I never deliberately teased my boyfriends—I made my boundaries clear from the get-go, and I was more than generous in the oral sex department.

I learned the ins and outs of pleasing a man early on, and spent years honing my technique. With all the men I burned through, one theme held true. Nothing brought them to their knees faster than when I got on mine. Again, it was a power thing for me, a chance to feel in charge of the situation, especially after everything else spiraled out of control.

I remember how impotent I felt when my health crashed. Before my diagnosis, it was the unknown that plagued me. What was happening to my body? The swelling, my inability to pee, the seizures. Why did I feel so nauseous and weak? My symptoms improved with dialysis, but the depression got worse, growing so deep and dark, I never thought I'd shake it. I stupidly believed I was in the clear after I got Wes's kidney. Turns out I was in a different forest. A darker, thicker forest with taller trees and more predators. Lupus wreaked havoc on my mind and body—and continues to do so. It has affected every facet of my life, especially my love life.

I never craved sex because lupus robbed me of my libido before it even had the chance to develop. My first flare of sexual desire happened when I kissed Jake. Since then, no one's come anywhere close to the way he made me feel. I forced those relationships because that's what I was supposed to do— date boys my age and have sex—but I never felt anything for them. Southern Australia's riddled with men I've left in the dust of sexual frustration.

No one is dustier than me.

Countless nights, whether I was single or not, I'd lie awake thinking about Jake. Without fail, the memory of our kiss ignited me. I'd replay it over and over again until I was burning with need. Then I'd take it further and imagine what it would feel like to have him touch me, hold me in his arms, and make love to me. One night, I explored those feelings with a touch I knew wouldn't hurt me—my own. I had my first orgasm alone in the darkness, thinking of Jake. In fact, I've had *every* orgasm with him in mind, so it bothers me that he'd be embarrassed to do the same. Granted, he never heard me moan his name . . . but he will. It's only a matter of time before I give him my virginity.

Right now, there's something in his eyes that heats my insides. They're pinned to mine, burning with profound lust and something darker—like possessiveness. Lena was wrong when she said Jake isn't an alpha like my brother. Yes, he's a gentleman at heart, but the alpha inside him is climbing the walls, waiting for its chance to break free.

Jake finds his voice. "*What?*"

I stiffen my spine. "You heard me."

"I'm sure your boyfriends loved that."

I cross my arms over my chest. "Never found it necessary to tell them."

"Then why'd you tell me?"

"Because it pisses me off that I'm a source of embarrassment for you."

"*You* aren't the reason—" He takes a deep breath and meets my gaze. "Look, I'm confused—" He shakes his head. "No. I'm not confused. I'm frustrated. Extremely frustrated. Not at you—or anything you did or didn't do—but with the circumstances."

"Which is why I'm going to a hotel tomorrow."

He releases the doorframe and advances on me, stopping mere inches away. "No, you are *not*."

"You don't make decisions for me."

He backs me to the wall, bracketing me with his arms. "Isla, please don't leave."

I give him a slow smile. "I'll stay if you kiss me."

Pain flashes in his gaze. "I can't."

"Why not?"

"Because you're off-limits for me."

I narrow my eyes. "Because of my brothers?"

He sighs. "That's part of it. I know at least one of them would gleefully feed me my balls. Or peel off layers of my flesh. Probably both."

"Wes doesn't run my life."

"He doesn't run mine either."

I throw my arms in the air. "Then what's your issue?"

"I respect him, Isla—almost as much as I respect you."

"I'm not asking for your respect."

He presses his forehead to mine. "You're getting my respect whether you ask for it or not."

"You look like a cyclops right now."

He laughs and hugs me. "I was thinking the same thing about you."

I close my eyes and return his hug. "Fine. If you won't kiss me, please keep hugging me."

"I *am* hugging you, Sprite."

"Yeah, but you cut it short last time." I lean into his embrace. "Don't do that again . . . it made me sad." I blink back the welling tears. "Please hold me for a few minutes."

The air leaves his chest in a rush. "Honey, you're breaking my heart."

"Well, it's true. No one ever holds me."

He tightens his arms around me and whispers, "If I had my way, I'd never let you go."

I bury my face in his neck and cling to him as the tears slide down my cheeks. I didn't plan on crying, but it happened. It's no surprise—I'm tired, hormonal, and in the arms of the man I love . . . a man who claims he can't have me. It's a personal hell for which I have my fucking brothers to thank.

"Why are you crying?"

"Because I'm frustrated too. I'm tired of being lonely."

Jake hugs me tighter and gently strokes my hair. "Me too."

I cling to him, allowing the emotion to pour out of me. From yesterday's long flight, to losing my meds, to the tension between us, I'm spent. My ankles are swollen. My head is throbbing. I'm nauseous and my hips hurt, but none of that compares to my heartache.

He pulls back and cups my face, brushing my tears away with his thumbs. "Please don't cry, Sprite."

"I'm sorry."

"Don't apologize either."

I give a watery laugh. "Then what *can* I do?"

"Get some rest. Tomorrow, I'll take you to see my studio."

"Remember, my car's coming at eleven."

He kisses my forehead. "There's your kiss, now fucking cancel it."

"That doesn't count."

He clenches his jaw. "Isla, *please.*"

"Fine. You win."

"It's not about winning." He runs both hands through his hair. "It's about me wanting you here."

I nod and head for my room. I dig through my purse, pull my phone out, and call the car service to cancel.

Jake appears in the doorway. "Don't forget the hotel."

I point to my phone. "Working on it."

He smiles, and it steals my breath. "Thank you for staying."

"Thanks for having me," I let my gaze burn into his, "even though you think you can't."

"Just because I can't, doesn't mean I don't want to."

I dramatically flop onto the guest bed. "This is America . . . home of the free, pursuit of happiness, and all that jazz, right?"

"Sweetheart, if I was free to pursue my happiness, I'd be in that bed with you right now."

He's gone before I can respond. The door to his bedroom closes behind him with a soft click.

I change into my pajamas, grab the bottle of face wash Jake bought me, and head for the bathroom to ready myself for bed.

Who knows? Maybe I'll fall asleep moaning his name.

I wake with a jolt and throw the covers off. Swirling tendrils of the nightmare I was having retreat to the corners of my mind. I'm sweating, which is a normal occurrence when I'm hormonal. I drag myself out of bed for a pad change and a glass of water.

I tiptoe downstairs to the kitchen and pull a glass from a cabinet. Leaning against the counter, I press a hand to my lower abdomen. I'm extremely crampy, which means tomorrow's going to suck. My periods are fucking brutal, thanks to lupus. I swallow a couple of pain pills and head back upstairs.

I round the corner at the top of the steps and walk smack into Jake, spilling the glass of ice water. He yelps and I shriek as freezing water saturates both our shirts. The glass slips from my grasp and shatters at our feet.

"Fuck! Are you all right?" He flicks the hall light on. "Why are you creeping around?"

I squint against the brightness. "I was thirsty. Why are *you* sneaking up on me?"

"I didn't even know you were up." He flashes a grin. "I'm hungry and that rice was calling my name."

"Well, shit. Don't let me get between you and your food." I chuckle and step aside, my bare foot finding a shard of glass. "Ouch!"

He snags me around the waist and carries me into the bathroom, setting me on the counter by the sink. "Don't move. I'll go grab the first aid kit." He leaves the room.

The ball of my foot's oozing blood. I press a hand to stop the flow and try to find the piece of glass.

Jake returns a moment later with a red box. His eyes widen, and he snatches my foot. "Why are you bleeding so heavily?"

You have no fucking idea.

"I'm on blood thinners." And come to think of it, I really need to find a doctor in New York so they can monitor me. I shouldn't be bleeding this heavily. My dosage may need an adjustment.

"Why?" He shrugs out of his wet shirt and quickly wraps it around my foot, applying pressure to my wound.

"Lupus causes blood clots, and I've already had a few. The one in my lungs could've been fatal. My doctors make me take blood thinners to protect my kidney and keep me from having a heart attack, stroke, or another pulmonary embolism. They don't want to take any chances." I shrug and force a smile. "They'd rather I bleed to death."

"I'd give *anything* to take this illness away from you."

"Thank you," I whisper.

"I swear to God," he meets my gaze, nostrils flaring, "if there was a way I could have it, so you didn't have to, I'd do it in a fucking heartbeat."

Lips parting, I press my hand to my heart. "You have no idea how much your ferocity means to me."

"I'm serious. It makes me livid you have to deal with all this shit."

"I'm used to it now." I shrug. "I try not to think of myself as sick, you know? For the most part, I lead a normal, healthy life. Yeah, some days it slows me down more than others, but I try not to let it stop me. God knows there are plenty of people with lupus who have it way worse than I do."

At least, for the time being. In its advanced stages, lupus can be downright debilitating, which I've seen firsthand. Sadly, unless they find a cure, that's what my future holds. I push the dark thoughts aside.

"Did you meet any of them?" He peeks at my bleeding foot.

"Yeah, Mum forced me into a support group back home. I've formed several close friendships over the years. It's mostly women, but we do have one guy."

"I'm glad you have that kind of support system."

"Me too. It's nice to have people who understand when I feel like bitching. Friends who get what I'm going through. Unfortunately, many of my mates from childhood have given up on me."

He frowns. "What makes you say that?"

I pick at my nails, trying to figure out a response that doesn't make me sound bitter. "Let's put it this way. Just because many of my symptoms aren't visible to others, doesn't mean they aren't there. Sure, I might *seem* fine, but it doesn't take much for me to overdo it."

"Wait, your friends think you fake your illness?"

"To be honest, I don't know what they think. But it's no secret they've stopped inviting me to gatherings."

"Why?"

"Probably because I flaked out so many times. I'd agree to do something—or go somewhere—but by the time it got close, I couldn't handle it. It's not that I wanted to cancel at the last minute, ya know? But I *had* to. Sometimes, the pain or nausea is so intense, I can't move. My old mates acted like I ditched them to take naps because I'm boring or antisocial. No one sees what I really go through."

"I'm sorry people haven't been there for you, Sprite."

"That's why I have my lupus group. They keep me afloat and give me the support I need. Besides, it's good for me to see what others deal with. It's healthy to keep my perspective. Shit could always be worse."

"It's great you have such a positive mindset. What's the worst part of it for you? All the meds?"

"No, not really. They're a necessary evil. Physically, my worst symptoms are joint pain and severe fatigue. But, if I'm being honest, it's the emotional impact that hits hardest. It's an isolating illness. It's tough to stay positive when I'm feeling lonely or angry. Or just plain depressed. But like I said, I'm used to it. And it could always be worse."

"You shouldn't have to be used to it. They need to cure you." He runs a hand through his hair. "What can I do to help?"

"It's an autoimmune disease. There is no cure. There's nothing you or anyone else can do." I shake my head. "Other than contributions to medical research."

"I already do that."

My brows shoot upward. "Really?"

"Money's been automatically deducted from my account every month since your diagnosis. Double comes out during your birth month. My mom and my friend Jesse's wife are breast cancer survivors, so I donate to the Cancer Society too."

I try to speak but can't find the words. My eyes blur. I blink back the tears and place my hands on his shoulders. "Thank you."

"My pleasure."

I peer into his gorgeous eyes. "You're an amazing man."

He smiles, stealing my breath and what remains of my sanity. "You are an incredibly strong woman, Isla Rose."

I love you.

Overwhelmed by what I'm feeling, I flush and avoid eye contact, focusing on his chest.

It occurs to me I haven't seen Jake shirtless since before our kiss, so I take a moment to enjoy the view. His shoulders and pecs are well defined and heavily muscled. A smattering of dark hair covers his broad chest, tapering to his abs before disappearing beneath his waistband.

His abs.

Holy fuck, his abs!

"When did ya get so fucking sexy?"

His gaze sweeps the length of me, coming to rest on my boobs. It dawns on me that my sopping wet, *white* shirt is plastered to my skin, leaving little to the imagination. "Probably around the same time you did."

I reach out and touch his naked chest, palms flattening against warm skin. With both hands still applying pressure to my wound, he's powerless to stop me. I know I shouldn't, but I can't help myself.

Jake sucks in a sharp breath and his gaze darts to mine. "What are you doing?"

"Touching you," I murmur, allowing my hands to drift lower, over his pecs to his mouthwatering washboard abs. I trace each ridge with my fingertips, watching his nipples pebble and goose bumps bloom.

He groans, his eyes fluttering closed. "Isla—"

"Hmm?"

"Honey, you're killing me." His chest heaves with each breath and the pajama pants do little to hide his erection. "You. Are. Fucking. Killing. Me."

"Not trying to kill ya, Jake. I just wanna put my hands on you."

"You can't."

"Actually, it looks like I can." I nod to my hands and smile. "I think what you mean is that I *shouldn't*. But those are two entirely different things."

"Do you have any idea what you're doing to me?"

My gaze drifts to his erect cock. "I think I do."

"I'm talking about inside," he snaps, releasing my foot to thump his chest with a fist. "What you're doing to my fucking heart."

I jerk my hands away and meet his pain-filled gaze. "I'm sorry. I didn't mean to upset you."

He nods and unwraps the shirt. "Now that the bleeding has slowed, I'm going to take the glass out. Hold still." He pulls a pair of tweezers from the first aid kit and braces my foot on his knee. He carefully removes the shard, cleans the wound, and bandages me.

"Thank you."

He tosses me a towel. "Stay here while I clean up the glass." He leaves the room with an abruptness that matches his clipped tone.

I squeeze my eyes shut, hating that he's angry with me. Furious with myself for losing control. Why did I have to put my hands on him, stroke him like he's some exotic creature for my entertainment? All I wanted was to feel his warmth, touch his hard body, soothe the restlessness inside him—and me. But I fucked up. I made him uncomfortable and hurt him.

Tears prick my eyes again, but I blink them away. No sense crying over spilled milk. It's not like I can un-touch him.

He reappears with a broom and dustpan and sweeps up the glass, emptying the shards into the bathroom trash can.

"Am I allowed off the counter yet? Or am I still in time-out?"

He leans the broom in the corner and walks over to me. He grips my knees, the touch sending sparks up my thighs. "First, we need to set some ground rules."

I raise a brow. "Ground rules?"

"Yeah," his lips twitch into a smirk, "since *someone* lacks the ability to keep their hands to themselves." He leans in close, the tips of our noses touching. "I'll give you a hint. That someone isn't me."

"I'm *able* to keep my hands to myself . . . but I don't want to."

"Which is exactly why we need ground rules."

"What if I promise to control myself? Can we skip the rules?"

"I dunno, Isla. Do you keep promises the way I do?"

"I don't know much about the promises you make, or whether or not you keep them, but I do know my goal isn't to hurt you."

His expression softens. "Listen, I'm sorry I snapped at you. I respect the hell out of you, Isla. I care for you and—" His grip on my knees tightens. "And I want you more than I want to breathe, but we can't act on this."

"I respect you too, and I've cared about you for longer than I can remember. By that, I mean my whole life." My hands settle on top of his and squeeze. "I can understand why you feel like we can't get involved. But I need you to understand something too. Despite what anyone thinks, my brother doesn't get to tell me what to do. I follow my own path."

A wry grin crosses his features. "Which is precisely why I'm giving you ground rules."

I give him my sultriest smile. "Rules are meant to be broken, Jacob Bennett." I stroke my thumbs over the tops of his hands. "Often and well." I hop off the counter and sashay from the room, purposely swaying my hips. I pause in the doorway and peer over my shoulder at him. "You can tell me your rules in the morning."

The lust in his gaze is volcanic. He opens and closes his mouth a few times before speaking. "What happens then?"

"I'll spend the afternoon breaking them."

He steps closer to me, fists clenched at his sides, his body vibrating with tension. "Then I'll make new ones."

"And I'll spend the night breaking those too."

Jake's gaze reaches inferno level. "Why?"

"Because I'm an Emerson and I get what I want." I lick my lips, allowing my gaze to roam his body. "You're *mine*, Jake . . . even if you aren't ready to accept it yet."

CHAPTER 8

Jake

Mood: "Sledgehammer" by Peter Gabriel

Is it possible to die from lust? To want another person so deeply, so intensely, that it literally fucking kills you?

As I stand in a lukewarm shower with my cock in my hand for the second time in hours, I know for me, death by lust is not only a possibility, but a fucking probability.

I stare at my chest, my abs. I can still feel her fingertips exploring me, burning me alive. It took every ounce of strength not to spread her thighs and bury myself deep inside her. As I stroke my shaft, my veins simmer with the need to claim her, the desire to wipe out memories of any other man she's been with and replace them with me. My kiss. My touch. My cock moving inside her. I want to be all she knows. All she needs. I want her to love me as deeply as I love her.

You're mine, Jake. Her words echo in my mind. What she doesn't realize is she's mine too. I close my eyes and picture her sultry smile, the curve of her breasts, the way her hardened nipples showed through the wet shirt. I want to suck them between my lips and flick my tongue. I haven't forgotten her little whimper of pleasure from when we kissed years back. I wonder how she'd moan if I licked her. Would she pull my face closer? Knot her fingers in my hair and tug on the strands? I groan and squeeze my cock tighter. A few more strokes and I'm there.

It's a release I desperately need, but nowhere near the one I crave with Isla.

I yawn and stretch in my bed. I slept like a rock. Oh, the wonders of a midnight orgasm. Too bad it was self-administered. Again.

I still can't believe Isla heard me in the bathroom. Then how I almost blew my cover with that text to Wes. I never even replied to the guy. My life is a clusterfuck of embarrassment lately. Needing a dose of sanity, I grab my phone and dial Jesse's number.

He answers on the second ring. "Yo."

"Dude, I can't make this shit up." I quickly fill him in on my jerk-off snafu and how Isla called me out on it. And then the texting debacle.

He laughs his ass off. "You need to write a book about all the shit that happens to you."

"I really should. I mean, I've got material from *way* back."

"Forget the archives—you have enough from this week alone. Anyway, how's Isla been toward you? Do you think she's still interested after five years?"

I clench the phone. "Yeah, man. She came right out and said it."

"So, see where it takes you."

"You know I can't do that."

"You keep saying that, but sooner or later shit's gonna hit the fan. You'll have to decide what holds more value to you—her family tree or what you feel for her."

I sigh heavily. "I know."

"It sounds like Wes isn't the only thing stopping you."

"He isn't. You know how I am, Jess. I don't want to overwhelm her with my neurotic ways. Besides, she's only in New York for a year. With all the dudes she's dated, I'd be lucky if I could keep her interest for a month, let alone an entire year."

"Pretty sure she's crushed on *you* for years."

"A crush isn't love. Once she's around me enough, she'll get over it quickly. Then what? She'll move back to Melbourne, and I'll still be here jerking off by my lonesome."

"You don't know that."

I stare out my bedroom window. "It's inevitable, man. Women don't stick around for me. Bottom line, she can't give me what I need."

"I get that it's scary, but you'll never know how good it could be unless you take a chance. Allow yourself to live a little, Jake. Let *her* decide what she's capable of giving you. Listen, I hate to cut this short, but I gotta go. Hannah's on the other line."

"Tell her I said hello."

"Will do. Later."

"Bye."

I shrug a shirt on and brush my teeth before heading downstairs. The coffee's been brewed, and Isla made muffins, but she's nowhere to be found. I call her name and search the main floor before running back upstairs.

I knock on her door. "Isla?"

"Yeah?"

"Can I come in?"

"Yes."

I push the door open. "Hey, sleepyhead."

"Hey." She's curled into a ball on her side, eyes squeezed tightly shut. "Good morning."

I rush to her bedside. "What's wrong?"

"I'm fine," she says in a strained voice.

"You're doubled over in pain. What the hell's going on?"

"It's always like this for the first day or two."

"Is this lupus related or your period?"

"Period," she mutters, tightening her arms around her midsection. "Can I take a rain check on visiting your studio? I don't think I can handle it today. My uterus is on a one-organ mission to shred my insides."

"Of course. Can I get you something? A glass of water?"

She points to a bottle on the nightstand. "I've got water, thanks. Would you mind grabbing the heating pad, please? I left it in the living room. And the paracetamol."

"Be right back." I jog downstairs and swing into the kitchen to put the kettle on. I know she didn't ask for it, but tea will make her feel better. Snatching the care package from the living room, I rush back into the kitchen and glare at the kettle, which isn't doing its job of heating the water fast enough. I count laps as I circle the kitchen island, replaying Jesse's words in my mind.

I've always considered him wise—especially when it comes to women. Let's be real, his wife is a dream come true. Hannah and Jesse are meant to be. I want what they have. I want someone who will stand by my side, no matter what life dishes out. A woman who will be there when it matters.

The kettle whistles, jolting me into action.

Armed with the items Isla requested, I head back upstairs a few minutes later. "One heating pad, pain meds, and mango coconut tea for the lady."

She smiles, stopping my heart. "You're the best. Thank you." She presses herself up and positions the heating pad on her abdomen before accepting the Tylenol. Popping three tablets in her mouth, she chugs some water and releases a heavy sigh. "What's on your agenda for today?"

"I need to review some community center stuff and meet up with Garrett to discuss the signage." I hand her the tea. "Careful, it's hot."

"Thank you."

"Anytime, Sprite. Do you want honey in it? I can run back downstairs ..." I'm ready to bring her the world on a platter if it will make her feel better.

She takes a slow sip and smiles. "No, it's perfect."

Although I realize it's only a cup of tea, her satisfaction warms me as much as if I were the one drinking it.

Isla tilts her head. "Wait, who's Garrett? Is this the same Garrett that Wes knows? Lena's friend?"

"Yep, that'd be him. Garrett lives on the bottom two floors of Lena's brownstone. They've been best friends for decades and neighbors for nearly as long. Anyway, Garrett is a phenomenal graphic designer. He's donated his time to help with all the publicity stuff, like signs, brochures, and our website."

"That's awesome."

"Yeah, he's a good guy, despite what you may have heard from Wes."

She snorts. "He's so fucking hotheaded sometimes."

"You should've seen him at my gala. I thought the two of them were gonna brawl."

She rolls her eyes. "Too bad Garrett didn't knee him in the balls."

"It reminded me of the clash of the Titans."

"The whole thing was a bloody clusterfuck, but Wes brought it on himself. I was with him the day those pictures surfaced."

"You were?"

"Yeah. Sitting right next to him when your text came through."

I line up her pill bottles on the nightstand. "Did he lose his shit?"

"You have no idea . . . I think he scared Mum a bit with his behavior. She cried when he left. Personally, I wanted to slap him. Lena's amazing, you know?"

"She truly is. I feel like I've known her forever."

Isla nods. "Me too. When I hung out with them in LA, it was funny to see her put him in his place. She doesn't take any of his shit."

"You should've seen her in Alaska. I've never seen Wes so off his game and speechless."

"Yeah, and the stupid fuck nearly lost her. Enough about my idiot brother. Tell me more about your community center. I heard there's going to be a fashion department?"

I twist her bottles, so the labels face outward. "Yeah. The facility will be divided into wings. I plan to have an area for costume and fashion design upstairs. I ordered a fleet of sewing machines."

She grins. "Is it odd that sewing machines excite me?"

"Not really." I laugh. "Judging by the size of your tattoo, it's clear you're into needles."

"You don't like it?"

"Not what I said."

"Do you like it?"

"I only saw it the one time, but yeah, it's sexy." I'm sure the view would be sexier if I saw it while I gripped her hips and thrust inside her, but that's another story. "Extremely. Sexy."

She bats her lashes. "Would ya like another look?"

Fuck yes. My cock twitches at the thought. "Not right at this moment."

Isla shrugs. "Suit yourself. Tell me more about the community center."

"Well, it's been a dream of mine for as long as I can remember. I hope to make it a safe place for kids to explore all things music, fine arts, graphic arts, photography, theater, fashion design, and more."

"You're doing it through your charitable foundation?"

"Yes. I'm footing most of the bill, but my benefit gala raised over five hundred grand for the cause. Wes and Austin each pledged half a million too."

"Wow, he never mentioned that."

"You know Wes likes his good deeds to go unnoticed."

She smirks. "That's a good way of putting it. I'm curious, though . . . you mentioned a lot of art stuff, but music's your thing. Tell me more about that."

"So, the facility's lower floor will house our music program, with workshops and lessons provided to eligible kids free of charge. We already have a lot of stuff planned for the kids. For instance, Austin agreed to drop in for an eight-week Memphis blues course. Once our collaboration album—and possible tour—is wrapped up, I'll be giving piano lessons and serving as the resident vocal coach."

She wiggles her fingers. "Will you give me lessons? You said my internship is near your studio. Maybe I could meet you there?"

"You wanna learn piano, Sprite?"

"I'm sure I'll suck royally, but yeah."

"I'd love to show you around the keys. We can start tomorrow."

"Excellent. I'll try not to getcha all keyed up."

I snort a laugh. "Well played."

She touches my arm with cool fingertips. "In all seriousness, I think what you're doing for those kids is amazing."

"Thanks. When my parents split up, the Art Haven in Brooklyn was a place where I found comfort. I wouldn't be where I am today if it weren't for the experiences there." I rub my jaw. "I wanted to use my resources to create something similar—a place for kids to turn to when they're sad or lost or simply bored. I'm thrilled it's finally happening. It gives me the opportunity to give back to my community and make a legacy for myself."

"I am so proud of the man you've become." She shakes her head in appreciation. "I always knew you'd go places with your talent, and never doubted that you'd give back to the community, but to see it happen is awe-inspiring."

I settle on the edge of the bed and take one of her hands in mine. "You have no idea how much that means to me."

"What're you naming the center?"

Shit.

My face gets hot. "Uh ... The Phoenix. Garrett came up with some gorgeous phoenix designs to use for our marketing blitz."

"The Phoenix? Like my tattoo—" Her mouth drops open. "Wait ... did my tattoo inspire the name?"

The rest of the capillaries in my face explode. "Not your tattoo." I force a swallow and look over her shoulder at the wall behind her. "Just you."

Before I can react, she throws her arms around my neck and pulls me into a hug. Her lips brush the outer shell of my ear, sending jolts of electricity down my spine and hardening my cock. "And here I thought the only thing I inspired was 'Crave.'"

"Crave" is a hidden track featured on my last studio album. It's extremely sensual—a darkly provocative foray into the pleasures of sex. It's my voice with the piano, and the *only* way I had the balls to release it was by embedding the song ten minutes after the album's final track. I'd be willing to bet most of my fans never noticed it was there. But, apparently, Isla did. I wonder if she picked up on the track's deliberate placement—following "If Only" by ten minutes. Both tracks are about her and the ten-minute break is symbolic of our age difference. I sweated bullets on release day.

"Who said *you* inspired it?" I rub a strand of her hair between my fingers. I know I should pull away from her, but I can't. "Maybe I wrote it for someone else."

I'm bluffing because I may let her kiss me if I admit she was my muse. Hell, I may let her kiss me anyway.

A low laugh sounds at my ear. "Well, if it isn't about me, I've been playing the wrong soundtrack."

"Soundtrack?"

She clasps the back of my neck and pulls my ear to her lips. "Yeah, for when I moan your name."

My breath leaves me in a rush. "This qualifies as rule breaking."

"I don't recall being given rules." She kisses my jaw. "Besides . . . I already told you I was planning to break them."

Pull back, you stupid fuck.

"Rule number one. Stop trying to seduce me."

She kisses my neck. "I'm not *trying* to seduce ya."

My hands clench the down comforter. "Let me rephrase. Stop seducing me."

"Okay." She releases me and flops back against the pillows.

Now I'm fucking reeling because I didn't actually expect her to stop—nor did I want her to. I rub a hand over my face. "That was unexpected."

Isla laughs and sips her tea. "I'm full of surprises."

I stare at her plush, mouth-watering lips but don't respond. I'd give anything to uncover her secrets.

She tilts her head. "So, is 'Crave' about me?"

"Maybe." I smirk and climb to my feet. "If 'Crave' gets you off, you should hear the others I've written for you."

Her eyes widen. "Others?"

"Yeah. Maybe I'll let you listen to 'Indulge' sometime." I flash a wink on my way out the door. "If you're capable of behaving yourself."

"That's doubtful."

I laugh. "At least you know your shortcomings. I'll be at Garrett's. Call me if you need me."

Twenty minutes later, I plop onto Garrett's couch and shake my head.

He hands me a can of seltzer and a manila folder filled with community center stuff. "Rough day?"

"You have no idea, man."

"Is Crocodile Dundette giving you a run for your money?" He waggles his brows, his golden lionlike eyes alight with amusement.

"I'm fucked. Completely and utterly fucked. Left, right, sideways, and upside down."

Garrett swigs his seltzer. "You pick out your coffin yet?"

"Nah, but I found a nice urn. I'm writing my obituary tonight. When they find my body—*if* they find it—have someone cremate me." I hold up a finger. "Oh! And give my piano to charity."

"I thought you said you were keeping your distance?"

I laugh. "She's *in* my house, dude. How the fuck can I be distant?"

"Wait, Lena said she was getting a hotel—"

"She had a reservation." I rest my face in my hands. "But I told her to cancel it."

"You and I are more alike than I thought."

I lift my head to meet his knowing smirk. "What do you mean?"

"We're both gluttons for punishment."

"I take it Ella's keeping you on your toes?"

He rubs at his wrists as a dark expression crosses over his features. "You could say that."

I recently introduced him to my friend Ella Sammons. As a photojournalist for the *Tribune*, I wanted her to get first dibs on interviewing Garrett about his lead role in the upcoming Broadway production, *Prodigy*. Ella's intensity rivals Garrett's. They're a match made in heaven. Or hell. Depends on how you look at it. She's certainly hot as hell. And the definition of an enigma.

"Put it this way," Garrett places a hand on my shoulder, "I, too, am fucked beyond repair, my friend. Fucked with a capital F." He clenches his jaw. "Bold print. Highlighted *and* underlined."

"Yeah, but at least Ella doesn't have brothers."

"True that. Why don't you save yourself the stress of secrecy and come right out and tell him?"

I bark a laugh. "Because I'd prefer not to die."

"Maybe he'll surprise you. I mean, Lena's been keeping him pretty occupied—you know, when they fuck their furniture through my ceiling."

"I don't know how you deal with that."

"Dude, you have no idea. The guy's a fucking machine." He gestures to a set of headphones on the coffee table. "I got noise-canceling ones so I can cope. If they keep it up, I may need to invest in a tranquilizer gun."

"Oh?"

"Yeah, I'm about two fuck fests away from darting Tarzan up there in the ass." He lets loose a battle cry of sorts, followed by a mock feminine moan. "There's nothing like listening to a porn soundtrack with your morning coffee. And all fucking day thereafter." His golden eyes meet mine. "It's unnerving."

"Have you tried talking to them about it?" I sip my seltzer.

He snorts. "And say what? Lena, please don't vocalize so much when you orgasm. Hey, Dundee, try to keep it down while you're deep-dicking my best friend."

My laugh sends seltzer out my nose, the bubbles burning like a bitch.

Garrett hands me a napkin. "There's no easy way to approach that conversation. Besides, I kinda deserve it." His lips curve into a devious grin. "My friend Anya is pretty loud in bed, so Lena has overheard more than her share of frenzied fuckery. But anyway, back to what I was saying, Wes knows you're a good guy, why wouldn't he embrace the idea?"

I finally recover from my coughing fit, and my knee starts to shake with the idea of having that conversation with Wes. "You want a list?" I rake a hand through my hair. "To start, I'm too old for her."

"Age of consent in New York is seventeen. How old is she?"

"Twenty-three."

"Seven years into legal territory. You're my age, right?"

"I'll be thirty-four in February."

Garrett waves a dismissive hand. "Ten years is nothing, dude."

"Now you sound like Lena. The fact remains that she's his little sister. I don't think you understand their closeness."

"No, but if I had a sister, I think I'd want her involved with a man whose character I can vouch for. Wes speaks highly of you."

"She and I are at different stages of life. She's finishing college, while I recently had my ten-year reunion."

"What are her plans for the future?"

"I have no fucking clue. She's not a planner like I am. She doesn't stay in one place, or with one person for too long. She burns through men like a wildfire."

Garrett scratches his chin. "What about you?"

I sigh heavily. "I'm over the dating scene. I want to settle down with someone who will be there when it matters."

"Would she ever settle?"

"Doubtful," I mutter. "So, can you understand why it's a bad idea? Why she's wrong for me?"

"Yet you *still* told her to cancel her hotel room. What is that old saying?" He chuckles. "Oh yeah, something so wrong, it's right."

I turn my head at the loud knock on his door. "Expecting company?"

"Yep." Garrett flashes me a grin. "Take a wild guess who this is."

Fuck.

"It's open," he calls.

"What time are we going to the brewery, mate?" Wes's booming voice reaches my ears. He stops in the doorway. "Bennett! What the hell're ya doin' here? I thought you had to go to your studio today?" He walks over and claps my shoulder.

I clear my throat. "I didn't feel like driving into Manhattan, man."

"Good. You can come to the brewery with us."

I glance between them, wondering about their chosen activity. Garrett's a recovered alcoholic. Bars and breweries aren't the wisest place for him. There must be some compelling reason. "What's happening at the brewery?"

"Craft beer," Wes says with a grin.

"There's an open mic tonight," Garrett explains. "They have one every week. A few of my employees are going. It's usually a good time. Remember that singer I mentioned the other day?"

"Your coworker's cousin who sounds like a mix of Adele and Florence Welch?"

"Yeah. Zara will be there again." He jerks his thumb at Wes. "Dundee can drink all the craft brews he wants, but *I'm* going for the music and parmesan truffle oil fries."

"And to ensure my safe transport," Wes adds.

Normally, I'd leap at the opportunity to drink beers with the guys and listen to live music. Tonight's different, courtesy of the beauty in my guest room. The siren who is hell-bent on seducing me. I don't want her there alone. Beyond that, I can't seem to stay the fuck away from her.

"I think I'll sit this one out."

Wes cocks his head. "Why? You love craft beer."

"My eyesight's been fucked up all day. I think a migraine's brewing." I feel like a dick for lying to him, but Lena wants Isla's presence at his party to be a surprise, and I don't want to let anything slip.

He frowns. "You get way too many migraines, mate. Have ya had that MRI yet?"

"Yeah. It was normal." I sip my seltzer and let the bubbles fizz in my mouth.

"Good." He turns to Garrett. "Looks like it's just you and me, mate."

"Where's Lena?" I ask.

"She's having a ladies' night with one of her girlfriends. She told me to find something to do."

"Hence, it's my night to babysit," Garrett adds with a chuckle.

Wes leans back and rests his feet on the coffee table. "You gonna let me stay up late and feed me treats?"

Garrett snorts. "You gonna antagonize me the whole fucking night?"

Wes grins. "Would I be me if I didn't?"

I laugh. "Garrett, in case you're wondering, the answer to that is *no.*"

"Yeah, I had a feeling," he mutters.

"It's nice to have someone to share the joy with—usually Emerson's busting my balls. You're welcome."

"You love me, Bennett." Wes leans forward. "By the way, Lena invited some of her nurse mates to the post-Thanksgiving party."

"Yeah, I assumed she'd have friends there since she's calling it *Friendsgiving.*"

He snorts. "You must not be feeling well—you usually aren't this dense."

"Help me out. How am I being dense?"

"*Women*, mate." He punches my shoulder. "There will be women there to introduce you to."

"For what?"

He wags his brows. "*Piano lessons.*"

"I'm not giving private lessons nowadays."

He narrows his eyes on my face. "Jesus Christ, do ya have a fever or something?"

I throw my arms in the air. "No, man. You're talking in fucking riddles."

Garrett snickers and elbows Wes. "Go easy on him—he's had a long day."

"Step one: Bennett meets woman. Step two: Bennett speaks to said woman. Step three: if all goes well and he doesn't fuck up, Bennett gets himself a date."

"Who the hell said I want a date?"

"I dunno, mate, but you're cranky as fuck lately. Maybe you need to go out and get yourself laid." He perks up and slaps his knee. "Wait a minute, I forgot about that little piece of somethin' somethin' you texted me about." He winks and my face grows incredibly hot. "*Are* you getting laid?"

Fuck.

"No. Definitely not."

Wes grins. "Then who's hearing you call out her name when you jerk off in the shower?"

Double fuck. Think, Jake. Think!

"Uh . . . Rosa."

Wes raises a brow. "Who the fuck is Rosa?"

"My cleaning lady."

"Since when did ya get a cleaning lady, mate?" He shakes his head. "You never mentioned her before, and I find it hard to believe you'd let somebody inside your space. No offense, but you're far too anal for that. Do ya follow behind her and check her work? Re-wipe the counters and shit? That's a helluva way to make yourself *more* anxious."

I give him the finger. "I'm trying to get ahold of my compulsions, thank you very much."

Garrett gives me a knowing smirk. "So . . . tell us about Rosa. Is she hot?"

Damn it, Garrett.

"Yeah." I pinch the bridge of my nose. "She's smoking hot. Hence the jerking off part."

Wes claps my shoulder. "Make it happen, mate."

"I don't have time for any of that shit, Emerson."

Garrett grins. "Make time."

"Rosa's recently divorced, and I don't have the time or energy to deal with anyone's baggage. I've got way too much on my mind lately. You know, the whole community center and all that."

Wes chuckles. "I think what I'm hearing is a lot of excuses. Let's cut to the chase. You don't want a date because you're scared."

No, I'm not scared. I'm in love with your little sister.

"Yeah, that's it." I line up the remotes on Garrett's table, then straighten his stack of magazines. "I'm terrified of women."

"I think you need to let Rosa come after ya with a feather duster and see what happens," Wes pokes my side. "A little tickle won't hurt ya. Or maybe her *vacuum* skills will ease some of that fear inside you—I've heard suction's good for phobias. Give it a go, mate."

CHAPTER 9

Isla

Internal playlist: "Turning Tables" by Adele

There's nothing quite like a rainstorm showerhead to soothe one's senses. The hot water felt amazing on my achy joints. I would've melted into the tile if it were possible. Toweling off after my evening rinse, I head back to my room. I dress in yoga pants, a purple shirt, and Jake's old Brooklyn hoodie before making my way downstairs.

Jake glances up from his place at the kitchen island. "Hey, Sprite." His gaze lands on the sweatshirt's block lettering and flares in surprise. "You kept it all these years?"

That's not all I've held on to for you.

I smile and settle on the stool beside him. "You asked me to, right?" I toy with the tattered ends of the hood strings. "I wear it all the time. It doesn't smell like you anymore, but it helps with the loneliness."

He opens and closes his mouth a few times before clearing his throat. "Isla, I—" He looks away and squeezes his eyes shut. "I don't know what to say."

Maybe something like, you're glad I kept it, or you think about me when you're lonely too?

I shrug and change the subject. "How was your visit with Garrett?"

"Great. I'm reviewing the designs right now."

"May I see?"

"Sure." He slides a stack of images in front of me.

I thumb through them, admiring Garrett's phoenix drawings. Vivid, colorful, and richly detailed, it's some of the most exquisite artwork I've ever seen. "My God, these are incredible. Too bad I didn't have *him* design my tattoo."

"Yeah, Garrett doesn't fuck around."

"You should see if he'll teach the graphic design workshops."

"I'm sure he'd love to, but he's swamped with preparations for *Prodigy*."

"What's *Prodigy*?"

"A new Broadway show coming next year."

"Is he designing their set?"

"No. Garrett scored the male lead role."

I can't put my finger on it, but something about his tone feels abrupt, almost like I'm bothering him. I realize he's busy, but I'm genuinely curious about his friend.

"Wow, Garrett can act?"

"Yep."

"What kind of production is *Prodigy*?"

"Musical."

What's with the one-word answers?

"Does he have a good voice?"

Jake nods. "Thanks to some of my theater contacts, I was able to view his audition tape. His voice is phenomenal."

"You two should collaborate musically."

"Maybe." He shrugs and stares out the window. "You never know what the future holds. *Prodigy*'s director approached me about writing a song for the show."

"Are you gonna consider it?"

"Already in the works. It's called 'Undone.'"

"I'd love to hear it. Along with the *others* you mentioned . . ." Batting my lashes, I playfully squeeze his shoulders.

Jake tenses in my grasp, his gaze snapping to mine. "I'm rescinding my offer to play those."

I cock my head. "Oh? And why's that?"

Sighing, he purses his lips and mutters, "Because it would be a *huge* mistake."

"A mistake?"

He stares out the window again. "Yeah, and I don't want to bring that kind of trouble onto myself." He clenches his jaw. "I don't have time for drama."

I cross my arms over my chest and grip my biceps. "When you say 'trouble' and 'drama,' are you referring to me?"

"Yeah." He rubs at the back of his neck. "Isla, listen, I need to apologize for my lapse of judgment . . ."

My heart sinks. "What're you talking about?"

"It was a mistake when I asked you to cancel your hotel reservation," he replies without looking at me.

I stiffen at the ice in his tone. "You're saying you want me to leave?"

"It's not that I *want* you to leave." He shrugs and taps his pen on the counter. "But—"

"But it's best if I do?"

He keeps his gaze fixed on something outside the kitchen window instead of answering.

Standing, I push my stool under the island's edge. "Got it. I hear you loud and clear. I'll be upstairs."

"Isla—"

Ignoring him, I rush up the steps, wincing at the throb in my swollen ankles. I close the bedroom door behind me and lock it. I snatch my phone from the nightstand and reserve a room and car service for an hour from now, then burrow under my blankets.

I'm not sure what happened at Garrett's, but there's a change in Jake since his return. His familiar warmth has dissipated, leaving me colder than I've ever felt. He's dark and broody, resonating with a moodiness I'm not used to seeing from anyone other than Reed. I curl my lip.

The last thing I need in my life is another Reed.

The tears fall freely as I chastise myself for my idiocy. *What the fuck was I thinking?* I was stupid for hoping Jake could see past my family tree and think of me as someone other than Wes's little sister. I adore my brother, but I'm so tired of living in his shadow. I'm tired of *being* a shadow. Jake always made me feel like I was in the spotlight whenever I was around him. Like I *was* light. Color. Beauty.

Did I imagine our connection? Our chemistry? I shake my head. No, I didn't imagine it. He wants me. More now than he did when I first kissed him. Beyond that, he cares for me. But it looks like that's not going to be enough for us.

Maybe seeing the effects of my lupus turned him off. Maybe he thinks I'm too needy with all my meds, naps, and restrictive diet. Or I'm too much of a burden, a harbinger of trouble and drama as he alluded to earlier. One thing's for damn sure, I refuse to be anyone's burden.

Jake knocks on my door. "Isla?"

"Go away."

"Let me in."

"Please leave me alone. I don't wanna talk right now."

"Well, I do." The authoritative edge to his tone pisses me off.

"Tough shit."

"Open the door, Isla."

"What part of 'I don't wanna talk' are you having trouble understanding?"

"I understand you perfectly, but I hate being shut out."

Says the man who effectively dismissed me from his kitchen.

"Sucks to be you."

"Listen, I'm making dinner. I'll let you know when it's ready so you can come down and eat."

"Not hungry."

His heavy sigh reaches my ears through the solid oak. He can huff and puff all he wants, but I'm sure as hell not eating dinner with him—I'm ordering room service from the hotel. A place where I'll be a paid guest and won't be in anyone's hair, especially not moody Jake Bennett's.

"C'mon, Sprite. Talk to me." When I don't answer, he jiggles the doorknob. "Okay, suit yourself. When you're ready to stop being stubborn, dinner will be waiting."

I don't bother with a response because I have nothing to say. Instead, I listen for his footsteps to clomp down the stairs. Once he's out of earshot, I fold my clothes and stuff them inside my suitcase, then make the bed and tidy the room. After everything is in its place, I sneak into the bathroom to grab my toiletries. I shove a wad of tissues into my pocket for when I let my emotional dam break.

Once back inside the safety of my room, I scrawl a note and leave it on the dresser with enough cash to cover the cost of my groceries and medication. I fold up the scarf I made him and leave it by my note. Removing his sweatshirt, I neatly fold the garment and leave it on top of the bed, my heart shattering into a million pieces. A tear slides down my cheek as my hand lingers over the worn fabric. For years, that shirt symbolized warmth. Familiarity. Comfort and love. Now, the sight of it pains me.

My phone chimes with a text alerting me of the driver's arrival. I let him know I'll be right out and do a quick room scan. Once satisfied, I trudge downstairs to the kitchen.

Jake hums to himself while checking on something in the oven. It smells incredible, but I ignore my growling stomach.

I clear my throat, blinking against the tears that want to seep out. "Jake."

He looks over at me and smiles, his dimples in full force. "Oh, hey. You finally came down—" He eyes my suitcase. "Wait, what are you doing?"

"The driver's outside to take me to the hotel. Thank you for your hospitality. I appreciate everything you've done for me."

He knots his hands in his hair. "You're leaving?"

I force an even tone. "I think it's the wisest course of action for me."

"No." He drops a spatula onto the counter and crosses the room. "I won't let you leave." His eyes are wide, sheer panic tightening his features. "Cancel your car."

"You said earlier you made a mistake by asking me to stay in the first place. My presence is making you uncomfortable, and I would feel more comfortable staying on neutral ground."

"But I don't want you to leave."

I cross my arms. "Jake, you clearly don't know *what* you want."

He grits his teeth. "Yes, I do."

"I'm sorry, but I can't handle your mind-fuckery right now. Thanks for everything. I'll see ya at Friendsgiving." I drag my suitcase behind me and walk out the front door.

The driver greets me and loads my stuff into the car.

Jake bounds down the front steps. "This is bullshit, Isla."

The driver eyes him warily before opening the door for me.

"I'll see you in a couple of days," I tell Jake. "And thank you for your hospitality."

"Don't fucking walk away from me!"

I bristle at his snarl and the words themselves. "Before you take that tone with me, I suggest you look in the mirror, Jacob Bennett. You *pushed* me away." I climb into the car and slam the door.

The driver speeds away as I rest my forehead on the window and cry big, fat tears.

CHAPTER 10

Jake

Mood: "Let Her Go" by Passenger

I cling to a lamppost and watch the sedan disappear from sight. I fucked with Isla's head and made her feel unwelcome. Now she's gone—she left—because I pushed her away. Picturing the tears that filled her beautiful eyes, a part of me dies inside.

Way to go, dick.

I trudge up the stoop and reenter the kitchen. No longer hungry, I turn off the oven, then retrieve my phone. I dial Isla's number, rubbing at the ache in my chest while I wait for her to answer.

She doesn't.

I try three more times, but it only rings. And rings. And rings some more before going to voicemail.

The fifth time I try to call, it goes straight to voicemail, telling me she turned off her phone. She shut me out. *Like I did to her.* I don't leave a message because I can't find the words to say.

I climb the stairs to the guest room and flick on the light, spotting my old Brooklyn sweatshirt neatly folded on the pillow. I cling to the doorframe for support. Hours earlier, she'd confessed that it brought her comfort in times of loneliness.

I cross the room and pick up the shirt. I was once a source of comfort for her, and as I rub the frayed drawstrings between my fingers, I realize how deeply I hurt her.

A wad of cash on the dresser catches my eye. My lip curls at the sight. I paid for her meds and groceries because I wanted to. I didn't expect—or want—to be reimbursed.

For anything.

I lift the money to find a dark green scarf beneath. I remember when she sat cross-legged on my couch, the sun's rays warming her face while she knit—no, *crocheted*. How adorable she looked correcting me, schooling me on the ways of yarn, needles, and hooks. Little did I realize she was making something for me. Safety-pinned to the scarf is a scrap of paper.

> For all the years you've kept me warm,
> I thought I'd return the favour.
> Thank you for being you.
> xoxo. Sprite.

My eyes burn, vision blurring on her handwriting.

I don't consider myself a crier. In fact, the last time I remember shedding a tear was in Alaska, when Lena's arms gave out during CPR and Wes still had no pulse. Staring at his blue lips, knowing it was over, I wept for the certain loss of my best friend. Before that was at my father's funeral. I didn't cry when I broke things off with Nadia. But now, in my cold gray house, dark in Isla's absence, my floodgates falter.

There's another note on the dresser. I clench my jaw and unfold it.

Jacob,

First, I want to thank you for your kindness and generous hospitality. I appreciate everything you did for me—especially the care package. Your gesture moved me in ways I can't explain. YOU move me in ways I can't explain.

When Lena let me know that she couldn't pick me up from the airport, I called you instead of a car service. I admit, perhaps it was unwise, but you'd already offered to show me around New York. I figured you wouldn't mind. My goal was never to make you uncomfortable—I only wanted to be close to you.

Jake, I've felt a lot of things for you. Friendship. A schoolgirl crush. My teenage heartthrob. After that kiss on the beach, things changed for me. I'm a woman now, and whether or not you're willing to admit it, we're drawn to one another. I can't explain the attraction, but I can tell you how it feels for me. While its nature and magnitude have evolved over the years, it remains a soul-deep awareness. I've tried to ignore it, but I can't. I think you know I want you, but I doubt you realize exactly how much.

Well, let me enlighten you.

I want you. I want your closeness. Your warmth. You. You're everything I've EVER wanted.

Reread my last sentence as many times as you need to.

Anyway, I went out on a limb by hoping you felt the same about me. It turns out I picked the wrong branch—maybe the wrong tree entirely.

Speaking of trees, I didn't choose my family tree or the people I share a branch with. I'm fucking tired of being expected to bloom in my brother's shade. While I understand and respect your loyalty, I hoped you could see beyond him. I hoped you could see ME. I get the feeling you can't, so I'll help you out.

I'm a grown woman. My own entity. I have goals and dreams, strengths, and shortcomings. I'm proud. Stubborn. Fierce. Let me repeat, *I am my own person, not an extension of Wes. I make my own choices and follow my own path.*

I know in my heart our paths intersect, but I'm tired of lingering at the crossroads while you keep changing direction. Your push and pull hurts me, Jake. You either want me or you don't. Pick one and commit to it because I'm tired of circling your tree. I'm tired of waiting for you to give me a place to land.

Isla Rose

I wipe at the tears streaming down my cheeks and refold her note. Sinking onto the bed, I roll to my side, clutching my old sweatshirt. I bury my face in the fabric and breathe in Isla's scent, warm coconut with a hint of mango. The tears come in waves, soaking the fabric.

I've never had such a visceral response to heartache that my fucking soul feels like it's fracturing apart. Crumbling. The emotion behind Isla's words—and the fact that I hurt her—rips me to shreds.

I need her to understand where my heart stands in this mess. She needs to know how much I care. I try her number again. Still nothing. I switch gears and call Lena instead.

"Hello?"

"Lena-Bean, I need your help."

"Oh, hi, Rita. Are you on your lunch break?"

I frown. "It's Jake, silly. Do I sound like a woman?"

"No. What time does your shift end?"

"Is Emerson right next to you or something?"

"Yes."

Now it makes sense—she can't speak freely. "Got it. I'll make this quick. You've spoken to Isla?"

"Yes. Talk about workplace drama!"

"I need to talk to her, and she's not taking my calls. Please text me the name of her hotel and her room number."

"Can't do that."

I hold the phone between my ear and shoulder. "Why not?"

"Trisha asked me not to."

Balling my fists, I grit my teeth hard enough to make my jaw pop. "Are you serious right now? Why the fuck not?"

"You know how Trisha gets. She's proud. Extremely proud. She put herself on the line and things went to shit. She needs time to lick her wounds."

"Look, I know I fucked up. I think *you* can understand I'm stuck between a rock and a hard place."

"Oh, absolutely. But it doesn't have to be like that."

"You make it sound like I can throw caution to the wind and go after her. It's not that simple. There's a lot at stake here."

"I'll remind you that's the case for *both* parties involved."

"Please text me the info. I'm begging you."

"Rita, you know I love you, but I pride myself on being there for *all* my friends. Trisha placed her trust in me, and that's not something I take lightly. You need to figure out whether you plan to accept the position or not. Don't try to fix things with Trisha until you know what *you* want. The strength of the department depends on a united front. No faltering. No wavering. Make a decision and step up to the fucking plate. Now, lemme go. I'm trying to watch a movie with my man."

"If you should happen to speak to Trisha, tell her to answer Rita's calls," I mutter before hanging up.

I slam my fist on the nightstand. I get that Lena made a promise to Isla. I respect how she's a damn good friend to both of us, but the fact that Isla shut me out pisses me the fuck off.

I try her number once more, but it goes to voicemail.

"Hey, it's Isla. You know what to do." The irony of her recorded greeting is a punch to my gut.

I listen for the beep. "Sprite, it's me. Thank you for the scarf. I absolutely love it. I, uh . . . I read your letter. I can assure you we're in the same tree." I clench the phone and force a swallow. "We're on the same branch too. The same fucking leaf. Please answer my calls. Honey, I'm sorry I hurt you. Please don't give up on me yet." I hang up and hug my sweatshirt tighter.

CHAPTER 11

Jake

Mood: "In My Blood" by Shawn Mendes

After two trips back to my car to make sure I locked it—even though I heard the fucker beep six times when I pressed the button on my keys—I finally ring the buzzer to Lena's brownstone. It feels like I'm yanking the pin from a grenade. Today is Friendsgiving Saturday, which means I haven't heard from Isla in three fucking days.

Three agonizing, torturous days.

I spent the Thanksgiving holiday with Chinese takeout, reorganizing my collection of vinyl records and the bookshelves in my office. I also washed my curtains, cleaned the leaves out of my gutters, and changed the batteries in my smoke detectors.

On the plus side, my house is cleaner than it has ever been, and I was musically productive for once. I wrote two brand-new songs—both about Isla. Last night, I had a come-to-Jesus conversation with Jesse where he told me to stop fucking around and commit to a decision about what kind of relationship I want. Then, because my anxiety wouldn't let it rest, I called my mother and got a two-hour "follow your heart" lecture. Now I'm ready to face Isla.

I think.

I clench my hands to stop them from shaking. My regular anxiety meds may as well be placebos, and the Xanax I took isn't doing shit. Then again, the espressos I guzzled probably won't help calm my nerves either. My fingertips brush my fly to make sure it's zipped.

Garrett answers the front door. "Hey, man. Lena's elbow deep in a turkey's ass right now, so she asked me to let you in."

"Wow. I didn't know Emerson was into butt stuff."

He guffaws in response, clapping my shoulder as he laughs. "I fucking love you, bro. And I am definitely stealing that joke at some point tonight."

"It's all yours, man."

"How are *things*?"

"Utter shit, my friend." I follow him up the stairs. "She here?"

"Not yet. Lena told her to come a little later."

"How's your situation?" I ask.

He forces a dark laugh. "I'm in way over my head."

"I know the feeling."

We enter the living room, which is already decked out for Christmas—Lena's favorite holiday. Evidently, she's one of those people who starts celebrating as soon as Halloween's over. I gravitate toward the enormous tree decorated with twinkling white lights. Garrett introduces me to Nate and Daria, a pair of graphic designers who work for him.

Wes's *Aegean* co-star, Ronan Flynn, claps my shoulder. "Jake Bennett. Long time, no see. What's going on, man?"

"Not much. How about you? Are you all settled in at your new place?"

"Yeah, pretty much. It's a bit of an adjustment."

Ronan recently moved from California to Manhattan because the love of his life got engaged to someone else. Alainna Baker, the actress who plays Aphrodite in the *Aegean*, has no idea her best friend is in love with her. She's all set to marry some dickhead Italian model who treats her like shit. Meanwhile, poor Ronan suffers in silence.

Heartache for the win.

I give his shoulder a sympathy squeeze, then follow Garrett into the kitchen. I take one look at Wes and laugh. "Nice dress, Emerson."

Wes gestures to his apron and curtsies. "Thanks, mate. Lena makes me wear it in bed."

She hands him a peeler. "You can bet your ass I will if you don't get the rest of those carrots done."

Saluting her, he turns his attention to the carrots on the island. "I'm on salad duty."

Lena kisses my cheek. "Happy Friendsgiving. Thank you for coming."

"Thanks for having me, Lena-Bean. Is there anything I can do to help?"

"Nope. We're good. Your job is to *relax*." She gives me a lingering look and dries her hands on a towel. "I think we're almost ready."

"Bennett, you want a beer?" Wes jerks his chin toward the fridge.

I'd love one, but I'm not stupid enough to mix alcohol with Xanax. "Nah. I'm good, man. Thanks."

A few more people arrive, including a trio of attractive women—Lena's nurse buddies, I assume.

"Jake, these are my friends, Kristie, Rita, and Trish. We work at the hospital together. Kristie and Trish are usually in the ER with me, and Rita's in labor and delivery. Girls, this is my dear friend, Jake Bennett."

"He was mine first," Wes points out. "I never officially said I'd share him."

Lena rolls her eyes. "Whatever, Ace. Ten bucks says Jake would rather hang out with me than deal with you."

"She's right." I chuckle and shake hands with her friends. "Nice to meet you, ladies."

Wes motions to Rita and Trisha. "I'm glad you two sorted everything out. Lena was worried."

Rita raises a brow at Lena, who stiffens. Her subtle nod is nearly imperceptible to anyone other than Rita and me.

Rita elbows her. "'Splain, Lucy."

Lena mouths, "later" and they share a look.

I love witnessing communication between women. They are truly fascinating creatures.

Trisha is busy staring at my crotch, so she missed Wes's comment in the first place. I'm in a mood where I have a mind to fuck with her, so I consider rolling my hips.

Wait, is my fly zipped?

Kristie notices her friend ogling my junk and pokes her ribs. Trisha flushes and looks away. Kristie smirks. "Nice to meet you, Jake. Wes was telling us about your community center the other night."

Rita touches my shoulder. "He mentioned you plan to offer Latin dance classes, so if you're in need of a salsa instructor, I'm happy to donate my time."

I perk up. "Really? That would be amazing. I've got people lined up to teach the ballet and hip-hop classes, but I haven't been able to find anyone for the salsa."

Rita grins and shimmies her hips. "Oh, honey, I do the bachata, the samba, and the rumba too. I love to dance. Right, Lena?"

Lena wraps an arm around her friend. "No one can move like Margarita Suarez."

"Besides, it will give me some time away from my hubby and twin boys," Rita says. "Mama needs a break."

Kristie laughs and nudges Rita. "I've been telling you that for years."

Meanwhile, Trisha's staring at my crotch again.

Please tell me I zipped it.

Since I can't check my zipper, I pull out my phone. "Rita, may I please have your contact info?"

"Of course."

We exchange numbers and I tuck my phone away.

Trish is still staring.

This is ridiculous. You want a show? I roll my hips.

She flushes and her mouth drops open. While I admit, I'm hung, I'm generally not one to tease women. Regardless, her reaction amuses me.

I check my fly as soon as it's safe to. It's zipped. Too bad that won't stop me from checking it again in five minutes.

Lena shifts gears and turns to Wes. "Uh, did we remember to preheat the oven for the pies?"

"Did it an hour ago, love. See? I listen when you tell me to do things."

Lena's friends retreat to the living room. A guy enters the kitchen with Garrett. The fucker is huge—nearly as tall as Wes and just as broad, if not broader.

"Connor! You made it." Lena throws her arms around his neck. "Wes, this is Garrett's cousin, Connor. He works for the FBI, and he's the one who installed my security system."

"Nice meetin' ya, mate. Thanks for doing that for her on such short notice."

Connor shakes Wes's hand. "No problem. I've known Lena since I was little. She babysat me, so the least I can do is help protect her."

"I'm fine, you two," Lena says with an eye roll. "They arrested the guy. Everything's good."

Lena's shithead father hired some thug to steal her grandmother's jewelry last month. Fortunately, she was across the country with Wes when it happened. Garrett *was* home and handled matters his way—which included beating the guy's face in.

Connor crosses his massive arms over his chest. "I still think you should take the classes I mentioned."

"What classes?" Wes asks, handing Connor a beer.

"Connor teaches self-defense classes at his gym," Lena explains. "He's been trying to get me to take them for years."

Wes perks up. "You own a gym?"

"I'm part-owner. The FBI takes up too much of my time, so I took on a partner. I still teach martial arts and self-defense classes every Tuesday and Thursday night. I told Lena she can join free of charge."

Wes points to Lena. "You're taking the classes, sunshine. No ifs, ands, or buts about it."

Lena waves them off. "I can handle myself."

"They've got a point, Leens," Garrett chimes in. "If you weren't in LA, shit could've gone down differently. I hate to think what could've happened if I weren't here to intercept the fucker. And with Wes traveling . . ."

"No one thinks their neighborhood is dangerous until it *is*," Connor adds. "I don't wanna see anything happen to you."

Lena props both hands on her hips. "What is this, gang up on Lena day?"

Connor gestures to himself. "I'll stop pressing the issue when you show me you can fight off a man of my stature. Until then, you can bet your ass I'm gonna keep hounding you."

"I like this guy." Wes claps Connor's shoulder and presses a finger to the middle of his chest. "In fact, I like you so much, I'm gonna introduce you to my sister."

I stiffen. Every drop of my blood starts to boil. Lena's eyes dart to mine and widen. I meet her gaze briefly before zeroing in on Connor. Garrett shifts uncomfortably in my periphery.

"You have a sister?" Connor asks with a smile I want to punch off his fucking face.

"Yeah, she's moving to the area in December." Wes motions to me. "She'll be across the street from my mate, Jake, which is just a few blocks from here. Anyway, Isla needs a security system installed too."

Connor grins at Wes. "I look forward to meeting Isla. If she's interested, I'm happy to enroll her in self-defense classes. Hell, if Lena agrees to come, I'll instruct your sister free of charge."

And I'll fucking kill you.

Wes nudges Lena. "Did ya hear that, sunshine?"

"Loud and clear." She meets Garrett's gaze, and they share an unspoken message.

Garrett turns to Connor. "Come help me move some chairs."

Connor sets down his beer. "Sure, man."

Wes removes his apron. "Hold up, I'll join ya. The chairs are in the attic and there're quite a few of them. Connor, how old are you, mate?"

"Twenty-nine."

"Isla's twenty-three," he explains as they leave the kitchen.

Lena appears in front of me. "Breathe."

"Squash it." My voice is someplace between a growl and a snarl. "Fucking squash it."

She clamps her hands on my shoulders. "I will, but you need to calm the fuck down."

My gaze snaps to hers. "Calm down? You want me to calm down when he's offering up the woman I love on a silver fucking platter?"

"He's not offering her up on a platter. He wants her to take self-defense classes."

"He thinks that meathead can protect her? Better yet, he thinks Isla will go for that? Fucking karate classes? Her ankles have been so swollen, she limps on the goddamn stairs. She's constantly in pain. How the fuck is she gonna do martial arts?"

Lena's jade eyes narrow on my face. "First of all, don't call him a meathead. He's a damn good guy. He's Garrett's family and a good friend of mine. Secondly, you need to calm the fuck down. I know you're upset but acting like a dick won't get you anywhere with Isla. She'll be here shortly. Stop focusing on wanting to kick Connor's ass—because guess what, you can't—and keep your focus where it needs to be. On *her.*"

Taking a deep breath, I close my eyes on my exhale. "I'm sorry."

Lena grips the front of my shirt. "She told me what she wrote in that letter. She wants *you,* so cut the alpha shit. Don't act like a fool and give her any reason to change her mind."

"I love you, Lena-Bean."

"I love you too, Jake. I'll do everything in my power to help you, but you have to be willing to help yourself." She points in the direction the other guys went. "Don't worry. Garrett's on board. He'll rein in his cousin as soon as it's clear to do so."

"Isla is *mine*."

Lena arches a brow. "Oh? What happened to the I'm-too-scared-to-go-after-what-I-want-because-Wes-will-kill-me version of yourself? You ditch that asshole?"

"No, I'm still here." I chuckle and rub my jaw. "Wrote my obituary and got my affairs in order, so at least I'm prepared for when it happens."

Lena giggles. "Don't be ridiculous. He adores you."

"Promise me something."

She cocks her head. "What's up?"

"When they find my body, you know, after I've choked to death on my balls, please make sure someone looks after my mom."

Lena laughs and pinches my cheek. "You got it, babe."

"I'm serious. I'm all she's got left."

After a few minutes, Wes and the others reenter the kitchen. Lena raises a brow at Garrett, but he shakes his head.

Wes rubs his belly. "What's our ETA on food, love? I'm withering away to nothing over here."

Garrett snorts. "Actually, I was thinking Emerson's put on some weight since he's been with Lena."

"Damn right, I have. It's all the cookies she feeds me."

"Um, excuse me, but I do not force cookies on you, Ace. That's all on you."

Connor turns to Wes. "Like I said, I've got a full gym you can use."

"He doesn't even need to go that far. I already told him he can use my weight room downstairs." Garrett cracks open a seltzer and hands a can to me.

"Thanks."

Connor sticks his hand out. "Sorry, man, I didn't mean to be rude and skip the introduction, but Lena distracted me. I'm Connor Geraghty."

Lena flashes me a warning glare, so I shake the fucker's hand. "No worries. Jake Bennett."

He tilts his head. "*The* Jake Bennett? As in, the singer?"

"That'd be me."

"Wow. My boss is obsessed with you."

Wes punches my arm. "There ya go, mate. Connor, what's your boss like? Is she single? Attractive? Preferably not a frigid ice queen like his last girlfriend."

Connor clears his throat. "Oh, uh . . . my boss is a man. I mean, he's not *unattractive* . . . for a dude." He gestures to me. "He's older though. Probably around your age—maybe like forty, forty-two."

Are you fucking kidding me? This guy is asking to get throat punched.

Wes laughs heartily. "Jake's only thirty-three."

"The older the better." I hold my arms out in sarcastic invitation. "By all means, please send him my way."

Lena touches Connor's shoulder. "Jake prefers women."

"Oh. What I meant was—" He clears his throat. "I didn't mean to assume—"

"Actually, I'm asexual when it comes to humans. Bestiality's more my thing . . ." I pause and lightly touch my chin in thought, "mainly turtles. Something about that hard shell, soft underbelly bit. It *really* gets me going."

Connor gapes.

"Jake wields sarcasm nearly as well as I do. Right, Bennett?" Garrett's lionlike gaze burns into me. His strange, golden eyes catch me off guard every time I look at them, but his warning is crystal clear.

Get your shit together, Jake.

"Sarcasm's my drug of choice." I force myself to smile at Connor. "I'll send you home with an autograph for your boss."

"Thanks, man."

Lena's phone chimes and she nods to Garrett, who glances at his watch. "Excuse me for a minute."

He leaves the room and Lena meets my gaze.

Isla.

My stomach twists into knots and I can't seem to pull air into my lungs. My scalp prickles and my ears start to buzz.

Damn, I need my anxiety meds if I'm going to feel like this all night.

Wes appears at my side and clasps the back of my neck. "You all right, mate? You're not yourself tonight."

I nod. "I'm good. Been sleeping like shit."

He pins his concerned gaze to mine. "You sure that's it?"

"Yeah, man. I'm fine."

"Jesus Christ. Lena says *fine* when she's anything but. Now I've got both of you using that fucking word."

Garrett reenters the room with a wide grin. "Hey, Crocodile Dundee."

Wes turns to face him. "I never expected Crocodile Dundette to look so much like you."

"Huh?"

Garrett steps to the side, and Wes's jaw drops open.

Isla taps the kitchen doorframe. "Got anything to eat? I'm bloody starving."

Her slender legs look even longer encased in black leather pants with high-heeled boots. The porcelain skin of her neck, shoulders, and upper back are revealed by an off-the-shoulder peasant shirt that matches her royal blue eyes. Chunky silver bangles decorate both wrists, jingling as she brushes the hair back from her face. Silver hoops hang in each ear beneath a pair of diamond studs. Even without the beach, she's got beachy, golden-brown waves. She looks like a fucking mermaid. A goddess. A runway model. I already know her warm, coconut-mango scent and the way she feels in my arms.

"Holy fuck," Wes sputters. "What the hell're ya doin' here, Imp?"

"Well, I was in the area, so I figured I'd pop by." She flashes him a cheeky smile, and my heart stops. "Surprise."

I lean against the counter as Wes charges across the kitchen, wrapping her in a hug. "I can't believe you're here."

"You're crushing me, ya big brute."

Wes releases her. "Oh, sorry."

Isla loudly cracks her neck. My stomach turns like always, but I barely notice it over the butterflies. No—fuck butterflies—it's a herd of buffalo galloping in my gut.

"Christ, Wes, I need a bloody chiropractor now. You can't squeeze me like that. You're built like a brick shithouse."

Wes runs a hand over his face. "Who orchestrated this?"

Lena comes up behind him and squeezes his ass cheeks. "Happy belated birthday, Ace."

Snagging her around the waist, he plants a kiss on her lips. "I love you more each day, sunshine." Wes turns back to Isla. "How'd ya get here?"

Isla laughs and the sound curls my toes. "Spent a long time in a rowboat. Unfortunately, I encountered a whale and that sank, so I switched to a kayak. Lost my paddle somewhere off California's coast. Then, I hitchhiked across the country with some shady truck drivers. One of them got mouthy, so I handled that. Finally, I crossed paths with a caravan of nuns who dropped me on your doorstep."

Connor laughs and motions to Wes. "Doesn't sound like she needs classes."

Isla raises a brow at Connor. "Classes?"

Wes shakes his head. "Sorry. Where're my manners? Isla, this is Garrett's cousin, Connor. He contracts with the FBI's cybersecurity team and teaches self-defense classes."

Isla shakes Connor's hand and something inside me short-circuits. "Nice meetin' ya, Garrett's cousin, Connor. I'm Wes's sister, Isla."

Connor grins. "Figured that one out."

"Connor will install a security system in your brownstone, and you and Lena will be his students."

"Students?"

Wes crosses his arms over his chest. "Yeah. You're taking self-defense classes."

"Oh, am I really? Says who?" Isla narrows her eyes on Wes's face.

He levels his typical no-bullshit glare on her. "Says me."

She cocks her head. "Last I checked, your name wasn't Luke Emerson. And even if it was," she jabs a finger in his chest, "I stopped following Dad's orders years ago." She smiles at Connor. "I'll agree to the alarm system, but I must respectfully decline the classes."

"Sounds good. If you change your mind, my offer stands."

Wes grips her shoulders. "Isla, I need to know you're safe."

"I'll be fine, Wes." She stiffens her spine. "I can take care of myself."

"Isla doesn't fuck around." Lena snakes an arm around Isla's waist. "Besides, I've heard the neighborhood watch team in that area is hypervigilant, and I'm sure she'll have neighbors who'll keep an eye on her."

Damn right I will.

"That may very well be the case, but I'm not gonna task Jake with that." He jerks a thumb in my direction. "With Rosa around, he's got better shit to do than babysit."

Fuck.

"Who's Rosa?" Lena asks, cocking her head to the side.

"Jake's new cleaning lady. He's got the hots for her."

Fire flashes in Isla's gaze. Furious blue orbs burn into mine, stealing my ability to breathe. "Well, I'd hate to distract him from a potential love interest."

"She's not my—"

"Besides, I do *not* need a babysitter."

"Alrighty, peeps." Garrett comes to the rescue. "How about we take our seats before the turkey gets cold?"

"Good idea." Lena motions to the dining room. "Everyone get settled, and we'll bring the food in."

As Garrett and Connor file out, Wes turns to Isla. "My goal wasn't to piss you off, Imp. I wanna keep you safe. Please don't be angry with me for the rest of the night."

"I'm not angry."

Wes chuckles and draws her in for a hug. "You're a shitty liar, love."

She sighs. "If we're gonna live so close to one another, we need to set boundaries. I need you to trust me to handle my shit. I'm not a child, or some damsel in distress who needs rescuing. Please try to stop bulldozing me, okay?" She levels him with a look. "Also, just because I'll be a few blocks away, that doesn't mean I'm cool with the pop-ins. I won't pop in unannounced at yours, and I expect the same from you."

"I'm sorry." Wes hugs her tighter. "I promise to try."

"Good. I'm thirsty. Lena, do ya have any wine?"

Wes frowns, his gaze dropping to her midsection. He touches his own abdomen where his matching scar resides. "Is that a good idea?"

Isla props her hands on her hips. "Wesley James, what did I just say?"

He holds his hands up in surrender. "All right, all right. I'm sorry."

"I can have *a* glass of wine. My doctor said it's okay in moderation, remember?"

He nods. "Yeah, I remember. Doesn't mean I like it."

"You liking it has no bearing on my actions."

Lena motions to a little black wine fridge. "I have white and red."

"White, please. Have you got anything on the sweeter side?"

"Moscato work for you?"

Isla grins. "That's perfect."

Lena pours her a glass and Wes leaves the room shaking his head.

"What's his issue?" Isla asks.

"Ignore him," Lena murmurs. "His alpha side's in overdrive."

"That's nothing new." Isla sips her wine and makes her way over to me. "Hello, Jacob. Tell me more about *Rosa*." Lip curling on the fictional name, the pain in her gaze is a knife to my chest. "Should I expect a wedding invitation?"

CHAPTER 12

Isla

Internal playlist: "Water Under the Bridge" by Adele

Well, *fuck. Looks like I had it all wrong.* I really need to get my head out of my arse.

Jake told me he cleans his own flat. Now he's suddenly got a cleaning lady? Funny, he never mentioned her before. Maybe she's the reason behind his coldness the other day. Who is this Rosa, and what's the extent of their relationship? What does she have that I don't? Does he hold and kiss her freely? Is she the woman he's willing to open his heart to? The one he'll draw closer instead of pushing away like he did with me?

Doesn't matter. His love life is none of my business. The crack in my heart widens, threatening to swallow me whole.

Jake's eyes darken. "Isla *Rose*. Long time no see . . . or *talk*."

He's pissed that I've ignored him for three days, but that's his problem. I needed to get a handle on my emotions before I could even attempt to deal with his mind-fuckery. I've spent three days kicking myself for writing that letter.

Written in the heat of the moment, I regretted leaving it for him the second he faded from view. It's too honest, too vulnerable. I left my emotional underbelly on that dresser, and I don't know whether he plans to caress it or stab a knife through my heart. Clearly, it's the latter.

I lift my chin. "Had a lot on my mind."

"Likewise."

Steeling my shoulders, I meet his gaze. "I still do, actually."

"Did you listen to my voicemail?"

I don't answer because I'm afraid I'll tell him I listened to it over a dozen times. How his voice simultaneously soothed me and broke my heart into pieces. I fear I'll tell him how I curled up in my white terry robe and lay in bed listening to his music. How I wished I hadn't left his sweatshirt behind. How I cried a monsoon of frustration and loneliness.

Jake steps closer to me. "Got nothing to say?"

"I have plenty to say, but now's not the time or place for it."

He gestures to the front door. "Then let's go. We can relocate to someplace more *private*." The word simmers with heat, anger, and something else. *Possessiveness.*

Who the hell is he to be possessive? What a hypocrite!

"I don't think *Rosa* would appreciate that."

"There is no Rosa." His low growl is little more than a vibration, but I hear him clearly. "I sent Wes a text meant for someone else and needed a cover. Isla *Rose . . . you* are Rosa."

"That's nice." Despite the relief coursing through my veins, I give a lazy shrug. Jake's eyes dart to my bare shoulders, and I stiffen my spine. "But I still don't feel like talking."

After his gaze sweeps the length of me like a physical touch, he purses his lips. "I need to talk to you before this tension between us goes on any longer."

My brother enters the room and, for once, Jake doesn't flinch and move away from me. Wes grabs a stack of napkins and waves them at us. "You two joining us for dinner?"

"In a minute," Jake answers darkly. "I'm not done talking."

"Well, I am. I like my food warm." I give Jake a tight smile and follow Wes to the dining room.

I sense Jake behind me even before he clamps a hand on my hip and tugs me back, bringing his lips to my ear. "We *will* talk, Isla." He releases me and pulls out a chair.

Instead of taking the seat he offers—the place beside him—I opt for a spot across the table between Garrett and his cousin.

Connor smiles as I take my seat and drape a napkin over my lap. "I hear this is your first time having an American Thanksgiving feast."

"It is. Everything looks and smells amazing, and I can't wait to try it. What's your favorite dish?"

"That's a tough one. I'd say stuffing and sweet potatoes are tied for first place."

I give him a smile. "Then I'll start with those." I reach for a casserole dish, but he stops me with a hand on my wrist. I peer up at him in surprise. Connor is brutally gorgeous—a hulking, muscled behemoth with dark hair and emerald-green eyes—but his gentle touch does nothing for me. No sparks. No tingles. No butterflies. Meanwhile, I can still feel Jake's grip on my hip, his breath at my ear. His body so close behind me. I sense him watching me from his place across the table. I raise my brow at Connor, who releases my wrist.

"Careful. The stuffing's extremely hot." He shows me a red spot on his palm. "Found that one out the hard way. I'll help you." He spoons some onto my plate. "That good, or do you want more?"

"More, please."

Connor smiles. "Your wish is my command."

"Thank you."

He nods and repeats with a spoonful of sweet potatoes. "Anytime."

One of Lena's nurse mates catches his attention and asks something about the FBI. Wes's booming laugh rings out at Garrett's jokes—one of which I wish I caught because all I heard faintly was Wes and turkey butt stuff.

All around me, people are laughing and chatting in a warm, jovial cacophony of festivity. Friendship. Love. I watch my brother for a bit, warmed by the way he looks at Lena. It wouldn't be an exaggeration to say everyone in the room can feel the depth of their bond. I envy the earth-shattering love they share. The kind where two flames burn as one. Lena and Wes are the definition of soulmates.

I peer across the table at *my* twin flame. Like the embers on a lit cigarette, flaring with each puff, his molten chocolate irises seem to glow with his fury. Arms crossed over his chest, fists clenched, Jake seethes with a volatility I've never seen from him. A turbulence I've never seen from *anyone*.

He presses his lips into a thin line. A muscle tics in his shadowed jaw. Despite his broody glower, the fine lines at the outer corners of his eyes—that crinkle when he smiles—are still visible. His dimples hint at their presence. Yes, my Jake is still in there, but with his entire body vibrating on the brink of an explosion, the man across the table is an active bomb.

And I'm ready to strike a match.

"Jacob," I say his name with a deliberate purr, "please pass the turkey."

"How much do you want?" His voice reverberates around me. Inside me. Through me.

I lick my lips, flash my sultriest smile, and toss him my lit match. "Fill. Me. Up."

His gaze is a solar flare. White hot. Blinding. A pulse of energy radiates across the table, stealing my breath, forcing me to lean back in my seat and clutch my chest. Thunder rumbles in the distance. Then I realize it's my heartbeat.

The corners of his mouth twitch into a cocky smirk as he skewers a few slabs of turkey and plops them onto my plate. "Tell me *when*." Unable to speak, I stare back at him as he piles on more food. "Hungry?"

His voice is laced with a dark challenge that heats my insides. My nipples prick the cups of my bra, and I silently thank every deity known to man I wore one.

Jake is a volcano. I'm peering over the edge, ready to fall into him, let his lava coat and burn me. Launch me into the sky when he erupts. I'm not sure what's on the horizon, but I do know this. Something's changed between us. I can't wait to stretch my wings and soar.

"No, Jacob." I ladle some gravy over the top of my food. "I'm *starving*."

Another solar flare, this one hotter than the first.

"Careful, Dundette. You're pushing him to his breaking point." Garrett's low murmur reaches my ears with a warning only I can hear.

My gaze snaps to his. "Oh, I'm counting on it."

Something flickers in his lionlike gaze. "I hope you're ready for the fallout."

Connor touches my shoulder. "Wes mentioned you have an internship lined up in Manhattan."

"Yes, it's in fashion design."

"Like sewing and such?"

While his interest in my field seems genuine, I cringe. It's a major pet peeve of mine when someone assumes all I do is hang out with some needles and my thimble. I open my mouth to correct him. "Actually—"

"No, not sewing. She designs clothes. Big difference." Jake squints at him. "And she's damn good at what she does."

Connor holds his hands up in surrender. "Sorry, I'm not familiar with—"

"You don't say." The words drip from Jake's lips like acid.

Garrett's foot brushes past my leg as he kicks him beneath the table. Jake's scowl deepens with the reprimand.

I flash him a warning glare and turn my attention to Connor. "My internship is part of a unique pilot program. I'll be working with a few women's shelters to help give them professional attire. It's a community outreach program aimed at getting disenfranchised women back on their feet." I sip my wine and continue, "The goal is to give them the confidence to get jobs and, hopefully, improve their situations."

Connor nods his approval. "Good for you. That's fucking admirable."

"Thanks. I have a soft spot for people at rock bottom. It makes me happy to watch them climb."

Connor smiles warmly. "Sounds like you have the ability to make them soar."

"Gimme a break." Jake lurches to his feet and storms from the room.

Leaning across me, Connor taps Garrett. "What the fuck is that dude's problem?"

Garrett rubs his jaw. "It's complicated."

"Me," I say. "His problem is with me. You did nothing wrong."

Connor raises his eyebrows. "Are you two together?"

"*Also* complicated," Garrett answers on my behalf.

"Jesus Christ, I was only trying to have a conversation with you," Connor mutters, shaking his head.

I touch his shoulder. "And you can. I'm enjoying our conversation immensely. I seldom get the opportunity to talk about my work."

"Well, if he keeps mean mugging me like that, I'm gonna ask him to take a walk outside."

"No," Garrett clamps a hand on his cousin's arm, "you will not."

The men share a look. Connor nods and turns his focus back to me. "What made you leave Australia? Don't they have programs like that?"

Jake returns, carrying a glass of water, and settles into his seat, his temper tantrum seemingly forgotten. He loosens his collar and gulps his drink. Something about the way his throat moves on his swallow makes me forget Connor asked a question.

He speaks up, "I imagine the bigger cities would cater to the fashion industry. I mean, maybe not like Milan or Paris, but still . . ."

"Oh, they have various programs back home, but I've always been drawn to New York. Once I read the description for this internship, I knew I had to have it."

"I'm sure it'll be nice living so close to your brother." His warm smile tells me he doesn't have much experience with Wes.

"That remains to be seen. In case you haven't noticed, he's a wee bit on the overprotective side."

Connor smirks. "Yeah, I gathered that."

I stiffen my spine. "And I don't take well to being bulldozed."

"Well, knowing Lena for as long as I have, I think it's safe to say she'll keep him in check."

"I adore Lena," I say, casting a glance in her direction.

"Yeah, me too. She was there for Garrett during some of his darkest times and I'm eternally grateful to her for that."

"Dundette, did you try the cranberry sauce?" Garrett plops a spoonful onto my plate.

"Not yet, but it looks like I'm about to." I laugh and nudge him. "Do ya have nicknames for everyone?"

He grins. "Pretty much. If you aren't a fan of Dundette, I can think of something else."

"No, it's fine."

"How come you never asked how I felt about Crocodile Dundee?" Wes laughs.

"Because unlike with my new friend, Dundette, over here, I don't care whether you are a fan of your nickname."

Soon, everyone finishes their meal and people pitch in to clear the table. The food was amazing—so different from what I'm used to. Especially considering my restrictive diet.

I make my way into the living room and chat with Lena's friends and some of Garrett's coworkers. Everyone is friendly and approachable, the conversation coming easily. Right now, I'm a normal chick—not someone who's immunocompromised, bowing to the authority of her illness. I enjoy the sense of community here. After being alienated by my mates, it gives me hope that I *do* belong somewhere.

Connor approaches from behind with a low whistle. "Holy shit. Your tattoo is incredible."

"Thank you. My brother has a matching one on his wrist. He took me on my eighteenth birthday. I don't think he expected me to get such a big one."

"It's a phoenix, right?"

"Yes."

"I can certainly appreciate quality ink when I see it, and yours is fucking exquisite." He rolls up his sleeves to show me the Celtic knotwork on his forearms.

"Are those full or partial sleeves?" I ask, intrigued by the intricacy of the design.

"Full sleeves. Got ink on my back and chest too."

"It's addictive, right?"

He nods. "My mother hates them."

"I don't think mine is too thrilled either," I say with a giggle.

Jake enters the room with Garrett, and they pause near the fireplace.

"Does the phoenix cover your entire back?"

I move my hair to the side so he can get a better look. "The wings extend across my shoulders and her tail feathers stop right above my bum. Not gonna lie, that part hurt like a bitch."

"You should try getting one on your ribcage. I remember being afraid to breathe because I didn't want her to fuck up the design. But now that I think about it, I'd say the underside of my arms hurt the most."

"Oh, I bet."

Garrett appears at Connor's side. "Come with me."

"Having a conversation, man."

"Now."

Connor curls his lip at Garrett before meeting my gaze. "I'm sure I'll see you around, Isla. Let me know when's a good time to install your system."

"I will."

He hands me a business card. "Here's my contact information in case you change your mind about the self-defense classes."

I pocket the card and thank him. Garrett ushers him out the door, likely downstairs to his flat.

I turn toward the kitchen and collide with Jake. "Excuse me." I move to step around him.

Our chests bump when he blocks my path. "What are you doing, Isla?"

"Uh, getting something to drink. What're *you* doing?"

He doesn't answer. His gaze flits to the front door, and there's an air of smugness about him that raises my hackles.

"Wait a minute." I shake my head in disbelief. "Jacob Warren Bennett, did ya just cockblock me?"

He grips my arm and pulls me down a darkened hallway, away from the other guests. "And what if I told you I did?"

I narrow my eyes on his face. "Then I'd say you pissed me the fuck off."

Jake backs me against a wall. Nose touching mine, he growls, "Well, color yourself pissed off, sweetheart. They don't call me Cockblock Bennett for nothing."

CHAPTER 13

Jake

Mood: "Blow" by Ed Sheeran

*B*ait taken.

Isla's gaze flashes fire. "I don't appreciate being cockblocked *or* manhandled in a fucking hallway."

"I would never manhandle you." I grip her chin and lean in close. "But for the record, I don't appreciate you flirting with another man in front of my face."

"Oh, really?"

"Yes, really."

"We. Were. Talking."

"Yeah, uh-huh."

She lets out a little feminine growl. "Who the fuck do you think you are? First, you have a temper tantrum and stomp out of the room like a little boy who didn't get his way. Then, you have the balls to interrupt my conversation? Jake, I swear to God, I wanna slap ya."

"So, slap me, then." I release her and hold out my arms in invitation. "Go ahead. Kick me, punch me, bite me—I don't give a fuck. The fact remains you are mine."

Her perfect nostrils flare at my statement. "Who says I wanna be?"

"Your letter said plenty."

She crosses her arms. "Maybe I changed my mind."

"You didn't." I trace my fingertips along her jaw, and her eyelids flutter closed. "I'm everything you've ever wanted, remember?"

Her eyes fly open. "Don't mock me."

"Honey, I'm not mocking you."

"Well, don't throw my words in my face." She waves a finger at me. "Or call me honey."

"I'm not throwing anything in your face; that was simply a gentle reminder."

"I'll give ya a gentle reminder," she warns, jabbing her finger into my chest. "Upside your thick noggin."

"Please do." I smirk and twirl a piece of her hair. "I'm pretty dense sometimes."

"No shit." Her softened tone doesn't match her words.

"So, are you willing to listen to what I have to say," I flash a grin, "*honey?*"

"Depends on whether or not you mean it."

"I've never meant anything more in my life."

"You're infuriating, by the way."

"Well, don't expect me to stop pushing your buttons, sweetheart. You're incredibly sexy when you're angry."

Isla opens and closes her mouth a few times, but she doesn't have a comeback for that. God love her, she's trying to stay pissed at me, but it's not working. Her posture softens in surrender. Her lips tremble as she looks into my eyes. She leans into my touch when I cup her face.

I brush my thumb over her lips. "Come home with me."

"No." Her breathless reply surprises me.

"Why not?"

"Maybe because my last experience there left me feeling—"

"Angry?" I offer.

"I was gonna say heartbroken."

I squeeze my eyes shut. "I'm sorry. I had a lot of shit going through my head. Please let me make it up to you. Tomorrow I'll show you around the city like we planned. We can swing by my studio—"

"I fly back to 'Straya tomorrow."

My heart sinks. "What time?"

"My flight's at eleven."

"Cancel it."

Isla shakes her head. "No. I need to get my flat in order. I have a ton of packing to do, and I need to move some shit into storage at my parents' house."

"When will you come back to New York?"

"Probably in two or three weeks. Depends on when the closing is for my brownstone. Wes mentioned something about negotiating for early occupancy, which would be ideal, especially since I wanna get settled before my internship starts."

"You can come back sooner and stay with me."

"No. I'm not doing that again. I refuse to make you uncomfortable in your own home." She blinks rapidly. "And I don't have the energy to feel like a fucking intruder."

"Listen to me." I clutch her shoulders. "I want you."

"I can't do the back-and-forth shit with you, Jake. It's too painful for me."

I shake my head. "I'm done with that."

"You're saying you had a change of heart?"

"No. My heart's been in the game since you kissed me on the beach. It took me a long time to get my head on the same page."

"Are you sure?" Her lip quivers like she aches to believe me but is waiting for the other shoe to drop.

"Yes." I brush my thumb over her lower lip to still the trembling. "Come home with me and I'll explain myself."

"No." She pulls my ear to her lips. "But you can drive me back to my hotel and show me how you feel. Actions speak louder than words, *honey*."

My cock stiffens. "Sweetheart, I'll show you all night long."

She fists the material of my shirt. "If we get there and you change your mind again, I *will* slap you."

"You won't have to. I'm all-in this time."

"Even if my brother eventually finds out about us?"

"Yes, but I'm not in a rush for that to happen."

"Neither am I."

I brush the hair back from her face. "Please make sure they play some good music at my funeral. Also, I need someone to look after my mother. She kinda loves me, so I'm sure she'll be sad when Wes kills me."

She snorts. "You say it like I'm his daughter."

"Oh, he'd *definitely* kill me then."

"Yeah, you're probably right about that. God help his future daughters."

"C'mon, let's get the hell out of here so I can kiss you."

"Oh?" Isla quirks an eyebrow. "You mean you're gonna give me something beyond a forehead peck?"

"You'll have to wait and see."

"Jake, I've been waiting an eternity for you to kiss me."

"We've kissed." I chuckle and rub my jaw. "Unless my memory of that night is somehow distorted . . ."

"That's not what I mean. Five years ago, *I* kissed you. Tonight, I need *you* to initiate. I need to know you want this as much as I do. That I'm not the only one who—"

"I've waited my whole life for you." My chest tightens. "And every moment without you felt like an eternity."

She narrows her eyes. "Then prove it."

Isla

Internal playlist: "Follow Me" by Craig David

Jake leans back and peers down the hallway. Satisfied we're alone for the moment, he turns toward me. His eyes seem to glow as he grips both sides of my face and rests his forehead against mine.

"Let me make myself abundantly clear . . ." His voice is gravelly as he brushes his lips over mine. "I want this more than you could ever imagine."

He covers my lips with his own, seizing me in a kiss that steals my sanity.

His tongue nudges the seam apart and slips inside my mouth, stroking against mine. I tangle my fingers in his hair, and his chest rumbles on a groan.

All too quickly, he breaks off the kiss. "Honey, that doesn't scratch the surface of what's in store for tonight." This time his lips find my neck, trailing kisses across my shoulder. The warm wetness mixing with the scrape of his stubble sets me on fire.

"Oh, God, Jake." My breath leaves me in a rush. "That feels amazing."

"Listen closely. You suddenly don't feel well, so we're gonna have to leave the party." He flashes a devilish grin. "But first, since we don't want to be rude, we'll say goodbye to your brother and Lena. You with me so far?"

"Yes."

"Good. You'll wait up here while I pull the car around. I'll text you when I'm outside." He grips my hips, yanking me up against him. "Don't keep me waiting."

"I won't." I gasp the words, feeling his hard cock pressed against my lower belly.

"Let's go." Jake releases me and heads down the hall, carrying himself with a swagger that makes my insides heat.

Wes stands by the fireplace chatting with Connor and Garrett.

Jake marches over to them. "Isla's not feeling well. I'm gonna drive her back to her hotel so she doesn't need to wait for a car."

"Oh, all right. Thanks, mate."

I appear at Jake's side. "I think I overindulged. My belly hurts."

Wes wraps me in a hug. "Feel better, Imp. Thank you so much for being here tonight—it means the world to me."

I squeeze him tightly. "I love you. Keep me posted with news from the realtor."

"Will do, love. Do ya have a ride to the airport tomorrow?"

"Yes, I booked a car service."

He nods. "Safe travels. Make sure you say goodbye to Lena."

"Where is she?"

"In the kitchen chatting with her girlfriends. I love you, Imp."

"Love you more." I quickly hug Garrett. "Bye, Garrett."

"Later, Dundette. Don't be a stranger."

Wes hugs Jake. "Thanks for looking out for her, mate."

"My pleasure."

More like mine.

I flush and turn to Connor. "It was nice meetin' ya."

"Likewise, Isla." He clasps my hand and squeezes. "Remember what I said."

Jake bumps fists with Garrett. "Later, man."

"Let me know how you want to proceed with The Phoenix's webpage."

"You have time next week?" Jake asks.

"I'm free every night except Thursday." Garrett rubs his jaw. "Unless Ella calls . . ."

"She'll call, dude. I talked to her this morning."

Garrett perks up. "Really?"

"Yeah, I'll call you tomorrow and fill you in." Jake turns to Connor. "Nice meeting you. Sorry I was a dick."

Connor shakes his hand. "I get it. Nice meeting you too."

Jake leads me into the kitchen. We approach Lena and he touches her shoulder. "Lena-Bean, thank you." He wraps his arms around her. "For everything."

"Wait, you're leaving?"

"*We're* leaving," I say, meeting her jade gaze.

A slow grin crosses her face—a smile that rivals the Cheshire cat. "*We?*"

I flush and glance at Jake. "Yes."

Lena pinches Jake's cheek. "Like I told you, Dolly Gallagher Levi ain't got nothing on me."

"Who's Dolly?" I ask.

Jake grins. "I'll explain in the car."

Lena waggles her brows. "Don't worry, you two. I'll keep the big guy occupied."

CHAPTER 14

Isla

Internal playlist: "God is a Woman" by Ariana Grande

I drop the key card to my hotel room while fumbling to stick it into the slot. Jake stoops to retrieve it. Instead of handing it back, he slides it into the reader. The door clicks, and I stop breathing.

He turns the knob and holds the door open for me. "After you."

I'm so acutely aware of Jake's eyes on my body that my legs tremble. His gaze burns into me, through me, with each wobbled step. I venture inside and stop to place my handbag on the desk. My hands are shaking so badly I nearly drop that too.

Jake comes up behind me. "Look at me." I spin around to face him. "If I'm making you too nervous, I'll head out. We don't have to do this—"

My heart sinks, landing someplace near my swollen feet. I kick off the murderous heeled boots. "You changed your mind?"

He holds up a finger. "That's not what I said. Before you take a swing at me, I need you to hear me out."

I lean back and cross my arms. "I'm listening."

"Everything you expressed in that letter mirrors what I feel for you. You laid it all on the line for me. Now it's my turn to do the same. I want you to fully understand what held me back these past five years. You weren't the only source of my hesitance."

"How can you say that when it's my brother in the forefront? All you kept saying was that he'd kill you. How does that not have something to do with me?"

"I mean it goes beyond your parents and brothers." Jake leads me to the bed, motioning for me to sit. He settles beside me. "Let me explain where I'm coming from. Wes is one of my best friends. I love and respect him. I'm sure you can imagine there'd be some guilt associated with desiring his little sister. Let's start from the beginning, the night you kissed me. Do you remember it as vividly as I do?"

"I've thought about it every day since it happened—even when I was involved with someone else. No kiss has ever felt the same to me. No one has ever come close."

"The same goes for me. Isla, I've dreamed about you, fantasized about you. I've written songs for you." He rakes a hand through his hair and takes a few breaths like he's gathering his thoughts. "Anyway, we hadn't seen each other in a few years, so I had no idea the gorgeous young woman who approached me on the beach was you. I've always cared for you, but I wasn't prepared for what I felt that night. When you handed me that shell and smiled, I swear a switch flipped inside me. I felt like I was seeing you for the first time. I wasn't prepared to *want* you. And I certainly never expected you to want me."

"I wanted you long before that," I confess. "Probably since I was twelve. You were my first crush."

He smiles and touches my cheek. "For the record, I did not feel anything like that for you until our kiss on the beach."

That makes perfect sense given our age difference.

"Back to that night. You were barely eighteen. I was twenty-eight. We were at Wes's birthday party. But the way you looked at me across that fire . . ."

"Pretty sure you were giving me the same look."

"You're goddamn right I was. I couldn't take my eyes off you. I saw you shiver, so I gave you my hoodie. Isla, in that moment, I wanted to give you my *everything*." He touches the tip of my nose with his finger. "I'm giving you back that sweatshirt. I asked you to hold on to it for me, so I'd appreciate it if you would."

"I will," I whisper. "I was hurt when I left it behind."

"I know. And I'm sorry."

I run my fingers through his hair. "Me too. Please tell me the rest of your story."

"I didn't want to leave the party, but I needed to get back to my hotel. I was exhausted and had an early flight the next morning. When I got to my Jeep and realized I'd lost my keys, some little voice in my head told me it was a sign I wasn't supposed to leave. Maybe it was my conscience, my heart. Who knows? Maybe it was fate. I remember asking myself *why*. What was my reason to stay? Then, all of a sudden, you appeared. You collided with me like a confirmation. The answer. *My* answer." His chest heaves with each breath. "My world stopped turning when you kissed me. I wanted to scoop you up and bring you with me. I wanted to spend the whole night kissing you. I wanted to hold you in my arms and make love to you. I wanted *everything* with you . . . and that scared the shit out of me." He grips my chin. "It destroyed me to see those big, beautiful, blue eyes fill with tears when you asked me to stay. And it fucking killed me when I walked away from you. But I had to."

"Because of Wes," I whisper.

Jake shakes his head. "My reservations went beyond Wes. You being my forbidden fruit was only the tip of the iceberg. I'm the root of the problem, and I need you to understand a few things about me." He takes my hands in his. "I'm a needy man. I battle anxiety and an obsessiveness that is all-consuming at times."

"You already told me you have OCD. I'm well aware of the implications there."

"Are you?"

I squeeze his hands. "Yeah. I did some research after I left your house the other day. I wanted to try to understand you better. Make sense of what was happening. I read about obsessions, compulsions, all of it. And I think I have a firm grasp on anxiety, in general."

"My compulsions are intense. *I* can be intense. I don't want to overwhelm you. I don't want to ask for more than you can give me. I'm terrified I'll make you my obsession." He rubs the backs of my hands. "You deserve better than that. I pushed you away to protect you."

"But what if I don't want to be protected?" I steel my shoulders. "What if I want you—all of you—exactly as you are? What if I want your intensity, your obsessiveness, your compulsions? What if I want the possessiveness I got a taste of earlier?"

His gaze flashes fire. "I wanted to hit him."

I smirk. "No kidding, Cockblock Bennett."

"You're mine, Isla."

"And you are mine. You've always been mine—even before your switch flipped." I tilt my head. "Since we're both on the same page with that, I'm wondering what else is stopping you."

"I feel like I'm standing on the edge of a cliff and you're the ocean beneath me. I want to fall. I'm ready to fall—"

"I know I said I'd slap you, but I'd certainly never drown you." I grip his hands. "Jump. Fall into me and let me carry you to shore."

"Honey, there's no going back for me. When I dive into this, into you, I'll fall hard. I need to know you'll be there to catch me. If we cross this line, I need to know I'll get to keep you. That you won't freak out and leave me adrift somewhere. I don't ever want to feel the way my mom did when my father left."

"What happened with your parents?"

"Mom deals with a lot of the same mental health shit as I do. My father couldn't handle her constant panic, the bouts of depression, or the way she clung to me and him. He wasn't the kind of man equipped to handle someone needing him. Then Mom got breast cancer. She really needed him then. He left us when his presence mattered the most." He runs his hands over his face. "I guess what I'm trying to say is, I'm needy as fuck. I need to know you'll be there when it matters. But most of all," he meets my gaze once more, and the profound vulnerability in his eyes makes me tear up, "I need to know you can handle me loving you—as deeply and obsessively as I plan to."

"Not only can I handle it, but I look forward to it." I hug him, burying my face against the crook of his neck. He tightens his arms around me and strokes my back. "I've spent years hoping one day you'd love me." I kiss his neck and watch goose bumps appear. His breath hitches as I trail kisses over his throat to his earlobe. He clutches at the material of my shirt. I continue kissing him because I love his scent, his warm skin, and stubbled jaw. I slowly lean back, pulling him on top of me. "Kiss me."

Jake nudges my legs apart, settling between them. He toes his shoes off, and they hit the floor with a thud. Bracing his weight on his elbows, he cups my face and seals his lips over mine. His kiss is deep, plundering. A kiss of starvation. He spears his tongue into my mouth, and it tangles with mine. Wrapping my legs around him, I thread my fingers in his hair. His rock-hard length presses between my legs. He rolls his hips, making me moan at the friction.

He pulls his lips from mine. "You have no idea how long I've wanted to hear you moan."

"Not as long as I've wanted you to make it happen." I give him a sultry smirk. "And by that, I mean *directly*."

He raises a brow. "Directly?"

"Yeah, like I mentioned previously, my experience moaning your name has always been . . . *indirect*." I brush my lips over his ear. "Self-induced."

"Why don't you tell me a little bit more about that." The huskiness of his tone heats me. "I'd love a play-by-play."

"Are you gonna tell me about when I heard you say mine?"

"Nope."

"Well, since I'm clearly the better sport, I'll tell you. It always started as a daydream, usually at an inconvenient time or place, sometimes both. The day you released the *Shades* album was the first time. I remember being in my afternoon classes and staring at my watch, willing the time to pass. Finally, classes ended, and I went back to my flat to listen. I made myself some tea, put comfy clothes on, and climbed into bed. Your voice has always done amazing things to me, and that time was no exception. Then I got to 'Crave' . . ."

"I wrote that on the flight home after our kiss."

"That song is so fucking sexy that I literally moaned aloud. I listened over and over again, took off my clothes—" I flush. Maybe I can't spell it out for him. "And I . . ."

Jake kisses my neck, the shell of my ear. "I'm listening."

"I think I'll leave it to your imagination."

He grips my chin. "How about we reenact it . . . together?"

"Can't do that."

He kisses my jawline and throat. "And why's that?"

"That region's off-limits for a few more days."

There's no way I'm doing anything while I have my period. No fucking way. It grosses me out enough, and the last thing I need is Jake being near all that. *It's bad enough he knows what kind of pads I use.* My face flames at the thought.

"You think that bothers me?" He brings his lips to my ear once more. "That's what showers are for, sweetheart."

Eyes darting to his, I curl my lip in sheer horror. "Absolutely not! It bothers *me*, so it won't be happening. Ever."

Jake chuckles, sitting up. "Got it. Message received." He touches my cheek. "I won't pressure you."

"Thank you."

He flashes a wolfish grin. "But I'd like to take you up on that offer to get a better look at your tattoo . . ." He straightens. "Uh, if you're comfortable with that, of course."

I give him a slow smile. "*That*, we can do." I sit up, scooting around so my back is to him. I lift the shirt up over my head. His breath catches. I place my shirt on the bed and move my hair aside.

"This is the most beautiful thing I've ever seen," he murmurs, tracing the phoenix's wings.

I reach behind and unhook my strapless bra. It falls around my waist. Jake's ragged breaths send goose bumps over my skin. "Touch me, Jacob." His shaky fingertips brush my shoulder blades. I peer over my shoulder at him. "Don't be nervous."

He flushes. "I'm not."

"Liar." I move closer to him, so I'm seated between his legs. I grip his wrists and pull his arms around me, placing his warm hands on my breasts. "Please touch me," I whisper, leaning into him. Jake exhales roughly and kisses the side of my neck. His huge palms cover me. I'm a B cup at best, but I feel flat-chested in his hands.

He drags his thumbs over my nipples, massaging them.

"Oh, God, Jake." I clutch the comforter.

"Turn around and let me see you." His voice rumbles in his chest, sending flares of heat through me.

Suddenly feeling shy, I slowly turn to face him. His gaze travels down my neck, to my breasts, then lower, pausing at my navel piercing. "Is that new?"

I shake my head. "Been a couple of years now. One of my mates from uni convinced me to go with her when she got her nipples pierced. But there was no way in hell I was doing that."

He toys with the purple jewel for a moment before his gaze snaps to mine. "It's sexy as fuck." His hands slide to my breasts, cupping them. "Everything about you is sexy." His thumbs find my nipples once more and I gasp. "I wanna kiss you here, if that's all right."

"Yes." My voice is a throaty whisper that makes him smile.

"Lie back for me."

I lower myself onto my back and Jake leans over, bracketing me with his arms. He dips his head and kisses me. It's a slow, deep tango of tongues that makes my head spin. He breaks the kiss and works his way down to my neck, sucking and kissing my skin. I weave my hands into his hair.

He moves lower, nibbling my collarbone, then my shoulders. One of his hands cups a breast as his mouth finds the other. He kisses the lower curve of my breast, my sternum, slowly edging closer to the nipple. I moan when his lips surround it, his tongue rubbing the peak in circles. His hand mirrors his mouth on my other breast.

"Oh, Jake, that feels so good . . ." I pull his head closer. "Please don't stop." He groans and gives my nipple a hard suck. "*Yes.* Just like that." My back arches as I absorb the sensations spearing through me.

Since the extent of my sexual experience with men is limited to my breasts, I'm extremely attuned to them. I can easily get myself off with nipple play, and over the years, I had a couple of boyfriends who were successful. Good thing those poor fools never knew I was imagining Jake when they kissed me. And now that I have the real Jake, instead of the phantom lover I envisioned, everything's more intense.

If he keeps doing what he's doing, he'll bring me over the edge in no time. His mouth is working my left nipple, which is more sensitive. Pinching and rolling my right one between his thumb and forefinger, he's got my toes curling.

"Don't stop." I gasp, tugging the strands of his hair. "Oh, Jake . . . do it harder." He increases the suction, rapidly flicking his tongue, and I fall apart. "Oh, fuck . . . Jake . . . Yes!" I wail my pleasure, throwing my head back. Hips bucking, back arching, I ride the waves of my release until my nipples are so sensitive, I can't take it anymore. I push at his head, and he immediately pulls back.

Jake stares down at me in utter bewilderment. "Did I just make you come?"

"I can assure you I wasn't fakin' it," I say on a gasp.

His eyes are wide and filled with wonder. "I've heard it's possible, but I've never seen it happen."

"Seriously? You've never given a chick a nipplegasm?"

"No. That was a first for me." He shakes his head. "Swear to God."

"Then how come you're so good at it?"

He runs a hand over his face. "Honestly, I just wanted my mouth on you. I had no idea what the hell I was doing."

"You're good at taking direction."

"Isla, that was the hottest thing I've ever experienced," he licks his lips, "and I can't wait to do it again."

I flutter my lashes. "Same. But they're too sensitive right now." I press myself up. "And that can only mean one thing." Still reeling, Jake raises a brow at me. Rising to my knees, I grip the front of his shirt. "Your turn."

"You don't have to—"

"Lie down," I command, pushing him onto his back. My fingers rapidly work the buttons on his shirt, revealing his muscular chest. I straddle his hips and shove the material over his shoulders. Between my legs, his cock presses against me. I roll my hips and it jerks.

"Isla," he groans my name, "you're killing me."

Leaning forward, I kiss and suck on his neck. "Just getting started, love." I work my way down, dragging my tongue over his hard nipples. I know I can make him come like this, but what I'm interested in is much lower. I give his nipple a series of rapid tongue flicks, followed by deep suction.

"Oh, *fuck* . . ." He spears his hands into my hair.

I kiss the hard ridges of his abdomen, my fingertips finding his belt. I rear up, making eye contact as I unbuckle it. "I'm gonna make you moan, Jacob." I pull the length of leather from its loops and toss it aside. Scooting back, I unbutton his jeans.

Jake grips my wrist. "I don't expect you—"

"I want to." I pull from his grasp. "I've imagined doing this to you for years." I shove his jeans over his hips down to his ankles. He kicks them off. I trail my fingertips along the waistband of his boxer briefs and kiss his abs once more. Sliding my hand up his thigh, I rub his hard cock through the material.

His hips jerk with my touch. "Isla . . ."

I grip his waistband with my teeth. "Hmm?"

"You're gonna burn me alive."

I tug his boxers down, freeing him. He's the perfect length—well above average, yet not monstrous like Lucas was. But Jake is thick, much girthier than anyone I've been with, which makes me mildly nervous for the future.

I grip him, sliding my hands up and down his shaft, absorbing his skin's softness, like silk-covered steel. Warm. Hard. *Mine.*

Jake groans, hands fisting the bedspread. "That feels so good."

"Just wait, love. I'm gonna give you more than a rub and tug." Our eyes meet and his widen. I feel the sultry smile take over my face. "You're mine now, Jacob Bennett." I slowly lean down, brushing my lips over the head. "Let me show you what that means."

CHAPTER 15

Jake

Mood: "Lick It" by Chris Watts

B low jobs are better than an ice cream sundae with a shitload of hot fudge. Or, in my case, leagues better than rubbing one out in the shower by my lonesome. Isla peers up at me with those eyes, her lips barely grazing the tip of my cock. I pray to every deity known to man that I don't embarrass myself.

Fuck being a minute man, I give it thirty seconds.

Her firm grip on my shaft tells me she means business. Her lashes flutter closed as she flicks her tongue over the slit, through the bead of moisture that collected. I clench my jaw, my thighs, my ass cheeks—anything that can be clenched, is clenched. She presses a series of butterfly kisses to my cock as her other hand cups my balls.

"You're gonna fucking kill me," I sputter. I'm not even in her mouth yet and I'm ready to come.

"No, Jake. I'm gonna love ya." She takes me to the back of her throat.

"*Fuck.*" My eyes roll back in ecstasy. As much as I want to look at her, I can't—I know damn well the sight will make me bust.

She starts to move, tongue massaging the underside as she takes me in. She pulls back and swirls it over the head, alternating rapid flicks with slow, deliberate licks. Like I'm a motherfucking popsicle. Like she's actually *enjoying* it.

My experience with getting blow jobs is somewhat limited—mainly because Nadia hated it. I wasn't allowed to touch her head or move my hips. And I sure as fuck couldn't come in her mouth. Right now, I'm not entirely sure what flies with Isla and what's off-limits, so I figure the safest bet is keeping my hands off. I clutch the blankets even though I ache to tangle my hands in her hair.

Isla pulls back and looks at me. "You're a bit tense."

"I don't want you to think I'm a fucking minute man."

She smiles. "Stop worrying and enjoy it. My goal's to make you come. If it happens quickly, then I'm doing it right." She drags her tongue up my shaft. "But I'm in the mood to tease ya a bit." She rolls my balls in her hand, massaging them.

My reply comes out as a garbled mess.

Isla takes me deep in her throat, lightly trailing her nails over my sack. Releasing her grip on my cock, she snatches my clenched fist and brings it to her head. I knot my fingers in her hair and she moans around me. She slides a hand to one of my nipples, pinching and rolling it between her fingers. I've never experienced anything like this. It's like her hands and mouth are everywhere.

"Isla, honey, *fuck* . . ." My hips jerk upward. She pulls back moments before I'm going to come and kisses my inner thighs, dragging her tongue over my skin. Sucking and nibbling everywhere *except* my aching cock. She licks my balls with the same level of attention. The impending orgasm subsides. The pressure inside me builds, sending fire through my veins.

She kisses my belly, my sides, and my kneecaps before finally coming back to center. Flashing me a devious grin, she takes the tip inside. She sucks and flicks her tongue until I'm about to blow, then stops suddenly, leaving me teetering on the brink of an eruption. She resumes her kisses on my hip bones.

"Do you like how this feels, Jacob?" she purrs, kissing my groin.

"Oh, fuck, *yes* . . ." I hiss the word, hips jerking, cock begging for her tongue. "Please."

"Please, what?"

"Let me come." I tighten my fingers in her hair and groan.

Isla grips the base of my cock and brings her mouth over it. "Well, since you said please. . ." She takes me to the back of her throat, moving her hand and mouth in tandem.

It only takes a few strokes.

"I'm gonna come," I warn, pushing at her head. She slaps my hand and keeps moving, increasing her pace and suction. My cock pulses, releasing harder than ever in my life. I couldn't stop if I wanted to. "Oh, fuck." My hips thrash and I pull her hair. Isla keeps moving—milking me until I can't take it any longer. "Isla . . ." Her name rips from my chest.

Pulling back, she wipes her mouth and flashes me a cocky grin. Right now, I know beyond a shadow of a doubt, I'm obsessed.

Isla

Internal playlist: "Feelin' Love" by Paula Cole

If I were a queen, I'd want to be revered by my subjects. Exalted and treasured. I'd want them to love me with a wholehearted purity that infuses who they are as people. Looking into Jake's eyes at this moment, I feel that reverence. I'm the queen he'd follow into any battle and gladly die on his sword for.

I give him a smile. "Did ya enjoy that?"

He runs both hands over his face. "You—" Shaking his head, he tries again, "You're just—I fucking can't . . . I—"

I giggle. "Not makin' much sense, Jacob."

"You blew my fucking mind."

I nudge him. "Wasn't your mind I blew."

He laughs, pulling me into a hug. "Come here." I settle alongside him, resting my head on his chest. His heart hammers his ribs and his breaths come in gasps. He holds me close, stroking my hair. "Isla, you're—"

I press a kiss to his chest, halting his words. "Stay with me tonight." I look up at him, hoping I don't sound too desperate. "Please, hold me. I wanna sleep in your arms."

Jake brushes the hair from my face and kisses my forehead. "Not going anywhere, honey."

We pull back the covers and scoot beneath them, tugging the crisp sheets up around us. I resettle in his embrace and close my eyes. For years, I've dreamed about Jake holding me. I've fallen asleep wrapped around a body pillow, wishing it were him, praying that one day our paths would intersect. Aching for a time when it could be just us—free from distractions, from whys and what-ifs, shoulds and should nots. I've wondered what it would feel like to rest my head on his chest and listen to his heartbeat, his breath, without time or distance to separate us.

I never imagined it would feel this good cocooned in the warmth and safety of his arms. The way he strokes my hair and brushes his lips over my forehead settles me. Alone in the darkness, an ocean away from where I grew up, he feels like home.

Jake hums "Desert Rose," a song he wrote for me. The lyrics run through my mind, bringing tears to my eyes.

I want to watch you bloom, see you rise and soar above me. Feel the wind from your wings on my face.

You inspire my heart to shed the pain, to break the chains that crush and bind it. To reach with you, to seek with you, until we find bliss.

My desert rose, the rains will come. Grow with me, our day is young. Free as birds, we'll stretch our wings. I'll let you know my heart and hear it sing.

Grow, my love, soak me up. Feel the waters that I bring.

Rise, my dove, drink me in. Just unfurl those pretty wings.

Fly above, hear me sing. Bloom for me, my desert rose.

CHAPTER 16

Jake

Mood: "Lights On" by Shawn Mendes

It's daybreak. Outside, the blaring horns and distant sirens remind me I'm in Manhattan. But it feels like heaven in this warm bed with Isla nestled in my arms. Lashes resting on her cheeks, lips slightly parted, a soft snore whistles from her.

We both passed out last night. Me, from mental exhaustion and post-orgasmic bliss. I'm sure she was simply tired. We never even changed for bed. That's okay—pajamas are overrated anyway. At some point during the night, the telltale buzz of an electric toothbrush and some crinkling plastic told me she'd freshened up. I thought about joining her but couldn't bring myself to leave the bed.

Currently, I'm butt naked, sporting my typical morning wood while Isla's still wearing black leather pants with nothing on top. Facing each other, her warm chest is pressed to mine. Soft, perfect breasts I want to lick incessantly. My cock twitches its agreement. Nothing compares to the ecstasy from last night. I can't imagine how good it will feel to be inside her. My mind fills with images of Isla on her back beneath me, legs wrapped around me, hips moving with mine.

I bet she's a hellion in bed. She *has* to be. Any woman who sucks cock like that is sure to annihilate a man during sex. Too bad she has reservations about her period because I'd be more than happy to bend her over in the shower. I clench my jaw and fight the urge to mount her. I can't wait to go down on her, taste every inch of her, know the secrets of her body. I'm still in shock that I made her come so easily last night. In the seventeen years I've been sexually active, I've never given a woman an orgasm simply by licking her nipples. Part of me figured it was a myth, but this gorgeous creature in my arms proved me wrong.

Isla is perfect. She's a goddess. A queen. *My queen.* I wish I could tell her how deeply I want her, but I'm afraid to overwhelm her. She says she can handle it, but she's never seen me in action. The last thing I want is to cage or smother her. It goes beyond love, delving into the primitive. I need her. I want her to need me too. I want her to be mine like I need to be hers.

What's going to happen when Wes finds out? Will he kick my ass? Or worse, cut me off entirely? I hate to admit it, but I need him too. Since I don't have siblings, Wes, Austin, and Jesse are my brothers. They're the ones who were there when it mattered—like when my mom had cancer and my parents split up. Those guys stood by me during my emotionally unstable teenage years and when my dad died. We've had each other's backs for the good stuff too. I'll never forget celebrating with them when my first album went platinum or when I won my first Grammy.

I'd like to think they feel the same about me. I know I've been there for Jesse—we've been friends since kindergarten. We've been part of each other's every milestone. I went with him to buy an engagement ring and proudly stood by his side on his wedding day. He was so nervous waiting for Hannah to enter the church. But when she walked down that aisle, gorgeous in her long, white dress, the adoration on his face will live in my memories forever. I remember the tears streaming down his cheeks during their vows. I spent days preparing my best man speech and surprised them with a song I'd written for their first dance. Then, a few years later, I gave him a shoulder to cry on when Hannah had a double mastectomy at twenty-eight. When she endured radiation and chemo for months on end. She's in remission now, but I'll never forget Jesse's pain.

Even with an ocean between us, I tried to be there for Wes when it mattered. Like after Reed's accident and during his agonizing recovery. Then, when Isla got sick. I was there for the Rachel fallout too. Austin's childhood was smooth sailing, but he's dealt with plenty of industry bullshit like crazed fans and stalkers. Wes and I were there when he met Katie. We'll be there for the birth of their child in a few months, and their eventual wedding.

Sure, the three of us might get pissed at one another now and then, but it's always short-lived. We've never had a true fight or been angry enough that our friendship was in jeopardy.

I glance at Isla. I know I'm crossing a line here. The thing is, I don't care anymore. I'm tired of being lonely. I'm done watching my three closest friends live out their happily ever afters while I wallow in misery and pine from a distance. I'm tired of holding myself back and pushing away the woman I love. I deserve happiness too. Right?

I love how Isla's spirit filled my home with warmth and color. How she challenged my OCD—ruffled and smoothed my feathers enough to keep me on my toes, but not too much to send me spiraling. I love how brave she was for going out on a limb with that letter. How she's beautiful and bold and free. The way she enriches and livens every room she enters and every life she touches. The depth of the despair that gripped me during the three days without her was one helluva wake-up call. I'm done with distance. Done with the push and pull. From now on, I need her close.

Yeah, Wes can come after me with a whole fucking army, but there's no way I'm letting her go now.

"What're you thinkin' about?" Isla's voice jolts me from my thoughts.

"You," I whisper.

"That scowl was for me?"

"I wasn't scowling."

She sits up. "Tell me the truth. You're worried about Wes finding out."

I sigh heavily. "Yes and no."

Isla rolls her eyes. "That's helpful. Now I totally understand what's swirling around in your noggin."

I chuckle. "Sadly, there's always a storm brewing in my noggin. Some days it reaches F5 on the Fujita scale."

"Fujita scale?"

"Yeah, it's the tornado measurement scale. Kinda like the Richter scale for earthquakes. But I've usually got rain and lightning and shit, so a hurricane is probably a more accurate analogy. I'd say my brain's normal state is similar to a category two hurricane."

"Got a thing for weather?" she asks with a laugh.

"Weather and natural disasters fascinate me."

"Why?"

"Because they scare the shit out of me. So, naturally, I fixate on them.

Monsoons, tidal waves, you name it. Earthquakes freak me out the most. Did you know there's a fault line near the city?" I shake my head. "Never mind, how the hell would you know that?"

Isla tilts her head. "Are you really that worried about an earthquake?"

Skirting her question, I explain, "It's called the Ramapo Fault and it runs from New Jersey through New York and Pennsylvania. Seismic activity could be catastrophic for the metro area. There's also a nuclear power plant a little way up the Hudson River. It's not currently active, but you never know—"

She grips my chin, forcing my gaze to hers. "Sometimes knowledge isn't power." Her royal blue eyes focus on mine. "There's no sense torturing yourself with every possible what-if, when ninety-nine-point-nine percent of them will never happen."

"I know," I mutter. "But it's that point-one percent that keeps me up at night."

"You need to chill the fuck out, love." Isla kisses me softly. "Live your life instead of living in fear. Because this is it. This life is all we get. Each moment is a gift and that's what you need to focus on."

"I wish it was that easy, honey."

"Maybe I can help." Her lush lips curve into a sultry smile and before I know what's happening, she pounces.

"Whoa." I flop against the pillows. "What was that for?"

She straddles my hips, and the morning wood that had dissipated makes a hard comeback. She leans forward and kisses my neck. "I'm gonna help you clear your noggin."

I gasp as she trails her tongue over my throat.

She nibbles my collarbone, and gripping my hands, interlaces her fingers with mine. She presses them into the mattress at my shoulders. "Stop thinkin' and feel."

"You gonna ravage me again?"

She grins. "Are ya gonna let me?"

"Fuck yeah, I am." I squeeze her hands in mine. "Because in three weeks, I plan to return the favor."

"Oh?" She flicks her tongue over my nipple. "And how do you plan to do that?"

"Something along the lines of having you writhing beneath me."

She squeezes my hips with her thighs. "You think so?"

I tug her hands so she flops forward onto me, her body pressed to mine.

I roll us over and settle on top of her. Flexing my hips, I deliberately rub my cock between her legs. The friction of skin against buttery smooth leather makes me groan. I bring my lips to her ear and whisper, "No, sweetheart, I *know* so."

Isla

Internal playlist: "Like a Virgin" by Madonna

Now would probably be a good time to tell him I'm a virgin.

I open my mouth, but for whatever reason, the words won't come. Part of me wants Jake to know he'll be my first, but a bigger part is afraid to tell him. What if my inexperience turns him off? Or worse, what if he decides he doesn't want the responsibility of devirginizing me? For Jake, it's bad enough that I'm Wes's little sister. I worry if he gets too deep into his own head, he'll torture himself for popping my cherry, or some archaic bullshit like that. No. I can't tell him. I'll just claim it's been a long time and ask him to go slowly. Which would be a solid plan if I hadn't already seen his thickness.

He rolls his hips again. The granny undies and monstrous pad I'm wearing keep bunching, but somehow, it only intensifies the sensations on my clit, pulling me from the whirlwind in my head. Jake buries his face in my neck and slowly flexes his pelvis. The pressure and friction set me on fire.

"I wanna be inside you, Isla," he whispers against my neck. "So fucking badly."

"Soon." I clutch his shoulders and wrap my legs around him, digging my heels into his arse. He groans and thrusts his hips. I reach down to stroke him, but he stops me.

"Just let me rub you, honey."

Jake moves his hips in a grinding motion. He's naked, and I've got pants on, but the pressure of his weight rubs all the right places. Opening my legs a little wider so each thrust of his hips massages me, I moan my pleasure.

"I'm gonna come if you keep doing that."

"I'm counting on it. I wanna hear you, sweetheart." He clutches my hips, pulling our bodies closer.

"Oh, Jake . . ."

"Come for me." A few more rolls of his hips bring me over the edge.

My back arches. "Jake! Oh ..." I dig my nails into his shoulders to keep me from going into orbit.

He keeps moving, then suddenly rolls off me, his hand flying to his cock. He roughly strokes it as he nears his release.

I take him into my hands. "Let me do it." He settles on his back, and I give him a good rub and tug.

"Isla, *fuck*." Legs shaking, he moans his pleasure. "I'm gonna come."

I tighten my grip. His cock pulses and releases onto his stomach. Mouth open, eyes squeezed shut, Jake's O face is sexy as fuck.

"You look hot when you orgasm."

Gasping, he barks a laugh. "Uh, thanks?"

"Well, it's true." I lean over him. "I love making you come, Jacob."

"The feeling's mutual." He cups my face. "I can't wait to make love to you."

Tell him.

"I hope I don't disappoint you," I say, chewing my lower lip.

He snatches his shirt to clean himself off. "That's probably the most ridiculous thing I've ever heard you say."

"Well, it's true. I'm not sure what your expectations are of me ..."

Tossing the shirt aside, Jake points to himself. "Do you see my face right now? I'm grinning like an idiot because we dry-humped like a couple of kids in the backseat of a car. You shattered my expectations when you kissed me five years ago. Isla, you ..." he swallows tightly, "I don't think you understand what you do to me. I'm enamored with you. Captivated by you. To be honest, I'm fucking smitten. So, you can stop worrying about *my* expectations." He grips my chin. "Because I'm scared I'll fall short of *yours*."

Tell him.

"Lupus has sexual side effects," I whisper, flushing. "Lubrication and skin hypersensitivity are issues for me." I meet his gaze. "I'm not someone who can go all night."

He chuckles. "I've never gone all night. I'm old. I want to sleep at some point."

"That's not what I mean—"

"I understand what you're getting at. We'll use lube and I can go as slowly as you need me to. I won't hurt you. When you feel like stopping, we'll stop. You let me know what you like, and I'll give it to you."

I'm a fucking virgin. I don't know what I like yet.

"Jake, I'm—" My phone rings on the nightstand. I glance at the screen. "It's my brother." I silence the ringer.

"You're not answering him?"

"I don't feel like dealing with him right now."

Jake snorts. "Don't worry. He'll call back." As if on cue, my phone rings again. "Told you."

I sigh. "Hello?"

Wes's booming voice reaches my ears. "Imp. How're ya feeling?"

I frown. "I'm great. Why?"

"Thought your stomach was bothering you?"

Right. "Oh, it's much better now."

"Glad to hear it. Thank you for coming all that way to celebrate my birthday."

"Of course! I love you. I'm sorry I had to cut out early."

"No worries. I always overeat when Lena cooks, so I get it. I'm glad Bennett offered to drive so you didn't have to wait around for a car."

"Yeah, me too. He's a good bloke."

"I know you haven't seen him in a while, but did he seem strange to you?"

Tensing, I glance at Jake. "Strange, how?"

"I dunno. He wasn't himself. Seemed like he was on edge. Was a bit of a dick to Garrett's cousin."

I shrug. "Jake seemed fine to me." *He's naked in my bed right now, wanna have a chat?* Jake stiffens and raises a brow. I shake my head.

"Did he say anything?" Wes asks. "He gets lost in his noggin sometimes, and I wanted to make sure he's all right. I've been preoccupied with Lena, so I feel like a shit for not checking in on him more."

"You're not a shitty mate, Wes. Jake has a lot on his mind with the community center. That's the only thing he mentioned."

"Good. I'll call him and see if I can help."

"I'm sure he'd appreciate that," I muse, running my fingers through Jake's hair.

"Anyway, I won't keep you. Just wanted to check in. When's your flight? I'm sorry I didn't offer to drive you to the airport. I'm a shit."

"No worries. My car will be here shortly."

"I also wanted to give you the news . . ."

"What news?" I ask.

"The realtor called me. The lawyers moved up the closing. You can move in on December tenth."

"Wait. What's today?"

Wes snorts. "You still on Aussie time? Today's Sunday. November thirtieth."

"Holy fuck, that's so soon. I've gotta pack up all my shit. Mum and Dad will still be in France."

"I called Cora. She's gonna help ya."

"Ugh." I curl my lip. "Does that mean Moody Melvin will be in attendance?"

Wes laughs. "They're a package deal, are they not?"

"Yup."

"Reed loves you, Imp. He's just—"

"He's just Reed."

"Right. Anyway, I'll letcha go. Text when you land. Love you."

"Love you, too. Bye." I hang up and turn to Jake. "My brother's worried about you. Thinks you're in a funk."

Jake smirks, gesturing to my half-naked body. "If this is a funk, bring it."

I roll my eyes. "No, he's seriously concerned. You should call him and spend time together—drink beers or whatever the hell you do."

"I'll call him later."

"Oh, and guess what . . ."

Jake eyes me. "What's up?"

"They moved up the closing, *neighbor*."

A broad grin crosses his face. "To when?"

"I'll see you in ten days."

His brows pop. "Seriously?"

"Yes. I move in on December tenth."

He pulls me into a hug. "That makes me ridiculously happy."

"Me too." I wrap my arms around him. "He enlisted Cora and Reed's help with packing my shit."

"I'll help you once you get here. So, wait, are you shipping furniture from Australia?"

"No, but I need to empty out my old flat and move stuff to my parents'. I'm bringing my clothes, shoes, electronics, and such. Wes bought the brownstone fully furnished, so the only thing I need to buy is a mattress."

"Or you can sleep on mine . . ."

"I intend to, Jacob. But it might look suspicious if I move into a place without a bed."

He chuckles. "A valid point. What were you going to say earlier?"

"Huh?"

"You started to say something, but Wes called."

Shit. "I'm a . . ." I pick my nails and debate the idea of getting the discussion over with, then decide against it at the last minute. "I don't remember."

Jake strokes my cheek. "You sure?"

Tell him. "Yes, I'm sure." I give a nervous laugh. "It's probably not important if it slipped my mind so easily."

"If you think of it, let me know." He leans in, our lips brushing in soft, tender kisses. "I want to know everything on your mind, sweetheart."

You probably don't want to know this.

I'm willing to bet Wes's kidney that Jake's stance on being my first would involve a whole lot of tail tucking and running in the opposite direction. We've come so far since our fallout at his brownstone, and I can't bear the thought of him pushing me away again.

CHAPTER 17

Jake

Mood: "If You Could Only See" by Tonic

Absence makes the heart grow fonder. That's what I keep telling myself as I ease into the last free spot in the short-term parking lot at JFK airport.

I peer at Isla in the passenger seat. "Are you sure you have everything? Your meds?"

"Yes. They're right here." She points to her purse.

"Okay, good. C'mon, I'll walk you in."

"You're not worried people will see us?"

Glancing in the rearview to do a quick scan of our surroundings, I squeeze her knee. "Like I told you, I'm all in now."

She smiles. "Me too."

"However, this is more appropriate in private." I lean in and seal my lips over hers.

Isla's breath leaves her in a rush. Her hands threading into my hair, she kisses me with a ferocity that mirrors our first kiss. A groan rumbles deep in my chest as I give her everything I've got.

Gasping, I break the kiss. "C'mon. You don't wanna miss your flight."

She grips my face. "Tell me you'll still want me when I come back." Her gorgeous eyes are wide and vulnerable, lips quivering. "Tell me you won't change your mind again. Promise we'll still have this."

"Honey, I'll want you for all eternity, so you don't need to worry about that."

"We've gone years without seeing each other, so why does ten days seem like an eternity?"

"It'll go fast," I assure her. "We can talk and text every day. If you want, we can FaceTime too."

"I'd love that."

I smile. "Me too. I'm gonna miss you, Sprite. More than you know."

I love you.

"I'll miss you more." Isla unclicks her seat belt and steps out of the car.

I grab her suitcase and carry-on—which the airline located two days ago and delivered to her hotel—and follow her into the airport. We check her baggage and make our way to security. Someone calls my name, but I ignore them. I'm not letting myself get distracted this time.

"I'll letcha know when I land." Isla wraps her arms around my neck and mine find her waist.

"Please do. Safe travels, Sprite." I tighten my embrace. "I'll see you in ten days." I give her a goofy grin. "Then I'm gonna take you on a date."

"A date?"

"I wanna wine and dine you. Minus the wine."

Isla laughs. "I'm allowed to have a glass."

I grunt instead of answering.

"When I get back, we can compare notes." At my raised brow, she kisses my cheek and gives me a megawatt smile. "I'll letcha know how many times I moaned your name during my 'alone time.'"

My breath whooshes out of me, and I glance at my crotch. "Put a mark in my column for forty-five minutes from now. Or sooner . . . if I decide to pull over. Hell, you should probably give me at least four for tonight."

She laughs and hugs me once more. "Jacob Warren Bennett, you're a filthy man."

"I guess I could say I'm sorry?" I shrug and flash her a grin. "But I'm really not."

"Don't be sorry, I love it."

"Honey, if you want filth, I'll give it to you."

Her lips brush my ear. "I want everything."

My cock throbs, and I remind myself we're in public. "I'll give you everything."

She releases me and adjusts the purse on her shoulder. "I'm gonna hold you to that."

I waggle my brows. "No, I'm gonna hold *you* to it."

"I can't wait." She chews her lip for a moment, then opens and closes her mouth like she's going to say something, but no words come out. Swallowing tightly, she smiles and gives me a wave. She makes it a few steps away, then spins back around.

Our eyes meet and the air between us shifts. Suddenly, I'm back at Wes's thirtieth birthday, staring across the fire at her. My chest tightens and the ability to breathe escapes me. The noise and bustle of the airport fades away and all I can hear is my heartbeat. All I can see is Isla. Cheeks rosy, reddened by my stubble. Blue eyes shining, she looks at me, through me, inside me, and I swear she can see my soul. Her lips are swollen from our kiss. I smell her perfume on me and can still taste the sweetness of her lips. Isla is exquisite, radiant, and *mine*.

"I love you, Jake Bennett."

Before I can respond, she disappears through the gate to security.

CHAPTER 18

Isla

Internal playlist: "Versions of Violence" by Alanis Morissette

There's something about rendering Jake speechless that makes me giddy. I'm not sure if it's the way his eyes widen on rapid blinks or how his mouth opens and closes like a pouty angelfish, but either way, I love it. I love *him*, and that's why I told him.

My phone buzzes in my pocket. I withdraw it and smile when I see his name on the screen.

Jake: We'll pick that conversation back up in ten days.

Smirking, I text my reply.

Me: Was a closing statement, not a conversation starter.

Jake: They're one and the same for me. It WILL be addressed.

I clutch my phone to my chest. Deep down, I know he loves me, but some verbal confirmation would make me feel more secure.

I'm finally back in Australia after an eternity of flying and travel bullshit. Reed and Cora met me at the airport, and we've been packing up my flat for the past few hours. While it's somewhat bittersweet to leave my apartment behind, I'm excited to start the next chapter of my life in New York. *With Jake.*

The thought makes me grin like a bloody fool.

Cora eyes me, hands on her hips. "Spill it, little bird."

I glance over my shoulder. Reed's down the hall, shoving my books into boxes. "Not now. Melvin might hear."

"Melvin's too busy being pissed at me to focus on anything but that."

"What's his problem, now?"

"I'll tell ya later."

"I'll fill you in later too. I don't need him knowing about this."

Reed limps into the room, carrying a box. "Christ, you have a lotta books. Do you even read?"

"I prefer communicating with pictures, but the written word grabs me from time to time."

He snorts. "This is the last of them. I'm not fucking with your clothes—that's all you."

"I'm hungry," Cora announces, batting her lashes at my brother.

His whiskey-colored eyes soften. "Whaddya feel like having, love?"

"I'd kill for a burger and some chips. With extra pickles."

Reed jerks his chin at me. "You?"

I know I should stick to my lupus diet, but it was a series of long, boring flights. The plane meals sucked, so a burger sounds incredible right about now. "Same as Cora, please. Hang on, I'll grab some money."

He narrows his eyes. "Wasn't askin' you to pay."

"I know that. I wanted to treat you two for helping me."

"Oh." Reed clears his throat. "Thanks."

I nod and hand him a wad of cash. "Here. Can you stop past a bottle-o for a piña colada wine cooler too, please?" He raises a brow and I sigh. "Yeah, yeah, I know. You sound like Wes."

He snorts. "Didn't say anything, but okay."

"Your brows did the talking. I'm only having one. It was a long trip. Cora, are you drinking with me?"

"Not today, little bird."

Reed turns to Cora. "You want anything else?"

"No, I'm good. But make sure they don't forget my pickles."

He cups her cheek, and a genuine smile lights up his handsome face. "Anything for you, love."

Cora flushes, the pink accenting her emerald-colored eyes. "Thanks, babe."

"Be back in a bit." He points at Cora. "No lifting."

"Okay."

Reed steps closer to her. "I mean it, Cora."

She gives him a thumbs-up. He nods and leaves the room.

I listen for their car to start before speaking. "He's rather attentive today. Did ya give him a BJ or something?" I ask the question, even though the last thing I want to hear about is my brother getting a blow job.

Cora laughs. "No. Definitely not."

"He doesn't seem pissed at all."

"Oh, I can assure you, he is."

"Why?" I flop onto the couch, stretching out my back.

Cora settles beside me. "I'm pregnant."

I bolt upright. "*What?*"

"You heard me."

No wonder he's pissed. Reed hates kids. "Oh my God! How far along?"

She flushes. "Thirteen weeks."

"Holy fuck." Tears spring into my eyes as I hug her. "I'm ridiculously happy right now."

"Me too."

"I thought you guys didn't want kids?"

"We didn't. I'm thirty-eight, and you know how Reed feels about children." She gives me a small smile. "But he surprised me."

"Thought you said he was pissed?"

"He's not upset that I'm pregnant . . . he's pissed I kept it from him for so long. I only told him two days ago."

"Why'd ya keep it from him?"

"To be honest, I didn't know for a while. My cycle's always been irregular. I'm on the pill, but with Mom passing—" She blinks rapidly. "I think I missed a few doses. I haven't been thinking clearly, and it just kinda happened." She releases a heavy sigh. "I've known for about a month, but I was terrified of his reaction. I was so afraid he'd leave me."

"How *did* he react?"

Cora's eyes well with tears. "He cried. He held me in his arms and told me how much he loves me."

"Do ya think he's okay with being a dad?"

"He's slowly coming to terms with it. We saw some kids playing outside on our way here and his lip didn't curl, so I guess that's a good sign."

I smile and hug her tighter. "I love you so much, Cora. Thank you for making me an auntie. Does anyone else know?"

"Not yet. We'll tell your parents after my ultrasound. Reed wants to tell Wes in person. Please don't let on that you know anything."

"I won't." I extend my pinky to her. "Pinky promise."

"Thank you. When I told Reed I've known for a month, he was furious. He doesn't like being blindsided. I never should've kept it secret for so long."

"Can he at least understand why you did?"

"I think he does, and that's what bothers him. He's upset I'd feel afraid to tell him something, which is why he's being so attentive. You know, like proving himself a bit."

I smile. "I feel like I love him right now."

"Jesus, if I'd known this would bring you two closer, I would've let him knock me up sooner." She leans in. "We don't have much time. I want every fucking detail about New York."

I quickly fill her in on everything that happened with Jake, sparing nothing. That's what I love about Cora—her willingness to hear my stories and live vicariously through my excitement.

"Well, if my situation can teach you anything, it's that you shouldn't keep things from each other. And while it technically isn't any of his business, I still think you need to tell him you're a virgin."

I shake my head. "He'll freak out."

"He'll freak out *more* if he goes at you full throttle and hurts you."

"I don't know what to expect," I say on a sigh.

"Let me help you out. Don't expect to enjoy your first time, and you can give up on any hope for an orgasm. From my experience, it hurts like a bitch, and you may even bleed a little, but it'll be over quickly if you're lucky."

I snort. "Ah, so my brother's a minute man."

Cora laughs. "No. Definitely not. I'm a little older than him, remember? Reed wasn't my first." She tilts her head and lets out a wistful sigh. "But I wish he was."

I study my hands. "I'm afraid I'll disappoint Jake."

"You need to be open and honest with him from the get-go. Especially with your illness. If you have trouble with tampons, you're gonna have a helluva time with a cock. I'm not trying to scare you, but I wanna make sure you tell him so he's gentle with you." She squeezes my hand. "Sex is a beautiful way to connect with someone, so even if your first time does suck, rest assured it gets better the more times you do it."

"Yeah?"

"Oh, absolutely. Once you learn each other's bodies, the feelings of intimacy deepen."

The sound of an engine outside reaches my ears. I stiffen and meet Cora's gaze. "Please don't tell my brother any of this."

"Are you crazy? I'd never tell him any of *our* secrets."

"Thank you."

Reed enters my flat moments later. "Bad news. They didn't have pickles." Cora's face falls. "Damn."

He grins and hands her a takeaway bag. "Just kidding."

She lightly slaps his arm. "You're a shit sometimes, Reed Emerson."

"Wouldn't be me if I wasn't." He hands me my food and a wine cooler. "They didn't have piña colada, so I gotcha mango."

I perk up. "I love mango."

"I know."

Shocked he remembers or cares about anything I like, I smile. "Thank you for going."

"Thanks for treating."

"Yes, thank you," Cora says around a mouthful of burger. "This is divine."

He kisses the top of her head. "No, *you're* divine."

I smirk and stuff a pickle into my mouth. I'm not used to seeing anything but a scowl on Reed's face, so the newfound pleasantries amuse me. The thought of him covered in baby shit amuses me even more. He gags when his dog farts—how the hell is he going to change a shitty nappy?

Reed eyes me. "What?"

I shrug and give him an innocent shake of my head. "Nothing."

He glances at Cora. "You told her?"

Her eyes widen, so I try to cover for her. "Told me what?"

Sighing, Reed steals one of my chips and settles on the couch between us. "What happened to keeping it a secret? I see that lasted all of five minutes. Did ya even wait until the car was out of the driveway before you spilled your guts?"

"What're you talking about," I ask, cocking my head to the side.

Cora frantically chews her food, avoiding eye contact with him. A flush creeps across her face, spreading to her neck and ears.

"Please. I know how you two gossip." He levels his cognac stare on me, brow quirking. "Keep your mouth shut. Understood?"

Cora touches his arm. "Don't worry. She won't tell anyone."

I give my brother a broad grin. "My lips are sealed, *Daddy*."

Reed snorts and runs a hand over his face. "I mean it, Isla. This stays under wraps. We're not telling Mum and Dad yet, and we plan to tell Wes after Christmas."

"Like I said, my lips are sealed. It's your news to share—not mine." I squeeze his shoulder. "And congratulations."

"Thanks."

"Are you planning to find out the gender?"

"That's up to Cora. I'd rather not know until the birth. The whole thing's a surprise, so why not keep the theme going? But she's gonna want to decorate the nursery in something other than green and yellow."

"Colors don't have a gender," I point out.

"Not saying they do."

"Then what does it matter?"

"Maybe I don't like pink?" He flicks my arm. "But, like I said, it's up to Cora."

"I'm undecided," she explains. "I get what he's saying—there are so few surprises left in life—but still, I wanna be mentally prepared."

"What if it's twins?" I say.

The color drains from Reed's face. "Then we're giving one of them to you."

"Twins don't run in either of our families," Cora says.

I sip my wine cooler. "There's a first time for everything. And I'll happily take one off your hands if that's the case."

"If we have twins, someone needs to medicate me," Reed announces. "Preferably with a hallucinogenic."

I shake my head. "Nah, that won't work. You can't change shitty nappies when you're hallucinating. What if you think it's sunblock? Or worse ...pudding?"

Cora laughs, shooting pickle out of her mouth. It lands on Reed's arm. Lip curling, he flicks it off and wipes his hand on *my* sleeve.

"You're disgusting," he informs me, his face turning a little green.

"I'm simply pointing out the problem with your plan. I'm looking out for ya. Really."

He shakes his head. "I'm so fucked."

"Oh, stop. You'll be fine. Do you hope for a girl or a boy?" I snort. "Or one of each?"

Reed straightens. "I'd prefer a boy."

"I'm hoping for a girl," Cora says wistfully. "I keep picturing all the pretty dresses you'll make for her."

I grin. "I can create a wardrobe for either gender . . ." I nudge Reed. "All the more reason to have twins."

He groans and climbs to his feet. "I need a water. Anyone want anything from the kitchen?"

Cora and I both decline.

When Reed's out of earshot, I lean in. "Who is he, and what have ya done with my brother?"

"I love him so much," she whispers, her eyes misting. "He doesn't know it yet, but he'll make a great dad."

I squeeze her hand. "You're gonna be an amazing mum."

Reed returns with a strange expression on his face. He limps to the couch and stands over me, gaze locked on mine.

"What?"

"You tell me." He sips his water.

"Tell you what?"

Cora touches his arm. "Reed, what's wrong?"

He steps closer to me. "Does Wes know?"

"You and your riddles." I throw my arms in the air. "Does Wes know *what?*"

"Did ya tell him you and Bennett have a thing?"

My throat goes dry, and my scalp prickles. "Huh?"

He points at my face, clearly not buying my feigned innocence. "You heard me."

My eyes dart to a bewildered Cora, who shakes her head. I turn back to Reed. "Not sure whatcha mean."

"You know you can change the settings on your phone, right?" His brown gaze burns into me. "Your texts don't have to flash across the screen when they come in."

Oh my God.

I blink. My mouth opens and closes a few times.

"Or you can leave your phone in your bag, instead of out in the open like that." He raises a brow. "You were supposed to call him when you landed."

"He dropped me off at the airport," I say, grasping at straws. "It's common courtesy to let someone know you've arrived safely."

"Well, you must lack that courtesy," he informs me with a smirk, "because you didn't let him know."

I stiffen. "Why're you snooping in my phone?"

"It's not snooping when it's left out in the open, birdie. I was looking for a glass and it was on the counter. That chime is a bit annoying. If Bennett's gonna blow up your phone like that, someone nearby is bound to notice." He flashes a wicked grin. "Like I said, you should change your settings."

"I like my settings just fine, thank you very much."

Reed nods. "That's wonderful. Make sure you put another check mark in his column. He's winning your contest."

Oh. My. Fucking. God.

Heat floods my face. "I . . . uh . . ." I cough and try again. "Um—"

Reed leans in close. "Oh, I almost forgot to tell ya."

"What?" I croak.

"He misses the taste of your lips."

A strangled noise escapes my chest.

Cora chokes on her water. Ears buzzing, I bury my face in my hands. Reed settles between us, resting his feet on my coffee table.

Why the fuck did I leave my phone on the counter?

Why do my texts show up on the screen?

Why the fuck is this happening to me?

Reed chuckles. "Busted."

Cora regains her composure. "Reed Matthew Emerson, don't you dare say a word to Wes."

"Ah, so he *doesn't* know. Interesting."

She grips his shoulders. "And *you* won't be the one to tell him."

He shrugs. "He's not stupid. He'll figure it out sooner or later."

"Reed, please," I whisper, meeting his gaze. "Please don't say anything. I'm still trying to sort through it."

"Let Bennett help you. He likes sorting things."

I bristle. "Don't go there." I'm not going to sit back and allow anyone to poke fun at Jake's anxiety.

"Well, it's true. He's already making columns and tally marks."

"That's none of your business."

"C'mon, Isla. There weren't enough blokes at home? Now you gotta move across the ocean and seduce Wes's best mate?"

"I did not seduce him. And my romantic history is none of your business," I snap.

"You're wrong on that one." Reed shakes his head. "It became my business."

"How so?"

"We happen to share a last name and you've got quite the reputation." He curls his lip, nose wrinkling in disgust. "It's common knowledge you burn through men, Isla."

"Again, my love life is my business."

"Except when people come to me with reports that my little sister's blown half of Melbourne."

"Reed!" Cora smacks his arm.

"Is that why you hate me?" I say, my voice reaching a shrill pitch. "Because you think I'm a slut?"

Reed doesn't even have the decency to look at me. "I don't hate you."

"But you think I'm a slut?"

He shrugs. "Well, if the shoe fits . . ."

Angry tears spring to my eyes. "Get out."

He raises a brow and climbs to his feet. "Excuse me?"

"Get out of my flat."

"Why? Because I'm stating a fact?"

Cora starts to cry. "Reed, for the love of Christ, that's enough."

I wave a finger in his face. "No, because you're a dick."

He smirks. "I guess you'd know, being the resident dick expert here, right?"

"Fuck you."

"Stop," Cora sobs.

Reed takes a step toward me. "You're upsetting my wife."

I square my shoulders, not about to back down. "And you're upsetting me. Now get the fuck out!"

Reed narrows his eyes on me and motions to Cora. "Let's go."

Sobbing, she climbs to her feet and grabs her purse. "I'm sorry, little bird."

"You have nothing to apologize for, Cora. I love you." I glare at Reed as hot tears spill down my cheeks. "Even if your husband's a dick."

He points. "Maybe you shouldn't have fucked everyone in town."

Instinctively, I slap him across the face. The loud crack reverberates through the room. My brother stares back at me, wide-eyed and open-mouthed, fury flashing in his gaze.

"You're out of line," he snarls, nostrils flaring.

"No, *you* are. For the record, I can fuck whomever I want. Now get the hell out."

Cora tugs him to the front door. They leave, with Reed slamming the door behind them. Outside, their car peels out of my driveway.

I curl into a ball on my couch and cry, my tears stinging my cheeks as they fall.

CHAPTER 19

Jake

Mood: "Demons" by Imagine Dragons

I know Isla's plane didn't crash because I already investigated that possibility. She landed in Melbourne, as scheduled, *eight* hours ago. Since I hate doing math in my head, I set my watch ahead to account for the time difference. She promised to call me when she arrived. I gave her some leeway and factored in an additional hour and a half for luggage retrieval and transport to her place, but I still haven't heard from her.

Why the fuck didn't I tell her I love her when I had the chance?

I don't want to come across as some crazy stalker, but I need to know she's safe. My brain offers about thirty terrifying possibilities, and two rational options. Maybe she forgot to take her phone off airplane mode. Or maybe she was jet-lagged and decided to nap. That makes more sense than her being caught up in human trafficking. Too bad I don't feel less anxious.

My brain taunts me with images of her bound and gagged, stuffed in someone's trunk. As much as I try to push the thoughts aside, they keep coming back. They collide with my psyche like a battering ram. Over and over and over again.

Tears on her cheeks.

Wrists bleeding.

Eyes wide with terror.

This is the terrifying part of OCD. The vivid, disturbing imagery and clawing panic it brings. No matter how hard I try to redirect, it's like someone's holding my eyelids open, forcing me to watch a slideshow of my darkest fears.

The endless montage of a tortured Isla violates me. I collapse onto my couch and try to breathe.

My phone rings. Unfortunately, it's only my mother.

"Mom." I inject false calm into my voice. "How are you?"

"Hi, dear. I wanted to see how your dinner party went."

"Great. Food was amazing."

Mom snorts. "Oh, c'mon, Jacob. You've gotta give me more than that."

"What would you like to know?" I ask, knowing damn well what she's getting at. She's never been a subtle woman, which is likely where my lack of filter stems from.

"Did you make amends with Isla?"

"Yup."

"She was receptive?"

"Uh-huh."

"What's wrong? You sound off."

"Nothing."

"Don't lie to me, Jacob."

I sigh heavily and clench my phone. I press the heel of my other palm into one of my eye sockets to combat the developing ache. If I don't give the woman something, she's liable to fly up here to "fix" me. Then I'll have two traveling women to worry about.

"I'm anxious, okay? I don't wanna talk about it."

"Because of Wes? I know he's hotheaded sometimes. How did he handle finding out about you two?"

"Well . . ."

"Oh, Jacob, don't tell me you're still keeping it from him . . ."

"It's not that simple, Ma. You don't know Wes like I do."

"I know him well enough to know that you need to be the one to tell him. Not for nothing, but I think you should do it before he figures it out on his own. He may be pissed, but he'll respect your honesty."

"I know."

"You say that you know, but I get the feeling you won't tell him."

I sigh and rest the phone between my cheek and shoulder so I can rub my temples. She makes a valid point, but it would be nice to adjust to mine and Isla's new normal before the shit hits the fan. Give us a moment to enjoy each other before he maims me.

That is, if Isla is still alive.

Ropes.

Blood.

Pain.

Mom chuckles. "I don't hear you talking. Is it because you know I'm right?"

My phone beeps with an incoming call. Now it's my psychiatrist. *Oh great, they're tag teaming me.*

"I gotta go, Mom. I'm getting another call."

"Bullshit."

"No, I'm serious. It's Dr. Ortiz."

"Oh. Okay, then you'd better take it. I love you. Think about what I said."

"I will. Love you too." I take a deep breath and switch calls. "Hello?"

"Jake, it's Dr. Ortiz. I'm calling to see if we can postpone next week's appointment. I have to fly out to Denver to take care of my mother after her surgery, and I'm not sure I'll be back in time."

"Sure, that's fine," I say, disappointed because I could desperately use our session. I get it. Family comes first. Her mom is overdue for a knee replacement and recently suffered a fall. "Do what you need to do. You know I'm flexible."

"Thank you. I really appreciate it. As far as rescheduling, what works better for you, before or after Christmas?"

Before. "After is fine."

"All right. How about I call you when I return, and we'll set something up then?"

"Sounds good."

"Are you good with all your meds? Need any refills?"

I sigh and clench the phone tighter. I hate asking for medication, which is why doc always asks how I'm doing with it. Still, whenever I have to admit I need more, I feel like I'm losing control.

Because you are.

"I could use more Xanax. I'm getting low."

"Is everything all right?" she asks. "I've got a few minutes if you want to chat."

Relief washes through me. I didn't realize how much I needed that option at the moment. I fill Dr. Ortiz in on the events of the past few weeks, starting from the point when I learned Isla was moving across the street from me. I spare little detail in my explanation because she's well aware of my history with Isla—including our kiss five years ago. I tell her about the disturbing images too. I never understood those people who lied or withheld information from their shrinks. What the hell's the point?

"Wow, Jake. Your brain is overflowing right now."

"Yeah."

"Let's take a step back and talk about why. So, it sounds like you're finally ready to embrace your feelings for Isla, which brings a whole new level of what-ifs," she muses. "Knowing you, there are endless possibilities and unknowns. Start with what you do know. The plane landed safely. She's firmly on the ground. Isla deals with chronic fatigue and just traveled halfway around the world. It makes sense she'd nap. You mentioned she needs to pack up her apartment. She has a lot to accomplish before she uproots her life to move."

"I know." *But what if?*

"How was she getting from the airport to her place?"

"Her brother and his wife were supposed to pick her up."

"Okay, so, don't you think you would've heard by now if something had gone wrong?"

"Yes." *Maybe?*

"No news is good news. Try to take comfort in that, Jake. You'll hear from her when she's able to give you a call. Then, soon enough, she'll be back in New York."

"Yeah. Now if only I had the balls to deal with big brother."

"Well, you already know what I'm going to say about that."

I chuckle and rub my jaw. "Yep. Stop hiding behind my anxiety."

"You got it. Listen, I gotta run, but we'll catch up soon. I'm sending a script to your pharmacy as soon as I hang up."

"Thank you. Have a safe trip to Denver."

"Thanks. Take care." She disconnects our call.

I stretch and look at the clock. Still no word from Isla. *Where the hell is she?* One thing's for damn sure—I can't pace around here worrying all day because I'm going to lose my shit. With a heavy sigh, I dial her number, surrendering to the panic that's been gripping me for hours. To my delight, she answers.

"Jake, I'm sorry I forgot to call you."

I breathe a sigh of relief. "It's okay, Sprite. I didn't mean to hound you." *Please don't think I'm obsessing already.* "I just wanted to make sure you're safe and happy."

"I'm safe," she mutters, her tone raising my hackles.

Maybe I'm coming on too strong. Was I too pushy? Is she annoyed with me?

I clear my throat. "You all right?"

"No." She sniffs. "I've had a shitty day."

"Sorry to hear that. The flight turbulent?"

"The trip itself was fine." Her voice breaks, and her shuddered breaths are a dead giveaway.

I clench the phone. "Then why are you crying?"

"Reed is a dick."

"We already knew that."

"He knows about us," she whimpers.

"How is that even possible? Austin swore not to say anything to him or Wes."

"Austin knows?"

I clear my throat. "He's known how I feel about you for years. So does my friend Jesse. Like I said, I don't talk to Reed much, so Wes is the only one I've kept in the dark."

"My phone was in the kitchen when Reed and Cora were here. He went in for a water and saw your texts flash across the screen."

"Fuck." Stiffening, I run a hand over my face. "Which ones?"

"All of them."

"I didn't say anything inappropriate." *Thank fuck I only alluded to our name-moaning contest.* "Most of them were just me checking to see if you were safe."

"He saw the one about you missing the taste of my lips. He knows, Jake."

"While it's a true statement, I never sent that in a text. Didn't you read them?"

"Wait, what? No, I haven't read them . . . We got in a huge fight and I told him to leave. This is the first I've looked at my phone."

"He played you, Isla." *Typical Reed, smart and manipulative.* "He said that to get you to confess."

"That conniving fuck!" she sputters. "Now he's gonna run to Wes."

I sigh heavily. "Wes will find out anyway."

"He'll tell him while I'm over here, across the ocean and fifteen hours ahead. I won't be there to defend you."

"I don't need you to defend me, Sprite. While I joke about it, I don't think Wes will actually murder me. If he wants to hit me, I'm fine with that. I can survive a few punches."

"You don't get it," she says on a sob. "Wes will go ballistic, and you'll decide I'm not worth the trouble. Then I'll lose you again."

I clench the phone. "Isla, listen to me. I'm not going anywhere. Fuck the ocean. Fuck time, age, and distance. And fuck your brothers. Both of them. Like I told you, I'm all-in."

She's quiet for a minute, her voice soft when she asks, "You mean that?"

"*Yes,*" I growl. "Every word."

"I wish you were here. I could really use a hug."

"I'll hug you when you return and every day after that. I'm sorry Reed got you upset. To be honest, I'm surprised us being together is such an issue for him. He hasn't given you the time of day in years, so why should it matter who you're involved with *now,* when you're about to be an ocean away from him?"

"We share a last name, so I'm a reflection of him," she mutters.

"How does that have anything to do with us?"

"It doesn't. The fight wasn't about us." She sighs. "I don't wanna talk about it. He left two hours ago, and I finally stopped crying."

"You're still crying," I remind her. "Which means you're still upset."

"Yeah, but now I'm crying over you, not him."

A loud buzz reaches my ears. "What the hell is that?"

"My doorbell."

"Who is it?"

"Dunno. And I don't feel like getting off the couch to look."

The buzzing becomes persistent, and it's joined by a knock. The person bangs on her door loud enough that I can hear the doorframe rattle. My heart pounds with the knowledge that she's over twenty hours away by plane and there isn't a damn thing I can do if she's in danger. I want to crawl out of my skin if it would only shorten that distance.

"Jesus Christ, is the SWAT team at your place?"

"I'm gonna look out the window." A moment later, she groans. "You've gotta be fucking kidding me."

"What?"

"It's Reed." I hear her stomp across the room, slide the lock, and open the door. "What do you want?"

"To talk," Reed says.

"I have nothing to say to you."

"Too bad."

"Uh, excuse me. Who do you think you are, pushing in here like that? Get out of my living room." Isla's voice is shrill. "I mean it, Reed. I'll call the police."

"Do whatcha need to do. I'm not leaving."

"Jake, I'll call ya back."

Click.

Deep down, I know Reed won't hurt her, but if he's pushing his way into her place, I can't help but wonder if he'd push her around. The fact that he made her cry makes my blood boil.

Clutching the phone, I pace the room and await her call.

CHAPTER 20

Isla

Internal playlist: "Bad Reputation" by Shawn Mendes

"Why're you here, Reed?" I snap, setting my phone on an end table.

My brother settles on the couch, placing his stupid feet on my coffee table again. "Already told ya. I wanna talk."

I sneer at him. "What, did Cora send you over to apologize or something?"

"No. Cora's not speaking to me right now," he mutters, crossing his arms over his chest.

"I don't blame her." I stand in front of him, my hands on my hips. "I still can't believe she married such a dick."

It baffles me sometimes. Okay, *most* times.

He looks up at me. "Yeah, well, I never claimed not to be."

"It's not something to be proud of. You wear it like a bloody badge of honor. *World's biggest dick.*"

Reed smirks. My handprint is still visible in the slight bruise on his cheek. If he doesn't wipe off his smirk, I may give him a matching one on the other side.

"You'd have to ask Cora about that."

I curl my lip. "Excuse me?"

"That's a bit of a stretch. Besides, I think Wes has me beat."

Gross. "You're disgusting. I wasn't referring—"

"Trying to get you to relax, Isla."

"Why should I relax? My entire childhood you acted like I didn't exist. You've made it clear you hate me—"

"I do *not* hate you."

"Whatever. I'm sorry I ruined your life, but I didn't ask to be born. And I don't know what I did to deserve your disgust."

"I'm sorry." Reed sits up. "I'm sorry for how I treated you growing up. And for today. Before she stopped talking to me, Cora made it clear my opinion is based on falsehoods. She told me to pull my head out of my arse and learn the truth, so here I am. What happened with the high school cricket team?"

I frown. "What do you mean?"

I attended a handful of games over the years, but nothing eventful ever happened. Except that one time when Dan Muller broke his leg. The fucking bone protruded through his skin, and I wanted to barf.

"From what I heard, you told the team to line up with their cocks out."

I blink a few times at his statement, which sounds like something out of a porno movie. "I'm sorry, *what?*"

Reed rubs his jaw, his gaze burning into me. "He said you blew every single one of them beneath the bleachers."

"What the fuck are you talking about?" Tears spring to my eyes. "Who told ya that?"

"Doesn't matter." He leans in. "Is it true?"

"Of course not. I have *never* done that to someone I wasn't in a relationship with. Ever. Your source is a fucking liar."

"Did you fuck Chase Wells in the back of his father's truck?"

"I've never so much as hugged him." My body trembles with shocked fury. "Who's tellin' you these things?"

"What about Donny Sampson? Did you fuck him while his cousin watched?"

"I've never fucked *anyone*," I screech, flailing my arms out to the sides.

Reed narrows his eyes. "What?"

"I'm a virgin, Reed. Someone pressured me for sex before I was ready, so I haven't let anyone touch me since. I push them away before it gets to that point."

"Repeat that . . . one more time." Reed's voice is low and dangerous. "Someone tried to rape you?"

"No. I'm saying he *pressured* me. He got a little handsy, but I took care of it." I narrow my eyes and swipe at my tears. "Don't act like you care."

"Who was it?"

"Carter Dawson's younger brother." I stiffen my spine, determined to look him in the eye. "Lucas. My first boyfriend."

"Lucas Dawson is the one who told me all those things about you."

"Oh? Did he tell you how eight months into our relationship a blowie wasn't enough for him anymore? How he pressured me to fuck when I wasn't ready? Did he tell you about the bet he made with his friends that he'd get me to give it up on his birthday?" My jaw trembles as I spit out the words.

"No."

"Let me fill you in. Remember that time you went to the cricket match in Melbourne with Carter? You know, when you were trying to get a job with his media company, so you thought you'd schmooze him with tickets to a game?"

"Yeah."

"Well, it was Lucas's birthday. I made him a picnic lunch and went over to his place. We were on his bed, fooling around. He tried to take it further. When I refused, he called me a dick tease and stormed out of the room. I quickly got dressed to leave, not understanding why he was so angry. I mean, I'd turned him down plenty of times before, and he'd always taken it in stride. Anyway, his phone was on his dresser. It kept chiming with texts from his mates. I was angry he ruined our birthday picnic with his mood, so I snooped."

"And?"

"He had a group message going with Chase Wells and Donny Sampson. They'd bet him five hundred dollars he couldn't get me to give him a birthday fuck."

"An actual *bet*?"

"Yup."

"That doesn't make any sense. He could've simply lied and claimed you two banged. Why go through the trouble?"

"You don't get it, Reed. Lucas had set up a hidden camera in his room."

"*What?*"

"I was on video. They were going to *watch* him devirginize me."

His eyes glow with rage. "What happened next?"

"I scanned the messages for clues and located the camera on his bookshelf. I stuffed the bloody thing into my backpack. When Lucas came back to his room, he tried to act all lovey-dovey, so I kicked him in the balls. I told him I knew all about his bet, and I dumped him right then and there. I stormed out of the house at the same time you and Carter stopped by. Remember how I collided with you when I ran out the front door?"

He nods. "Why didn't you tell me what happened?" There's an edge of guilt to his tone that niggles at my conscience.

"Because I was hurt and angry. I trusted Lucas, but he clearly didn't care about me. I wanted to get the fuck out of there."

"Was there . . . footage?"

"Yep. On the camera's storage card were several videos of us making out. A few blow jobs. My tits."

Reed squeezes his eyes shut. "I'm sorry."

"Why are you sorry? I destroyed the SD card and moved on with my life. Lesson learned, ya know?"

"I'm sorry because I believed him." His chest deflates on a sigh. "You left, and Lucas came upstairs crying, saying you broke his heart. He told me he caught you cheating and found out you'd been slutting around for months, then claimed you kicked him when he confronted you."

"Oh, did he now?"

"Yeah. He told Carter and me all those other things too."

I shake my head bitterly. "Wow, Reed. Thanks for the vote of confidence. So happy the topic of who I welcome into my body became such a controversy." I give him a thumbs up. "Thanks for having such a vested interest in my pussy. Rest assured, now you can go update your coital archives where I'm concerned. Hymen intact? Check. Slut status? Let's call it reformed."

"Isla, stop."

"Why? Does the glaring proof of your misogyny make you uncomfortable? Gotta tell you, it feels awesome being slut-shamed by my own brother. So much for benefit of the doubt. Nice to know my family has faith in me."

He looks at his hands. "Why didn't you tell me what he tried to do?"

"Because I was ashamed of my stupidity. Besides, you've hated me since the moment I was born. Maybe I should've mentioned it, but I didn't think you—or anyone else—would care." I clench my jaw. "Looks like Lucas cut me off at the pass and filled your head with shit. I guess that's why you treated me even worse afterward."

"No." He runs a hand over his face. "That's not why. It's because I'm a selfish prick."

"That isn't news."

"The job was yanked out from under me."

"Wait, I thought you turned it down? That's what you told Mum and Dad."

He shakes his head. "Carter offered me the job while we were at the game. I was ecstatic. After Lucas spewed all that shit, Carter rescinded his offer. Said he didn't want to bring any drama around his growing business. Then he stopped talking to me. Completely cut me off. I was fucking furious, and I blamed you."

"Reed, I'm sorry. I didn't know."

"No, Isla. *I'm* sorry." Tears well in his eyes. "All these years—"

"You've harbored anger for your slutty little sister who unknowingly cost you a job."

He squeezes his eyes shut. "I'm sorry," he whispers. "Your sex life is none of my business, but I held my assumptions against you because I'm a piece of shit. I was too bitter about losing the media connection to ask your side of it."

"Well, look at you now. CEO of Emerson Media. You and Wes have built an empire of your own. Sounds like it was a blessing in disguise." I give him a cheeky smirk. "You're welcome."

"I wouldn't be CEO of anything if it weren't for Wes." A shadow passes over his face. "I work hard to keep this family's reputation in the public's good graces."

"You say it like Wes is out there doing drugs and impregnating women by the dozen. He's a good man, for fuck's sake."

"He *is* a good man, but his behavior has been exceedingly reckless." Reed rubs his temples. "If you recall, he skipped the bloody premiere for *The Aegean* to chase after that girl. The whole situation was—and still is—a fucking train wreck. After pulling a stunt like that, he'll be lucky if he gets another contract, period."

"I know he fucked you around by missing the event, but he had to smooth things over with Lena."

"Which could've happened *after* the premiere."

"What can I say? He's in love."

"Like I said, he's fucking reckless."

Pinching the bridge of my nose, I release a heavy sigh. "Don't be bitter about it, Reed. Lena's amazing."

"I'll take your word for it," he mutters, staring out the window. After a moment, he meets my gaze. "I didn't know you were a virgin." I open my mouth to make a smart comment, but he holds up his hand. "And you're absolutely right—it's no one's business but yours. Your virginity has no bearing on your value and I'm sorry I let false information cloud my opinion. Like I said, I'm a selfish prick."

I consider telling him it's all right, but nothing about the situation is okay—his behavior has hurt me for years. The chip on his shoulder shouldn't be my burden to carry.

"Say something," he mumbles.

I sigh heavily. "My lack of a sex life isn't something I broadcast, but yeah. After Lucas, as soon as a guy pressured me to fuck, I was done with him. That's why there were so many of them, and they never lasted more than a few months. Turns out they all wanna fuck."

"What about Bennett?"

I shake my head. "Jake is different."

"Different, how?"

"He treats me like royalty. I've loved him since I was a kid, and I knew he'd be mine after Wes's thirtieth birthday party." I give a small smile. "He just didn't know it then."

Reed's brows pop. "You guys have been together for five years?"

"No. I kissed him that night, but he walked away. He had too much respect for you and Wes. And I was only eighteen. I didn't see him much for a while, but we recently came to an understanding."

"An understanding?"

"Yeah. I don't care whether you, Wes, or anyone else likes it, but Jake is mine. I love him, and I'm going to marry him one day. I know it in my heart and soul."

"Seriously? He's a lot older than you and looking to settle down. Are ya sure he's right for you?"

"Absolutely. He's mine and I'm his. This may surprise you, but your birdbrained, virgin sister who cost you a job, saved herself for Jake Bennett all this time."

"So, what's your plan? Move to New York and have a secret relationship under Wes's nose? You know he's not gonna be happy about this, right?"

"I know, but he's gonna have to deal with it. We've always been close, and I'd like to think he'd want me to be with a man who respects me. Someone whose character he can vouch for."

He nods. "What about Jake? Isn't *he* concerned about Wes's reaction?"

"He's agonized over it for five years. The last thing he wants to do is disrespect Wes—or you."

Reed sits quietly for a moment, gazing at me. "To be honest, I don't have a problem with it. Jake's not disrespecting me. Lucas Dawson disrespected me when he hurt you and filled my head with shit. I disrespected *you* when I believed him. I'm so sorry, Isla. I swear, I'll make it up to you."

"You can start by not running to Wes about me and Jake." I poke his chest. "Also, I'm not thrilled with how you played me."

He tilts his head. "How'd I play you?"

I cock a brow. "Oh, I dunno . . . maybe with that 'taste of my lips' statement."

He smirks. "Never claimed not to be manipulative."

"Yeah, well, cut that shit out." I flick him on the head. "And do not say a word to Wes."

"I won't." Reed places a hand on his chest. "You have my word. However, if Wes *asks* me about it, I won't lie to him."

"That's fine. He won't ask you. He thinks we don't talk, remember?"

He gives me a sheepish look. "I've always been jealous of your bond."

"With Wes?"

"Yeah. I idolized him for ten years. He was *my* big brother. Then you were born, and everything changed. Wes adored you from day one. With your big, blue eyes, you even looked like him. You were the sun and moon for Wes—and Mum and Dad—and I suddenly felt like I didn't matter. I hated my eye color and everything else about myself. Instead of embracing you, I resented you." He shakes his head sadly. "Then you got sick, and it was Wes's kidney that saved you. I wanted it to be *mine*." He flicks his gaze to mine, and I know he's being truthful. "I remember being so disappointed I wasn't a match. I wanted some connection with you. I wanted to be part of that bond. But no, you and Wes got closer. And what did I do? I believed lies fed to me by a filthy piece of shit. Instead of asking you what happened, I treated you like crap. I'm sorry," he whispers. "It was never you. I'm the issue, always have been."

I wrap my arms around him. "It's all right, Reed."

"No, it's not. You're my sister and I treated you like an outsider. I've given strangers more kindness than I've shown you. I'm so fucking sorry. Especially since *I'm* the bloody outsider." His voice breaks along with my heart.

"What are you talking about?"

"Nothing." His tone is hollow when he adds, "Forget I said it."

I shift and take his hands in mine. "Let's move forward. We're both starting new chapters in life. We can be there for one another from here on out. I'm beyond excited about the pregnancy."

"I'm bloody terrified. If something happens to Cora, I'll die."

"Cora will be fine. All you need to do is be there for her. You're already doing a wonderful job—it moved me to see you be so attentive earlier." I ruffle his hair. "I think you're gonna make a great dad."

"Thanks. I thought I didn't want kids, but I'm genuinely happy. She was so afraid to tell me. I don't want my wife to ever be afraid of me." He meets my gaze. "And this may seem strange, but I feel like I'm getting a second chance."

"How so?"

"I know in my gut she's carrying a girl. I fucked up my relationship with you, but this baby girl will be different. I'm gonna do it right this time."

Fat tears roll down my cheeks as I hug him tighter. "I love you, Reed."

"Love you too, little bird." He tightens his embrace. "Jake's a good man. I'm happy for you." He chuckles. "But I can't believe you two fell in love at the party I didn't even invite you to."

I laugh. "For whatever reason, I knew I needed to be there, which is why I went over your head."

"Jake wasn't even supposed to come. He told me he couldn't make it. I still can't believe he flew all that way to sit on the beach for four hours and then leave."

"What's meant to be will be."

"How did he keep it secret for five years?" He perks up, eyeing my face. "Wait a minute, his songs—"

I flash a coy smile. "Are about me."

"Holy fuck. He's got it bad for you."

"I can assure you it's mutual. The ocean between us helped him keep his distance. Now I'm moving across the street from him, so it's not like he can walk away. And he made it crystal clear he's done pushing me away. Plain and simple, he wants me, and I want him."

Reed chuckles. "You have a way of getting whatcha want, Isla Rose."

"Damn right, I do."

CHAPTER 21

Jake

Mood: "Heavy" by Linkin Park

Best friends make the world go around. The following day, Jesse eyes me from across the table, amused satisfaction dancing in his gaze. "I'm glad you finally got your shit together, Jerk-off Jimmy."

I snort and give him the finger. "Don't remind me."

We hit up Ralph's Tavern for lunch because we both felt like having burgers. I take a massive bite of mine and shake my head while I chew.

"I love that you created a fictional cleaning lady on the fly, but anyone who knows anything about you—or has been to your place—would see right through that."

I nod. "Wes definitely did. He asked if I follow her around and redo everything."

"Sounds like he knows you better than you think." Jesse sips his beer and leans in. "Which is why you need to be careful, man."

"I know," I mutter.

"I mean it. Don't weave a web so tangled you forget what lies you've told. I know you keep a lot of shit from people, like your anxiety and stuff, but it isn't like you to outright lie to someone—especially a dude like Wes, who you call one of your best friends."

"He *is* one of my best friends." I pinch the bridge of my nose. "I'm not lying because I want to deceive him or something. If she weren't his baby sister, he'd know all about this."

"Be careful," Jesse repeats.

I nod and change the subject. "How's Hannah? You said she hasn't been acting like herself lately."

He sighs heavily. "I think she's depressed. She's been really distant and avoiding shit she loves to do."

"Yeah, that sounds like depression to me. Just be there for her, man. Sometimes our moods happen without a reason behind them. Knowing someone is there makes it easier to cope."

"I'm her husband. I'll never *not* be there for her."

I squeeze his shoulder. "You're an excellent husband, Jess. And the best friend I could ever ask for."

Austin sets down his guitar and crosses his arms over his chest. He flew in from Memphis so we could record a few songs at my studio.

He raises a brow. "Well?"

"What?"

"What's goin' on with you, man? You ain't actin' like yourself."

I sigh and rest my head in my hands, peering at him from between my fingers. "I'm so fucked, dude. I can't even begin to tell you how incredibly fucked I am. Over, under, and inside-out. Fuckity-fuck-fuck-fucked."

Austin's baby blues narrow on my face. "You gonna explain or keep talkin' in riddles?"

"Wes told you Isla's moving to the city, right?"

"Yeah. Of course, he did." He snorts. "But I still can't believe he bought her a place. When's she movin' here officially?"

"In eight days."

"All you gotta do is keep your distance. You been doin' it for five years."

"Too late."

"What do you mean?"

I rub my temples. "She was here a few days ago."

"Oh? He didn't mention that. I take it she showed up for Lena's Thanksgiving party? I was sad we missed it, but with Katie being so nauseous all the time, I didn't wanna push her to travel."

"I get it. Yeah, Isla was at the party, but she stayed a couple of nights at my place first."

"Wait . . . what?" Austin's jaw drops. "How'd that come about?"

I bring him up to speed and watch the amusement in his eyes grow. "It's not funny, man."

"I'm not laughin'. I've never seen you this twisted over a woman. And of all people, little Flight Risk Isla." He shakes his head. "You gonna tell Wes?"

"No fucking way."

"You should. Wes doesn't like being in the dark." He points at me. "He should hear it from you instead of stumblin' upon it himself. Y'all need to have a chat."

"Dude, I'm already hanging naked from a tree. I'm not gonna give him a stick, spin him, *and* take off his blindfold. What the fuck do you think I am? Stupid?"

"Nah, but you're right about the piñata." He chuckles. "Except somethin' tells me you ain't got candy inside."

"Just the nasty ones like black licorice."

"Hey. Don't knock black licorice. I kinda like it. In all seriousness, I think you should talk to Wes. Sometimes he's reasonable."

I scratch my head. "Are we talking about the same Wes?"

"I said *sometimes*." He sighs and plucks a few strings on his guitar. "Look, you've known Wes and Reed almost as long as I have—"

"Oh, Reed knows."

His brows pop. "Really? How'd *that* happen?"

"Long story. Anyway, he and Isla had a big talk."

"Now *I'm* confused. Are we talkin' about the same Reed?"

"Yeah. She didn't give me details about their heart-to-heart, but apparently, he's fine with it." I shrug. "I guess they sorted shit out and they're on good terms now. And thank fuck for that."

"Yeah, I never understood why he was mean to her."

"Me neither. Like I said, she didn't elaborate—just told me it was a misunderstanding and she's really happy they worked through it."

"Do you think he'll say somethin' to Wes?"

"He assured Isla he wouldn't, so I guess we'll see." I pin Austin with a hard stare. "And you're not gonna say anything either, right?"

"No. I won't. If he asks, I'll send him your way."

"Fair enough." I lean in. "Did you broach the tour topic with Kate yet?"

We've been discussing the possibility of a six-month world tour next year, after our joint album releases. We're both viewing it as a last hoorah. While we plan to record music for as long as we're able, the touring cycle has gotten old. He's going to be a dad. He wants to be present in his family's lives. I'm tired of the endless travel. I need to focus on The Phoenix instead of city hopping. I have lofty plans for the community center. Goals that are more aligned with the phase of life I'm entering. Aka, the "make a legacy for myself" chapter.

His chest deflates on a sigh. "Yep. She ain't happy about it. Said all I ever do is travel and leave her behind. I think she's still feelin' the aftereffects of us being lost in Alaska. She told me she'd gotten to a point where she accepted the fact that I was dead. She lost all hope, man."

"That doesn't sound like Kate."

"No kiddin'. I know a lot of it is pregnancy hormones, but she's been really irritable. Clingy, yet weirdly distant. I want my old Katie back."

"Be patient with her, Memphis. Have you set a wedding date?"

"Not yet. She wants to wait until after the baby comes. She's currently pissed at me for letting it slip to the media that we're expecting."

"Oh? How'd that happen?"

"Well, it was after our ultrasound appointment. There was a news crew outside doing a story on the medical center's expansion. I was excited and said somethin' to one of the reporters. Katie ain't too happy with me." His face transforms into a broad grin. "But we found out we're having a little girl."

"That's awesome!" I clap him on the back. "She'll have you wrapped around her pinky finger in no time."

"Got that right." He pulls out his phone and taps on the screen. "Look at how cute. She wasn't cooperating for the technician, so we didn't get the best picture. Check out her little hands and feet."

I peer at the ultrasound image and smile. Austin and Kate's daughter currently looks like a tiny Martian in gray scale, but her hands and feet are perfectly formed. "She's got some long fingers. Her daddy's gonna have to teach her the guitar."

He squeezes my shoulder. "And Uncle Jake is expected to give piano lessons."

"I'll be honored to, man." My phone rings. I glance at the screen. "It's Jesse. Lemme take this real quick."

"Do what you gotta do. Tell him I say 'hi.'"

I nod and answer the call. "Hey, Jess." He's silent for a moment, so I glance at my screen to ensure I'd actually answered. "Hello? You there?"

"J-Jake . . . It's back."

"Huh?"

"The cancer—" Jesse's voice breaks.

No. Please, dear God, no.

"Jake, it came back," he cries, "it spread to her fucking lungs and brain."

"Oh my God," I whisper, clutching the phone. The room starts to spin. "How do you know?"

"She wasn't making sense—kept talking about my old repair shop. She said she needed to get payroll done."

"But you closed your shop five years ago."

"Yep. And I never had any employees." He sniffs. "Took her to the ER and they sent us to Sloan Kettering."

I shut my eyes. "Can they do surgery or chemo?"

"No," Jesse sobs. "It's all through her, man. They put her in hospice. Gave her a month, at most."

"Jesus Christ." My eyes fill with tears and spill over. "Whatever you need, I'm here. I mean it, Jess. I don't want you worrying about a fucking thing. Mortgage, bills, nothing. Stay with your wife."

He says something, but I can't understand him.

His news drove a cleaver into my chest. Anger bubbles in my veins. How the fuck can this happen? Hannah was in remission. Why does she have to suffer? Hasn't she been through enough? Chemo, nausea, hair loss, a double mastectomy, her skin charred by radiation. That wasn't enough agony? Why does my best friend have to watch his wife die? It's times like these when I question everything I believe in. Bile rises in my throat, turning my stomach.

"Jesse, listen to me. I love you, man. I'm on my way over." I stand and grab my coat and keys. "I'll be there in twenty minutes."

"Thank you," he says between sobs. "I don't wanna be alone."

CHAPTER 22

Isla

Internal playlist: "Remedy" by Adele

I stare at my phone, willing it to ring. I haven't heard from Jake in almost three days. He'd mentioned Austin was flying in for a week so they could record a few more songs, so maybe he's preoccupied. I get it—he wants to finish up this album so he can focus on the community center after the tour. Yet, I can't help feeling like I'm out of sight, out of mind. I know the time difference makes it challenging, but he's a night owl. I glance at my watch.

It's night and there's been no owling.

Of course, I'd feel less alone if I hadn't become so isolated from my mates. I wrap my arms around myself and lean against the counter in my parents' kitchen. I miss my pre-lupus friendships. I miss the sleepovers, parties, and beach days. Most of all, I miss feeling connected to people. It's not that my friends have totally shunned me, but there's an awkward undercurrent that makes me wonder what we had in common in the first place. Maybe I'll meet some nice women in New York to form new friendships with.

Opening my parents' fridge for the third time, I sigh and grab some carrots. I don't want carrots, but nothing's magically appeared since the last time I checked. Not that I expected a stocked fridge—they're in France—but they could've left me something other than carrots. *Of course, I could always pop over to the supermarket.*

Since I'm so bloody exhausted, I curl my lip at the thought of adding anything else to my list. Reed and Cora helped me box everything and move it out of my flat. Anything that's going to New York has already been shipped to Lena's place. My furniture crowds my parents' den, and I've spent two days sorting my clothes. I know I don't need to bring every piece of clothing I own—especially the beachy stuff—but it's hard to choose. While it's hot as hell here, the fact remains it's almost winter in New York.

Christmas is coming. I'm excited for a New York Christmas with snow, frosty air, sparkling lights, and everything else I've seen in movies. I want to visit that enormous tree they put up by the skating rink. I want Jake to kiss me under some mistletoe. Snatching my phone, I decide to text him that idea. Heated by the visual, I type the words with a smile.

His response is almost immediate.

> **Jake: We can arrange that.**

I grin at my phone, formulating a cheeky comeback.

> **Me: Crikey! You do exist!**

> **Jake: I'm sorry I've been MIA. My friend Jesse's wife is dying. Been at the hospital with him.**

I feel like a whiny arse now.

> **Me: OMG! What happened? I thought she was in remission?!**

> **Jake: So did we. Hannah has triple-negative breast cancer, which means it's extremely hard to treat. She had a double mastectomy, chemotherapy, and radiation. The cancer came back and spread to her lungs and brain. All they can do now is keep her comfortable.**

> **Me: How is Jesse coping?**

> **Jake: He's a fucking mess.**

I squeeze my phone.

> **Me: How about you?**

> **Jake: I'm heartbroken. I've known Hannah since we were kids. She's one of the sweetest people I know. It's fucking gut wrenching to watch this go down. There's NOTHING I can do to help her or ease Jesse's pain.**

> **Me: You being there for him is what matters, Jacob.**

Jake: I feel so helpless. And angry. I'm fucking livid she's suffering. I'm furious Jesse must lose the love of his life when there are rapists and murderers walking the streets. Why the fuck does she have to die?

Me: I wish I had an answer for you. Life is cruel sometimes. My heart breaks for them. And for you. I'm here, Jake. Any time of day or night, I'm here.

Jake: Means the world to me, Sprite. I can't wait to see you again.

Me: Likewise. Hugs to you and your friends. If there's anything I can do, please let me know. Xoxo.

Jake: Thank you. Xoxoxoxoxo.

I set the phone aside and wipe my eyes. I can't fathom what he's dealing with. I remember when Cora lost her mom to cancer. Reed kept Cora on her feet even as her world crashed down around them. I want to do that for Jake—be his comfort, his support. I want to be his everything.

Me: I love you.

Jake doesn't respond—not that I expect him to—but I wanted to tell him anyway. He can use some love right now. He can use some love, in general.

I think about Hannah and Jesse. Jake's talked about them a lot, so I know how close they are. Wes has mentioned them too. He referred to Jesse as a quiet, good-natured bloke and called Hannah sweet. It's not fair they have to suffer like this. I don't even know them, and I'm angry. Naturally, that means I'm going to crochet something. Crocheting is my go-to activity when I'm feeling emotional. Whether it be anger, frustration, loneliness, or joy, if I'm overwhelmed by my feelings, I dig out my yarn. This time's no exception.

Settling on the couch with my supplies, I start a pair of purple baby booties. Hopefully, I'll have a niece who can wear them.

CHAPTER 23

Mood: "Find Me" by Boyce Avenue

Giddiness. It's not a feeling I'm used to, so it took me a while to figure out what it was. Despite spending hours every day this week at the hospital with Jesse, I'm giddy today. Isla's flight lands at two, and I can't wait to see her. I've cleaned my house and stocked the fridge with stuff I know she can eat. I even shaved and got a haircut.

Lena's picking her up this time, which is fine because it gave me some time to chill with Austin before he left. We only got two songs recorded instead of the five we had planned, but shit happens.

I'm completely gutted over Hannah. My throat's raw, and I've cried more this week than I have in the past ten years. I can't even look in Jesse's eyes because the pain I see in them suffocates me. A wave of emotion swells. I clench my jaw and hold it back.

My doorbell rings, so I make my way to the foyer. I spot the top of Wes's head through one of the glass panes.

I open the door. "Howdy, surfer boy."

"Hiya." He steps inside. "Do ya have a screwdriver?"

"Yeah, hold on. I'll grab my tools. What are you screwing?"

He waggles his brows. "Lena prefers to be called a *who*, actually."

I snort. "Your bedroom pet names are none of my business."

"I like to share the wealth." He elbows me and laughs. "I'm putting a chain lock on Isla's front door."

"Doesn't she have a deadbolt?"

"Yep. But I'm adding a chain lock. Bought a slide bolt too."

I smirk. "Are you expecting an invasion?"

"Nah, I just want her to be safe. That reminds me . . ." Perking up, he pulls something from his pocket and places it in my hand. "I had this made for ya."

My fingers close around the key. "For what?"

"I dunno. In case she runs into trouble."

"This is a safe neighborhood. You need to stop worrying."

Wes snorts. "Says the professional worrier."

"I don't deny I'm a hypocrite," I say with a grin. "But I'm right."

"I know you are. To be honest, I feel much better about her being in New York with you across the street."

Guilt squeezes my heart. "Yeah, man. I'll look out for her." I cock a brow and hold up the key. "This won't work for the chain lock or slide bolt though. While it may be able to saw through the barbed wire, I doubt I could breach the laser force field with it. I'm gonna need a bigger key."

Wes laughs, following me into the kitchen. "I know I'm overprotective. I can't help it. She's my baby sister, ya know?"

Oh, that's something I can never forget.

"She's not a baby anymore, Wes. Give her some credit. She's tougher than you think."

"I'm still gonna insist she take those self-defense classes."

Fucking Connor.

I stiffen, forcing a neutral tone. "Do you really think she'll go for that?"

He sighs. "I dunno. I'll talk to her about it again when Connor comes over later to install the security system."

And I'll pop his tires.

Wes cocks his head. "What?"

"Huh?"

"You're making a face. What's your issue with Garrett's cousin?"

"I don't have an issue with him."

"Don't bullshit me, mate. You were a real dick to him at Friendsgiving. What gives?"

I rummage through my toolbox. "Philips or flat head?"

"You're avoiding my question."

Fuck. Think, Jake. Think.

I sigh. "Maybe I don't like the way he looked at her."

"Whaddya mean?"

Oh, so now I got your attention, huh? Deciding to appeal to his protective side, I say, "Like she was a piece of meat. I've known her since she was little. Didn't sit well with me."

He shakes his head. "You were a dick before she got there."

"You mean when he tried to hook me up with his forty-something boss?"

Wes chuckles. "Right. Never mind."

"You know I'm totally cool with gay dudes, but I'm fucking thirty-three. Don't say I look like I'm in my forties already. Jesus, all I could think was that I'm losing my hair and getting a fucking beer gut. My self-esteem's shitty enough. Sorry, but the guy rubbed me the wrong way from the jump. Then he started salivating when Isla got there. Guess what? Maybe *I'm* a little overprotective too."

He claps my shoulder. "I get it. Sorry for grillin' ya. I guess I'd feel better about her dating someone I'd met, you know? He's Garrett's cousin and he's with the FBI, so I figure he's not a creep."

"How about you let Isla worry about who she wants to date?" I challenge. Wes bristles, so I backpedal. "Maybe she wants to be single. I mean, her focus should be on her internship, am I right?"

"Good point. Lena told me I should mind my own business."

"Lena's right." I close my toolbox. "Let your sister get settled. Stop trying to hook her up with every meathead you come across in the tri-state area just because you think he can protect her."

"Connor's not technically a meathead—"

"Not for nothing, but he looked at her like she was meat. Therefore, he's a meathead in my book."

Wes grins. "Looks like I can count on Cockblock Bennett to cockblock my little sister."

"You're goddamn right you can." Guilt churns my gut. I can't look him in the eye, so I yank my fridge open. "Want a beer?"

"Nah. I'm good. I need to lay off the beer and cookies for a bit." He pats his stomach.

I hand him a water. "That'll be a challenge with Lena as your woman. Holy shit, those brownies she sent me home with were incredible."

Wes laughs. "Had one for brekkie." His phone rings, and he pulls it from his back pocket. "Hello, sunshine."

I chug a water while he talks to Lena.

"I'm at Jake's right now. Hold on, I'll ask him." He nods to me. "Lena's having a little housewarming thing at Isla's place tonight. Gonna order take-away. Lena and I will be there. Garrett's coming too. You wanna pop over?"

"Sure. Ask if I can bring anything."

"Jake wants to know what he can bring." He sips his water. "Just yourself."

I smile. "Oh, I'll be there."

CHAPTER 24

Isla

Internal playlist: "The First Taste" by Fiona Apple

My lower belly flutters as I wait for Lena to hang up. "What did he say?"

"Of *course* he's coming," she bats her lashes, "and I'm sure there will be plenty of *that* later."

I flush, adjusting my sunglasses. "About that . . ."

Lena switches lanes. "Don't be nervous; this is Jake. His sun rises and sets with you."

"I'm a virgin."

Her head jerks to the side. "*What?* You never mentioned *that* before."

I twist my fingers together. "I know. I'm a little shy about it."

"Are you waiting for marriage or something?"

"No. It's not a purity or innocence thing. I wanted Jake to be my first ever since I kissed him at Wes's thirtieth. The stupid fucks I dated made it easy to hold out."

"That is beyond swoony and adorable. What does he think?"

I chew my lip. "So . . . he doesn't exactly know yet, and I'm not telling him."

Lena pulls into a parking space outside a deli. "Why not?"

"Because he'll freak out and push me away again."

She narrows her eyes. "Why would he freak out?"

"He already feels like he's betraying Wes." I shake my head. "Taking my virginity would be the cherry on the cake."

"Your cake—and your cherry—are no one's business but yours. Wes shouldn't have any part in that conversation. This isn't the Middle Ages— it's *your* body. No offense, but I hate when people use the '*taking* one's virginity' phrase."

"How come?"

"Because it implies the person loses value after having sex for the first time. This is especially true for women." She squeezes the steering wheel. "Don't even get me *started* on the patriarchy."

"No, go ahead. Get started. I wanna hear your thoughts," I say, since I enjoy witnessing Lena's ferocity.

"Well, this may be my inner feminist ranting, but I feel like there's a double standard. Dudes can fuck whomever they want, but if a woman does, she's slut-shamed. That doesn't fly with me. In my opinion, sex is—or should be—a shared experience. It's about gaining an awareness of sexuality and pleasure itself. It's deepening the connection between two people. The first time can hold tremendous significance for both people involved, but I hate how society acts like a woman's virginity is the Holy Grail. Yes, you're sharing a piece of yourself with another person, but that doesn't diminish your value. You're still you. If anything, a healthy sex life enhances you." She laughs. "Of course, I can only say this now that I actually *have* a sex life, but you get the idea." She eyes me. "That being said, I still think you need to tell Jake."

"Christ." I sigh heavily. "You sound like Cora."

"I'm serious, Isla. I've been in the same room as you two. Your chemistry is off the fucking charts. When you and Jake finally collide, it's gonna be explosive." She shimmies in her seat for effect.

"I know," I whisper, a shiver coursing through me.

"Look at you . . . you're fucking trembling just thinking about it."

"Twenty-three years is a long time to wait."

"My point exactly. You don't want him going buck wild in there. Since you're a virgin, it more than likely *will* hurt. While I know nothing of Jake's bedroom preferences, I know him well enough to know he'd die before he hurt you." She squeezes my hand. "I know you're keeping a secret from Wes, but don't build your relationship with Jake on a foundation of secrecy. Be open and honest with him. That man loves you. He deserves your honesty."

My heart flutters. "You really think he loves me?"

Lena rolls her eyes. "Does a bear shit in the woods?"

I snort. "I imagine they shit in fields too."

Unclicking her seat belt, Lena laughs. "Bears shit anyplace they want. Big, steaming piles of shit, and they don't give a flying fiddler's fuck who steps in it."

"You're perfect for Wes." I shake my head. "Honestly, Lena, I swear some of the things that come out of your mouth could come straight from him."

She flashes a cheeky grin. "You should see what goes *in* it."

Plugging my ears, I squeeze my eyes shut. "For the love of Christ, do not reference sucking any dongers that share my last name." I shudder and curl my lip. "Reed gave me enough of a visual when I called him the world's biggest dick."

She laughs. "Got it. I'll try not to gross you out. I'm getting chips. You want to come in the store with me?"

"My ankles are a bit sore, so I'm gonna hang in the car."

She nods. "You want anything?"

"No, I'm good. Thanks."

Lena returns a few minutes later with some groceries. "I meant to ask you this when we spoke on the phone, but I forgot. I saw a flyer for karate classes in there, and it reminded me. Did Wes say anything to you about those self-defense classes?"

"You mean the ones with Garrett's cousin?"

"Yeah. Your brother's riding my ass about them," she mutters, starting the engine. "He wants me to take them in January," she pops her shoulder, "but I don't feel like rolling around on a gym floor when I could be home."

I smooth some gloss on my lips. "Tell *him* to take them and then teach you."

She snorts. "Are you kidding? All it would take is one tackle and he'd be trying to fuck."

"Knee him in the balls." I stuff the gloss in my bag. "That'll teach him."

"I'd rather let him fuck me." She laughs and pulls into traffic. "Apologies for the donger reference."

"It's fine."

"The reason I brought the classes up is because Wes thinks he's making *you* take them with me. Figured I'd give you a heads-up in case he mentions it tonight."

"Nope. Not happening. While Connor's gorgeous, I have no desire to get sweaty with him. Besides, Jake would lose his shit." I give her a coy smile. "Wes can *think* all he likes, but he doesn't *make* me do anything."

Lena smirks. "Remember that when the stomping and chest pounding starts."

After a pit stop at her place to grab the last of my things and retrieve Garrett, we pull up outside my brownstone. Jake leans on the stoop scratching his head while Wes does something to the front door.

"Oh, shit. Emerson's got tools," Garrett calls as we exit the vehicle. "Got a permit for that?"

"No, but I got one for this." Wes gives him the finger. "Jake, hand me the other screwdriver."

"What're ya doing to my door?" I stand at the bottom of the stoop with my hands on my hips.

Jake gestures to my brother. "He's boarding up the place like Fort Knox. Hope you're ready to use your windows, Sprite."

"I'm givin' ya another lock, Imp."

"How many locks does she need?" Lena asks, climbing the steps. She hugs Jake and kisses Wes. "Hey, babe."

"Hi, sunshine." He returns her kiss and points to the door. "I dunno. I may pop over to the hardware store and pick up a few more. Haven't really decided yet."

"Don't go putting all kinds of holes in my door," I warn. "You'll have to patch them so I can paint it purple."

Wes curls his lip. "Purple? Why the hell do ya want a purple front door?"

"Because I like purple." I hug him. "But don't worry, I cleared it with my neighbors. Right, Jake?"

Jake chuckles. "You can paint it any color you want." He gestures to the chain lock my brother installed. "As long as you use these."

I laugh and point to the windowsills. "Wes, are ya gonna put some spikes on here too?"

Wes nods. "That's actually not a bad idea." He turns to Jake and Garrett. "Where do they sell spikes?"

Garrett claps his shoulder. "They've got 'em at the porn shop a few blocks over."

Wes grins at Lena. "Hey, sunshine, looks like we're going shopping later."

"Hi, neighbor," I say, giving Jake a quick hug.

"Welcome to the hood. Trash collection's on Tuesday and we have a noise ordinance. Don't forget to clean up after your dog."

"I'll keep that in mind if I get one." I squeeze his shoulder, and when my brother's not looking, let my fingertips slowly slide down the back of his arm. Jake's gaze heats and lingers on mine for a moment before he flushes and looks away.

"I'm hungry," Wes announces.

Garrett snorts. "What else is new?"

"What does everyone feel like having?" I ask. "Lena bought stuff for nachos as an appetizer."

"You decide," Jake says. "I printed out menus for all the local food places and left them in your kitchen."

"Thanks, Jacob. You're the best."

Everyone steps inside, and Wes gives us a tour of the brownstone. Other than the realtor's website, this is the first I've seen my home's interior. The first floor's layout is identical to Jake's, but I keep that morsel of information to myself. With spacious rooms and glistening hardwood floors, it's far more beautiful than I imagined. The walls are all a soft white, and sunlight streams through the windows. While the house is fully furnished, the pieces feel a bit too formal for my taste. The jacquard-patterned couch needs to go. I love color and texture in my wardrobe, but I'd prefer to have neutral furniture, especially when I think about all the pretty accent pillows I can buy to jazz it up.

My brownstone is warm and inviting, but in desperate need of personal touches. I can't wait to paint and decorate with an eclectic mix of wall art. I also love blending nature into my home environment. Hopefully, there's a nursery nearby so I can get some plants for my living room. My flat back in Australia boasted several plants, each one residing in a piece of homemade pottery from one of my lupus support group mates.

We make our way into the kitchen, which to my delight, boasts granite countertops and new appliances.

Lena points to the pantry. "We stocked you up with some basics. There's an air mattress and sheets you can use until you get a real bed."

"And you need dishes and linens and shit, but you should be good with everything else. We'll take you shopping tomorrow." Wes holds out his arms. "Whaddya think?"

"It's perfect." I fling my arms around his neck. "Thank you so much. I love you." I kiss his cheek.

Wes gives me a bone-crushing hug. "Love you too, Imp. My pleasure. I'd rather have you close by than alone somewhere in Manhattan."

"I've decided I'm gonna pay you rent," I inform him. "It's only right."

He scowls. "Absolutely fucking not."

"I mean it, Wes. While I appreciate this more than words, you shouldn't have to buy me a place just because I wanna do an internship in New York."

He crosses his arms over his chest. "You're my sister. I'll buy you whatever the fuck I want."

Garrett squeezes my shoulder. "Looks like you aren't winning this one, Dundette."

"She's not." Wes grips my chin. "Sorry, but I'm not budging on this." Suddenly, he perks up, and a devious grin crosses his face.

I narrow my eyes. "What?"

"Actually, there *is* a way you can pay me back . . ."

"Oh, yeah? And what might that be?"

"You and Lena are taking self-defense classes in January."

Lena chuckles. "Remember what I said about the chest pounding?"

After the grand tour, our group feasted in my new kitchen. Lena and I used the stools at the island while the three men leaned against the counter.

While it's not part of my anti-inflammatory diet, I figured my first night as a New Yorker was the perfect time to try their world-famous pizza. Wes has been talking about it for years, and when I sank my teeth into cheesy goodness, I realized he wasn't exaggerating. It was well worth the cheat on my diet—and the potential for achy joints. After all, I *did* just fly across the damn ocean. Doesn't a girl deserve some cheese with her jet lag?

Connor came by around seven to install my security system. Wes and Garrett helped. Meanwhile, Jake stayed in the kitchen with Lena and me, and helped us wash the insides of my cabinets. I can't wait to load them with pretty dishes, now that everything's squeaky clean.

I'm not typically a shopper, but I must admit I'm excited to buy some stuff for my new place.

It's after nine now. Everyone except Connor is still here.

Jake's getting ready to head home. "All right, everyone. It's been a long, draining week. I'm gonna go to bed." He gives me a quick hug. "You need anything, I'm only a phone call away." His gaze burns into me. "You know where I live."

My insides flutter with his unspoken message. "Thank you for coming. I really appreciate your help tonight."

"Always." He hugs Wes and Lena and gives Garrett a fist bump before turning to me once more. "I'll *always* have your back."

"Thank you."

He nods. "Later, Sprite."

I watch him leave and glance at Lena, who smirks and looks away.

"I think we should head out too. Isla's exhausted from traveling, and we did a lot of work in the kitchen. C'mon, Ace."

Wes wraps me in a hug. "I love you, Isla. Welcome to New York."

"Love you too." I bury my face in his chest. "Thank you. For everything."

He squeezes me. "Get some sleep. Call us tomorrow when you're ready to shop."

"I will."

Lena hugs me. "Night, chicky. See you tomorrow."

"Can't wait. Thanks for all your help."

Garrett claps my shoulder. "Later, Dundette."

They leave and I flop onto my couch. My phone rings five minutes later. *Jake*. My insides flutter and heat.

"Hello?"

"Come over."

"I'm exhausted, Jake. I'm ready to fall asleep."

"Come sleep in my arms. I want to hold you."

"You know what? I'd love that. I'll be right over." I hang up and snatch my keys. Shrugging into my coat, I lock the door and bound down the steps. I duck between two parked cars, look both ways, and cross the street.

Jake opens the door as I reach his porch. "Hurry up or you'll freeze."

"Too bad I don't have someone willing to keep me warm," I say, stepping past him into his foyer.

He closes the door. "It's a damn shame, isn't it?" The click of his deadbolt matches my heartbeat.

I slowly turn to face him and gesture to his T-shirt and pajama pants. "That was quick."

He shrugs. "Felt like being comfortable."

"Shit. I left my pajamas at home." I turn for the door. "I'll be right back."

Jake stops me. "Don't go back out in the cold. You can wear mine. Come upstairs with me."

I kick off my shoes and leave them on the doormat.

He takes my hand and I allow him to lead me to his bedroom. Aside from my self-guided tour—which he doesn't know about—it's my first time in there.

"This is a spacious room. Ceilings are lofty. What's the square footage?" I ask.

Jake smirks. "Do you actually want to know or is this nervous chatter I'm hearing?"

I flush and look at my hands. "Am I that easy to read?"

He tips my chin up. "Sometimes." His warm chocolatey gaze softens as he looks at me. "Don't be nervous. It's *us*. We don't have to do anything to-night. Like I said on the phone, I just want to hold you." He pulls me into his arms.

I rest my head on his shoulder. "You give the best hugs."

"I love hugging you."

I close my eyes and breathe in his scent. "I love you," I whisper.

His breath catches, and Jake tightens his arms around me. While I des-perately wish he would, he doesn't say it back. "C'mon. Let's get you some clothes." Leading me into his closet, he flicks the light on. He hands me a white T-shirt and gray plaid pajama pants. "These okay?"

"They're perfect. Thank you." I survey his immaculately organized ward-robe. "We need to do something about this."

"What do you mean?"

I brush my hand over the section of long-sleeved shirts. "All the gray."

He chuckles. "I like gray."

"No kidding." I point to the hangers. "You're extremely organized."

"I know."

Pulling a hanger from the bar, I hold up a long-sleeved shirt. "What happens if I do this?" I walk over and hang it with his pants.

Jake's eyes dart from his shirt's rightful position to its new home, then back to me. "It freaks me out."

"You can't ignore it?"

His jaw tightens. "No."

"At all?"

"Nope. Even though I know it's ridiculous, it'll eat at me until it's back where it belongs."

I nod and move the shirt to its original location. "I was curious about how your mind works."

"It's an endless loop of worrying, chastising myself for worrying, and worrying some more."

"About things you can't control?"

"Almost always," he points to his clothes, "which is why I control what I can."

"Is there anything I can do to help you?"

"Yeah," he gives me a sheepish smile, "don't rearrange my stuff."

I ruffle his hair. "I want to shake up your world a little like a snow globe."

"Honey, you shook my world up the moment you kissed me and every day since. It may as well be a blizzard because I've got snowflakes all over the fucking place."

"Is that a bad thing?"

He squeezes my hand. "No, but it scares me a little."

I force a swallow. "Why? Don't you wanna be with me?"

"Absolutely." Jake cradles my face in his hands. "But sometimes I'm afraid of how much I love you."

My heart swells, and I bite my lower lip. "You haven't said it, so I was beginning to wonder . . ."

"I love you more than I can put into words. It overwhelms me sometimes. Especially when the voice in my head tells me I'm gonna lose you."

"Why would you think that?"

"You want to know how my mind works, right?"

"Yes."

"Well, that's what happens to me. An inkling of doubt creeps in and multiplies. I obsess over it until it consumes me. It feeds off my insecurities and plants ideas in my head. I've always had a deep-seated fear of losing the people I love, mainly because it's happened more than once."

"You mean with your dad?"

"Yeah. First, he left. Years later, I finally developed a relationship with him, and a heart attack took him. I've lost other people too."

"Nadia?"

"No. To be honest, I never loved Nadia. I went through the motions with her."

"Why?"

"She was a distraction from you."

"How was that fair to her?"

"Trust me, Nadia didn't love me either. It was a publicity thing arranged by her agent. I went along with it because I was lonely."

"Have you ever been in love?"

"Yeah. My first love was a girl named Molly. She was a counselor at a music camp I went to after my junior year of high school."

I raise an eyebrow. "She was older than you?"

"Yeah, by seven years. She was my first *everything*."

"Wow. What happened?"

"I fell hard for her that summer. She promised things would stay the same, but she went back to college and forgot about me. I went up for a surprise visit only to find she'd moved on with some fellow grad student. Supposedly, she wanted a man who could take care of her." He rubs his jaw. "Interestingly enough, she contacted me six months ago. Guess I finally meet her qualifications."

I nod. "Funny how a little fame and success brings them out of the woodwork."

"Yup." He runs a hand through his hair. "I guess I'm trying to explain how normal shit—like a breakup or whatever—affects me differently. Things hit me deeper than most people. Everything's amplified by my OCD. I take what-if to a new dimension, and my mind tortures me with scenarios and possibilities. I can't control it, so I get insecure. Needy. Moody. Possessive." He squeezes his eyes shut. "Isla, I love you. Never, ever doubt that. But I'm scared."

"Tell me what you're scared of."

"I'm afraid I'll overwhelm or drain you."

I squeeze his hand. "You won't."

"You don't know that. I'm needy as hell. I need to know you'll stick around if I bare myself to you. I need to know you'll be there when it matters. Plain and simple, I need you to stay. Even when I'm out of my mind. Even when I'm moody and quiet. Even when I push you away. Just . . . stay."

"I'm not going anywhere, Jacob. I'm yours for the taking."

"I never want to take from you, honey. I only want to give. If you let me, I'll give you my everything. But I need to know you want that much from me."

"I want everything with you, Jake. Only you." I stroke his cheek. "Sounds like you need some reassurance."

"I need—"

I grip his face, silencing him with my lips. Groaning, Jake pulls me up against him. His tongue tangles with mine, urgently spearing into my mouth. We pour ourselves into the kiss. Lust and passion wash over us, sluicing off our bodies and pooling at our feet. Hands roaming, mine slide beneath his T-shirt to stroke the warm flesh of his back. Between us, the hardened length of him presses into my belly.

"You've had a long day. I told you I just wanted to hold you." His roughened voice heats my insides. "You should probably stop touching me."

I lightly trail my nails down his back. "And what if I don't wanna stop?"

"Isla . . ." He draws a few steadying breaths. "Put your pajamas on and get in bed so I can hold you."

I hold up the pajamas. "What if I want you to put them on me?"

"Your clothes would come off, and I can't guarantee I'd be able to follow through with the rest."

"How about I take off my clothes, and you can pick up from there?" I slowly unbutton my shirt.

He reaches out to stop me. "Honey, I'm trying to be a gentleman."

"Maybe I don't want a gentleman right now," I say, pulling from his grip. He releases my hand, and I unbutton my shirt the rest of the way.

"I'll always be one with you." Fists clenched at his sides, he watches me shrug out of the shirt and drop it on his closet floor. His eyes widen at the sight of my purple lacy bra.

I flutter my lashes and toy with the straps. "Should I keep this on?"

His eyes flare with heat. "That's up to you."

I nod and slide the straps off my shoulders. "I think it needs to come off." I reach around and unhook the back, letting the garment land by my shirt.

Chest heaving, his gaze wanders my body. "You're so beautiful," he whispers.

I smile and unbutton my jeans. Shoving them down over my hips, I step out of the jeans and kick them aside. Jake eyes my matching lace panties and licks his lips. Heat floods my core. I slowly spin around, giving him a view of my arse. Perfect, since I'd chosen a thong for the occasion.

He sucks in a sharp breath. "Oh my God."

I peek over my shoulder at him. Lust rolls off him in waves, each one slamming into me.

"Turn around and look at me," he commands roughly. I turn to face him and meet his gaze. "Do you want this?"

I nod.

Jake steps closer to me. "There's no going back from here, so I need to hear you say it."

"Yes."

He grips my chin. "Yes, what?"

"I want you to make love to me."

"You sure?" His low growl makes me even wetter.

"Yes," I say with conviction, because at this moment, I need him inside me more than I need the air in my lungs.

Tell him.

He brushes his lips over mine. "God, I was hoping you'd say that." He nips my lower lip. "You're absolutely sure—"

I grip the hem of his shirt and lift it over his head. Balling it up, I heave it in the corner of his closet.

He chuckles. "Guess that answers my question."

"Damn right, it does." Sliding my hands down his chest and abs, I find the waistband of his pajama pants and shove them down, shocked by my immediate view of his cock. "You're free balling!"

"It's my house. I can go commando if I feel like it."

"True. I guess I didn't expect it."

"Kind of like how I didn't expect that view of your ass a moment ago?"

"Yeah, something like that." I study him appreciatively. "You're a beautiful man, Jacob."

"Thanks. Now get your sweet little ass into my bed."

I salute him and sashay from the closet, swaying my hips dramatically. I reach the edge of his king-size bed and peek over my shoulder.

Jake leans against the closet doorframe, no doubt enjoying the show I gave him. "You're so fucking sexy, Isla."

I shimmy my hips. "How about you come and get me?"

He's behind me in an instant, his hands gripping my hips. His cock presses against my lower back. He kisses my shoulders and the side of my neck. "Get in," he growls at my ear.

I crawl up the bed and slide beneath the sheets. I settle, resting my head against his pillows. "I'm waiting."

Jake prowls up the mattress to me like a male lion, his lips seizing my neck once more as he settles on top of me.

"Aren't you getting under the covers?" I ask, pointing to the sheet and blanket between us.

"Pacing myself," he whispers, teeth grazing the shell of my ear. "I've waited years for you, so I'm gonna take my time."

"Get under the damn blankets," I command, pulling at him. "It's cold in your room. Besides, I wanna feel your warm skin on me."

Grinning, he peels back the covers and slides inside. "Yes, ma'am." He nudges my thighs apart and settles between them, resting on his elbows.

I absorb the warm, heavy weight of his body and pressure between my legs. He rolls his hips, making me gasp.

He grips the waistband of my panties. "These need to come off."

"Then take them off me."

He rears up so he can watch as he slowly slides the panties over my hips. His breath catches at the sight of me. Completely bare, my skin's no doubt glistening with my arousal.

"Shit," he whispers reverently.

I smile and kick the panties to the bottom of the bed. Jake drinks me in like an expensive whiskey. He's the first man to see me fully naked, and I can't help but feel exhilarated.

He snatches a condom from his nightstand drawer and rolls it on. My heart rate picks up speed.

Tell him.

"Kiss me," I whisper, threading my fingers in his hair.

Jake brings his lips to mine and obliges me with the most passionate of kisses. Tender, yet urgent, his tongue unravels me. Here, naked in his bed beneath him, bracketed by his strong arms, I'm at home.

His cock glides through the moisture that's collected between my legs. He grips himself and lines us up.

Tell him.

Jake pulls back. I can tell he's going to check for my consent again, so when he opens his mouth to speak, I press a finger to his lips. "Yes. I'm sure."

He kisses my finger. "Not what I was going to say, but I appreciate the reassurance."

"What were ya gonna say?"

He smiles and brushes the hair off my face. "I love you."

My breath leaves me in a rush. "Love you too."

Tell him.

"Jake, I . . ." I force a swallow. "I, uh . . ." He raises a brow, so I clear my throat and try again, "I'm . . . um, well . . . So, the thing is—" My legs tremble on either side of him, and I tightly clutch his shoulders.

"I'm nervous too." His gaze focuses on mine. "I don't know what your expectations are of me, but I'll do my best to meet them."

"I don't know what they are either."

"That's good. I guess. What I'm saying is, you're in control. You tell me what you like, and I'll give it to you."

"I don't know what I like," I blurt.

"Yeah, okay, Miss-I've-Been-Moaning-Your-Name-For-Years. I'll believe that when pigs fly." Chuckling, he starts kissing my neck again. "I already know you like this."

"I'm serious." I draw a shaky breath. "I don't know what I like because I've never done this before."

Jake stills, his lips at my throat and the head of his cock nudging my pussy. "What?"

"You heard me."

"Wait a minute." He lifts his head and meets my gaze. "Are you telling me—"

"Your sweatshirt isn't the only thing I've held on to for you."

CHAPTER 25

Jake

Mood: "Lost" by Dermot Kennedy

I'm hearing things. Or, at the very least, misinterpreting them. She can't possibly be a virgin. Correction, there's no fucking way she's a virgin. She's had dozens of boyfriends—dudes all over Australia are obsessed with her.

I blink a few times. "I'm sorry. *What?*"

"Are you even listening to me?"

"I'm listening, but I think I misunderstood you."

"I'm a virgin, Jake."

No misunderstanding that. How is it even possible? Obviously, I know *how* it's feasible, but why would she want *me* to be her first?

Your sweatshirt isn't the only thing I've held on to for you.

I shake my head to clear it. "Not possible."

"Oh, I can assure ya, it's both a possibility and a reality."

"You've really never had sex?" I whisper, dumbfounded at a level I didn't think existed.

"That's what virgin means, Jacob," Isla snaps. She pushes against my chest, so I move off her and sit up.

I scratch my head. "But why?"

"Did ya miss the part where I told you I saved myself for you?"

Okay, so I didn't imagine it. Why the fuck would she save herself for me?

Who would do that? I'm a needy, moody bastard with a fucked-up head and more issues than I care to remember. I'm no prize.

"I guess I find it hard to believe."

Pain flashes in her eyes. "Are you calling me a liar?"

"I'm not calling you anything. I'm simply trying to make sense of it."

"What's there to make sense of? I'm tellin' you I'm a virgin."

"Isla, honey, you don't need to pretend with me. Don't be coy about your skills in the sack to make me feel better about my insecurities. Virgins don't give head like that."

Isla's mouth drops open and tears well in her eyes. She blinks rapidly—her futile attempt to hold them back—but they spill over.

Fuck.

"That came out wrong." Running both hands over my face, I backpedal, "What I'm trying to say—"

"Oh, I think you've said enough." Isla scrambles from the bed and yanks my sheet free. It's quite the feat, given the neurotic way I tuck in my bedding.

She wraps the sheet around her body. "Gotta tell you, Jake, this isn't the reaction I expected." She waves a finger at me. "And for your information, virgins who've never allowed anyone to touch them below the waist have ample opportunity to hone their cock-sucking skills." She rushes from my room into the adjoining bathroom, slamming the door behind her.

Is there an award for dumbest fucker on the planet?

Because I'm definitely the winner. No. Forget the planet. I take the win for universe's biggest idiot.

I pull the condom off and toss it into my trash can, then lurch from my bed. I head for the bathroom, yanking my shirt and pajama pants on as I go. On my way across the room, I trip over my shoes and nearly face-plant.

"Fuck!" I catch myself in time but knock some shit off my dresser.

Double fuck.

It's my cactus. The one Mom sent to keep me company. I tend to kill plants, so I didn't have any. Mom decided I needed some "color in my gray-scape," so she mailed me a fucking succulent garden. Ignoring the dirt everywhere, I follow Isla.

"Sprite?" I tap on the door.

"Go away." Her muffled voice cracks with hurt and anger.

"Can't. I live here. Let me in."

"Leave me alone."

I try the doorknob. "Isla, unlock the door."

"No!"

I force an even tone, despite the rising panic in my chest. "I wanna talk to you. I need to explain myself better."

"I don't give two fucks whatcha want right now, Jake Bennett, so you can stuff that notion up your arse."

I clench my jaw. "Let. Me. In."

Instead of opening the door—or answering me—she turns on the shower. The metallic scrape of the shower hooks gives me an idea.

CHAPTER 26

Isla

Internal playlist: "Happy" by Leona Lewis

I guess I thought it would mean something to Jake that I wanted him to be my first. Clearly, it doesn't. Maybe all he cared about was getting his piece of my pussy. Or worse, what if I'm simply his token virgin? Part of his sexual bucket list like Lucas, and so many of the guys back home, who desperately wanted to fuck me.

I remember Lucas saying he couldn't wait to be inside me because he knew I'd be tight. Men love tight women. Especially, the patriarchal fucks who want to be the first ones to explore unchartered territory. I believed, to the depth of my soul, that Jake was different.

But nope.

He's just like the rest of them—eager to stuff his dick in whatever hole I'm offering.

A sob wracks my frame, stealing my breath. How could I have been so fucking stupid? Hot, bitter tears stream down my cheeks. Hugging myself, I lean against the cold tile and kick myself for my naivety.

A clicking sound scrapes on my nerves. The stubborn fuck is still outside the door trying to get in.

Well, tough shit.

I have no trouble staying in this shower all night. I'll use up all the hot water in Brooklyn before I face him again.

There's a shuffle and another click.

I peek around the curtain. Jake is *inside* the bathroom, leaning against the closed door with a smug look on his face.

"How the fuck did ya get in here?"

He holds up something metal—a skewer. "I have my ways."

"Oh my God, you picked the fucking lock?"

He tosses the skewer on the vanity. "What if I did?"

"Then you're a dick who doesn't respect a woman's privacy!"

"Guess I'm a dick, then."

I point to the door. "Seriously, get out."

Jake doesn't budge. "Nope."

"Please leave me alone."

He crosses his arms over his chest. "Honey, I'm not going anywhere until we talk."

"I have nothing to say."

"We both know that's not true."

"Calling me a liar again?"

He shakes his head. "Never called you one in the first place."

"Whatever." I snatch a bottle of his shampoo and squeeze some in my hand.

"You weren't going to tell me, were you?" His tone is low and calm, a stark contrast to the emotion raging inside me.

I ignore him and lather my hair, the invigorating mint opening my sinuses. No, I wasn't going to tell him. I decided at the last minute when I felt him between my legs. When Lena and Cora's warnings flashed through my mind and trepidation crept in. When I remembered I've never successfully used a tampon—let alone a dildo—and it occurred to me that he could really hurt me.

"Asked you a question, Sprite."

"Don't call me Sprite. You lost that privilege."

He gives a low chuckle. "Yeah, okay, Sprite. Did you plan to tell me or not?"

"No, I didn't."

"Why not? Why would you be afraid to talk to me about something?"

"Uh, maybe I was worried about your reaction?" I rinse my hair, working my fingers through it to loosen any tangles. Too bad the knots in my stomach won't go quietly down the drain.

"Why would you be afraid of my reaction?"

Is he serious right now?

I curl my lip. "Looks like I had a bloody good reason to be, now doesn't it?"

"Answer my question."

I peek at him again. "Are ya dense?"

He nods. "Sometimes. Why'd you keep your virginity a secret from me?"

"My sexual history is none of your business."

"You're absolutely right about that." He steps closer to me. "But you made a point to mention it as I was about to push my cock inside you. Why not tell me sooner? We've had multiple conversations about sex."

"Do ya want a list of reasons?"

"Yeah. I do." Crossing his arms, he steps closer, his gaze burning into me.

"I didn't say anything because I thought you'd freak out and push me away again." I tangle my fingers in my wet hair and pull. "Because I wanted to be more than the token virgin in your collection."

He stiffens and narrows his eyes. "My collection?"

I squeeze some conditioner into my palm. "Because I hoped I was more than a notch on your bedpost."

"Are you fucking serious?" he growls. "You think that's what you are to me?"

Deep down, I know that isn't the case. It's Jake—not Lucas. But, since he pissed me off and embarrassed me, my pettiness takes over.

I square my shoulders. "I dunno what to think."

"Really, Isla? I haven't made my feelings known?"

The pain in his voice makes me look away. He's right—he's been open with me from the start. I'm the one withholding information.

"Oh, you have no response for that? Now you're shutting me out. Nice." He throws his hands in the air. "If you were so conflicted, why tell me at all?"

"Because I thought you should know you were about to fuck a virgin."

He takes a few steps closer. "Why?"

"Because I was scared," I spit out the words as I rinse.

Pain flashes across his face. "Of me?"

"No. I was worried about the mechanics of it . . . fittin' you inside me." I meet his gaze. "I was afraid you wouldn't be gentle."

Closing the distance between us, he looms at the edge of the shower. "Do you think I'd *ever* be rough with you?"

"I have no idea what to expect. You know, that whole inexperienced *virgin* bit."

"All those boyfriends you've had . . . They never touched you?"

The disbelief on his face is a punch to my gut. He must think I'm some slutty chick who's fucked half of Australia.

Fresh tears rain from my eyes. "I haven't allowed *anyone* to see me naked or touch me below the waist. I dated because it was what I was supposed to do. Believe me, I'm well aware of my reputation." At his raised brow, I clarify, "Did I burn through men? Absolutely. Have I given plenty of head? Call me a fucking professional. But that's as far as it went."

"Why?"

"They all wanted one thing from me—something I had zero desire to give. The moment they pressured me for a fuck, I cut them loose. When I kissed you five years ago, everything changed. You're the *only* person who I've ever wanted to have sex with." I shake my head sadly. "You weren't my first kiss, but I wish you had been. I vowed not to make that mistake twice, so I saved the rest of my firsts for you."

"I wish you would've told me sooner."

"Why? So you could leave me sooner?"

Pain twists his expression. "Isla—"

"You're right, Jacob. I purposely kept it from you until the last minute." Tears stream down my face. "I finally told you because I thought being my first would mean something to you, but I guess I was wrong. Clearly, you think I'm a slut too. I'm done talking now." I close the curtain.

Jake yanks it open and steps into the shower, fully clothed. "What did you just say?"

"You heard me."

"Never call yourself that again," he snarls, pressing me up against the wall, effectively caging me with his arms. Nose touching mine, his furious gaze burns into me. The shower's stream saturates his hair and clothes but does nothing to douse his fury. Pain and anger war in his gaze as I stare at him in shock. "For the record, I don't care that I'm your first."

My heart cracks down the center. "Thanks, Jake. That's exactly what I needed to hear right now."

"You took that the wrong way." He holds up his hand. "Let me explain. What I mean is, it doesn't matter to me if you slept with zero or one hundred men—all that matters is *I* get to have you."

"Making me feel like some sort of conquest isn't helping your cause."

"Let me finish," he snaps, gripping my chin. His gaze is a solar flare of heat and pain that singes me to ash. "If you think your little revelation doesn't affect me, you're dead wrong. The fact that you—a woman so far out of my league, it's ridiculous—would even *consider* letting me touch you . . ." He releases me and rubs a fist over his face. "I've loved you for years, Isla. I've dreamed about you, fantasized, lusted, pined, ached, you name it. I never imagined you wanted me too. I'm not worthy of the ground you walk on, let alone your heart. The fact that you wanted your first time to be with *me* feels like a mathematical impossibility—a fucking *gift*—so forgive me if I was a little taken aback!"

"Why would you say you're not worthy?"

"Because I'm not." He cups my face. "Isla, you are light and color and joy—all the things I'm not. Your strength and resilience surpass anything I'd be capable of."

"That's not true, Jake."

"We'll have to agree to disagree." He shakes his head. "Like I said, I don't care if I'm your first or your sixty-first. The number's irrelevant." He grips my chin once more and brings his forehead to mine. "Do you know why?"

"Why," I whisper.

"Because I'm going to be your *last*." He presses his body up against me. "I'm going to be your first. Your last. And everything in between. I'm gonna be your *only*. I want to be all you know. All you want or need. I wanna be your everything." He squeezes his eyes shut. "Because you're everything to me."

"You already are my everything. You always have been."

"You're it for me." Water drips off the tip of his nose onto his lips. "I love you more than I have a right to, and it scares the shit out of me."

Fresh tears stream from my eyes as I throw my arms around his neck. "I love you too."

He pulls me close. "I'm sorry my reaction and word choices hurt your feelings. I'm an idiot sometimes." He slides a hand to my hip. "And I'm glad you told me because I could've unknowingly hurt you."

"I should've told you sooner, but I was afraid you'd pull back again." I rest my head on his shoulder. "You're already conflicted about Wes, so I figured I shouldn't fuel the fire. I thought knowledge of my un-popped cherry status would freak you out."

He snorts. "Don't call it that. The visual freaks me out." I raise a brow, so he clarifies, "I imagine a bunch of dudes holding pins. They're all chasing giant red balloons and trying to pop them."

I laugh. "Well, for what it's worth, my balloon willingly seeks your . . ." I glance to where his wet pants are plastered to his crotch. He's thick and perfect and the farthest thing from a pin. "Baguette."

Jake throws his head back and bursts out in a rich and hearty laugh. "My baguette is currently on the soggy side. How about we stop wasting water?"

I turn off the faucet. "Good call."

He hands me a couple of towels. I wrap one around my body and secure my hair with the other. He quickly sheds his clothes and dries off with a hand towel.

"Don't be ridiculous," I say, handing him one of mine.

"Thanks." He towels himself dry and wraps it around his hips.

"I'd rather you keep it off."

He chuckles. "I'm sure you would, but it's cold in here."

I press a finger to the middle of his chest. "The last thing you need to worry about is shrinkage—you're huge."

He snorts. "I am definitely *not* huge."

"I'm the better judge. I guarantee I've seen more dicks than you have."

Jake wraps his arms around me and laughs. "You have a way with words, honey."

"Well, it's true. You're the girthiest man I've ever seen."

"Uh . . . thanks?"

"You're welcome." I pinch his arse. "You're welcome to bring it my way—"

"Look at me."

I meet his gaze. "What's up?"

"It's not happening tonight."

Shrugging, I force a smile. "Yeah, I kinda figured I ruined the mood."

He shakes his head. "You didn't ruin anything. We're not doing it tonight because you're jet-lagged and emotional." I open my mouth to protest, but he continues, "After the week I've had, and us fighting, *I'm* emotional too."

"You seem fine to me."

"Isla, I just got into a shower fully clothed, pinned you to the wall, and screamed in your face. Trust me, I'm not anywhere close to fine." He retrieves a new toothbrush from his medicine cabinet, squeezes some toothpaste on it, and hands it to me. He puts toothpaste on his own and starts to brush.

Standing side by side, we brush our teeth like an old married couple.

He finishes up and smiles at me, dimples and eye crinkles on full display. I loop my arm around his waist and return his smile.

He turns to face me. "I love your smile."

I kiss his lower lip. "I love yours."

"C'mon, let's go to sleep." He leads me to the bed with a warm palm on the small of my back. "And don't try to seduce me this time."

I drop my towel and slide between the sheets. "No guarantees."

"You should probably put clothes on."

Stretching my arms and legs, I flail like I'm making a snow angel. Not that I've ever actually made one, but what I'd do if given the opportunity. "Nah, I like your thread count too much to wear clothes."

His eyes flick to the growing bulge beneath his towel, then back to mine. "Wasn't a request." His gravelly tone hardens my nipples. Tendrils of need unfurl in my lower belly.

I smile. "Doesn't change much on my end."

"Isla . . ."

I flutter my lashes. "Yes, Jacob?"

"You're killing me, honey. You have no idea how much I want you."

"Then get your arse in here and kiss me until my noggin explodes."

CHAPTER 27

Jake

Mood: "First Time" by Lifehouse

I groan low in my chest as delicate fingers grip my shaft and stroke it. I've never had a dream this realistic. Probably because I've never had Isla in my bed before. It feels like she's actually touching me. A warm wetness surrounds the head of my cock.

"Don't tell me you're gonna sleep through this, Jacob."

My eyes fly open. Sure, I'm flat on my back, but it's definitely *not* a dream. "What are you doing?"

Isla chuckles and licks the tip. "Take a wild guess."

I blink a few times and try to gather my wits. She's nestled between my thighs, giving me a blow job I didn't ask for. *What universe is this?*

"I was asleep."

"No kidding. You were also hard, so I took the hint."

"Happens in the morning," I say it like the concept of morning wood is exclusive to me.

"Mm-hmm." She sucks the head of me between her lips.

"*Fuck*, that feels good."

Sunlight filters through my blinds, casting a soft glow on her. Isla peers up at me with those eyes, the blue more vivid than ever.

"This is what happens when you get hard and rub yourself against me in your sleep." She takes me to the back of her throat.

"Oh, fuck, yes," I hiss. "You're a little vixen."

Chuckling, she lifts her head. "Yeah, well, my vixen abilities are limited to this, so shut up and enjoy it." She cups my balls and flicks her tongue. "Because I hate to break it to ya, but you're gonna be the one doing all the work with everything else."

"I can assure you it won't be work."

"Mm-hmm." She moves her head and hand in tandem, stealing my ability to think.

I absorb the sensations and fist the sheets. She chuckles again; the vibration making my hips jerk. She moves my hands to her hair, so I lightly tug it, which seems to spur her on. Her enthusiasm ratchets up a few notches while my longevity falters.

"Isla, honey, fuck—" I squeeze my eyes shut. "You're gonna make me come already." Tightening her grip, she increases the pace and sucks me deeper. "Oh! Isla—"

Feral moans rip from my chest as I orgasm. She keeps going until my cock is so sensitive, I can't take it anymore.

She lifts her head and flashes the sultriest sex kitten grin I've ever seen. "Did ya enjoy that, Jacob?"

"You have no fucking idea."

She wipes her mouth, smooths her hair, and cozies up beside me. "Good morning, love."

"Damn right, it is." I shake my head in disbelief. "You're a goddess. You know that, right?"

"No. I'm just a girl who loves her man."

I pull her close. "I'm a man who loves his woman and wants her to know she can wake him up like that anytime she wants."

She peers into my eyes. "I'm your woman?"

I raise a brow. "Uh, I think we've established that."

"No, what I mean is, do you think of me as your girlfriend?"

"I'm not one for labels, but you could say that, yes." I brush the hair off her face. "But I feel like soulmate is a more fitting term."

Her eyes well with emotion. "You mean that?"

"Yeah, I do."

She grips my face and kisses me. Deeply. Passionately. Pouring her heart and soul into it. She breaks the kiss after a few minutes. "You're my twin flame, Jake Bennett."

"Twin flame?" I tilt my head. "Is that like true north?"

"Yes, but in my opinion, it goes deeper. Look it up sometime. I'll start crying if I try to explain myself." Isla brushes her thumb over my lower lip. "I know you don't do labels, but I figure I should give you a heads-up."

"A heads-up?"

"Yes. Consider yourself warned," she gives me an earth-shattering smile, "you're gonna be my husband one day."

Time stops, along with my heart. *She wants forever with me.* How is it possible this beautiful, amazing, resilient goddess chooses *me* to share in her forever?

I smirk. "Oh really?"

"Yes, really. Gird your loins, love."

I laugh and pull her close. "You're something else, Sprite."

Hours later, we're both showered and dressed. Sadly, a series of phone calls from my mother, Jesse, and the community center's foreman interrupted our sexy time. We don't want any interruptions when we finally make love, so we decided it wasn't meant to happen this morning. Besides, I've waited too damn long for her—the *last* thing I want is a quickie. Currently, she's making omelets while I read through my neglected emails.

"What's on your agenda for today?" she asks.

"At some point, I need to swing by the hospital for a bit. I think I'll bring some lunch for Jesse. What are you doing today?"

"Wes and Lena are taking me to some stores. I need dishes, sheets, a mattress, décor stuff," she runs down her list while twirling a piece of hair, "food, batteries—"

"Batteries?" I flash a wolfish grin. "What do you need them for?"

"Torches and stuff. Why?"

The cute little thing missed my reference. I shake my head. "Thought you needed them for something *else* . . ."

Her eyes widen as realization dawns. She flushes deep crimson. "No, I don't use one of those."

I chuckle. "Ah, so you prefer the ones that don't run on batteries for your solo moan sessions?"

Redness creeps down her neck. "I don't use dildos, either."

I cock my head. "Then how do you . . . *you know?*"

"With my hand." She looks away shyly. "On the outside."

"*Only* on the outside?"

"Yes." She swats my arm. "Now, stop. You're making me blush."

I snatch her around the waist and pull her to me. "Let me get this clear—"

"Jacob, I wasn't kidding when I told you I saved the rest of my firsts for you. *Nothing* has been there." She looks away shyly. "I'm afraid of tampons, for fuck's sake."

"Isla Rose Emerson, you were going to let me inside you when you've never even used a *tampon?*"

"Can we please not talk about tampons?"

"You brought them up."

"No," she flicks me on the nose, "*you* went down that road when you assumed that I needed batteries for the vibrator I don't have."

"Looks like I'm gonna have to change my approach." I brush my lips over her ear. "I hope you like foreplay, sweetheart."

Her eyes widen and she points to the stove. "Right now?"

"Nah, I'll let you eat your eggs first." I pinch her ass. "And do your shopping. I need to run some errands of my own."

Like to the pharmacy to buy some fucking lube. And more condoms.

"I'll probably be gone all day." She grimaces for a second before she perks up. "Do you have anything planned for dinner?"

I let my gaze travel the length of her body. "Oh, I sure do." Isla's shoulders rise and fall with each shaky breath, like she can *feel* my eye caress. Gripping her waist, I massage her hip bones with my thumbs. "You saved your first time for me, so you can bet your sweet little ass I'm gonna make sure I was worth the wait. Tonight, I'm going to show you what it means to be my woman." I kiss her neck and lightly nibble her collarbone. "First, I'm gonna wine and dine you."

"Then, what?" she asks, breathlessly. "You gonna deflower me, Jacob?"

"Goddamn right, I am. Prepare yourself, Isla," I trace the curve of her breast, "because I'm gonna worship every fucking inch of you."

CHAPTER 28

Isla

Internal playlist: "I Got You (I Feel Good)" by Jessie J

The flood of arousal at Jake's words is instantaneous and panty saturating. I've never felt desire like this. My entire body thrums with a hyperawareness of him. His scent, his dark lust-filled gaze, the sound of his breaths, everything. My nipples are hard and the hairs on my arms stand on end.

"Every inch?" I whisper, thinking of his lips and tongue on my body.

"Head to toe, sweetheart." He slides his palms to my arse and tugs me closer. Reaching one hand around the front of me, he cups between my thighs, making me gasp. "But I'm going to linger *here* for a while . . ." Stroking me over top of my leggings, he trails kisses to my ear and whispers, "And savor the taste of you."

Oh my God.

"Jacob—"

He holds a finger to my lips. "Save your voice, honey. You're gonna need it later."

"Huh?" I'm literally bewildered with lust.

His lips curve into a wicked smile. "For when I make you moan my name." I suck in a sharp breath as Jake kisses my neck. "Over and over and over again . . ."

"I'm canceling my plans with Wes and Lena," I say on a gasp.

"No, you're not. Besides, I've got things I need to do today . . . before I do *you*, that is."

"Holy fuck."

"Sweetheart, there will be nothing holy about it," he squeezes my arse once more, "but I promise you, I'll make an angel sing."

Wes taps the table. "Hello? Earth calling. Imp, are ya with me?"

I jump, my eyes darting to his. "What?"

"Asked you a question." He cocks his head. "What's up with you today?"

"I'm fine. Whaddya mean?"

"You're acting like you got roos loose in your noggin."

Chuckling, Lena steals the pickle from his plate. "Leave her alone. She's got a lot on her mind."

"Like what?" Wes probes.

"Gee, I dunno, let's see . . . I sat on a plane for over twenty hours, moved into a new home—in a foreign country, I might add. Got an internship starting in a few weeks . . ." I shrug. "You know, the normal stuff."

"Well, at least you don't have to worry about being safe in your home. That security system is top of the line."

"Thank you."

He waves me off. "Don't thank me. It's my duty as your brother to protect you."

"I don't need protecting, Wes. I'm a grown woman."

"I know that, but—"

"And I *will* pay rent."

"We've been over this, Isla. I won't accept money from you. I bought the brownstone because you needed a place to stay, *and* it was a good investment. It was a simple solution."

"You don't always have to be the one who fixes or solves things, you know? You can let others do their part." I stare into my brother's eyes. "Not every burden is yours to carry, Wes."

Lena flashes an I-told-you-so look in his direction. "Funny, I remember telling him something similar."

Wes rubs his jaw. "When it comes to protecting or taking care of my family," he points to me and wraps an inclusive arm around Lena, "I'll carry whatever burden's necessary."

"Figured you'd say something like that."

He steeples his fingers in front of his lips. "But there is something you *can* do. And this is extremely important to me."

"I'll do it." My kind, generous brother—the one who'll stop at nothing to solve my problems and to whom I'm forever indebted—needs something from *me*. I'll move mountains to make it happen. "Whatever it is, I promise to do it."

"Good. Classes start January fourth."

"Fuck," Lena mutters, slapping herself on the forehead.

"Wait. What?"

Wes grins. "You're taking self-defense classes with Lena."

Shaking my head, I grip his wrist. "I'll do anything but *that*."

"Too late. You already gave me your word."

"Wes—"

"I'm not budging on this, Isla. With me being in the city, attracting media attention, people are gonna figure out who you are. I don't wanna chance some lunatic going after my sister to get to me." He pins me with his gaze. "You and Lena are the people I cherish most in this world. Please understand my need to keep ya safe."

Lena gives me a pleading look. "It'll be fun. We can make it our twice-weekly girls' night."

I raise a brow at her. "I see he's already worn you down?"

"As much as I love pushing his buttons, I understand where he's coming from. I've seen how freaked out he gets over his family. I've also witnessed a few rabid fans who probably want to kill me. If the roles were reversed, I'd be doing the same. If I could protect *him*—or ease his fears—I'd do it. This is one way I can help."

Damn it, Lena.

I release the world's heaviest sigh.

Wes chuckles. "Christ, you're gonna blow down the Empire State Building with all that wind."

"I'm *not* happy about this," I mutter. "But I'll do it because I love you."

He squeezes my hand. "Thank you. It means a lot to me, Imp."

"I know."

"I filled Connor in on your limitations."

I stiffen. "Excuse me? How am I limited?"

"I'm not saying you are limited—"

"But ya told him I have limitations, which defeats the purpose of self-defense classes."

Wes's brows knit together. "How so?"

"Because he'll assume I'm weak and go easy on me. Pretty sure your rabid fans won't give a fuck about my swollen ankles."

"Let me get this straight. First, you're dead set against the classes. Now you're pissed at me because I warned him you may need some modifications? You've seen the bloke—do you really want him coming atcha full throttle?"

"I don't want him coming at me at all, but if I'm gonna do it, I'll do it right. You know how I feel about authenticity."

Lena giggles. "There's no mistaking you two are siblings. She's just like you, Wes."

He grins. "Yeah, I know she is. Which means she's gonna pout the rest of the day since she didn't get her way."

I give him the finger. "Stop gloating, ya fuck."

My phone vibrates in my purse. I glance at the notification and smile. To avoid a texting debacle like I experienced with Reed, I made sure to change my settings, so my texts no longer flash across the screen. And for an added layer of protection—on the off chance someone snoops—I changed Jake's name in my contacts to Dana, which is Cora's younger sister. We talk all the time, so no one would raise any eyebrows at our texting frequency. Now, I just need to be careful I don't send her something intended for Jake. Her real entry in my phone is Dana Priest, so it shouldn't be a problem. Hopefully.

Dana: Head to toe, sweetheart . . . that's a promise.

I type my response.

Me: Will the angels be playing harps?

Dana: Harps, accordions, ukuleles, you name it.

I smirk as my fingers fly over the touchscreen.

Me: Got any French . . . horns?

Dana: No, but I've got a Scotch-Irish one.

Me: I know. I played it this morning.

Dana: Well played. (FYI, I mean that in reference to your pun AND my horn)

Wes looks over my shoulder. "Who're ya texting?"

"Dana."

He nods. "Listen, I know you're pissed at me, but think of the positives."

I roll my eyes. "Which are?"

"Connor seems like a nice bloke. He's got a good job—"

"I am *not* interested in Connor." I wave a finger in his face. "Nor will I ever be, so you can stuff the matchmaker gig up your arse."

Wes shakes his head in confusion. "Why not? Sure, he's twenty-nine, but it's not *that* bad an age difference."

"What's wrong with age differences?" Lena asks with a smirk.

"Depends on the people involved. Isla's not at the settle-down phase yet. Older men often want that." He turns back to me. "I think Connor would be great for ya. I mean, he's good-looking. Got muscles and tattoos. You love those—"

"First of all, how do you know what phase I'm in?"

"Isla, you jump from bloke to bloke before I can blink. You mean to tell me settling down's even a possibility for ya?"

Dana's name appears on the screen once more, and I can't help my coy smile as visions of my future sexcapades dance through my head like wanton sugarplums. "Maybe you've been wrong about me all along." My brother's brows pop at my statement, so I lean in. "Maybe I dated all those guys because I was trying to force myself to want them. Did ya ever think of that?"

He holds his hands up in surrender. "Okay, okay. Whatever makes you happy."

"It would make me happy if you stayed out of my love life."

"Message received, Imp. Be with whomever you like."

I arch a brow. "You mean that?"

"Yeah. As long as they treat you right."

Let's see if he remembers that one when he finds out about Jake. Something tells me the notion will be long forgotten.

CHAPTER 29

Jake

Mood: "Desert Rose" by Sting

I empty my purchases onto the kitchen island and run down the seventy-two lists in my head, sure I've covered all my bases for tonight. Operation wine/dine/deflower is in full swing.

After two hours researching anti-inflammatory diets, I found some recipes that sounded appealing and hit up the grocery store. I purchased a six-pack of nonalcoholic piña colada wine coolers—because I care about her kidney and liver—which will pair wonderfully with the coconut-mango shrimp risotto I plan to make. For dessert, I snagged mango sorbet and dark chocolate truffles.

Isla loves roses and purple, so I went to four florists in search of purple roses. Since I'm a selective purist, I wanted *real* purple roses, not white ones that had been dyed. Apparently, they're hard to come by because they're a hybrid of naturally occurring rose colors. Who knew? The florist informed me that purple roses are symbolic of enchantment, rapture, majesty, and love at first sight. While I wasn't in love with Isla when we first met—because she was five—we connected immediately. When I learned the meaning behind them, I bought out the store, which sadly only amounted to three dozen beautiful roses for my Isla Rose.

My next stop was the pharmacy. The rogue rubber I found in my nightstand last night must've been left over from my time with Nadia. When I looked at the wrapper this morning, I noticed the expiration date was over a year ago. Clearly, it's been a long time since I needed condoms. Good thing we didn't go all the way.

Tonight, I'm well prepared. I bought a variety pack of ribbed, ultra-thin, and studded. Whatever the fuck that means. Thankfully, Sawyer was the pharmacist behind the counter instead of Maura. He didn't blink an eye at the three variations of lube, or the massage oils I plopped on the counter.

Lastly, I swung by a jewelry store and stared at amethysts for an hour before settling on earrings and a necklace. I imagine most women aren't given gifts after their first time, but I'm not like most men. Isla, herself, is a gift—one I'm not worthy of receiving—so if she's choosing to share herself with me, I'm going to make damn sure I show my appreciation.

My phone buzzes with a text.

Isla: Just got home . . . but W & L are still here. I'll come over when they leave.

A shiver of excitement runs down my spine.

Me: I'm ready for you.

Isla: Likewise. And it's been that way for YEARS.

My cock stirs. *This is it.* I can't believe I'll finally get to hold her in my arms and make love to her. In my mind, I've indulged in the fantasy for half a decade already. I hope I live up to her expectations. Beyond that, I hope I don't hurt her. I've never slept with a virgin, so I investigated that after my recipe search. Hence the surplus of lube. I've always considered myself average to slightly above, by no means huge, but it's not the first time a woman has called me girthy. I hope I'm not too much for Isla.

After I shower, shave, and dress for dinner, I compile a playlist of songs that remind me of her. I strategically add a few of my own. Leaving a vase of roses as the centerpiece for our meal, I deposit two dozen in my bedroom, scattering some petals around the room. I light a few candles in the kitchen before proceeding to pace my living room. *I'm not nervous. I'm not nervous. I'm not—*

My doorbell rings. *God, I'm nervous as fuck.* "It's open," I call out, tripping over my own two feet.

The front door swings open, and Wes enters the foyer.

Fuck. Wrong Emerson.

At this point, I can't do anything about the flowers and candles in the kitchen. Thanking sweet baby Jesus I decided not to scatter rose petals all over the house like I originally planned, I force a neutral tone. "Hey, man."

"Hey. Got a minute? I need to talk to you about something."

Double fuck.

"Sure, what's up?"

He plops onto the couch with a heavy sigh. "Did ya ever think you knew someone, only to find out you had it all wrong? That they kept something from you for years and you were too blind to see what was right under your nose?"

He knows. My insides shrivel. "What do you mean?"

"My sister." He rubs a hand over his face. "Isla sorta kinda came out to me today. Maybe. Possibly."

"Huh?"

I must look as dumbfounded as I feel because he laughs. "I know. I had absolutely no idea."

"When you say came out—"

"I think she likes women, mate."

I laugh hysterically. It's not that I find homosexuality amusing—because I don't. I'm one hundred percent an ally and respect everyone. The laughter is a natural response to the realization Wes isn't about to feed me my balls or slaughter me.

"Jake, I'm serious."

"Dude, what are you talking about?"

"I think she's in love with Dana."

"Who the fuck is Dana?"

"Cora's sister. The blonde. You've met her." He shakes his head. "All these years, I assumed Isla was boy crazy. Turns out, it's possible I was wrong. It bothers me."

I force a straight face and even tone. "That she's possibly not heterosexual?"

"No, mate. You know I'm totally cool with everyone. I'm upset she didn't tell me." He looks at his hands. "I've always considered us to be close."

"Maybe she just figured it out?" I offer.

"I dunno."

"Since you don't know for certain, maybe you shouldn't make assumptions about her preferences." I want to ask what they were discussing when the topic came up, but I'll save that question for Isla.

Pain flashes in his gaze. "Yeah, but why didn't she tell me sooner?"

Because her love life is none of your business? I straighten. "Maybe she was afraid of your reaction?"

"Why would she be afraid of me, mate? She knows I adore her—I'd die or kill for her in an instant."

"Not for nothing, but you have hotheaded tendencies and fly off the handle at times. Maybe your ferocity over her is the very reason Isla didn't say something sooner." I pat his shoulder. "Think about it. Maybe your approval means so much to her, she'd rather keep something from you than risk disappointing you."

"All I want is for her to be happy and safe," Wes meets my gaze, "and honest with me. I never want her to be afraid to come to me—no matter what she thinks my reaction might be."

Guilt pierces my heart and weaves through my ribs, squeezing my lungs. *Tell him.*

"Wes, I . . . uh . . ." I clear my throat. "You're one of my best friends—"

My cell cuts me off with an incoming call. Austin's name appears on the screen.

Wes points to my phone. "Don't tell Memphis what I just told you."

"I won't, but I've been playing phone tag with him all day, so I need to answer this."

Wes nods. "Do whatcha gotta do."

"Hello?"

"Hey, man. You're mighty hard to reach. How's it goin'?" Austin drawls.

"I'm good. Wes is here."

"Tell him he owes me fifty bucks. The Titans kicked Pittsburgh's ass."

I chuckle and glance at Wes. "You owe him money."

Wes gives me the finger. "That's what I think of his bet."

Austin laughs. "Lemme guess, sore loser over there has a nice gesture for me?"

"You got it, Memphis. What did you want to talk to me about?"

"Did Dave call you about the charity concert?"

"What charity concert?" I glance at my phone, surprised to see our shared manager's name in the notifications. "Actually, I have a missed call from him. I never heard it ring."

"They're putting together a Valentine's charity concert for the heart association. They want you and me to headline it."

"Oh? When's this happening? And where?"

"Valentine's Day. I think he said Radio City Music Hall. I figured we could raise some money *and* celebrate your birthday."

"I'm down if you are." I do some quick math in my head. "But it's kinda short notice to throw a concert together, don't you think?"

"Yeah, but between the two of us, we can make it happen. Dave thinks it'll sell out right away."

"What kind of show?"

"Dude, it's Valentine's Day. Fuckin' love songs."

I snort. "Got plenty of those."

"I know, me too. Dave said we've got free rein. We can do whatever the fuck we want. Only catch is that we don't get paid and we have to promote the charity."

"I'm fine with that."

"Also, it will be a live televised special." He grunts. "Not sure how you feel about those."

"It's no different than a live show for me. But I'm curious. Why don't they just tape it?"

"Because they wanna flash the organization's number on the screen and get people to call in and shit."

I nod. "Makes sense."

"So, what do you say, man? You feel like spendin' your birthday with my sorry ass?"

"I'm in if you are. It's not something I'd want to do alone. Besides, your name is the one that'll draw in the scores of screaming women."

While we're both singer-songwriters, our music styles are vastly differ-ent. Austin appeals to the younger crowd with his pop-soul hits. He's a wiz-ard with every guitar known to man, whereas the piano is my instrument of choice. I have a big voice and love my music orchestral. Between the two of us, we can draw a diverse crowd. Plus, it will give us a chance to perform some of our collaborations.

Austin laughs. "Dude, your women scream too. Usually when they can't find their readin' glasses or dentures, or struggle solvin' a crossword puzzle—but they scream."

I snort. "Ha. Ha. Ha. Aren't you hilarious? Lemme go, asshole."

"Later, man." Austin hangs up.

"What was that about?" Wes asks.

"Memphis wants me to do a Valentine's Day benefit concert with him."

"On your actual birthday?"

"Yep."

A knock sounds on my front door. *Isla.* Once again, my innards shrivel.

"Hello?" Lena calls. "I'm looking for a big behemoth who wandered in this direction. Have you seen him?"

I chuckle. "Got your sasquatch in here, Lena-Bean."

Wes snorts. "Yeah, but I'm less hairy."

Lena enters the room. "Thank fuck for that." She gives me a quick hug and points to Wes. "Let's go. I'm starving."

Wes climbs to his feet and claps my shoulder. "Later, mate. Thanks for the chat." He takes a deep breath. "Smells good in here. Are ya burning candles?"

"It's part of the new mellow Jake."

Wes barks a laugh. "That's a good one. Mellow Jake. There's nothing relaxed about you, mate."

"Uh, hence the candles. Hopefully, some serenity garden scent will chill my shit out." I laugh and shake my head.

"Wouldn't count on it. You'd better get yourself a flower or two, mate. Plant a garden. Smell some roses. Maybe that'll help."

I feel the wicked grin transform my face. "I do love roses."

CHAPTER 30

Isla

Internal playlist: "A.D.I.D.A.S. (All Day I)" by Ro James

My skin is smooth and fragrant, so now I need to figure out what I'm wearing. *Not that I'll be wearing it for long.* My insides flutter and heat. Despite being stuck with my brother, I've been aroused all day. I can't believe sex is finally happening for me.

With my Jake.

I hope I don't disappoint him. After Wes went over there, I asked Lena for some tips and pointers. When I mentioned Jake is well endowed, she informed me she has plenty of experience acclimating to a man of tremendous size. While she was careful to leave out any mention of my brother, it didn't take rocket science to figure out who she meant. *Gross.* She told me it *will* hurt the first time, but foreplay and lube are my friends. Hopefully, Jake has some.

I slip into a royal blue maxi dress. With its ruching on the bodice and buttons all the way down the front, it's one of my favorite designs. I layer a white cardigan over the top, then finish the look with silver flats. After my hair is to my liking, and I've applied one coat of mascara, I text Jake.

Me: I'm coming over.

Dana: Front door's unlocked.

Shivering with anticipation, I snatch my keys, phone, the overnight bag

I packed, and make my way outside. A bitter wind gusts up my dress, freezing my legs and arse. I cross the street and scamper up to Jake's front door.

A delicious aroma greets my nostrils in the foyer. Despite the lack of color, his home is warm and inviting—like him.

"Hello?" I lock the front door behind me.

Jake's voice drifts from the kitchen. "In here."

With a steadying breath, I shove my shaking hands into the pockets of my dress. I always put pockets on the clothes I design because I hate not having them.

I step through the kitchen archway. "Hello, handsome."

Jake spins around, and I lose my breath. He's gorgeous in dark dress pants and a crisp, white, collared shirt. He's rolled both sleeves to his forearms and left the first few buttons undone. Dark hair peeks out from beneath, and I already know how sexy his chiseled torso is. He changed up his usual stubbled jawline with a clean-shaven one, for which my sensitive skin is grateful. With tousled chestnut waves falling in his face, his hair is the perfect mixture of haphazard and sexy.

"Hello, gorgeous," he says with a smile that reaches the corners of his eyes. The warm chocolate depths unravel me, like always. "I've missed you today." He holds his arms out in invitation.

Crossing the room, I melt into his hug and wrap my arms around his waist. "I've missed you more."

"I highly doubt that." Jake tilts my chin up and peers into my eyes. "You look beautiful."

"Thank you. I made this dress."

His gaze sweeps the length of my body. "Lotta buttons there."

I flutter my lashes. "Maybe I want to watch you unbutton them."

Jake's breath leaves him in a rush. "Dinner first. Then I'll make that happen." His gravelly tone sends a flood of heat between my thighs.

"Kiss me."

"Honey, if I start kissing you now, we'll never make it to dinner." He pecks my forehead. "That's all I can manage without stripping your clothes off."

I chuckle. "Who said I feel like having dinner?"

He flashes a wicked grin. "You don't have a choice."

"Oh, really?"

"Yes, really." He hands me a piña colada wine cooler. "Operation wine/dine/deflower wouldn't be complete without dining."

I laugh. "You named our evening?"

"Sure did. But, for the record, *deflower* was your terminology—not mine. Although it's a bit patriarchal for my tastes, it works for the theme, so I went with it." He points to the bottle I'm holding with a sheepish smile. "There's your wine—if you can call it that. I may or may not have purchased nonalcoholic coolers."

"That's fine, Jacob." While I don't need or want a lupus reminder, I appreciate that he's being sweet while still keeping my health a priority. "The virgin ones taste just as good."

He steps closer, a carnal gleam in his eyes. "Oh, I bet they do."

Heat blooms on my face and neck. "I meant—"

"I know what you meant, but I plan to sample all things virgin this evening." He licks his lips. "And as for dining, I made coconut-mango shrimp risotto. I think you'll like it. I impressed myself, actually."

"You literally combined my favorite foods into one dish."

He smiles. "I know. Wait until you see what I have for dessert."

"Jacob, are you trying to romance your way into my pants?"

"Take out the trying part." Eyes darkening, he hands me a gorgeous purple rose. "Here's your flower in exchange for the one you're sharing with me tonight, Isla Rose."

Everything inside me catches fire. I've never wanted him more than I do right now. Any trace of trepidation flies out the window. I need him inside me, filling and stretching me, more than I need the air in my lungs.

"Let's skip dinner."

Jake smirks at my breathless request. "I've waited over half a decade for you. You've waited even longer. We're not rushing this."

"But I want you."

"I want you more." He grips my shoulders. "But we're doing this the right way. I want to give you a night worth waiting for."

"Jake, you didn't need to go to these lengths for me. I don't need extravagance to make my first time memorable. It's happening with you, and that's all that matters."

"Sweetheart, I'd go to any length for you. This is hardly extravagance—it's the way you deserve to be treated." He rakes a hand through his hair. "I wish you were my first, Isla. I can't go back in time, but I can make sure you know exactly what you mean to me."

I grip the sides of his face and kiss him. He groans and tightens his arms around me. Our lips and tongues dance. Threading his hands in my hair, Jake deepens our kiss for a moment before breaking it off.

"We have to stop." He leads me to a stool at the island. "Dinner's ready."

All I can manage is a nod. Jake fills our plates while I admire the floral arrangement.

"I've never seen a purple rose."

He grins. "Had a helluva time finding you those hybrid flowers, honey."

"Everything's perfect. You're officially the wizard of date nights."

He sets my plate in front of me with a chuckle. "Hopefully, you'll enjoy my bedroom wizardry."

I gnaw my lip. "I hope I can handle your . . . wand."

He settles on the stool beside me and squeezes my knee. "You will. We'll go slowly."

I take a mouthful of risotto instead of answering. The throb between my legs intensifies with each passing moment.

"This is delicious, Jacob. Thank you."

"Glad you like it. Did you know shrimp has anti-inflammatory properties?"

I smile. "Yes, but I'm surprised you do."

"I researched some things today. I've got several recipes tucked away so I can make dinner for you more often."

Overwhelmed by the care he put into our evening, my eyes water. "I love you."

"Love you more. Now eat up, so I can ravage you."

We devour our meal, and Jake clears the plates. My body sizzles with lust, making me shift position. I'm already wet, which surprises me, given my lupus.

He blows out the candles and turns to face me. "Are you sure you want to do this?"

"Yes."

"Wait here for a moment. I'll be right back." He jogs toward the stairs and takes them two at a time. I listen to his footsteps overhead while twirling a piece of my hair.

He returns after a few minutes and takes my hand. "Come with me, honey."

Jake leads me upstairs. My breath catches when we enter his bedroom. Lit candles cast a flickering glow on his gray walls. A bouquet of purple roses rests on his nightstand and he scattered rose petals in a trail leading to his bed. He replaced his gray comforter with a luxe plum-colored one. More petals litter his bed. Soft music plays in the background, his velvety voice reaching my ears.

He closes the door behind us and squeezes my hand. "You all right?"

"Yes."

Jake cradles my face in his hands. "Look into my eyes and promise you'll tell me to stop if it's too much."

"I will."

"I mean it, Isla. You're in control."

"Have you ever been with a virgin?" I whisper.

"No, but I know how to please a woman. I'll make sure your body is ready to take me. Tonight, I'm going to make you come so many times, you won't remember you're a virgin once we get there."

My breath rushes out of me.

A wicked grin curves his lips. "You're mine, sweetheart." He reaches for the top button of my dress and pops it open. "Every. Single. Inch." He punctuates each word with an opened button. He works his way down the bodice, fingertips brushing against my skin. Pausing at my belly ring, his eyes flare with heat. "This is so fucking sexy."

"Glad you think—"

Jake sinks to his knees in front of me, his fingertips toying with the waistband of my panties. "I'm sorry, were you saying something?"

"Holy fuck," I whisper.

He continues to free buttons from their moorings, grazing over my satin-covered clit as he moves lower. Finally, he reaches the last button. But instead of standing, he leans down and kisses my ankles. Peppering kisses on each calf, he works his way upward and lingers on my kneecaps, trailing his tongue in ways that make me forget my name.

"Turn around."

I obey his husky command and let my dress fall to the floor as I spin. He swirls his tongue behind my knees, eliciting my gasp. I realize why he told me to turn when I glimpse our reflection in the full-length mirror beside his dresser.

Jake flashes me a grin and slides his palms up the front of my thighs. Behind me, his mouth follows suit, pausing at the curve of my arse. Grabbing a fistful of each cheek, he rises to his full height. His lips find my neck. My head drops to the side to allow him access. He releases my arse and unhooks my bra. He nibbles my shoulders, then drags the straps to the sides and lets it land by my feet.

Lips never leaving my neck, Jake cups my breasts and pulls me back against him. I moan when he lightly pinches and rubs my nipples. He rolls his hips, pressing his cock into my back.

I meet his gaze in the mirror and wiggle my arse. "You staying clothed for this, Jacob?"

He nips my earlobe. "Be patient."

I reach behind me for his belt buckle. "Been doing that for five years."

"Tonight is about you." Jake shackles my wrists, stopping me. "Let me take my time." Releasing them, he turns me so our lips meet.

His plundering kiss unravels me.

I clasp the back of his neck and pull him closer. Our mouths meld, breaths and tongues mingling. He cradles my face like I'm treasured, like I mean as much to him as he does to me. A part of me can't believe I'm kissing Jake Bennett, the man I've loved for most of my life. The man who's going to make love to me for the first time.

The man I'm going to marry.

He leads me to the edge of his bed without breaking our kiss. I squeeze his arse cheeks. He groans and rolls his hips, so I do it again. He responds with a swat to my arse, sending a flare of heat through me. I moan into his mouth and squeeze his butt a third time.

Jake tugs his lips from mine and brings them to my ear. "I know what you're trying to do."

"And what's that?" I gasp.

"If you're looking for a spanking, it's not happening. Tonight, I'm going to make love to you." I give him a pouty lip, which makes him chuckle. "Don't worry, sweetheart," he licks the shell of my ear and yanks my hips up against him, "I'll toss you over my knee some other time."

CHAPTER 31

Isla

Internal playlist: "Lips on You" by Maroon 5

This is it. It's happening. My virginity will soon be a thing of the past. I lie on the bed, resting my head on Jake's pillows amid fragrant rose petals in shades of lavender and plum.

Jake smiles and slowly unbuttons his shirt, exposing the granite muscles beneath. As he slides it from his shoulders, he seems broader and taller than usual. Everything about him oozes with potency—a carnal strength I've never witnessed in him. My breath hitches as his hands move to unfasten his belt buckle. Eyes pinned to mine, he slides it from the loops. The length of leather hits the floor with a clunk. He unbuttons and sheds his pants, kicking them aside. All that remains are charcoal-colored boxer briefs slung low on his hips. My gaze lingers on the bulge they restrain. I'm ready to feel him thrust every hard, thick inch inside me.

Kneeling on the bed, he grips my ankles and lifts them to his lips. As he licks and kisses his way up each leg, he hums the melody for "Crave." Every nerve ending sizzles with his touch, stoking me hotter, making me wetter than I believed possible. When he reaches my upper thighs, he lowers my legs to the bed and—continuing his inward kissing quest—turns his attention to my wrists. His tongue travels up each arm to find my throat. He moves to my breasts. Wet heat surrounds my left nipple, and he gives me a hard suck.

"Oh, Jake." I gasp, clutching the comforter. "That feels good."

He licks and teases both nipples until my moans come freely. Nibbling a path down my abdomen, he pauses at the waistband of my undies. My legs tremble with the anticipation of him touching me below my waist . . . kissing me *there*. God, I hope my body doesn't disappoint him.

"This is what I had in mind when I wrote 'Crave.'" Using his teeth, he slides my undies down over my hips. I lift them to assist, and he drags the satin thong to my ankles before removing and holding it up. "You're not getting these back." He wads them in a ball, then stuffs them into his nightstand drawer.

My breath catches as Jake takes a moment to look me over. "You're exquisite, Isla. Fucking perfect." He leans forward and kisses the surgical scar on my abdomen. "Everything about you is perfect," he whispers, his lips moving lower. He nudges my shaking legs apart, his fingertips feathering over my inner thighs. "You okay?"

"I . . . uh. It's just that . . . no one's ever—"

"No one's ever kissed you here."

Nodding, I force a swallow. "I'm a little nervous." I chew my lip and look away. "I don't want to gross you out."

"Look at me." He waits for me to meet his gaze. "This is something I enjoy doing." He brushes his lips on the skin below my navel. "Relax and let me love you." Settling on his elbows, he kisses up each inner thigh, pausing at my center. His hot breath gusts over my pussy. "Open your legs wide for me, honey." I slightly part my trembling limbs. Jake grips my knees, spreading them wider apart. "I want you like this when I taste you."

He brushes the tip of his nose along the crease of my thigh and groans. His hands slide beneath me, palming the cheeks of my arse. Pulling me to him, he puts his mouth on me.

"Oh, God, Jake." I throw my head back.

He swipes his tongue through my opening and growls low in his chest. "Put your legs over my shoulders."

I obey his command. He licks up and down the center of me with long, dragging strokes of his tongue. He swirls it on my clit. My hips jerk, thighs automatically clenching together. "Oh, fuck."

Jake nudges them open once more. "Spread wide for me." He spears his tongue inside me, alternating thrusts and flicks with swirling licks and flutters. "You taste like fucking heaven."

Moans rip from my throat. "Jake, oh yes . . ." My hips jerk in his hold as he brings me higher and higher. He surrounds my clit with gentle suction. "Oh, fuck—" I tug on his hair. "You're gonna make me come."

His pace doesn't falter, but it's the tiny tongue flicks he adds in that take me over the edge. Back arching, I wail his name as I climax.

He backs off my clit but doesn't stop licking me. Sliding a hand from beneath me, he slowly slips a finger inside my pussy. He moves in and out gently, rubbing me inside, making me whimper and thrash. "Oh, Jake, that feels amazing . . ."

Jake's tongue finds my clit once more and rapidly flicks. I climax almost immediately. He seizes the opportunity to add a second finger. He moves them inside me, stroking places no one's ever touched. Lifting his head, he meets my gaze. "You okay?"

I nod.

"Is this too much?"

"No, it feels good."

Jake turns his focus to his hand, watching his fingers thrust in and out of me. "This will be me soon, honey. Do you feel ready?"

My hips press into his touch. "I want you *now*, Jake."

He smiles and lowers his mouth to me once more. The combination of his tongue and fingers brings me unprecedented ecstasy. An orgasm builds deep inside. I've only ever had them with my clit. Jake keeps rubbing and thrusting his fingers, bringing me closer and closer.

"Please don't stop." He picks up the pace and I fall apart. As I climax, he sucks my clit, making me come even harder. Back bowing off the bed, my pussy spasms around his fingers. I ride the waves of my release with bucking hips while he continues licking and stroking me. "Jake, oh, God, I can't take any more." I push at his shoulders.

He lifts his head and flashes a wicked grin. "Now you're ready for *me*."

My entire body trembles with the aftershocks. I can't think or breathe, let alone speak. Jake presses himself up and sheds his boxers. His thick cock juts proudly, moisture beading at the tip. He leans over, pulling a condom and some lube out of his nightstand. Tearing the package open, he rolls it onto his cock.

I reach for his hand. "Wait."

Jake stills, his gaze darting to mine. "What's up?"

"Is that latex?"

"I dunno. Most condoms are . . . Why?"

"I have a bit of a latex allergy," I whimper.

"A *bit* of an allergy?" He blinks a few times and snatches the wrapper. "*Fuck.*" He takes a few breaths. "That information would've been helpful earlier," he mutters, dragging a hand over his face.

"I didn't think about it. I—"

"It's okay. I'll go to the store tomorrow." He flops onto his back and removes the condom, flinging it across the room.

"Jake, please make love to me," I whisper.

"Not without a condom. I won't jeopardize your health with a pregnancy."

"Please . . . I need you. You can pull out of me before you come."

Jake rolls toward me, indecision warring on his features. "Isla—"

"Please . . ." I cup his face. "Make love to me. Even if it's only for a minute. I need you."

He glances at his cock, then at me. Swallowing, he squeezes his eyes shut. "Okay. Let me wash off, so the latex I've touched doesn't irritate you." He scoots off the bed and disappears into the bathroom.

I listen to the running water and mentally chastise myself for forgetting about my allergy. Jake must think I'm a total airhead.

He reenters the bedroom and settles on the bed. Hands shaking, he squirts some lube in his palm and smooths it on himself. He adds some between my legs too. "You sure you're ready?"

"Yes." I tilt his chin to meet my gaze once more. "I love you, and I want this."

He nods, settling between my thighs. He rests his weight on his elbows and peers into my eyes. "Tell me to stop and I will." He lines up the head of his cock with my pussy. "You promise?"

"Yes," I whisper, wrapping my legs around him.

He kisses me for a moment—a slow, deep tangle of lips and tongues—then brings his mouth to my ear. "I love you." Rolling his hips, he presses the head of his cock inside me.

I clutch his back. He eases in a little farther. The bite of pain makes me whimper.

"Tell me to stop," he whispers at my neck.

"I don't want you to stop."

He rocks his hips, going deeper. I gasp and dig my nails into his back. He pulls back slightly, then presses forward once more. It's a slow torture with tendrils of pleasure hovering on the periphery.

"Go ahead, Jake."

"You sure? I don't wanna hurt you."

"Do it," I say on a gasp, gritting my teeth. "Now."

Jake pulls his hips back and braces his weight with one hand. The other grips my hip. With a deep breath, he surges forward. I cry out as he buries himself to the hilt, his cock filling and stretching me to my limit. Tears spring to my eyes, and I clamp my legs around the back of his thighs.

"You all right?"

"Don't move for a minute," I whimper, squeezing my eyes shut. "Just hold me."

"We can stop—"

"No." I cup his face. "Please go slow."

He nods and kisses me. "I love you."

"I love you, Jake Bennett." I cling to him. "Now, make love to me."

Jake

Mood: "Our First Time" by Bruno Mars

With my jaw tightly clenched, I slowly rock my hips, barely moving inside her. I've never had sex without a condom. I've never even considered it. Now that I've felt her with nothing between us, I don't know if I can go back.

"Isla." I groan at her neck. "You feel so good."

She doesn't answer, clinging to me tighter. Her wet, tight pussy holds me in a viselike grip while I ease in and out.

"You okay?"

"Yeah. But we need more lube."

I squeeze some on my cock without taking my eyes off her face. "You sure you want to keep going?" A tear rolls down her cheek and I freeze. "You're crying. I'm hurting you."

Isla tightens her arms and legs around me. "No. I'm just . . ." She takes a breath. "I've wanted you—wanted this—for so long."

"Me too." I brush the hair off her forehead.

"I'm so happy I waited for you."

My chest tightens. "Isla, you're everything to me." Her vivid blue orbs flutter closed when I roll my hips. Burying my face at her neck, I continue my slow, deliberate strokes while raining kisses on her throat and shoulders.

My balls tighten as I edge toward my orgasm. I'm close, damn close. I need to keep my head in the game so I can pull out in time.

A few more strokes and I'm there. Gripping the base of my cock, I quickly pull out and stroke myself to release, moaning Isla's name as I come.

I glance down and freeze. My cock is tinged red with the evidence of her first time. While I knew it was a possibility, the amount of blood on the sheets alarms me. I pin her with my gaze. "I told you to stop me if it hurt too much."

"I'm fine."

"Honey, I made you bleed. Like, a lot."

"Virgins bleed sometimes. Honestly, I'm good. It's probably because of the blood thinners."

She clearly needs a fucking dose adjustment.

I grip her chin, forcing her gaze to mine. "I'm sorry if I hurt you." I pull her into my arms.

She buries her head in my chest. "No, I'm sorry I ruined your sheets."

"You know I don't give a fuck about the sheets. It's you I'm worried about."

"I'm fine. Yeah, it hurt a little, but I'm better now."

"Why didn't you say something?"

"Because I didn't wanna ruin the mood or disappoint you."

"Look at me." Swimming in unshed tears, vivid blue eyes meet mine. "It felt incredible, and you did not disappoint me." I gently stroke her back, then tighten my arms around her and breathe in her scent. "I promise it will be better next time."

"Everything leading up to it was incredible." She lifts her head to look at me. "Mind blowing, actually."

I trace her cheek. "You like my filthy tongue?"

Her eyes flutter closed. "God, yes."

"Good. I'll do that to you all night long. I love the way you taste." I press a kiss to her lower lip. "Sweeter than sugar."

She turns a deeper shade of pink and averts her eyes.

"Oh, I don't think so, honey. No need to be shy with me. We're beyond that now. No more secrets between us. But we do need to discuss birth control. Are you on the pill?"

"No. I can't take hormones."

Right. Another morsel of information that would've been helpful earlier.

"Then I'll stock up on non-latex condoms. I can't believe you forgot to mention your allergy. I mean, seriously. What if I put you into anaphylactic shock, trying to have sex with you?"

I can't even imagine that conversation at the hospital. *So sorry to inform you, sir, but it looks like your girlfriend's allergic to your dick.*

"I don't get anaphylaxis. It's usually only a rash." She chews her lip. "Not telling you wasn't intentional. The topic of condoms hasn't come up until tonight."

"I know. I'm teasing you. How about we get cleaned up? I could go for a nice hot shower. Come with me." She sits up and winces. I touch her cheek. "You *sure* you're okay?"

Isla nods. "Yeah, I'm good. Just a little sore."

I rake a hand through my hair, hating that I'm a source of pain. "I'm sorry."

"Let's make a deal." She meets my gaze. "How about neither one of us apologizes for the rest of the night?"

"I'm on board with that." I help her out of bed and carry her to the bathroom.

"I can walk."

"Felt like carrying my woman." I set her down and turn the water on. After retrieving washcloths, we step inside. The hot stream does wonders for my achy muscles. I wet a cloth and gently press it between her legs.

She wraps her arms around my neck. "Thank you for being gentle and taking care of me."

"I'll always be that way with you."

She grips the sides of my face and stares into my eyes. "Thanks for being my first."

"Thank *you* for waiting for me." I kiss her lips softly. "And for the record, I plan on being your last. Your only."

CHAPTER 32

Jake

Mood: "Make It Rain" by Ed Sheeran

Isla settles on a stool at the kitchen island and winces—which happens every time she sits. I hate that I'm the cause. At the same time, when I see evidence that I've been inside her, it awakens some weird primal streak in me. The whole thing's a bit archaic, but I can't help it. I feel like a pacing alpha. Possessive. Dangerous. A man who will stop at nothing to protect his woman.

Her current threat is the pickle jar. She grits her teeth and twists but can't get it open. As the new and improved alpha Jake, I jump in and hero-ically save the day. Removing the lid, I hold out a dill spear like it's made of gold. I hate the damn things, but she likes them, so I'm keeping up my supply.

"Thanks, hon. My wrists feel swollen today."

"How's your ... uh ... undercarriage?"

She laughs. "Do I look like a Mercedes to you?"

"No way. You're in Ferrari territory, or maybe a Rolls Royce." I scratch my head. "Lamborghini."

"My undercarriage is tender, but I'll be fine in a couple of days." She crunches on her pickle. "Then ya can take me for another spin. Preferably a slow country drive, down a long winding lane."

I glance down at myself. My erect cock is pitching a tent in my pajama pants. "How is it that everything you say turns me on?"

She giggles. "Did I mention I can drive a stick shift?"

"Damn right, you can. On a serious note, how are you feeling? I was a little concerned when you bled like that."

She flushes. "Blood thinners, remember?"

Right. My scalp prickles at the reminder. "Yes, I remember."

"Plus, you have a huge donger," she points out, snagging another pickle.

Her statement makes me want to roar and pound my chest. Alpha Jake shit. "Thanks for the ego boost, but I really don't."

"Well, you felt huge." Her gaze burns into me. "And even though I'm sore, I kinda like it." Unable to speak, I blink a few times and raise a brow. She places her hands on my shoulders. "It felt like you claimed me as yours, which is all I've ever wanted."

"You *are* mine. Last night was a gift I'll cherish for the rest of my life. Every part of you is *mine*." The stallion inside me rears up. "And I can't fucking wait to make you mine over and over and over again."

Her pupils dilate. "This side of you is hot, Jacob."

"You bring out the best in me, honey." I grin and kiss her. "So, what's our game plan for today? Did you make me a list of places you want to see in the city?"

"Yes, actually. There're quite a few—"

My cell rings. "Hold that thought," I say, retrieving it from the counter. It's an unknown number, but I answer it anyway. "Hello?"

"She's gone."

I clench the phone. "Huh?"

"Hannah—" Jesse's voice breaks on a sob. "She . . . she died this morning."

Tears spring from my eyes before he finishes speaking. "I'll be right there." I hang up the phone and sink to a stool, burying my face in my hands.

"What's wrong?"

"That was Jesse—" I can't finish my sentence from beneath the suffocating blanket of grief his words draped over me.

Isla wraps her arms around me. "I'm so sorry." I rest my head on her chest. She gently strokes my hair while my tears drench her shirt. "Go get dressed and be with your friend. Since you didn't have breakfast, and I'm sure Jesse hasn't eaten, I'll make sandwiches for you to take."

Nodding, I climb to my feet and head upstairs to change. I can't believe this is happening. Jesse's voice is on a continuous loop in my head, breaking my heart with each pass.

CHAPTER 33

Isla

Internal playlist: "Spectrum" by Florence + The Machine

My heart aches for Jake. I can't fathom Jesse's pain. Fucking *breast cancer*. First Cora's mum, and now, Hannah.

Jake comes back downstairs with red-rimmed eyes and tear-stained cheeks. I hand him the bag with the sangas I made and a travel mug of coffee.

He gives me a weak smile. "Thank you. I'm sorry, but we'll have to do your city tour some other time. I'm not sure when I'll be home."

"Go be with Jesse. If you need me, you know where to find me."

Jake wraps me in a bone-crushing hug. "I love you so much."

"Love you too." I kiss his cheek. "I'm gonna wash your bedding and then I'll let myself out."

"That reminds me." He retrieves a key from on top of his fridge. "I want you to have this."

"I'll have one made for you."

"Wes gave me one already," he reveals with a smirk. "You know, just in case."

"Oh, did he? I bet he wasn't counting on you tinkering with my undercarriage."

He gives me a watery laugh. "Thanks, Sprite. I needed that."

"Anytime. Please give my condolences to Jesse."

"Will do." He plants a quick kiss on my lips and heads out the door.

"So," Lena edges closer to me on the couch and lowers her voice to a whisper, "the suspense is killing me. Did you?"

Flushing, I nod. "We did."

Her jade eyes flash with intrigue. "And?"

I crane my neck to make sure Wes is still in the kitchen. His muffled voice reaches my ears. He's been on a conference call with his lawyer and Reed for over an hour, trying to sort through last month's contract breach.

Satisfied he's occupied for the time being, I turn my focus to Lena. "It hurt like a bitch."

"You kinda expected that, though. Right?"

"Yeah, but I bled a lot more than I thought I would." I chew my lip. "It upset him."

"That's not surprising. He's a gentleman." She tilts her head to the side. "When you told me your med list for Marc, you mentioned being on blood thinners, right?"

"Yeah. I used injectable meds when I first had the transplant, but they've got me on warfarin now. It's been around forever and has the most data in kidney patients, so my doctor feels most comfortable with that. Even though it's a pain in the arse." I frown, thinking of my frequent lab tests. "While taking tablets is certainly more convenient, he tends to fuck around with my dose. Honestly, I may consider going back on the injections, just so I don't have to get my INR checked all the time. No sense making a zillion trips to the lab—in an unfamiliar city—when I don't have a car."

"Good point. Were you able to give yourself the injections or did your parents have to help?"

"Mum and Dad did them for a bit, but I took over once I got the hang of it. I mean, it's not ideal, but clearly something's fucked with my warfarin dose."

"We need to make sure we find you some doctors in the area so they can properly monitor you. I know a few nephrologists, but I'll have to ask around to see who they recommend for rheumatology. There's a lupus specialist in Manhattan, but she's booked pretty far ahead. Maybe I can call in another favor. Marc knows everyone. At the very least, I'm sure he can get you some baseline bloodwork to switch you over to a low molecular weight heparin if that's what you wanna do."

"Yeah, I think so. The last thing I need's internal bleeding, and I don't have the time or energy for blood draws. I still can't believe your ex helped with my meds. Being Wes's sister and all."

She smiles. "I can. He's a good guy at heart. Just wrong for me."

"Has Wes met him?"

"Nope."

"That's good. He'd probably act like a dick instead of thanking the bloke for helping me out."

"Yeah, probably." She touches my arm. "But keep in mind, Wes doesn't know about your luggage snafu—or that you stayed with Jake. Anyway, enough about your brother. Tell me more about your night."

"Lena, he was so—"

"Are we doing the Statue of Liberty today, or would ya rather hit Rockefeller Center?" Wes's booming voice makes me jump. His long legs eat the distance across the room. "It's your call." He glances at his watch, then ruffles my hair with one of his enormous paws. "But we should probably get moving so we can hit everything on your list."

"While I'd love to see the statue, my knees hurt, so I don't think all those stairs are a good idea." Actually, everything hurts—and I desperately need a nap—but I'm not about to bail on my New York City tour.

"We could always ride the lift," he suggests. "You've been wanting to see the view since you got here."

"The elevators only go to the base of the statue, Wes," Lena corrects him. "If she wants to make it to the crown, there's a shitload of stairs. My middle school field trip was there, and I remember the spiral staircases being really narrow," she curls her lip, "and brutal on the thighs."

Wes chuckles. "You hated squats then, too, huh?"

"Fuck squats." She turns to me. "Why don't we check out Top of the Rock. It's the observation deck at Rockefeller Center. The views are stunning, and they have elevators."

"Yeah, let's do that." I nudge Wes. "Are you *sure* you wanna come?"

My brother narrows his eyes on my face. "Why wouldn't I?"

"Well, people will probably mob you—especially without Paul here."

The bodyguard Wes uses for events is still in Los Angeles, but Wes told me he has plans to move to New York.

Wes rubs his jaw. "I'm gonna try to blend in."

Lena snorts. "Good luck with that one, Ace." She straightens. "Isla has a good point. With the big Christmas tree up and everything, it's a zoo over there. Maybe she and I should venture out alone."

His face falls. "I get the feeling I'm not wanted."

"No. The problem is too many people want you," I say with a laugh. "Besides, I need girl time with Lena."

"For the record, she was mine first."

Lena wraps her arms around his waist. "I'll always be yours, Ace. Why don't you see what Garrett's up to?"

Wes nods. "Lemme hang the blinds for Imp. Then I'll leave you two alone. Where're your tools?"

I shake my head. "I don't have any tools."

"Whaddya mean, you don't have tools?"

"I mean, I don't have tools."

"I guess today's mission is tool shopping, then." He peers out the front window. "Shit. Where's Bennett when ya need him?"

"Have you talked to him today?" I ask cautiously. It hadn't occurred to me that Wes and Lena may not know about Jesse's wife. Regardless of whether Jake chose to tell them, he needs their support now.

"No. Why?"

"His mate's wife died this morning."

Wes's breath leaves him in a rush. "Fuck. Hannah was a sweet girl. Jesse must be devastated."

"Jake's not home. He went to the hospital to be with Jesse. When I saw him outside earlier, he seemed pretty upset."

"He's known them for a long time. Went to primary school with Jesse and Hannah."

"Like I said, he'd been crying, so you may wanna reach out."

Wes nods. "I'll call him tonight."

"I wonder when the services will be," Lena says.

"If Jake mentions anything, please let me know. I'd like to pay my respects," I say, even though I'm sure Jake will tell me before he tells Wes.

"I'll keep ya in the loop, Imp."

My phone rings. Dana flashes on the screen as I pick it up. "Excuse me a moment," I say to Wes and Lena before answering. "Hello?"

"I needed to hear your voice," Jake murmurs.

I make my way into the living room. "Are you okay?"

"Not really."

"Is there anything I can do?"

"Love me." He sighs heavily. "Please, always love me."

CHAPTER 34

Isla

Internal playlist: "Let It Be Me" by Ray LaMontagne

Jake hasn't been home in almost a week. He told me Jesse's falling apart, and he's afraid to leave him alone. I found out Hannah's favorite color was blue, so I crocheted a blanket for Jesse. I used several shades of indigo and cobalt with the ocean as my muse. Maybe it will give him comfort. The viewing for Hannah is tonight, so I'm riding over with Wes and Lena to pay our respects.

Lena took me to every place on my list this week. From the botanical gardens, to Broadway, to Central Park. We had a blast hanging out. After years of feeling isolated from my mates back home, I've finally connected with someone who gets me. Someone who understands my illness from a medical standpoint, and who has some fucking empathy. Wes is out of his mind if he doesn't marry that woman.

Sure, I've been busy, but I miss Jake—his hugs, his laugh, the way he looks at me. I miss everything about him.

My phone buzzes with Lena's text alerting me they've arrived, so I make my way outside. Hopping into the back seat of her car, I settle in for the ride to Manhattan. Wes spends most of the trip on the phone with his upcoming film's director, so I stare out the window.

We reach the funeral home in forty-five minutes. Wes is still finishing up his phone call, so he tells Lena and me to head inside. The line of people is out the door. Hannah clearly touched many lives in her thirty-three years on earth. We enter the waiting area and sign the guest book. It's a slow process, but we finally make it to the main viewing room. I breathe a sigh of relief that it's a closed casket.

I spot Jake in the front row, seated beside a man I assume is Jesse, their backs to us. He's got his arm wrapped around his friend's shaking shoulders in an effort to console him.

Jake sees Lena first and waves. When he makes eye contact with me, the emotion in his gaze takes my breath away. He leans in and says something to Jesse.

Lena and I kneel at the casket and say a quick prayer before rising. In my periphery, I notice Wes scanning the room as he approaches. Spotting Lena, he motions for us to wait for him in an empty row of chairs. Jake rises, turning to face us.

Jesse slowly climbs to his feet and stands beside him. My first impression is that he looks *exactly* like Reed. They share the same cropped chestnut hair, olive skin, whiskey eyes, and muscular build. Dressed in a black suit and tie, Jesse is the definition of tall, dark, and handsome.

Lena greets Jake and hugs him.

"Hi, Lena-Bean. Thanks for coming. Jess, this is Lena, Wes's girlfriend."

Lena clasps Jesse's hand. "I'm so sorry for your loss."

"Thank you." His deep voice resonates with a sadness that breaks my heart in two.

Jake turns and hugs me. "I miss you, sweetheart," he says in my ear. Releasing me, he looks at Jesse. "This is Isla."

"I've heard a lot about you, Isla."

"Likewise, Jesse." I hug him tightly. "My deepest condolences to you and your family."

"Thank you," he whispers, hugging me back.

I hand him the folded blanket. "Jake mentioned your wife's favorite color was blue, so I made this for you. Maybe it'll give you some comfort."

He clutches it to his chest. Clenching his jaw, Jesse blinks rapidly to hold back tears. It doesn't work. They slide down his cheeks as he hugs me once more. "You're an angel, Isla. Thank you." I kiss his cheek and squeeze Jake's hand before following Lena to the row of chairs.

I nudge her. "In case you're wondering what Reed looks like, Jesse is the spitting image of him."

"Really? I expected him to look like you and Wes."

"Nope. He may as well be Jesse's twin. If I didn't know better, I'd swear my brother was here."

"Wow, that's uncanny." She tilts her head toward where Jesse's standing. "You really knitted that for him?"

I nod. "Crocheted, but yeah. It's my hobby."

"That's incredibly sweet of you."

"Jake's told me so much about Jesse, I feel like I already know him. I wanted to do something to ease his pain."

Wes reaches the front and greets Jake and Jesse, hugging them both. Soon enough, it's time for us to leave.

On our way out the door, Jake gives me a lingering stare. The kind of look where if we had thought balloons, they'd be as big as swimming pools, filled with everything that's on our minds. I know some sign language from my primary school days, so I discreetly make a heart shape with my hands, then sign, "I love you." He smiles and does it back.

We reach Lena's car and settle into our seats.

"Well, that was bloody heartbreaking," Wes says on a sigh.

"Wes, how come you never told me Jesse looks like Reed?" I ask.

"He really does, right?" He shakes his head. "Almost felt like I was hugging our brother." He rubs his jaw and stares out the window for a moment before speaking. "There were a lot of people there. Not that I'm surprised. Hannah was incredibly sweet. I feel so fucking bad for Jesse."

"Jake's car hasn't been outside at all this week," I announce.

"Yeah, he's been staying at Jesse's," Wes says. "They've always been like brothers. This loss is hitting Bennett hard." He looks over his shoulder at me. "Did you make that blanket for Jesse? It looked like your handiwork."

Shit. I'd stuffed it in my purse on the ride over so he wouldn't notice. "Um, yeah. I texted Jake to see if he wanted me to bring his mail inside."

"What does that have to do with a blanket?"

"He asked me to keep an eye out for something from the Cancer Society. I guess he's making a huge donation in Hannah's memory. Anyway, I felt like doing something nice for Jesse too."

Thinking on my feet is not my forte. Neither is lying—especially to my brother. Guilt churns my stomach.

"Mum and Dad raised you right, Imp. You truly have a heart of gold."

CHAPTER 35

Jake

Mood: Time is a double-edged sword.

The crowd is finally winding down. Jesse's sister is staying with him tonight, so I can head home. It feels like I haven't been there in months. It's no exaggeration to call this the most emotionally draining week of my life. Tomorrow's Hannah's funeral. Jesse is broken. Completely devastated. It guts me to see him like this, and I'd give anything to ease his pain.

I hand him a bottle of water. "Don't let yourself get dehydrated, man."

"You sound like Hannah. She always forced water on me." Jesse squeezes his eyes shut, but fresh tears escape from beneath his lashes. "Why the fuck do I have to talk about her in past tense? How do I go on? How do I keep living when everything reminds me of her?"

"I wish I had something helpful to say, but I don't have the answer to that."

"I think I'm going to sell our house and move Upstate."

I wrap an arm over his shoulders. "Don't make any decisions right now. Give yourself time."

"Don't you get it, Jake? Time is *all* I have left. Seconds, minutes, hours," he knots his hands in his hair, "days, weeks, months, years—a fucking eternity without her." A sob rips from his chest. "I can't live the rest of my life in a house where every room is infused with her."

Hannah was an interior designer, so his statement holds heart-wrenching truth. She *is* present in every detail—from stenciled walls to light fixtures to the color of the paint. No room in that house lacks Hannah's touch, which means Jesse has no escape from his grief.

"You know you're always welcome to stay with me." I grip his shoulders. "I mean that, Jess. If you need me, I'm here."

"I may take you up on that once Maggie flies back to Seattle tomorrow." He wipes his eyes and whispers, "I'm afraid to be alone."

"You have a key. The guest room is yours, my friend, for however long you need it. All I ask is if my bedroom door's closed, knock first."

That forces a crooked smirk from him. "I definitely wouldn't wanna interrupt anything with Isla. Or see your hairy ass."

"While my five o'clock shadow shows up at noon, my ass isn't as hairy as you'd think."

"I'll take your word for it." He points to the blanket Isla made. "I can't believe she did that for me."

"I can. She's a sweetheart. Always has been—even as a kid." I hold up my scarf. "She made this too."

"Hold on to her, man."

"I will."

"I mean it. Never, ever let go of her." He grits his teeth. "Breathe her in and let her reach your soul. Don't hold back. Love her with everything you've got. But most of all, savor every fucking moment. Because you never know when or how she'll be taken from you." A tear rolls down his cheek. "In my experience, life always takes the ones you love most."

I peer into the haunted eyes of my best friend as he speaks a sobering truth. I open and close my mouth a few times, but I have no words for him. He lost his parents in a car crash at ten, and at thirty-three, his beloved wife to breast cancer. His sister Maggie is all he has left. And me. Fortunately for him, Jake Bennett is *always* there when it matters.

"Tomorrow afternoon, you're coming back to my place after the funeral. I'll order takeout. We can drink beer and watch the game. You're staying with me for the foreseeable future."

"But you have—"

I hold a hand up. "This is nonnegotiable, Jess."

"Thanks. I don't know where I'd be without you."

Hours later, I kick my shoes off in the foyer, smoothing the doormat with my foot. My home still smells like roses from my dinner with Isla last week. I make my way into the kitchen. On the island, the wilted flowers hang in a vase of cloudy water, but that's literally the only thing out of place. All the pots and pans are gone. Opening a cabinet, I discover Isla washed and put everything away—exactly where it belongs. My cookware, cutlery, and dishes are meticulously arranged like everything else in my home. Seeing how she made the effort to keep with my organization makes me love her even more.

I trudge upstairs to my bedroom, expecting to find a mess of dried rose petals. Nope. She cleaned those up too. In fact, she changed my bedding and did my laundry. I find a pile of clean, folded clothes in a basket near the dresser. My eyes land on a scrap of paper.

> Jacob,
> I hung up all your shirts and pants, but this stuff
> looks like it belongs in drawers. I'll let you do the
> honors.
>   xoxo, Sprite.

Smiling, I tuck the note into my pocket and peek inside my closet. Sure enough, everything's hung appropriately—by color, style, and sleeve length. A splash of color draws my attention to a dozen new shirts in varying styles. One of them has a note pinned to it.

Lena and I went shopping this week. Per our discussion about your wardrobe, I took it upon myself to spice it up a bit. Naturally, there's a method to my madness:

The green ones will pair nicely with your chocolaty eyes. Like a sexy forest of sorts.

Blue shirts for water because it makes me think of the ocean back home and the way you calm me.

The yellow ones remind me of warmth and sunshine, which is how I feel around you—and how I've felt since our sandcastle days.

The red shirts represent fire and the way you ignite me.

The purple ones (yes, I'm making you wear purple) represent love, passion, pleasure, and the rich, decadent fullness of life.

You fill me, Jake. Mind, body, heart, and soul. I love you more than I can put into words, so I thought this visual representation would help.

With all of me,
Your Isla Rose

My eyes water with the wave of emotion that slams me. Jesse's words echo in my mind like they've done since the moment they left his lips.

I pull my phone from a pocket and text Isla.

Me: Are you asleep?

Her reply is instantaneous.

Isla: No, I'm crocheting. You okay?

Me: I'd love for you to sleep in my arms.

Isla: When you come home, we can make that happen.

Me: I AM home, Sprite.

Isla: I'll be right there.

Despite the day's events, a wave of giddiness washes over me—just like it did when I spotted her at the funeral home. I quickly brush my teeth and change into pajamas.

The front door creaks open.

"Where are you?" Isla's lilting voice reaches my ears.

"Upstairs," I shout, attempting to do something with my unruly hair.

She enters my bedroom and flashes her gorgeous smile. "Hello, love."

"Hey, beautiful."

Isla looks down at her attire of yoga pants and my Brooklyn sweatshirt. "Uh, okay." She smirks at me. "Beauty's in the eye of the beholder, I suppose."

I sit on the edge of my bed. "How about you come a little closer so I can be*hold* you."

She rushes over, flinging her arms around my neck. Her enthusiasm knocks us off-balance, and I flop backward. She lands on top of me. "I've missed you like you wouldn't believe."

I brush the hair back from her face. "Honey, I've missed you more."

Straddling me, Isla brings her lips to mine in a kiss that steals my sanity. She threads her hands in my hair and pours her soul into me. With the week's emotional turmoil, and all the time I spent without her, I want her tonight, more than ever. I need her body and soul to coat me. Wash over me and soothe my rawness.

"I need you." I groan into her mouth.

"I'm here, hon." She kisses my jaw, my neck, her hands finding my waistband. "I'm all yours tonight."

We tug at each other's clothes, quickly shedding them. Isla's lips glide over my chest, licking and teasing my nipples. Her hair tickles my skin as she moves down my abs. She grips my cock, brushing her lips over the head. While I know the ecstasy that mouth brings, it's not enough. I need to be inside her.

"Isla."

She meets my gaze. "You don't want this?"

"I want you to ride me."

She flushes. "I doubt I'll be any good at that."

I point to my nightstand. "The lube's in there. Put some on us both. I'll help with the rest."

Retrieving the bottle, she coats my cock and reaches between her legs. She looks to me for direction.

"Guide me inside you and work your way down on top of me. Do what feels good. Add more lube if that helps." I fold my arms behind my head. "Don't worry about me—I'm gonna enjoy the show."

She smirks and lifts her hips. Lining us up, she slowly takes the head of me inside. Her breath hisses out of her. "Oh, God, Jake . . ."

"Fuck, you feel good." Unable to resist their softness, I cup her breasts and brush my thumbs over her nipples.

She lifts slightly, then slides farther down onto me. Snatching the bottle of lube, she squirts some on, the cool liquid a contrast to her heat. She slowly eases down. I watch my cock fill her, inch by rock-hard inch. Isla gasps and clutches my shoulders.

"That's it, honey," I say through gritted teeth. "Take me all in."

Her pussy accepts me to the hilt. "Oh, Jake . . ."

Some primitive part of me wants to flip her over and drive inside her, but I know that can't happen.

Yet.

I grip her waist. "Roll your hips and move them in a circle. See what feels best and do that."

She works my cock in a grinding rhythm, her fingertips clenching my shoulders.

I glance at her face. "Does it hurt?"

"Only a little." She lifts her body on a gasp. "Not like last time." She slides down, her pussy squeezing me.

"You feel so fucking good," I groan the words. "I love being inside you." I reach between us and find her clit. I massage it, and her eyes flutter closed.

"Oh, yes." Her hips jerk. "*Jake . . .*"

"I love hearing you say my name." I circle my thumb, rubbing and stroking her. I can tell she enjoys it by the way she presses into my touch. Little gasps and moans escape her parted lips. It doesn't take long to bring her sweet, responsive body to the edge.

"Keep doing that. It feels—oh, Jake . . ." Her nails dig into my shoulders. "I'm gonna come."

"Let me hear you, honey."

Arching her back, she wails my name as I play her body's keys. I'm the maestro and she is my muse. Her climax, the crescendo in our little symphony.

I roll us over without pulling out. "I'm taking over now. Tell me to slow down if it's too much."

She nods and wraps her legs around me.

I move with slow, measured thrusts, going deeper each time. "I love making love to you," I whisper, burying my face in her neck. With the funeral and everything else, I never made it to the store for condoms, so I've got to pull out when it comes time.

I roll my hips, making us both moan. She tightens her legs around me. I kiss her lips, neck, and shoulders as I move, working my hips in a slow, rocking grind. Isla's so goddamn wet and hot and tight, I won't make it much longer. Groaning, I move a little faster.

So close.

Yanking my hips back, I pull out and grab my cock, roughly stroking it. "Oh, fuck . . . Isla." I'm too caught up in my ecstasy to aim, so I release on her stomach before collapsing on top of her. She clings to me, pressing her face in my neck. "I'm sorry. I didn't mean to get that on you." I snatch my boxers to clean her off.

"No worries, love. You were in the moment."

I cup her cheeks, peering into those beautiful eyes. "Are you okay?"

"Yes. Stings a little, but nothing like last time."

"Good." I kiss her lips and flush. "I'm sorry I didn't last longer. I swear I'm capable of having stamina."

"Honestly, I'm glad you didn't. I was getting ready to stop you."

"I promise we'll get to a point where it feels good for you."

"Jacob, it does feel good for me—even when it hurts. Because it's *you*. I love feeling you deep inside me, claiming me as yours." Her lip quivers. "Being in your arms feels secure, and a place to land is all I've ever wanted."

I pull her close and kiss her. "You *are* mine, Isla Rose. Right here is where you belong."

CHAPTER 36

Isla

Internal playlist: "You Say" by Lauren Daigle

Two days later, I stand at Jake's kitchen sink and wash his blender while mentally running through my shopping list. We're going to the hardware store to pick up paint and stuff to build shelves in one of my closets.

Freshly showered, Jake strides into the kitchen and plants a kiss on my cheek. "Good morning, honey."

"Good morning, love. Your green smoothie is on the counter." His lip curls slightly, so I chuckle. "I barely put any kale in yours. I swear, it's mostly apple and blueberries."

He takes the tiniest of sips and smiles. "You're right. It's actually delicious."

"Good. Now drink up. Tomorrow you're gonna try a carrot one."

He brushes the hair back from my face. "Thank you for forcing your healthy habits on me."

"Well, I happen to love you, Jacob. Your health is important to me."

"I've never had this before," he murmurs.

"Yeah, you did. I made it the same way as last time, but with more spinach and less kale."

He shakes his head and gestures between us. "No, I mean, *this*. A woman in my kitchen taking care of me. I've never had anyone like you, Isla. You make my house feel like a home. You make me feel like I'm . . ." he pauses, searching for the right word, "home."

Tears prick the corners of my eyes. I turn off the faucet and dry my hands on a dish towel before throwing my arms around him. "You're my home too," I whisper, resting my head on his shoulder. "You always have been."

My phone rings on the counter beside us.

"It's Wes," Jake says. "Probably calling back about what they want us to bring."

I grab the phone. "Hello?"

"Good morning, Imp. What's on your agenda for today?"

I chew my lip and decide for an honest answer. "Well, since I figured you and Lena are busy getting stuff together for Christmas Eve, I asked Jake if he would mind taking me to the hardware store for paint and shelves."

"I had a feeling those white walls would drive you crazy. Make sure you get masking tape and a variety of paintbrushes. They make special ones for corners and shit. Ask Bennett, he'll make sure you don't forget anything. Actually, you should have him remeasure that closet for ya. I'd hate to have you buy shelves that are too short."

I snort. "You don't trust my measurements?"

Wes laughs. "I trust Bennett more."

I glance at Jake, and a twinge of guilt settles in my stomach. "Good idea. I'll ask Jake."

"Bennett built a huge walk-in closet off his bedroom. He's very meticulous, so you're in good hands."

Remember that, Wes.

"I know." I squeeze the phone tightly. "Did Lena decide what she'd like me to bring?"

"Just yourself. We've got it covered."

"All right, well, let me go. I need to shower so we can head out."

"Oh! I thought of another thing to pick up at the hardware store. See if they have any ice melt for your front porch. We're supposed to get some shitty weather this weekend. Ask Bennett. He'll know what kind to buy."

"Okay, will do. Love you."

"Love you too, Imp. Bye."

I hang up and sigh. "Wes would like you to remeasure my closet because you're more meticulous than I am."

Jake chuckles. "I noticed you didn't tell him I already checked your measurements."

"He also said to tell you I need ice melt, masking tape, and multiple sizes of paintbrushes."

He points to the list on the counter. "Everything's already on there. I've got you covered, Sprite."

I hug him tightly. "Thanks for taking care of me."

Jake tips my chin up. "I will *always* take care of you, sweetheart."

Hours later, we pull up outside a construction site on our way to lunch. I study the colossal structure and the workers with their hard hats and machinery.

"What's this?"

Jake turns off the car and unbuckles his seat belt. "I wanted to show you the future home of The Phoenix."

"Bloody hell, the place is huge," I exclaim, unclicking my belt.

He grins. "This is only the shell, but I've got big plans for it."

We step outside, and Jake leads me along the footpath with a hand at the small of my back.

"Shouldn't we have hard hats on?" I ask.

"Probably. We're only going to the office though." He gestures to a portable building with a cluster of men outside, looking over some papers.

One of them sees Jake and perks up. "Jake, how's it going?" he shouts over the jackhammer across the way.

"Good, man. How's everything coming along?"

"We're right on schedule."

"Excellent." Jake turns to me. "Isla, this is Dylan, my project manager. D, this is my girlfriend, Isla."

Dylan's gaze flares in surprise. "Nice to meet you, Isla. Welcome to The Phoenix."

"Thank you. Nice to meet you as well." I shake his hand.

Jake points to the office. "I wanted to show Isla the building plans."

Dylan smiles. "Sure, man. They're on my desk."

Jake takes my arm and guides me into the office. He locates the site's plans and unrolls them with a grin. "This is top secret stuff, Sprite."

"I'm honored to be here."

He explains the community center's layout and shows me the corresponding areas on the page. He points to a large section in the building's right wing. "This is yours."

"Huh?"

He meets my gaze. "I would love for you to run The Phoenix's fashion design program after you're finished with your internship."

My hand flies up to cover my mouth. "Oh my God."

"I'll technically be your boss, but I'd rather you think of it as a partnership. When I say, 'it's yours,' I mean it. You can have free rein to do whatever you choose—be it something similar to your internship, where you help underprivileged women, or something else entirely. I'll order any equipment you need or want, and I won't limit your budget."

"Jacob, I—" Blinking back the welling tears, I try to form a sentence, but fail.

"I know we haven't talked about what's on the horizon, so I'm not sure of your plans for your career. I don't want to pressure you, but The Phoenix needs your expertise. Tell me you'll do it." His chocolaty gaze is wide with vulnerability and hope. "Please be part of this dream with me."

I grip the sides of his face. "Yes."

Relief washes over his features. "Really?"

"Yes," I repeat, louder this time. "I would absolutely love to."

Jake crushes my body to his. "Thank you."

"I'm blown away right now, and I'm having a hard time with words, so please don't take my silence as a lack of excitement. This is my dream job, Jacob. You have no idea how much your offer means to me."

It means he sees our future as clearly as I can. It means he wants to be my partner in all that we do. It means we share the same horizon. There will always be an *us*.

Earth meets sky.

Jake tips my chin up. "Your 'yes' is the greatest gift I've ever been given." His tone gravelly, he blinks a few times and swallows before continuing, "You don't know how much you mean to me, Isla Rose."

CHAPTER 37

Isla

Internal playlist: "Tonight" by John Legend

Christmastime in New York is wildly different from back home. For one, it's summer in Australia, so I'm used to sweating my arse off. Instead of snow boots and a red suit, our Santa wears board shorts and carries a surfboard. Street parties, impromptu cricket games, and carols by candlelight are some of my favorite traditions. While I've always enjoyed the holiday, it invigorates me to experience the northern hemisphere's version.

I peek out my front window at the fresh blanket of snow. I have the sudden urge to make snow angels, but I don't have suitable attire—or a yard—to make them in.

Jake and I haven't had much alone time since Jesse came to stay with him after Hannah's funeral. Jesse is heartbroken, but Jake is doing his best to help him hold it together. I made them dinner last night and we all watched a funny movie.

Their friendship is a brotherhood. A bond so strong and enduring that after spending some time with them, I'd swear they *are* siblings. The closest thing I have to a sisterhood is my relationship with Cora. Here in New York, I've got Lena. Spending time with her is effortless and soul nurturing. Plus, I love watching her put Wes in his place.

Today is Christmas Eve, Lena's birthday. She's having a gathering at her house this evening to celebrate. Jake convinced Jesse to come so he isn't alone. Before we head over there, Jake promised to take me to see his recording studio—a mini date of sorts.

Across the street, Jake cleans off his car while Jesse shovels the porch. I step outside and gather some snow. Tightly balling it, I pelt Jake in the middle of his back.

"Whoa!" He whirls around. "We really going there, Sprite?"

I giggle and throw another. This one hits him in the thigh.

Jesse laughs. "You've got good aim."

Shaking his head, Jake returns to scraping the ice off his windshield. I toss one more, hitting his shoulder this time. He sets the scraper on the hood of his car and stoops to make a snowball.

"Three strikes, sweetheart," he calls, hurling it at me.

I duck and it hits my front door. "You've got shitty aim, love."

Jesse snickers. "Women have been telling him that for years."

Jake gives him the finger before making another snowball. "Who says I wanted it to hit her?" He eyes me. "That was a warning shot, Sprite."

"You gonna hit home this time?" I tease, shaking my arse at him.

He dramatically winds his arm like a major league pitcher and releases the snowball. He's too slow. I've already retreated behind the safety of my front door. A loud thud on the other side makes me laugh.

I pull the blinds aside and peek out the window. He's standing in the middle of the road with his hands on his hips. I blow him a kiss and make a heart shape with my hands. Smiling, he returns the gesture, then points to his watch and mouths, "Ten minutes."

I give him a thumbs-up and grab my purse and the bag of homemade gifts I crocheted. I love making things for the people I care about. Jake told me Jesse uses his blanket all the time, which makes my heart happy. I've made scarves for Wes, Garrett, and Jesse, as well as matching gloves. Lena doesn't wear scarves, so I made her a hat and mittens. Jake is getting gloves, a sweater I designed, and a poem I wrote for him.

I head outside once I have everything I need. Jake and Jesse are shoveling my front steps.

"Careful, it's icy," Jake warns. "Hold the railing."

"Thank you, gentlemen. Maybe we can stop at the hardware store on the way? I don't have my own shovel."

"You don't need one, you've got me."

"I don't expect you to do this every time we get a storm. I can shovel."

Jake smiles. "Yes, you *can* shovel, but you don't need to." He points to his car. "Get in."

I salute him and make my way to the vehicle. Placing the gifts in his back seat, I slide into the front and check my phone while I wait.

There's a text from Reed. My heart flutters in panic for a moment until I open the message.

Reed: My intuition was right.

It's an ultrasound picture. He's drawn an arrow to a trio of lines between the fetus's legs.

Reed: Girl parts.

I'm getting a niece! My grin stretches ear to ear as I type.

Me: Ahhhhhh!!!! I'm so fucking happy right now! Commence the production of little dresses.

He sends me a smiley emoji.

Reed: Please don't say anything to Wes. I want to tell him in person. Probably sometime in late February.

Me: I won't, Reed. I love you. I'm sorry for making you lose that job.

My phone rings, so I answer with, "I know it's in the past, but it's been bothering me."

"It was a blessing in disguise, Birdie." His deep voice lacks the usual annoyance. "You said it yourself: I've got an empire to run now." He snorts. "And a rogue brother to rein in."

"I know. You're doing a bloody good job of it. The empire running, that is."

"Thanks."

I giggle. "I don't think Wes is rein-able."

"No shit," he mutters.

"Don't worry about Wes. He'll charm his way through the contract breach stuff."

"Let's hope."

"I've been thinking about something you said."

"And what's that?"

"It made me sad when you called yourself an outsider."

He's quiet for a few moments. "Don't be."

"But I am. I hate that my illness—and the way I behaved

afterward—brought a darker cloud over our relationship. I mean, yeah, Wes and I got closer, but I always loved you." I squeeze my eyes shut. "Sorry for rambling. I guess I'm worried about us having lingering issues. I don't want you hating me again."

Reed sighs heavily. "I thought we went over this. I never hated you, little bird. I was misinformed and judgmental. I acted like a dick, plain and simple. You have nothing to apologize for."

"I love you," I say, squeezing the phone.

"Love you too."

"Please give Cora my love."

"Will do. Say hello to Bennett. By the way, did ya tell Wes yet?"

"No. I'm holding off as long as I can."

"You should tell him. He hates being in the dark. It's better if it comes from you. Oh, and what's this I hear about you having a secret love affair with my sister-in-law?"

"*What?* Wes is clearly off his bloody rocker. I never said—" I release a heavy sigh as the false connections he made from his interpretation of our chat fit themselves into place. "Look, I changed Jake's name to Dana in my phone to avoid another mishap like I had with you. Apparently, our idiot brother took it upon himself to make assumptions."

"He thinks you're seriously in love with her."

"Let him. My love life isn't his business."

"You're weaving a web for yourself, little bird. Be careful. Gotta run. Merry Christmas."

"Merry Christmas." I return the phone to my bag.

Moments later, Jake slides into the front seat and squeezes my knee. "Ready for our adventure?"

"For over five years now."

He chuckles. "I meant today. But yeah, me too."

"Jake, do you think we should tell Wes?"

He sighs heavily. "We *should*, but I don't want to. He won't be happy about this."

"I know, but I feel guilty for lying to him."

"Me too." He shakes his head. "Honestly, I've been avoiding him because it eats away at me. I feel like I can't look him in the eye."

I cross my arms. "It's not fair we have to feel like we're doing something wrong. This isn't Romeo and Juliet. Our families aren't at war. Why the fuck do we have to hide?"

He waves to Jesse and eases from the curb. "I know, Sprite. I hate it too."

"Reed thinks we should tell him."

"When did you talk to Reed?"

"A few minutes ago. He said Wes thinks I have romantic feelings for Dana."

Jake chuckles. "Oh yeah, I meant to tell you about that. Wes stopped by that day and told me his theories. I didn't bother to correct him. He wasn't upset about the possibility of it—just hurt you never told him."

"It's my fault entirely. He read too much into what I was saying, and he was pissing me off, so I guess I kinda let him." My sigh deflates my chest. "But I think I agree with Reed. We need to be honest with Wes."

"What if we tell him after the new year? Let's enjoy our holidays and save the drama for later."

"*How* will we tell him?" I ask, gnawing my lip.

"We'll go over there and sit him down—together. You and me as a united front. I'll warn Lena and Garrett ahead of time in case he goes off the deep end and slaughters me."

"I didn't mean to bring stress into your life."

"No, sweetheart, you've brought me *to life*. You're everything bright and colorful and happy. I love you and I want to be with you. Wes is a storm we'll need to weather."

Jake's studio is amazing. I follow him into the soundproofed space, which was designed for stellar acoustics. The eclectic lighting and abstract pieces that grace the walls lend it an artsy feel.

I marvel at the grand piano situated in the center of the room. "So, this is where the magic happens."

"Most of it, yes." Jake smiles. "As you well know, the rest of my wizardry happens in the bedroom."

I tap a few keys on the piano. "Did you ever think about bringing both worlds together?"

He cocks his head. "What do you mean?"

It's been several days since we last made love—and my period's due the end of next week, plus or minus a few days—so I'm feeling frisky.

"I mean, what if we made some music of our own . . ."

His eyes flare with heat and sweep over me. "Right now?"

"No time like the present." I bat my lashes. "Pretty sure you mentioned the place is soundproof."

Jake lunges, seizing me around the waist. He yanks me up against him and brings his lips down over mine. His kiss is deep and urgent, hands knotting in my ponytail.

"Strip for me," he commands, yanking his lips from mine. "I want to see every inch of you."

Flashing a sultry smile, I make a show of removing my clothes. His eyes darken, reflecting his growing excitement with each article I toss near the piano. The cool air hardens my nipples, but it's the way he licks his lips that sets me on fire. I take out my hair tie, allowing the tresses to cascade over my shoulders and down my back.

Jake circles me like a hungry predator. His gaze travels over my naked body, and the feral heat in his eyes makes my insides quiver. He points to the bench. "Lie down."

I saunter over and settle with my back on the cold wood. "Come and get me."

He grips my hips and yanks me to the edge, then kneels on the floor between my legs. He guides them over his shoulders and presses my thighs apart. "Spread wide for me, honey." Kissing his way up my inner thighs, he puts his mouth where I need him most.

My back arches. "Oh, Jake."

He tightens his grip on my hips and pulls me closer. He spears his tongue inside me, licking me up and down.

A groan rumbles in his chest. "I love the way you taste." As his lips and tongue tease me, he releases one of my hips and reaches for the keys.

The man literally plays the piano with his face between my legs. As the first few notes of "Crave" reach my ears, I'm lost in him. His wicked tongue. The toe-curling sensations. All I know is the ecstasy he's giving me. The second verse brings the finger he eases inside. Another one joins at the song's chorus. The melody reverberates in my head, each note and lyric coming to life between my thighs. The man licks my pussy like he'll die if he stops.

Moaning, I buck my hips. He surrounds my clit, sucking and tongue flicking until I fall apart.

"Jake! Oh, *yes.*"

He keeps moving, merciless in his crusade. "Oh, God . . . *Jacob.*" A second orgasm slams through me, stealing my senses.

Another.

And one more.

Jake lifts his head and flashes me a cocky grin, my juices glistening on his lips. "That was the interlude." He climbs to his feet and pulls me up. Before I realize what he's doing, my body's in the air. Tossing me over his shoulder, he carries me to the edge of the piano and closes the lid before setting me on top of it. "Symphony time."

"I don't wanna break your piano."

"We won't." He unbuckles his belt, then drops his pants to his knees and frees his cock. He nudges my thighs apart and stands between them. He's tall enough to make the position work. "And even if we do, I'll buy another. Wrap your legs around me."

I do as I'm told. He lines himself up with me and eases inside. "Oh, *Jake.*" I clutch his shoulders. He grips my hips and pushes deeper, stretching and filling me.

He draws his hips back and surges forward. We both gasp. Clenching my hips, he begins pumping. "You okay?"

"Yes. You feel so good." I tighten my legs around him. This time is different. His cock rubs places deep inside I previously hadn't noticed over the pain. It doesn't hurt at all, which is a damn good thing since we don't have lube.

"Isla, your body is heaven."

"Don't go slow. Give me everything."

"You sure?"

"Yes. Please don't hold back."

He surges forward, making me cry out. And for the first time, he thrusts his hips the way I imagined he would during all those years I spent fantasizing. Hard, fast, and deep. Possessive, claiming, and so fucking good.

"Isla, fuck—" He buries his face at my neck and keeps moving.

An orgasm builds inside me. "Oh my God, whatever you're doing, keep doing it!"

CHAPTER 38

Jake

Mood: "Sex on Fire" by Kings of Leon

Isla is seconds from orgasm, seated on top of my grand piano, porcelain skin against the sleek obsidian. Her pussy squeezes me as my cock strokes in and out. I ramp up the intensity, unable to stop the guttural sounds leaving my chest. My legs ache from standing on my toes.

"Come for me," I growl, clamping my hands on her hips.

"Oh, *yes!*" She throws her head back and wails her pleasure. "*Jacob.*"

Isla coming on my cock is the sexiest thing I've ever witnessed. Her pussy flutters and spasms around me, taking me to the hilt and bringing me to the brink. She digs her heels into my ass and pulls me deeper.

She's so goddamn perfect that I lose my mind and my control. "Isla, oh fuck, I'm gonna—" Hips slamming, I come hard.

Inside her.

Feral moans and groans rip from my chest. I keep moving until I've given her everything I've got.

Isla clings to me, gasping and shaking her head. "If I'd known it could feel like that, I would've seduced you years sooner."

A grin creeps across my face. "I wouldn't have let you."

"I call bullshit, Jacob."

I slowly pull out of her. "We need to swing by the pharmacy."

"For condoms?"

"Yeah."

Isla nods. "I wondered why you didn't stop yourself."

"I'm sorry, honey. It wasn't intentional. You feel so fucking good, my pull-out game clearly can't be trusted. While we're there, I'll pick up the morning-after-pill."

She shakes her head. "I can't take hormones, remember?"

"Shit. Why was that, again?"

"Blood clots."

Her words spear through the haze in my head. With lupus and a kidney transplant, a pregnancy would be extremely complicated. And quite possibly dangerous.

And I fucking came inside her.

"Fuck." Panic rises in my chest. "When is your next period due?"

She flushes and looks away. "We're not discussing my cycle."

I tip her chin up. "Oh, yes, we are. My recklessness put you in danger. I need to know this information."

She hesitates and meets my gaze. "Ten days or so. Around the end of next week, but I can't be sure because I'm usually irregular."

She's midcycle, which means she's probably ovulating. *Great.*

I run a hand over my face. "I need to know the moment it comes, okay?"

"Okay."

"And going forward, don't let me near you if I'm not wearing a condom."

"I'm sorry," she whispers.

"Don't you dare apologize. This was my responsibility, and I fucked up. I'm not a teenager, I'm a grown man who knows better."

"It takes two to tango. I could've stopped you, but I didn't. I don't want you beating yourself up over this."

I grip the sides of her face. "I will *always* take care of you." I force a swallow. "No matter what happens. I mean that, Isla."

"I know you do," she whispers. "But it's not only your responsibility. Maybe I'll get an IUD?"

"That's up to you. I don't want you to go and have a surgical procedure because I'm a fucking idiot. Besides, I thought there were hormones in them?"

"No, not all of them. I'd get the copper kind."

I cringe at the thought of a piece of metal inside her body. "I think it would be easier if I wore a condom."

She shakes her head. "I've been thinking about it for a while. I talked to Lena about them, and she said it's convenient."

"Like I said, that's your choice. It's your body, and I support whatever decision you make, but I'm not making love to you without a condom again." I wrap my arms around her. "You're too precious to me. I shouldn't have lost control and jeopardized your health. Promise you'll tell me when your period comes?"

"I will." She tightens her arms around me. "Was it all right for you?"

I cock my head. "The sex?"

She flushes. "Yeah."

I blink a few times. *Is she serious?* I just dropped trou and fucked her atop my grand piano. "It was the best of my life."

Her lips curve into a coy smile. "I enjoyed it immensely. Thanks for the orgasms."

"Gotta tell you, I feel like I'm a hundred feet tall right now. I love making you come. And your naked body on my piano is easily the hottest thing I've ever seen."

Isla smiles as she moves to grab her phone. She saunters back over to the piano and climbs up to lounge along the top. She silently messes with her phone before raising her arm. She pouts her lip and then bites it, trailing her fingers down her stomach. After a minute, she turns to me. "Better check your texts, Jacob."

CHAPTER 39

Isla

Internal playlist: "Utopia" by Alanis Morissette

Jake, Jesse, and I climb the steps to Lena's brownstone and ring the bell. I can't believe it's evening already. Our afternoon was amazing—especially the mind-blowing orgasms. Hours later, I can still feel Jake inside me. I bat my eyelashes at him and wink. He smiles and squeezes my shoulder.

After lunch, we stopped at the pharmacy as planned. I met his friend Maura, the pharmacist who helped with my medicine debacle last month. Jake bought out their supply of non-latex condoms while I nonchalantly played with my hair.

Garrett opens the front door. "Happy Festivus."

Jake claps his shoulder. "Merry Christmas, dude. This is my friend Jesse."

Garrett shakes Jesse's hand. "Hey, man. Nice to meet you."

"Nice to meet you too."

"How's it going, Dundette?"

I hug Garrett. "I'm great, and you?"

"Living the dream." He holds the door open, and we head upstairs to Lena's.

Her home is the definition of Christmas spirit. The enormous tree I admired at Friendsgiving sparkles with white lights and shimmering ornaments. Her living room boasts an assortment of reindeer and a miniature village, complete with tiny ice skaters. Holiday music drifts from the speakers, making me feel like I'm at the North Pole. My mouth waters at the aroma of apple pie.

Lena's in the kitchen, pulling cookies out of the top oven. On the island, there's an assortment of appetizers next to a rack of cooling pies and cookies. She's wearing a red sweater dress and a Mrs. Claus apron. Completing the look is a sparkly red and green elf-ear headband.

"I just gained five pounds walking into this room," Jake declares, hugging Lena. "Happy birthday, Lena-Bean."

She kisses his cheek. "Thank you. Merry Christmas."

I hug her. "Happy birthday, love. You take festivity to the next level."

Lena grins. "I'm not here to fuck spiders."

Jesse laughs. "That's a new one. And happy birthday."

"Thank you. That's one of my favorite Wes-isms. I steal all the ones I like."

"Speaking of that, where's Wes?" I ask.

Lena giggles. "You'll see."

As if on cue, my brother enters the room in a Santa costume.

"Mother of God," Jake says.

"Bennett! Come sit on my knee and tell me your Christmas list."

I stare at Wes. "Are ya wearing a fake belly?"

Jake snorts. "Nah, he's been indulging in too much beer and desserts."

"As a matter of fact, I am wearing padding." Wes lifts his Santa coat to prove it. "And it's hot as fuck, so I won't be wearing it much longer."

I hug him. "Merry Christmas, ya big brute."

"Same to you, Imp. Are you on the nice list this year?"

"Nope." I tug on his fake beard. "Never grow one of these."

"Mrs. Claus loves my beard." He rubs his belly. "But she's currently pissed at me."

Jake smirks. "And why's that?"

Wes points at Lena. "'Cause I've been bumping uglies with one of the elves."

Lena raises a brow. "Who you calling ugly?"

"Definitely not you, twinkle toes."

Jesse laughs again, and I'm glad we convinced him to come. I couldn't bear the thought of him being alone on Christmas Eve.

Lena gestures to the food. "All right, everyone. Help yourselves. For drinks, we have beer, wine, and seltzer. Who's having what?" She grins at me, pulling out a piña colada wine cooler. "Got something special for you, my dear. It's nonalcoholic."

"You're a goddess," I say, accepting it. My wrists hurt from all the crocheting I've been doing lately, so I hand the bottle to Jake, and he cracks it open for me. "Thank you."

"Anytime, Sprite." Jake grabs beer for himself and Jesse.

Lena pulls a turkey from the lower oven, and we all load up our plates with food. Everything tastes divine. We congregate in the living room after everyone's bellies are full.

Wes stands. "I'd like to make a toast to the birthday girl." Lena smiles up at him. "Happy birthday to the fiercest, most extraordinary woman I know. You're a spitfire and a supernova. My life started when I met you, and I look forward to sharing many more birthdays with you. I love you, sunshine."

Lena's eyes water. "Love you too, Wes. Thank you."

I stand and walk over to Lena. "I also have something to say. Lena, thank you for making my brother whole. You're his true north, and you feel like a sister to me. I adore you. Happy birthday."

She squeezes my hand. "Thank you, sweetie. I love you too."

Jake speaks up, "Since I don't like feeling left out, I'll put my two cents in. Lena-Bean, you're amazing. You've been my friend and confidante since the moment we met. Thank you for being you and for keeping the big guy in check. Happy birthday, my dear."

"Love you, Jake." Lena wipes her cheeks. "Dammit, guys, you're making me cry."

Garrett chuckles. "Sorry, Leens, but I don't want us drowning in your tears, so I'll save my speech for your wedding day." He kisses the top of her head. "But I'm pretty sure you already know how I feel. Happy birthday."

She hugs him. "Love you forever and always, Gar."

Jesse steps forward. "Lena, I just met you, but I can already see the kind of woman you are. Thanks for opening your home to me. Happy birthday."

"You are most welcome, Jesse." She gestures to all of us. "Thank you, everyone. I'm grateful to have you in my life."

We exchange our gifts, and everyone's impressed with my handiwork—all of them wearing some combination of scarves, hats, and gloves.

"Dundette, this is the coolest shit ever! How did you learn to do this?"

"I taught myself when I was on dialysis. It was my way of coping with the situation, and it made the time pass quickly."

Wes carries over a big package and places it in my lap. "I think you'll find these useful, Imp."

I unwrap it to discover a set of purple tools. "This is great. Thank you." I hold up the hammer. "I can't believe you found a purple set."

"Ordered them special." He chuckles. "Now I don't have to bug Bennett every time you need something fixed."

Jake shrugs. "You know I don't mind helping your family. My tools are her tools." He smirks at me. "But purple's way cooler than my boring-ass black ones."

"You know it, Jacob. Feel the squishy handle." I hold it out to him.

Jake squeezes the hammer. "None of my tools have squishy handles either. I believe you've taken it to the next level, Sprite. If you need any hard-handled, run-of-the-mill tools, wave a flag out your window or something."

I snort. "I'll hang it with my freak flag."

"You do you, neighbor. Wave whatever flags you want. Just don't spray paint my trash cans."

Garrett laughs. "You have that issue in your neighborhood too?"

Jake nods. "Who the fuck has time to make graffiti dicks on a garbage can?"

Wes cocks his head. "What the hell're ya talkin' about?"

"Some idiot has been spray painting bright yellow cocks on people's shit," Garrett explains.

"Mine haven't been hit yet," Jake says. "It's probably some kid who should be involved in music or sports. Makes me wish the community center were in Brooklyn."

I giggle. "If I was gonna draw a dick on something, I'd make it purple."

"Big surprise there, Sprite. My point with all that is the importance of not roaming the streets at night."

Wes claps Jake's shoulder. "I really appreciate you looking out for her."

Guilt squeezes my chest. I pick at my nails to avoid making eye contact with Wes.

Jake, on the other hand, looks him square in the eye. "Your family is my family, and I'm happy to treat her as such."

Wes nods. "Means a lot to me, mate."

CHAPTER 40

Isla

Internal playlist: "We Can Make Love" by SoMo

Christmas Day has always been a favorite of mine, but it feels more magical this year. I'm sure the snow has something to do with it. With the chaos of my move, I never got a tree or decorated at all, but the glistening streets make up for it. Maybe I'll convince Jake to have a snowball fight later. Giddiness flutters inside me at the knowledge I get to spend my first white Christmas with the man I love. We slept at our own homes, but he'll be here shortly for breakfast. I flip our omelets and pour us some coffee.

The front door opens. "Merry Christmas," Jake calls, stepping out of his snow-caked boots. "We got more snow last night. I'll shovel your steps after we eat."

"Merry Christmas, hon. And thank you."

He hangs his coat in my hall closet, makes his way into the kitchen, and wraps his arms around me. "Good morning, my sweet."

"G'day." I cup his jaw and kiss him, loving the taste of his minty lips, and his fresh, clean scent. "You smell good."

He chuckles. "I showered."

I drag my hand down his chest to his belt. "You'll likely need another by the time I'm done with ya."

He points to the growing bulge in his jeans. "I've been here for all of thirty seconds, and you already have me bursting at the seams."

"Did ya bring any frangers?" My insides quake and quiver as he pulls a strip of condoms from his pocket with a grin. "Uh, we won't be doing it twelve times today, love."

He laughs. "No kidding. Figured I'd stash some here, so we have them. I don't know how long Jesse plans to stay—and I'm not going to rush him out—but I'd feel more comfortable doing the dirty at your place."

"Are ya saying I'm too loud?"

"Fuck no." His gaze sweeps over me. "I *love* hearing you. Turns me on."

Setting the condoms on the counter, I turn my focus to our food. "Hope you're hungry." I place an omelet on his plate. "Brekkie is served."

"You expect me to focus on chewing right now?"

I lick my lips. "What do you *want* to focus on?"

"Getting you naked."

Heat flares inside me. "Your eggs will get cold."

Jake points to the microwave, arching a dark brow. "I'm sure we could remedy that one."

I gesture to the living room. "I started a fire."

He snorts. "That's a fucking understatement."

"I mean, in the fireplace." I laugh and shake my head. "Maybe you could ravage me in front of it."

"Fuck the eggs." Jake grabs the condoms and grips my arm, tugging me to the other room. We settle on the couch, and he withdraws a box wrapped in gold paper. "I bought these as an 'I love you' gift for after our first time, but things got crazy, and I never had the chance to give them to you."

"Jacob, you didn't need to buy me anything."

"I wanted to, sweetheart." He runs a hand through his hair. "I added something to complete the set and made it your Christmas gift instead. I hope you like it."

I carefully unwrap the paper to reveal a black velvet box. Opening the lid, I gasp. Amethyst drop earrings sparkle in the light. A weighty matching pendant on a platinum chain and a ring of interspersed amethysts and diamonds twinkle up at me. "My God, these are gorgeous."

Jake smiles. "Amethyst is actually my birthstone, but since you love purple, it seemed more fitting than sapphires."

My eyes water. "Jacob, I love them. Thank you so much."

"You're welcome, Isla Rose. Merry Christmas." He presses a kiss to my knuckles. "Will you wear them for me?"

"Of course."

"I mean, right now," he murmurs. "I want to see you in these and nothing else."

"We can arrange that." I lift the shirt over my head and toss it aside. Since I'm home, I never bothered with a bra. Jake dips his head, bringing his mouth to my breasts. I swat at him. "Control yourself."

He exhales roughly. "No guarantees. You're so beautiful, honey."

Standing, I shed my yoga pants and lace panties. My amethyst earrings have French hooks, so I easily put them in. Next, I slide the ring on the fourth finger of my left hand and wonder if he catches the significance of its placement.

He meets my gaze and smiles knowingly. "You're mine."

"Always," I whisper, fumbling with the necklace's clasp. "Help me."

Jake brushes my hair aside and fastens the pendant around my neck. His lips find my ear. "I want you."

I swiftly work the buttons of his shirt and slide it off him. Biting my lip, I caress his muscled chest and abs. "I'd swear someone sculpted you. You're perfect."

"Far from it, my sweet." He unbuckles his belt and drops his pants. Soon, he's naked as well. "Let's make this a bit more romantic, shall we?" He moves my sofa at an angle, giving us a better view of the flames. My curio cabinet full of koala sculptures looms behind the couch.

"Watch the lamp," I warn, pointing to the end table he shoved to the side.

Jake flicks it on. "Now I can see you better." I flush and cover my breasts. He cocks a brow. "Oh, I don't think so. I want them in full view at all times."

I lower my hands and slowly turn in a circle.

"Get on the couch," he commands, his tone gravelly. Snatching a condom, he rolls it onto his cock as I settle on my back.

"Come and get me, Jacob," I purr with a feline stretch. I fling one of my legs over the back of the couch, opening myself wide for him.

He prowls over, squeezing lube onto himself. I didn't realize he'd brought some, but I'm secretly thankful.

"Are you ready for me?"

"Yes." I roll my hips in anticipation.

Jake kneels between my thighs and strokes the leg draped over the couch.

"Keep this up here for me." He shoves a pillow beneath my arse. Bracing his weight, he hooks my other leg over his shoulder and kisses my ankle as he lines us up. He rolls his hips, pressing inside me. "Oh, fuck, you feel so good." He groans through his teeth.

"Make me scream, Jacob."

He leans forward and kisses me. "Don't worry, I plan to." His tongue and cock spear into me, stealing my breath. The angle brings him deeper than ever before.

I moan loudly and grip his shoulders. "Please don't hold back."

He thrusts his hips harder and faster. "You want it this way?"

"Yes." I arch my back. "Jake, give it to me."

CHAPTER 41

Jake

Mood: "Closer" by Nine Inch Nails

She's going to burn me alive. With one leg over the back of the couch and the other over my shoulder, Isla spreads herself open for me, welcoming me deeper. Her moans and pleas spur me on. The condom dulls it slightly, but I can focus my attention on her instead of pulling out in time.

"You all right?" I growl, pumping my hips.

"Yes." She pulls at my shoulders. "Kiss me."

Leaning forward, I bring my lips to her ear and whisper, "I love making love to you."

Isla grips my ass and pulls me deeper. "I want more this time."

"More?"

She peers up into my eyes. "I don't want to make love." Pupils dilated, cheeks reddened by my stubble, she brushes her lips against mine. "Kiss me, Jake." Her lower lip quivers. "I want your kiss while you fuck me."

My breath hisses out of me. "You're gonna wear me out."

She flexes her hips upward. "Make me scream."

I surge forward, my cock slamming into her. She cries out in pleasure. Seizing her lips in a slow, sensual kiss, I deliver hard, measured thrusts. The sofa slams against the end table with each one.

I tear my lips from hers. "Like this?"

"Yes! Oh, fuck, *yes!*"

I find her lips once more. Spreading her legs even wider, I power into her. The lamp tips over with a crash. We both chuckle but I don't stop to fix it. The couch bangs into the table, shoving it across the hardwood floor.

"I love fucking you, Isla."

"Harder." She makes the command and I deliver. "Oh, God. You're gonna make me come." She urgently meets my thrusts. "Yes! Don't stop—" Isla climaxes with a screaming wail and rakes her nails down my back. "Oh, *Jake* . . ."

I fuck her even harder, seconds from my own release.

Behind us, the curio cabinet shatters. I instinctively shield Isla with my body as shards of glass slice open my skin. My back, neck, and shoulders take the brunt of it, but my arms and legs don't go unscathed.

Something heavy slams my shoulder. "Fuck!"

Isla's purple hammer hits the floor with a thud. I lift my head. "Why the hell would you store tools in—"

My heart stops.

From the living room doorway, a pair of livid cobalt irises turn my blood to ice.

CHAPTER 42

Jake

Mood: Closed casket is better.

I'm dead.

Lurching upward at bullet speed, I pull out of Isla and jump to my feet. I snatch a throw pillow to hide my rapidly deflating cock and toss a blanket over Isla. Blood trickles down my neck and back.

Glass is everywhere.

Isla sits up. "How the hell did that happen?"

I can't answer her. I can't fucking breathe, let alone speak. Butt naked, blue-balled, and still wearing a condom, this is the start of my nightmare and the epitome of worst-case scenarios. Paralyzed, I stare at the ticking bomb and await his wrath.

She looks over her shoulder and shrieks, pulling the blanket around herself. "What the fuck are you doing here?"

Wes heaves her toolbox across the room. Wrenches and screwdrivers crash on the hardwood like shrapnel. "You forgot these."

Isla leaps to her feet. "I said, no pop-ins! You can't barge in here and start throwing shit!"

"I own the building and I knocked first," Wes growls, his nostrils flaring. "Then I heard ya scream. I thought someone was taking advantage of you. Let myself in to investigate." He clenches his fists at his sides. "Never thought it'd be Bennett I'd find balls deep inside my fucking sister!" His roar reverberates through the brownstone as he advances. "When I gave you a key, it wasn't an invitation to fuck her."

Isla steps in front of me. "He didn't need your invitation. I gave him mine."

Shut up, Isla.

Wes glares at her. "You must be *Rosa*."

"Goddamn right, I am."

Isla, please . . .

He pins me with his gaze. "Got anything to say for yourself, *Dana?*"

I open and close my mouth a few times, but the furious disgust in his eyes chokes my air and steals my words. I'm reduced to a limp-dicked mute.

A fucking coward.

"You're supposed to be my best mate." He narrows his eyes. "How could you cross this line with my family? Why'd you—" His chest heaves, and he clenches his jaw. "*When*. Did. This—"

"Jake didn't do a fucking thing to you!" Isla shrieks.

Wes shakes his head. "He lied to me. You both did."

Isla straightens. "How'd we lie?"

"You purposely misled me about a fucking cleaning lady and Dana. Then ya went behind my back. You kept me in the dark and made a fool of me. Had a good laugh at how dumb I am, did ya? Tell me." He glares in my direction, the blue lasers searing a hole through my chest. "How long?" When no one answers, he takes a step closer. "How. Long. Have. You. Been. Fucking. My. Sister?"

I steel myself for a punch. "That's none of your business."

"Like hell, it's not!"

"She's a grown woman."

Wes advances on me, his sneer making it look like he's baring his teeth. "She's my fucking baby sister!" His roar rattles the windows.

"I'm aware."

"Bennett, you'll be lucky if I don't beat the shit out of you. I suggest you lose the sarcasm."

"Wasn't sarcasm, Wes. If you think the fact that Isla's your sister hasn't eaten me alive for five years, you're dead wrong." Holding the pillow in front of myself, I stiffen my spine. "Believe me, I'm acutely aware of the family tree. Like I said, I've had five fucking years to think about it."

"Whaddya mean, five years?" His voice is low and dangerous. Wes spears his hands into his hair. "This has been going on since she was eighteen?"

"He means we aren't some meaningless fling," Isla snaps. "I loved Jake *long* before I turned eighteen, but that's when I finally did something about it. For the record, he never pursued me—he walked away and kept his distance out of respect for you and Reed."

Wes points to the pillow hiding my cock. "Ya call this respect?"

Isla talks over him, "I wanted Jake, so I went after him. Except *this* time, he didn't push me away. Accept it and move on."

"Accept it?" he snarls, inches from her face. "I will *never* accept it."

Isla jabs a finger in the middle of his chest. "Then get the fuck out."

Wes stiffens for a moment. His tensed muscles seem to pulse and vibrate as rage pours off him in waves. For a split second, I worry he'll hit Isla. I step closer, preparing to defend her, but he keeps his fists at his sides. All six foot five of him looms over her. He leans in so their noses touch. "Excuse me?"

Isla steels her shoulders. "You heard me. I'm not your property—or anyone else's—and you don't run my life. *You* don't get to decide who I involve myself with—*I* do." She lets her gaze burn into him. "I've chosen Jake. It's always been him, and that isn't gonna change. If you can't embrace us, then leave us the fuck alone."

Blood runs down the side of my neck and drips onto my chest. My attempt to brush it away results in a smear.

The movement draws Wes's attention. "You're bleeding."

"No shit. You threw a hammer at me."

"Threw it in your *direction* when I thought she was being raped. Didn't see your face right away." He gestures between us. "We're done here. I can't trust you, so I've got no use for you."

I shrug. "Sorry you feel that way."

"Get out, Wes," Isla repeats.

"Once again, I'll remind you I own the building."

She curls her lip. "If you're so keen on asserting ownership, consider me your tenant. Therefore, I've got rights. Don't worry, I'll drop off your rent later. In the meantime, you'd better respect my boundaries. I'll remind you that unannounced drop-ins will not be tolerated." She stands on her tiptoes and gets right in his face. "And if you ever hurt Jake again, I'll hurt you!"

"You already did that when you lied to my face." Wes turns on his heel and storms out, slamming the door behind him. Moments later, tires spinning on ice confirm his departure.

Isla's body starts to tremble. Knees buckling, she sinks to the living room floor. Her tears come fast and heavy, a deluge of regret and pain.

Yanking on my boxers and jeans, I kneel at her side and wrap my arms around her. "I'm sorry it went down like that."

I never heard Lena's car pull up outside, and I missed his knocks over the slamming furniture and Isla's screams. He couldn't walk in when we made love? When I kissed and held her close like she was precious to me? No, it had to happen when I fucked her, when I thrust inside her like a goddamn animal. I will never forget the look in his eyes. Brimming with fury and disgust, they stripped my dignity and broke my heart.

Decades of friendship lost. His trust shattered like the cabinet, its shards piercing my heart. I made this bed of glass, so now I must lie in it.

Isla sobs in my arms, curling her body into a ball. Defeat replaces her ferocity. She stood up to Wes for me while I fucking stood there like a coward. I should've defended our love, asserted myself, claimed her as mine as she did.

Instead, I did nothing.

"Let's get you dressed." I help her to her feet.

She catches a glimpse of my back and yelps. "Your skin's torn to shreds!"

"I'm fine," I mutter. "It's better than what I expected him to do. Throwing a hammer tomahawk at me certainly beats him bashing my skull in."

"He had no right to barge in and throw anything." She grips my arm.

"I shouldn't have put us in this position."

Isla's lip quivers. "Are you leaving me?"

"No, honey, I'm not going anywhere. I should've listened when you suggested we tell him. Maybe it would've been better received if he didn't walk in on me fuck—" I squeeze my eyes shut. "Having sex with you."

Isla shakes her head. "We both know it wouldn't have been well received in any circumstance."

"I hate that I'm the reason for tension between you and your brother. It fucking kills me, Isla."

"Don't worry about us. He can't stay pissed forever."

I rake a bloodied hand through my hair. "You don't know Wes like I do."

"No, love, I know him better than you. He'll get over it eventually. Now, come into the kitchen so I can get the glass out of you."

CHAPTER 43

Isla

Internal playlist: "Heavy in Your Arms" by Florence + The Machine

Studying the mess that is Jake's back, I decide I'm going to beat Wes. Slap his face like I did Reed's. Jake is seated at the kitchen island, resting his forehead on the granite. I plugged a desk lamp in for more light, but I can't see the glass shards through the blood.

"I think we need to go to a hospital."

"I'm fine. Just pick them out," he says on a sigh.

"You may need stitches."

"I don't need—" A knock at the front door cuts him off. "Oh look, he's back to finish me off."

"I slid the bolts, so he'll have to break the fucking door down." I march into the foyer and peek out the window. It's not Wes, so I open the door.

Wide-eyed, Lena steps inside. "What the hell happened over here?"

I cross my arms over my chest, wondering what bullshit Wes fed her. "Whaddya mean?"

"Your brother just blew in like a fucking tornado."

"What makes you think something happened?"

Lena eyes me. "Because all he said was, 'Bennett's bleeding. It's my fault. Go to Isla's and help him.' Then he disappeared downstairs. Garrett wouldn't let me inside to talk to him but from what I understand, he's currently going apeshit on the punching bag."

I motion for her to follow me into the kitchen. "Wes threw a hammer at Jake. It hit my cabinet and shattered the front. He's got glass slivers everywhere."

"Son of a bitch." Lena rushes over to Jake and plops her bag on the counter.

"Howdy, Lena-Bean."

"Hey. Don't worry, splintered glass is my trauma nurse forte." She quickly ties her hair back and washes her hands. "So, he barged in here and threw a tool at you for no reason?"

Jake sighs. "No . . . he had a reason."

"He walked in on us having sex on the couch," I explain, flushing. "Apparently thought I was being raped. He kinda witnessed a climactic moment for me, if ya know what I mean . . ."

Lena's eyes widen. "Oh, fuck."

"Yep. Dunno how long he was standing there, but if you look up 'getting caught with your pants down' on *Urban Dictionary*, you'll see my face." Jake squeezes his eyes shut. "He hates me, Lena."

"No. If he hated you, he would've fed you your dick and left you to bleed to death. He sent me here instead."

I curl my lip. "Well, isn't that noble of him?"

Lena rummages through her bag and pulls out tweezers, a magnifying glass, and gauze. "Isla, I need a roll of paper towels and a bowl of warm water." She drags a stool over and settles. Angling the lamp, she meets my gaze. "I'll take care of his back. Why don't you take a hot shower and try to calm down?"

"Good idea. I'm gonna clean up the living room first."

Jake grips my wrist as I pass him. "No, you're not. I'll take care of it. Last thing I need is you getting cut. *I'm* not on blood thinners."

Lena picks out a glass sliver and holds it up for him to see. "How did she not get sliced?"

"My legs have some cuts, but the rest of me is fine. Jake shielded me with his body. A heroic act if ever there was one."

Jake sighs heavily. "There's nothing heroic about me. Please let Lena check your shins."

"They're fine. I already picked the glass out. It's you I'm worried about."

Lena points to me. "Let me take a quick peek before I get started on him."

Placing my foot on a stool, I slide my pants leg up to my knee so Lena can examine me. My left leg is fine, but it turns out there is a sliver in my right ankle. She removes it and cleans the area.

"Am I good?" I ask.

She nods. "Yeah, thankfully, yours aren't too deep. After you shower, I'll put a bandage on the one on your ankle."

"Do you need any help with him?"

"Nah, I've got this."

Jake points to the ceiling. "Please go shower like Lena said."

I salute him and head upstairs. Pausing in front of the bathroom mirror, I'm shocked by the amount of Jake's blood on me. I step beneath the hot water and cry.

My relationship with Wes will never be the same. The big brother who adored me no longer exists. Now, he's a man who threatened the one I love.

No one threatens what's mine and gets away with it.

CHAPTER 44

Jake

Mood: "I'm A Mess" by Ed Sheeran

It takes Lena almost two hours to remove the glass from my back. She also picks pieces from my scalp, neck, arms, and thighs, placing the bloody slivers in a pile on the counter.

I turn to face her after she finishes bandaging me up. "Thank you."

"Got you covered, my dear." She meets my gaze. "Now, I'm gonna ask you a question and I need a serious answer."

"This sounds ominous," I mutter, noting her tone and grim expression.

"Do you feel like there's any glass elsewhere?"

"No, I think you got it all."

"I'm talking about *sensitive* areas, like the crack of your ass or your balls?" she clarifies.

Now that she mentions it, my ass does sting, but I'm not telling her that. I'll go explore with my handheld mirror and flashlight later.

"Nope."

"Well, I need to look either way."

"Uh . . . *nope.*"

"I'm a fucking nurse, Jake. Do you have any idea how many ass cracks and ball sacks I've seen in my lifetime?"

"No, but mine isn't gonna be one of them."

Lena rolls her eyes. "Isla, I need a flashlight."

"Lena Hamilton, you are *not* examining my ass crack."

"I'll do it," Isla says, approaching with a flashlight. "Bend over and spread 'em."

"No one is looking at my ass crack!"

Isla props her hands on her hips. "You'd do it for me, Jacob."

"That's different," I sputter, yanking on my hair like it will make this nightmare stop. "You're you. I'm a fucking *dude*."

"What does that have to do with anything?" Lena challenges. "Everyone has an ass crack, darling."

I clench my jaw. "I. Have. Hair."

"Oh, you mean you're human like the rest of us?" Lena scoffs and cocks a brow. "Now, drop your drawers."

She's fucking serious. I open and close my mouth a few times. *This can't be happening to me.*

"No."

"Jake, listen to me. I've picked a shitload of glass out of you. Some of it was too small for you to even feel. If you have a splinter that works its way in and gets infected, you're gonna have an issue." She wags a finger in my face. "So, unless you want to have pus crusting your ass hairs, I suggest you bend the fuck over."

I squeeze my eyes shut. "Fine. But Isla needs to leave the room. I'd like to hold on to a shred of my fucking dignity."

Isla hands over the flashlight. "Let me know when you're done."

"Isla Rose, don't you *dare* walk in on me," I warn. "If you love me at all, you'll give me some privacy."

She smirks and gives me a thumbs-up before leaving the room.

Lena flicks the flashlight on and adjusts the desk lamp. "I'm a medical professional—"

"Don't talk." I hold up my hand. "Just probe me and get it over with."

She snorts. "Jesus Christ, what is it with men and their assholes? I'm not gonna probe you, Jake. I'm only looking."

"I still hear you talking, Lena." Turning my back, I pull my boxers down. "If I don't hear your voice, I can pretend it's not you."

"Fine. Lean forward and stop clenching so I can actually fucking see."

This surpasses the level of humiliation I can withstand. I may actually die and take my hairy ass crack to hell with me, glass splinters and all. Satan and I can share stories about our ass hairs, although the hellfire probably burned his off. Then again, he's not actually human, so he probably didn't have them in the first place.

What *is* Satan? I think he's a fallen angel—do they have human characteristics?

Lena sighs. "You're still clenching."

"No shit, I'm fucking clenching," I snap. "I guarantee Satan clenches too."

"*What?*"

"Never mind."

"Okay . . ." Lena chuckles. "You've got two choices. Either *you* spread your ass cheeks, or *I* will."

"Mother. Fucker." Resting my face on the counter in hopes I suffocate, I lean forward and spread my legs apart. I grip my cheeks and expose my hairy ass crack to Lena.

She shines the beam of light, examining me more closely than anyone in my pathetic life has ever done before. "Don't move," she murmurs, reaching for the tweezers. "I see one." She painlessly removes it. "Okay, I'm done with your ass. You need to turn around."

"No fucking way."

"Jake, you have a piece of glass embedded in your balls. I can't get to them like this, now turn around. Or do you really want a scrotal infection?"

"I can't believe this," I mutter, covering my cock. I slowly turn to face her.

Lena squats in front of me with the flashlight. "Move your penis to the side."

"He should've bashed my skull in. That would've been better."

She peers up at me. "If my name was Helga and you were in a hospital, would you be giving me this much shit?"

"Probably not. And why are you still talking?"

"I'm a nurse. I'm damn good at my job and I care about *all* my patients. You're my friend, so I care even more about you. I'm sorry you feel embarrassed, but I'm only trying to help you."

"I know. Thank you."

She stares at me, arching an expectant brow.

"What?"

"Can you move your dick, please?"

"Right. Sorry," I mumble, pushing it to the side.

"Lift your balls a little. Or I can—"

"I got it."

"Good. Now, don't move." Lena removes two pieces of glass from my ball sack—ones that I didn't even feel stuck in it. Then again, my entire body throbs and stings like I got stung by a hundred bees, so it's a little hard to differentiate.

"Okay, I think we've got them all," she says, standing. She makes her way over to the sink to wash her hands. "I'm gonna call Marc and have him phone in antibiotics for you, just in case. I want you to take all of them. Some of the lacerations on your back went pretty deep. Keep the bandages on for the rest of today. I'll stop over tomorrow morning with some wound wash, and we'll do a bandage change."

I pull up my boxers, then wash my hands before wrapping her in a hug. "Lena, thank you."

She pats my shoulders to avoid putting pressure on my wounds. "That's what friends are for." She smirks. "If it makes you feel any better, I picked an engorged tick off Wes's balls after we went hiking. You were *way* more cooperative than his pansy ass."

I snort. "Gee, thanks. I feel like a million bucks."

She grabs a Ziploc baggie from a drawer and fills it with glass.

"What's that for?"

"Evidence."

I grip her shoulders. "Please don't show him that."

"He needs to see what he did."

"Yeah, well, in *his* eyes I deserved it. Don't give him the satisfaction."

"You didn't deserve a goddamn thing. Loving his sister is not a crime."

"Again, that depends on whose perspective you're looking from."

"Can I come back yet?" Isla calls from the living room.

"Yeah, Sprite. We're done."

"How'd ya make out?"

"As a matter of fact, I removed three pieces from his nether regions." Lena holds up the baggie. "I'm bringing this home as ammunition for when I rip Wes a new asshole."

Isla scowls. "My brother's damn lucky his girlfriend's a nurse. The media could've had a field day with this."

This is probably a bad idea.

No, it's *definitely* a mistake, but I'm doing it anyway.

I loudly rap on the door to Lena's brownstone. I waited until Isla fell asleep—for the joint nap I conned her into—before I snuck out.

Garrett opens the door, his eyes flaring in shock. "What are you doing here?" he asks in a hushed tone.

"I need to talk to Wes."

He shakes his head. "Not a good idea, man. Give it a few days."

"I assume Lena filled you in?"

"Heard both sides of it, which is why I'm telling you to wait."

"Where is he?"

"Downstairs in my gym. Earlier, he pulverized a punching bag. He's burning out my treadmill at the moment. He's been on it for hours . . . ever since he found out."

"You mean, since he walked in on us?"

"No, that was the boxing. The running started when he learned Reed and Austin knew about you and Isla and didn't tell him."

"Fuck. How'd he hear that?"

"Austin slipped somehow. Wes called Reed to confirm." Garrett looks over his shoulder before turning back to me. "Then Lena put the icing on the cake."

"How so?"

He sighs. "She told him she knew. Lena said people keep him in the dark because he reacts like an asshole. She called him a bully."

I run a hand over my face. "I'm sure that went over well."

"He lost his shit," Garrett mutters. "Now *they* aren't speaking either."

"Wonderful. So, what's the plan? Let him camp out at your place in solitude?"

"Yep."

"Please let me talk to him. His issue is with me, and me alone. Lena is the last person I want to see upset. She's been a friend from the start and spent half the day picking glass out of me."

"I know, she showed me when she got home. Then went upstairs and threw the bag at him." Garrett steps closer to me. "I'll let you in, but I'm coming with you."

"That's not necessary."

"I mean it, bro. Don't start any shit. I'm gonna be pissed if I have to pull him off you. Then I'll kick *both* of your asses."

"You won't have to. I'm good at de-escalating him."

Garrett snorts and holds the door open for me. "Maybe when you weren't the dude banging his little sister."

I follow him downstairs. Wes's heavy footfalls reach my ears, and I wonder how long he's been running.

"Wait here," Garrett says, once we're a few feet from the door. He enters the training room. "Hey, big guy, I need you to stop for a minute."

"What's up, mate?" Wes grunts without slowing his pace.

"Get off and I'll tell you."

The treadmill beeps and slows. "What's wrong?"

"Someone needs to talk to you."

"Tell Lena I've got nothing to say right now. She can try again tomorrow."

Garrett steps aside, and I move into the doorway.

"Got nothing to say to him either." He curls his lip. "Today, tomorrow, or *ever*."

"That's fine, Emerson. But I have something to say to you."

"Too bad." Wes crosses his huge arms over his bare chest. Sweat soaks his hair and pours into his eyes. "Not interested in anything you have to say."

"You misunderstood me." I step forward. "I don't care if you're interested—or whether or not you believe me. Right now, you're going to listen."

Garrett flashes me a warning look. "Remember what I said."

"Don't worry, Garrett, I'm not gonna hit him." Wes sneers, snatching a towel to mop his face. "Would've done it already."

I hold my arms out in invitation. "If you really wanna hit me, go ahead. Kick me, throw tools," I point to my shredded back where blood has seeped through the bandage to stain my shirt. "Go ahead and stab me with more glass . . . I don't give a fuck."

He narrows his eyes. "You'd let me hit you?"

"If it makes you feel better, yeah. Do what you gotta do." I close the distance between us. "But here's what I won't stand for." I point at his face. "You giving Lena, Memphis, Reed, or anyone else shit for *my* actions."

"They helped ya lie," Wes snarls.

"No, they kept their mouths shut about shit that wasn't their business to discuss."

"I should've been told. Isla *is* my business."

"No, she's a fucking grown woman. You are *not* her keeper. Thanks to you, she spent all Christmas Day crying."

He shrugs. "That's her problem."

I stiffen my spine. "News flash. Whether you like it or not, Isla is mine. That means her tears are *my* problem. I don't like seeing her cry, so now I'm going to make it *your* problem." I take a step closer. "I don't care if you own every building in Brooklyn—or the fucking state of New York—I won't let you bulldoze her. You want rent? Name your price and I'll pay it."

"I'm not gonna charge her rent. That's fucking ridiculous."

"Then you'd better respect her boundaries. Because if you think you're going to make her life hell or disrespect her, you can put the brownstone back on the market. She'll live with me."

"You've gone off your bloody rocker, Bennett."

"Have I? Tell me something, Wes. You were so eager to put Isla on a platter and serve her up to Connor—"

"I was not. You're twisting—"

"Then, you supported her when you thought she might be interested in a woman. But when Dana turned out to be me, *that* was an issue?"

"I saw you fucking my baby sister!" he roars.

Garrett moves closer. "Emerson, calm down."

To my surprise, Wes nods and takes a deep breath. Garrett's de-escalation powers are clearly superior to mine.

"She's twenty-three. She's not a baby anymore. And you would've had a problem regardless of whether you walked in on us today or ten years from now."

"You *both* lied to me."

"Yeah, we did. And I'm fucking sorry. I can't speak for Isla, but *I* lied because I didn't want to disrespect you. The last thing I wanted was to hurt you." I meet his gaze. "I realize I crossed a line, but it's not one I crossed lightly. I've agonized over this for years. I'm tired of hiding how I feel. I'm tired of wanting her from a distance, writing song after song about her while everyone else lives their lives."

He furrows his brow. "What're you talking about? What songs?"

I shake my head. "Doesn't matter. My point is, I didn't start things with Isla, and I kept my distance as long as I could. She came to me, man. I'm done fighting it. I won't push her away this time. I deserve to be happy too. After everything she's been through, Isla deserves to be happy. I'm sorry I hurt you, but I won't apologize for loving her." I clench my jaw. "I will *never* apologize for loving her, and I'll do it until the day I die."

He blinks. "You actually love her?"

"You say it like I'm the kind of guy who plays games with women. I think you know me well enough to know that I don't. Why do you think I haven't seen anyone in years?"

"You tell me."

"Because I refused to hurt someone by going through the motions when my heart wasn't in it. Because Isla ruined me for all other women, and I didn't care enough to try with anyone else."

"How long have you felt this way?"

"Since your thirtieth birthday party."

He raises a brow. "Elaborate."

"I can't explain it. We were just hanging out at the beach, and she kissed me. I was so stunned. I never expected her to do that. I didn't see her that way. Not until then. I panicked and walked away."

"Because of me?"

"Yeah, you were a huge part of it. Plus, the fact that she was barely eighteen." I shake my head. "I didn't ask for her persistence, and I certainly didn't expect her to move across the street from me. *That* was your doing. I guess what I don't understand is how Connor and Dana were acceptable options. You were fine with them, but *I'm* not good enough for her? Why is that, Emerson?"

"You're not the issue! For fuck's sake, Bennett. Are you blind?"

"Don't tell me no one would be good enough for her because we both know that's a crock of shit."

"I never said you weren't good enough for her." Wes shakes his head. "It's not about that."

"What's your issue?"

"She'll *destroy* you, mate. She'll fucking wreck you." He grips my shoulders. "Open your eyes. You need more than she can give. Did ya think about what's gonna happen after her internship?"

I press my lips in a thin line but don't answer. He doesn't need to know about Isla's plan to work at The Phoenix with me.

"Let me clue you in. She'll move back to Melbourne and leave ya behind."

"You don't know that."

"Listen to yourself. You know it as well as I do. Isla's a free spirit. You can't make her settle. All the sewing machines or koalas in the world wouldn't settle her. You're a temporary fix, a stop along the way. You're ready to settle, start new chapters in life, but she's not there yet—you're not her final destination. She can't give you the security you crave. She isn't ready for forever. Isla will *never* be ready for forever. I know you want them to, but your stories don't connect. She's in a different book, mate."

"You don't know that either."

"I know my sister better than anyone else." He tightens his grip. "You forget how well I know *you*, Bennett. Think about the future. Where do you see yourself in five years?"

With Isla.

When I don't answer, he says, "Settled. Stable. You've got roots, Jake." He slowly shakes his head. "That's not Isla. You two are like earth and sky— total opposites. You can't ground her. No one can. At the slightest hint of her taking flight, you'll panic and tighten your grip. By pulling her closer, you'll push her away. You'll try to cage her before she's ready, and you'll lose her." He releases me and takes a step back. "Then I'll lose you both."

"Maybe you're right," I say, forcing a swallow. "Or maybe you don't know her as well as you think you do. Either way, it's a chance I need to take. The way I see it, earth meets sky on the horizon."

It's a line from a song I'm working on for Isla.

"The horizon you see is an illusion. Earth and sky never truly come together in the end." He runs a hand over his face. "She'll wreck you."

"Maybe she won't."

He shakes his head. "I hope you know what you're doing."

"All I know is that I love her. If we're destined to crash and burn, then so be it. At least I got the chance to fly."

"Don't come crying to me when it happens."

"Don't worry. I won't come to you for anything." I step around Wes and head past Garrett for the door.

"Bennett."

I look over my shoulder at Wes.

"I'm sorry about the hammer. I didn't see your face. I never would've thrown it if I didn't think she was in danger. I didn't mean to hurt you."

I give him a curt nod and leave without a word. His apology surprises me but doesn't ease the sting. I won't tell him it's all right because it isn't. Now that the adrenaline—and ibuprofen—has worn off, my back burns like a bitch.

His foray into fortune-telling hurts more than any laceration. His words run laps through my mind, seeping into the cracks and chasms carved by anxiety.

What if I am only a stop along the way?

Will Isla return to Australia? Did she agree to my Phoenix proposal because I put her on the spot? Does she truly see a future between us, or is my time with her merely a brief layover during her journey?

The horizon you see is an illusion.

CHAPTER 45

Isla

One week later

Internal playlist: "Hear Me" by Kelly Clarkson

Our waitress leaves with our lunch order and Lena grips my hand. "You're too quiet today. Please tell me what's wrong."

"I dunno."

"Yes, you do. How was the weekend? Did Jake take you on a New Year's Eve date?"

"No," I mutter. "He said he wasn't feeling well and went to bed at eight."

Lena's brows pop. "Night owl Jake?"

"Yep." I deflect the topic back onto her before I burst into tears. "What did you guys end up doing?"

"Nothing eventful. Just a quiet dinner at home." She smirks. "And some make-up sex."

"Gross. Say no more." I shudder and sip my iced tea. "But I'm glad you two are talking. I felt terrible when you mentioned you had a row over us."

"Please don't stress about it. You know Wes—explode, simmer for a bit, then cool down. His temper isn't new to me, and I've weathered bigger storms with him."

"I don't know how you deal with his shit."

"He has endearing qualities." She squeezes my hand. "How's Jake's back? Wes feels like a piece of shit about it."

"He should." I meet her gaze. "Jake's back is healing, but his head's fucked up."

"What do you mean?"

"He's been . . . different."

She tilts her head. "In general, or toward you?"

"Both." I blink rapidly. "Other than a peck on the cheek, he hasn't touched me since it happened."

"Are you serious?"

I nod. "He's been with Austin in the studio all week, planning that Valentine's concert. Between that, having Jesse staying with him, and the community center, he's got a lot on his plate. I get it and I'm trying to be supportive and understanding. But . . ."

"But what?"

"He's been distant."

Lena furrows her brow. "Did you ask him about it?"

"Yeah. Said he has a lot on his mind." I chew my lip. "I tried to be intimate with him, but he turned me down."

"Like cuddling?"

I look at my hands. "Everything. I was gonna give him a blowie, but he rolled over and went to sleep instead." A tear rolls down my cheek. "I understand he's upset over his fight with Wes, and the sheer chaos of the last time we had sex, but I feel like it goes deeper than that."

"Talk to him."

"Lena, I've tried, but he's moody as hell."

"Do you think it's his depression?"

"Maybe. But somehow it feels directed at me. I've been walking on eggshells since Christmas, but it hasn't helped—he's still distant and cold." I swipe at some tears. "Maybe he's decided I'm not worth the trouble."

"Isla, stop. You know he loves you. I think he's having a hard time balancing his life right now. I mean, he's trying to be there for Jesse, his friendship with Wes went to shit, he's gotta deal with idiot contractors all day, and according to Austin, the Valentine's concert is more work than they'd expected." She tucks her hair behind an ear. "Just be you. Keep smiling and shining. He'll be back to himself soon."

"Let's hope," I mutter.

The waitress delivers our meals. The food looks good, but I don't feel like eating. I don't feel like doing much of anything. Wes and I aren't speaking, which is a first for us. Whereas when Reed and I had a rocky relationship, Wes was my rock. Now, the tables have turned. When I filled Reed in on the Christmas showdown, he told me to give Wes space and offered to talk some sense into him. Clearly, that hasn't happened yet.

Jake's behavior has my stomach twisting into knots. An invisible band squeezes my chest and the tears hover inside my eyes, waiting to spill over. It seems like he regrets being with me, like I somehow fucked up his life. I suppose I did to some degree since Jake and Wes aren't speaking either. The warm, welcoming man I fell in love with has become someone else entirely. An aloof, moody, disinterested version of himself, and I don't like it.

I miss my brother. I miss warm Jake. I'd give anything to bring things back to the way they were.

Maybe I was wrong to follow my heart.

"Do you need a ride to your internship?"

"No. Jake's taking me."

"Perfect. I can pick you up on the days I work." Lena perks up. "Don't forget about tomorrow night."

I look at her, puzzled. "What's tomorrow night?"

"Our self-defense classes, silly."

"Fuck. I forgot all about those."

Lena bites into her pickle. "How'd Jake react when you told him you agreed to them?"

I shake my head. "I never told him."

"Seriously?"

"I was going to mention it the next day at breakfast, but Jesse called with news of Hannah's passing and everything went to shit. I honestly haven't thought about the classes since." I rub my temples. "I can't believe I forgot to mention it to him. Do I really have to do them?"

Lena's face falls. "Don't tell me you're backing out on me."

I sigh heavily. "Do I have the option to back out?"

"Of course you do. I'm being selfish. I wanted someone to commiserate with, so I didn't have to exercise alone." She gives me a sheepish smile. "It's okay. I'll tell Wes you're not into it."

"No." I grip her wrist. "I'll do it. I gave Wes my word—if I back out, he'll never forgive me."

"Are you sure?"

"Yes. I won't abandon you. Besides, maybe this is the olive branch Wes and I need."

Lena smiles and hugs me. "That's my girl."

"Now I need to figure out how I'm gonna bring it up to Jake. Then again, he hasn't seemed interested in anything I do, so why should this be any different?"

CHAPTER 46

Jake

Mood: "An Evening I Will Not Forget" by Dermot Kennedy

I pace the kitchen and listen to the idiot architect ramble about having to move some load-bearing walls. I don't give a fuck which wall goes where, as long as they finish building the place.

Jesse walks in and opens the fridge for the third time this hour. He surveys the contents and grunts.

I cover the phone with my hand. "Do you think something's gonna magically appear?"

He shakes his head. "Can't decide what I feel like. Are you hungry?"

"Not really." I point to the phone. "Lost my appetite during this conversation."

"What's Isla doing tonight?"

I shrug. "No idea."

He narrows his eyes on me. "When you get off the phone, I need to ask you something."

I nod and turn my attention back to the architect.

The doorbell rings. I make my way to the foyer and open the front door for Isla. I raise a brow. "Pretty sure I gave you a key."

"It's in my other handbag and I didn't feel like climbing sixty-five steps." She gives me a small smile. "Hi."

"Hi." I kiss her forehead and point to my phone.

Nodding, Isla makes her way into the kitchen. I follow a few feet behind so I can wrap up my phone call. Her unsteady gait alarms me.

I hustle forward and grip her arm. "Why are you limping?"

"I tripped on the sidewalk and twisted my ankle."

"Are you all right? Is it bruised?"

"Not yet, but it will be," she mutters.

I open the freezer and reach for an ice pack. If she's already limping, I can guarantee its bruised—and swollen.

"I don't need ice, Jake. I'm fine."

She doesn't need you, the voice in my head whispers. "Okay, suit yourself," I mumble, closing the freezer door.

Isla settles beside Jesse. "Hey, Jess."

"How's it going, Isla?"

She shrugs. "I'm a little nervous about my internship starting tomorrow, but I'm okay. How're you holding up?"

"I'm taking each moment as it comes. Sometimes, I feel at peace knowing Hannah isn't suffering any longer. Other times, I can't breathe." He lets out a heavy sigh. "Comes in waves."

She squeezes his arm. "If there's anything I can do, please let me know. Have you two eaten?"

I end the call and shrug, focusing my attention out the window. I haven't been hungry in days. The last thing I need is a migraine, so I keep force-feeding myself. It would probably help if I took my anxiety meds, but I haven't made it to the pharmacy to pick up my refill. I also haven't found the energy to return Dr. Ortiz's calls about rescheduling my appointment. I don't feel like talking.

To anyone.

"Hello? Earth to Jacob."

"Not hungry," I mutter, avoiding her gaze.

"That wasn't my question." She weaves her hair into a braid. "I feel like cooking something. Maybe Jesse's hungry?"

He chuckles. "I'm always hungry."

"Okay, since Jake's on some sort of hunger strike, I'll ask you. Whaddya feel like eating?"

"Can we have pasta?"

"I've got tortellini or penne."

"You decide," Jesse says.

"I'll surprise you." Isla rises. "Let me head home and see what I can whip up." She looks over at me. "Can we talk?"

The voices in my head let loose a chorus of whispers. *She's done with you. She had her hookup and she's ready to move on.*

I give her a curt nod. "Yep."

"Alone?"

She doesn't want to embarrass you in front of Jesse.

Bile rises in my throat, but I force a shrug and follow her outside. "What's up?"

She doesn't answer until we cross the street. "You tell me."

"Pretty sure *you're* the one who wanted to talk."

"I want you to tell me what I did wrong." She limps up her stoop and unlocks the front door.

I scratch my head. "Who said you did something wrong?"

"Your attitude and body language." Isla props her hands on her hips. "I wanna know what's wrong."

"I've got a lot on my mind."

She enters the kitchen and fills a pot with water. Placing it on the burner, she shakes her head and mumbles something under her breath.

"What was that? Didn't hear you."

"I *said*, this is the part where you tell me what's on your mind." She cocks her head. "But it doesn't look like you're gonna do it."

I sigh heavily. "What do you want from me?"

"I dunno, Jake. Maybe your honesty? If this isn't working between us—"

Panic flares in my chest. "What the hell does *that* mean?" My voice rises an octave with my heart rate. "You're giving up on us?"

She narrows her eyes. "Is that what you want?"

That's her way of saying yes. Don't hold her too tightly, you're already losing her. Earth and sky never truly come together in the end.

"Is it what *you* want?" I challenge, clenching my fists at my sides.

Her lower lip quivers, but she holds her head high and stiffens her spine. "I asked first."

"No," I snap, moving closer to her. "That's *not* what I want."

"Neither do I, but why do we feel broken?" A tear rolls down her cheek. "I want my old Jake back. The one who smiled from his eyes."

"I'm sorry, honey, but I don't feel like smiling."

"Why?" she whispers.

I spear my hands into my hair. "Because everything went to shit."

"But we still have each other—"

For how long?

"What happens next week? Next month? Next year? What happens when your internship ends?"

"How the hell should I know? I can't predict the bloody future—I could get hit by a bus tomorrow. Or struck by lightning. No one knows what's gonna happen in life. We've gotta live it as it comes. Besides, as Jesse's circumstances prove, the future isn't guaranteed. For anyone."

Notice she didn't mention The Phoenix? She doesn't want that for her life. You pressured her into it. She's also not wearing any of the jewelry you gave her.

I clench my jaw, feeling my nostrils flare. "Not the answer I was looking for."

"What're ya talking about?" She throws her hands in the air. "Jacob, you aren't making sense."

The horizon you see is an illusion.

I swallow and blink my eyes against the sudden sting. "How long until it's over?"

"Until what's over?"

I stare at my feet. "When does it end for us?"

Isla holds her hand up to silence me. "Go home and get some sleep. You're spewing crazy shit right now, and I don't have the energy for it. Tell Jesse I'll bring his food over when it's ready."

She's checking out now. You're dismissed. She's ready to move on to the next one.

She's not ready to settle.

You're a temporary fix. A stop along the way.

"That's your answer?" I sputter, tugging on my hair. "That's your idea of reassurance?"

Isla points to the door. "Go home, Jacob. I can't deal with ya right now." She pours a box of penne into the boiling water and stirs.

My eyes blur with tears, but I refuse to blink. "First you wanted to talk. Now you're telling me I'm dismissed?" I force the words out in a strangled whisper.

"Yeah. For the rest of tonight," she replies without even looking at me. "We can try again tomorrow."

My head is spinning, so I leave without another word and head home. Jesse's still in the kitchen, reading a newspaper.

"That was quick."

"She said she'll bring the food over when it's ready."

He eyes me. "What's going on with you two? Am I putting a damper on things?"

"No. Not at all. It has nothing to do with you, man."

"Then what's up? It's been a while since I've seen this side of you."

I glare at him. "What the hell does that mean?"

"The side that comes out when you spend too much time in your own head." He folds the newspaper. "I've known you since you were five and I can read you like a book. I don't know what stories you're telling yourself, but you need to stop. Chill the fuck out."

CHAPTER 47

Isla

Internal playlist: "I'm Like a Bird" by Nelly Furtado

Lena picks me up outside the building that houses the internship program headquarters. I slide into the front seat of her car and wince at the throb in my ankles. We're on our way to Next Level, Connor's gym. I'm utterly exhausted from being on my feet all day. I don't know how productive I'll be at these fucking classes, but I gave Wes and Lena my word.

She grins at me. "I'm dying to hear how your first day was."

"Amazing. I really believe in this program and can't wait to help these women get back on their feet."

"Are you only designing work attire?"

"Mainly professional attire, yes. But the budget has some flexibility. I'm sure I'll get to make some pretty dresses too."

"What did Jake say when he dropped you off?"

"He didn't."

"Huh? The other day you told me he was taking you."

"I called a car service instead." Blinking rapidly, I stare out the window. "Tried talking to him last night, but he was being a dick, so I sent him home."

"What the hell is going on with him?"

I shake my head. "Dunno, Lena. But I won't be anyone's burden. I'll find my own way into the city."

"Was he pissed you called for a car?"

"I doubt he even remembers today was my first day, or that he agreed to take me. I wanted to arrive early, so I left the house at seven. Saw Jesse outside and he told me Jake wasn't up yet."

"Holy shit. I bet he blew up your phone when he woke."

I shrug. "Dunno. I left it at home."

"Wait, so you haven't talked to him *at all?*"

"Nope. My attempt to talk last night was a joke, so I decided not to bother. I was way too nervous about my first day." I stare out the window. "Would've been nice to have someone hug me this morning and tell me 'good luck,' but I digress."

Lena sighs. "I'm sorry he's acting this way, Isla. Let's enjoy our class and grab a drink afterward to celebrate your first day."

"Works for me."

CHAPTER 48

Jake

Mood: "Unwell" by Matchbox 20

I peek through the blinds at the sound of a car door, expecting to see Isla. Nope. It's our neighbor. I glance at my watch. It's after six.

Where the fuck is she?

Is she hurt or lost in the city somewhere, but too stubborn to call me? Or worse, did the driver abduct her?

I can't believe I overslept this morning. I had planned to stop at Nicolai's Bakery to grab breakfast for us on our way into the city. I rolled out of bed at fucking ten thirty instead. The reason why isn't a mystery. Thanks to my ruminating brain, I didn't fall asleep until after four. To make matters worse, I forgot to set my alarm.

I *never* do that.

When I rushed downstairs in a panic, Jesse informed me a car service had picked Isla up at seven. An hour earlier than I told her we'd leave.

She hasn't returned any of my calls.

This is the beginning of the end, a voice in my head whispers. I clench my jaw and try to stop my train of thought in its tracks.

But I can't.

It plows into me, shoving me forward as I trip over weathered railroad ties and gravel.

Jesse's words from Hannah's viewing flutter through my mind. *Savor every fucking moment. Because you never know when or how she'll be taken from you.*

I pace the living room. Headlights signal an approaching car, but it's not her. Bile rises in my throat. I try to think of other things—like the show I'm planning with Memphis—but it backfires. Thoughts of Austin immediately branch to Wes, the third Musketeer. I can still hear his voice in my head, his warning on a continuous loop.

You're a temporary fix, a stop along the way. You're ready to settle, start new chapters in life, but she's not there yet—you're not her final destination.

Her train is going to blow through my stop and run me over in the process.

I know you want them to, but your stories don't connect. She's in a different book, mate.

It seems she's already closed our book. Thanks to me.

By pulling her closer, you'll push her away. You'll try to cage her before she's ready, and you'll lose her.

I've tried to keep my distance, even when all I want to do is pull her close, hold her, and never let her go. I can't let myself stifle or suffocate her. I won't allow my love to cage her.

The horizon you see is an illusion. Earth and sky never truly come together in the end.

She'll wreck you.

She already has.

Jesse appears in the doorway. "You're pacing."

"No shit, man," I snap.

"Call her."

"She's not returning my fucking calls, okay?"

"Maybe she went to see Wes. Try calling him."

"Nope. I said everything I need to say to him."

Jesse cocks his head. "Then call Lena."

"I don't wanna drag her into this. Wes already gave her shit about me and Isla. She's gotta deal with him, so I won't add drama to her life." I make a lap around the couch. "What if something happened? What if she's hurt? Lost in the city? What if the driver abducted her?"

Jesse throws his hands in the air. "What if she sprouted a dick overnight and moved to Vegas?"

I glare at him. "It's not funny, man."

"I want you to realize how ridiculous you sound." He tosses me my phone. "Why don't you call Garrett and see if Isla is upstairs with Lena and Wes? This way, you keep Lena out of the mix, and you can ease your alien abduction fears too."

Scowling, I scroll through the contacts and locate Garrett's name.

He answers on the second ring. "Jake, what's going on, man?"

"Hey. Have you seen Isla lately?"

"I haven't seen her, but I know she and Lena went out tonight."

I clench the phone. "Out?"

"Yeah. I talked to Wes earlier. He said Lena wanted to celebrate Isla's first day with a few drinks after class."

"What class?"

"Dude, where have you been? The self-defense classes at my cousin's gym. Remember? They started tonight."

You never know when or how she'll be taken from you. My vision blurs and my ears start to ring.

Garrett's voice echoes in the distance. "Hello? Are you there?"

"Yep."

"So, anyway, Lena picked Isla up at four so they could make it to class on time."

"Interesting."

"Huh?"

"Isla never mentioned the classes. Not since Wes first brought them up."

"That's weird. She agreed to them weeks ago."

What else hasn't she told you?

I squeeze the phone tight enough to crack the plastic case. "Oh, did she?" I choke out the words.

"Yeah. Listen, I've gotta run. My director's calling. I'll catch up with you later." He hangs up.

Wheezing, I slowly sink to the couch.

Connor.

He made his move.

Connor is the one taking Isla from me.

Connor, with his huge muscles and tattoos, bigshot FBI job, a mind not riddled with anxiety and insecurities, and—let's not forget—Wes's full approval. My hands start to shake, making me drop my phone.

Jesse walks over. "What's wrong?"

"It's happening." A wave of nausea slams into me. The panini I inhaled during lunch lands on my best friend's feet.

"Fuck!" He jumps back as I heave a second time. I can't see Jesse or hear his next words through the suffocating haze, but Wes's booming voice echoes in my head. *You're a temporary fix . . . you're not her final destination.* His words reverberate against my skull, drowning out light, color, and sound. Flooding my veins and pulling me beneath the surface. *Earth and sky never truly come together in the end.*

Images of Isla in Connor's arms assail me. Her soft body beneath him. Her nails digging into his back. His cock stretching and filling her. The cruel montage etches itself into my brain. I'd claw my eyes out if only I could get it to stop.

You never mattered to her.

My universe fades from gray to black.

CHAPTER 49

Isla

Internal playlist: "Seven Devils" by Florence + The Machine

I slide from the passenger seat after hugging Lena. "Thank you for cheering me up tonight. I had a blast with you."

She grins. "Likewise, sweetie. Sorry we had to stay out so late so I could sober up. I didn't plan on that second margarita."

"No worries, love. I think I talked you into it." I grab my handbag. "We doing this again on Thursday?"

She giggles. "Hell yes! But only let me have *one* drink."

"I'll keep you in check. Night, love." I close the car door and limp up my front steps. Lena waits until I'm safely inside before leaving.

I lock up, sliding all my deadbolts, and toss my keys into the dish on my new accent table. I slide out of my coat and hang it up. I'm still wearing my gym clothes, which is fine because we really didn't sweat.

Tonight's class was an introduction. Connor spent most of it discussing the types of martial arts and the importance of situational awareness. Six women signed up for the class, and they all seem like cool chicks. Maybe I'll make some new friends, so I don't dominate Lena's time.

Speaking of Lena, my phone chimes from somewhere in the living room. She promised to text me when she got home. I make my way in there and try to remember where I left the thing. I open a desk drawer. Nope. Sifting through a stack of papers, I push items around and scratch my head. I know

I had it when I called the driver, but for the life of me, I can't remember where I left it.

"Looking for this?" Jake's voice comes from behind me.

Screaming, I knock the wicker desk chair onto its side and whirl to face him. He lounges on my couch and holds up my phone.

"Jesus Christ! You scared the piss outta me!" I shudder and make my way over to him. "I forgot the damn thing when I ran out the door this morning."

Face set in stone, he stares up at me but doesn't speak.

"What's wrong?"

The muscle in his jaw pulses. His gaze slices through me, dark brows meeting in the middle. He remains silent.

Cold.

Unyielding.

"Lemme guess. You're pissed I didn't call ya?" I point to the phone in his hand. "There's your reason."

"They don't have phones in your office?"

"They do, but I'm shitty with numbers. I don't have everyone's phone number committed to memory."

"You expect me to believe that?" He leans forward. "Or is *mine* the only one that slipped your mind?"

"The only one I remember is Wes's because it's been the same for years." I cock my head. "Like I said, I'm shitty with numbers."

"How was your day?" He asks the question but there's a disconnect between the words and his tone, making it crystal clear he doesn't give a fuck how my day was. This is a fishing expedition and I'm not biting.

"Good. And yours?" I chirp, snatching my phone.

"Hell."

"Sorry to hear that." I scroll through my texts and type a quick reply to Lena before turning back to Jake. "Did you and Austin nail down the set list for the show?"

"Yes." Jake stands. He's only got me by a few inches, but he seems much taller now. It probably has something to do with the fury in his gaze, but I'm not giving him the satisfaction of addressing it.

I yawn. "Are you around tomorrow? Maybe we can do something for dinner?"

"Why didn't you tell me?"

Again, I'm no marlin. He can cast as many lines as he'd like, but I'm not biting. "Tell you what?"

"Don't play games with me—you know what I'm talking about," he snaps. When I don't answer, he narrows his eyes. "Did you think I wouldn't find out?"

"About *what*, Jacob? I've had a long day, so I don't have the energy for your riddles."

Sneering, he steps closer to me. "Someone else wear you out?"

"What're ya gettin' at?"

"You never told me you agreed to take the classes."

"I didn't remember until yesterday."

He cocks a brow. "Do I look like an idiot?"

"Not usually, no." I cross my arms. "I told Wes I'd take them when he and Lena took me shopping for house stuff. I planned to mention it to you the next day, but Jesse called with news of Hannah's passing, and I completely forgot. Had Lena not reminded me at lunch yesterday, I would've missed the first one."

"You could've told me last night."

"You mean when I called you over here to talk and you refused to do so?"

His brows knit into a scowl. "I didn't refuse to talk—"

"Bullshit." I wave a finger in his face. "I asked what was on your mind, and you gave me nothing. I was nervous about today and wanted some reassurance, or maybe a hug, but you were cold to me. Didn't seem like the time to bring up the topic."

"Tonight's class was your last one. I don't want you going to any more of them."

I bristle at his command. "Too bad. I gave Wes and Lena my word."

His eyes darken. "And what about me?"

I shrug. "I've given you every part of me, but it doesn't seem to matter."

"What the fuck does that mean?"

"Number one, you need to change your tone. You're being combative for no reason."

His nostrils flare. "You snuck out an hour earlier than we agreed to this morning, didn't contact me all day—"

"We already covered that part. I'll memorize your phone number immediately."

He clamps his hands on my shoulders. "This isn't a joke, Isla!"

"Do you see me laughing?"

"I worried about you all fucking day. Then you didn't come home until after midnight. I found out from Garrett that you were rolling around with his fucking cousin!" The words leave his lips on a snarl, making me flinch.

I take a few deep breaths to calm my nerves. "I didn't roll around with anyone. I sat in a chair and listened to Connor talk about martial arts."

"So, you could listen to *him*, but you dismissed *me* last night?"

"Last night," I begin, shrugging out of his grasp, "I tried to connect with you, but you blocked me out."

Jake sneers. "How quickly you move on to the next one."

I steel my shoulders. "Excuse me?"

"Is that what I am to you? A stepping-stone? A stop along the way? We both know I'm not your final destination. The horizon is a fucking illusion."

I jab a finger in his chest. "This is the shit I'm talking about. You and your goddamn riddles."

"Then riddle me this. If you knew it would upset me, why'd you agree to the classes?"

"Because Wes backed me into a corner. I owe him—for the house, his fucking kidney. Self-defense classes are a small price to pay for all of that. It's all he's ever asked of me." I clench my jaw. "And I gave him my word."

"Since we know where Wes stands with me, I'm sure the fact that Connor has his approval eases the transition for you."

"What transition?"

"I mean, you and Connor are part of the same book. Think about it—he's the perfect age, he's got an FBI job, he owns a gym. Hell, you love muscles and tattoos—he's even got those. Wes planned to serve you up on a platter from the get-go. Tell me, did he arrange your marriage too? Where will you lovebirds be honeymooning? Did Wes assign a specific number of kids, or will you two get to decide on that?" His lips curl in disgust as he spits out the words. "Will you get any say in the names?"

"Jake, you're off your bloody rocker."

"Am I?" He steps closer to me. "Because it seems everything's falling into place. When will you stop being your brother's pawn?"

"I am not his pawn. And for the love of Christ, I'm *not* interested in Connor!"

"Why not? *Our* stories don't connect, so he'd be perfect for you." He shakes his head. "Tell Connor he can thank me later."

"What're you saying?" This feels a lot like being dumped, and I can't wrap my mind around what's happening. I open and close my mouth. "Connor can thank you for what?"

Curling his lip, Jake sweeps his gaze over my body. "Breaking you in for him. Now you're ready to ride with the big dogs."

Before I realize what's happening, my hand collides with his cheek. "How dare you!" I shriek, slapping his other cheek. "I fucking saved myself for *you*!"

"C'mon, Isla. Don't pretend I mean something to you."

"Get out!" I screech, shoving his shoulders.

"Dismissing me again?"

Bitter tears stream from my eyes, burning my cheeks. "Get the fuck out of my house!"

Jake stares at me for a moment, like he's trying to decide whether I'm serious. Then he stalks from the room without another word. He doesn't even glance over his shoulder at me.

I plop facedown onto my couch, crying so hard I can't breathe. The walls close in around me as the suffocating weight of my heartache crushes what's left of me.

CHAPTER 50

Jake

Five days later

Mood: Gel bleach is far superior to the spray.

Jesse leans against the bathroom doorframe. He's been there ten minutes. I keep waiting for him to say something, but he doesn't—just keeps watching me in silence.

I'm on my hands and knees, wedged between the vanity and toilet, scrubbing some rust from the grout with an old toothbrush. I wish dentists didn't steer everyone away from hard-bristled brushes because those fuckers are hard to come by.

"I think you got it, man."

I hold up a spray bottle. "The infomercial guaranteed this shit would remove years' old rust stains. They can stuff their Good Housekeeping Seal up their asses."

Jesse rubs his jaw. "I don't see any rust, dude."

No, it's definitely there. I point to the spot. "You can't see the reddish tinge?"

"Not on the grout, no. I think what you're seeing is blood."

I frown. "It's not bl—"

"Look at your hands." Jesse marches over, snatching my wrists. "They're fucking raw. Your knuckles are bleeding."

"I'm fine."

"No, man," he shakes his head, "you are not fine. Not even a little. When is the last time you ate?"

Two days ago. "I dunno."

"C'mon, let's go to Ralph's for lunch."

"I don't feel like eating. I want to get this bathroom clean." My gaze finds a smudge on the mirror. I'll take care of that next. *I need to buy more Windex. And bleach. I need—*

"Jake, the bathroom is clean. You've used every fucking chemical known to man. I'm light-headed from breathing the fumes."

"No one told you to stand there," I mutter. "I need to get this done."

"Or what?" He grips my shoulders. "What happens if the nonexistent rust stain stays there for the rest of eternity?"

I stare up at him. The rational side of my brain is mute, and I know he'll never understand the shit my anxiety voices spew.

"Tell me. Will the house be overrun with roaches? Or a stink bug infestation? Will the place burn down? Are the pipes gonna burst?"

I clench my jaw. "No."

"Is someone gonna march in and revoke your Grammy awards? Unwrite your songs? Make you unlearn the piano? Infect you with smallpox?"

"Stop, Jess."

"Will your spleen rupture? Will my spleen rupture? Will your teeth fall out? Will I get hit by a bus?"

What happens when you lose Jesse too? Or your mom? Who's gonna give a fuck about you then?

No one. You'll be alone like you deserve.

"Stop!" I bellow, knotting my hands in my hair. "I know it's ridiculous, but I can't control this. You don't get it, Jess. I *need* to clean or—"

"Or what?" Jesse barks. "What's gonna happen, Jake? I need to understand what's going on in your head because you're fucking scaring me." He shakes me by the shoulders. "This isn't you, man. You're strung out and manic. How much caffeine's in your system?"

About one thousand milligrams. Ten cups of coffee. The shakes aren't as bad anymore, as long as I keep my hands busy. I need the caffeine to keep the quiet times away. "I dunno."

"You're not eating or sleeping, and you've been drinking nothing but coffee. I'm surprised you haven't gotten a migraine yet. When do you see Dr. Ortiz next?"

Never. "Dunno."

"Bullshit. You told me she had to reschedule, so when is your new appointment?"

"Don't have one."

"Why not? She left a voicemail on your house phone last week. Didn't you call her?"

She left four messages on my cell too. "No, I didn't call her. I don't want to talk." I look away and start scrubbing the tile again. I'm probably the only thirtysomething who still has a house phone, but what happens if the cell towers fail and there's an emergency or something?

Jesse snatches the toothbrush and pulls me to my feet. "We're getting you out of the house for a bit. Let's get food."

I can't leave. I can't look at her door and wonder who else has been walking through it. "I don't wanna leave the house." I shrug out of his hold. "And I don't feel like eating."

"I don't give two shits what you feel like doing—you're coming. I'll fucking force-feed you if necessary." He grabs my face, tilting it to look at him. "Listen to me, I'm not gonna watch you crash and burn, my friend. Not now, not ever."

His face blurs as tears fill my eyes. They slide down my cheeks and drip onto my neck. Truth is, I've already crashed—it happened when I stopped my meds.

Now, I'm burning.

My eyes and nose burn from the chemicals I've inhaled. My throat burns from crying. Acid churns my empty stomach, gurgling into my throat. My lower back keeps spasming from crouching on the bathroom floor for hours. Everything's fucking burning and I can't stop it. But nothing compares to the hollow ache in my chest.

Jesse's lips are moving, but I can't hear him over the voices in my head.

CHAPTER 51

Isla

Two days later

Internal playlist: "Light On" by Maggie Rogers

Someone's knocking. I frown and glance at the clock. It's nine thirty. *Who the hell's popping over this late?*

Setting aside my crocheting, I rise and hobble to the foyer. I peer through the window and quickly open the door for Jesse.

"I need to talk to you," he says.

I squeeze my eyes shut and step aside so he can enter. I point to my couch. "Have a seat."

He settles with a heavy sigh. "I'm sorry to bother you this late, but I'm worried about Jake."

I stiffen and force a nonchalance I don't feel. "Is he all right?"

Jesse shakes his head. "Far from it."

"Serves him right for being a dick to me," I mutter, crossing my arms over my chest.

He rubs his temples. "Listen, I know he hurt you, but you've gotta understand that it's not him. *None* of this is him."

"*He* absolutely stood here and accused me of cheating." I clench my jaw against the welling tears. "Trust me, I didn't imagine my heart being broken."

"I'm not saying he didn't hurt you."

"He pissed me off too."

"He's a damn fool and you have every right to be angry. But I'm truly worried this time, Isla. We've been friends since kindergarten. I've seen Jake deal with a lot of shit, but I've never seen him like this." He pins me with his gaze. "He's not eating or sleeping—"

"Neither am I."

"Our friend Maura called me. Jake never picked up his refills. He stopped taking his meds after Christmas."

"She's a pharmacist. She shouldn't be telling you anything like that with the privacy laws. I'm not even from this country and I know that."

"Yeah, well, Maura's also known Jake forever, so she's doing the concerned friend thing. She reached out after Jake's psychiatrist called the pharmacy to see if he'd picked up his prescriptions."

Why isn't he taking his meds?

Jesse leans in. "Yesterday, I heard from Dr. Ortiz herself. Since I'm his emergency contact, she called to let me know she's concerned that Jake won't return her calls. She rescheduled his appointment from before Christmas, but he blew off the new one." He rubs his jaw. "Simply didn't show up—no call or anything. He's been her patient since his teens, and he's never done that. Jake's mom called me this morning. He's avoiding her too. He's super tight with Donna and has never shut her out before."

"Why is he doing this?" I whisper, hugging myself.

"He's sick, Isla. That's what I'm trying to tell you. Jake needs help. He's depressed and his OCD is out of control. He's fucking spiraling and I can't seem to reach him."

"What can I do?"

"That's why I'm here. I need to know where you stand."

"I love Jake with all my heart, but he shut me out and pushed me away. I gave him every part of me, but it wasn't enough. He doesn't want my help."

"That's not true. You're everything to him. This chaos between you two is only happening because of his mental illness—the anxiety and obsessions completely took over his mind. I need you to understand that. I don't even want to tell you about the compulsive behaviors he's using to cope." He rakes a hand through his hair. "I forced him out of the house the other night. *Forced* him, Isla. Begged him to give me a glimpse of what's in his head."

"Did he?"

"Eventually. I asked him to describe some of the images and inner mono-logue torturing him. And it scared the shit out of me." He motions between us. "We have no fucking idea how debilitating these obsessive thoughts are. The disturbing imagery taunting him wreaks havoc on his mind. Jake struggles even when he's medicated and having regular therapy sessions. Unmedicated? Forget it. His self-isolation and depression are making it worse. This illness is pervasive."

"What can we do?"

"I'm working on getting him some help. I've scheduled several appointments with Dr. Ortiz. I'm going to sit in on a few. I guess what I'm asking is whether you'd be open to trying again? I don't want to give him false hope if you plan to crush him."

I bristle and wave a finger at Jesse. "You need to understand something too. I *never* had plans to hurt Jake. He's the only man I've ever loved. He hurt *me*."

"I understand that." He pins me with his cognac gaze. "But would you let him back in?"

"My door is always open for him, Jesse. It's up to Jake to walk through it. I'll leave the light on, but I won't make it easy for him. Big changes need to happen."

"Was hoping you'd say that."

CHAPTER 52

Isla

Twelve days later

Internal playlist: "Linger" by The Cranberries

I hold my front door open for Lena and stiffen at the sight of Wes. "Why'd ya bring *him*?"

She sighs heavily. "Because he found out we were making cookies and wanted to partake."

"You could've said no."

"Didn't feel like dealing with any foot stomping today."

"What makes you think *I* wanna deal with him?"

"I'm sure you don't, but like I said, he insisted."

I cross my arms over my chest. "I'm not in the mood for his shit."

"Do either of you care that I can hear you?" Wes asks from the foot of the stairs.

"Nope," Lena and I say in unison.

"There's a shocker." Wes makes his way up the steps and stands behind Lena. "I don't wanna fight anymore, Imp."

"Who said we're fighting?" I hold the door open for them.

"You haven't spoken to me in close to a month. In my book, that's fighting."

I narrow my eyes on his face. "Gee, I can't imagine whatcha did to upset me."

"I'm sorry, Isla," he murmurs, touching my shoulder. "For all of it. I reacted without thinking or knowing what I was seeing. I feel terrible about Bennett's back. I'm disgusted with myself over the fact that I could've hurt you both. I'm a fucking asshole."

Taken aback by his apology, I blink a few times and glance at Lena. "Who is he, and what've ya done with my brother?"

Wes rolls his eyes. "Christ, you act like you're dealing with Reed. I'm not *that* much of a dick."

"Jury's still out on that," I chirp. "Let's make some cookies, shall we?"

Lena and Wes follow me into the kitchen. It's Sunday afternoon, so I assumed Wes would be watching the football game with Garrett. Lena hates football—almost as much as I do—so we planned a girls' night in.

"What's new, Imp?"

"Not much. I'm settling in at my internship and meeting some amazing women. My coworkers seem friendly enough, but it's the people we're helping who I'm drawn to. I outfitted a single mom with a business suit last week. Her job interview is tomorrow. I hope it goes well."

"How have you been feeling?" he asks, studying my face.

"Horrendous."

"How come? Are ya havin' a flare?"

"Yeah. A bad one. My day off was Wednesday and I spent too much time in the sun. I had to miss Thursday and Friday because I was puking my guts up."

Wes raises a brow. "It's the middle of winter. How the hell did you get too much sun?"

"I spent a few hours on the rooftop, crocheting." I stupidly thought the fresh air would clear my head, but I didn't account for the sun's reflection off the snow. "I skipped the sunscreen and left my sunglasses in the house. By the time I got inside, my eyeballs were sunburned, and I spent the rest of the day bent over the toilet."

He squeezes his eyes shut. "I hate that you have to deal with that."

I shrug. "I'm used to it."

Lena shudders. "Weren't you cold, sitting up there all that time?"

"Not really," I lie.

I'd hoped the frigid air would numb the hollow spot in my chest where my heart once was. The ache behind my eyes from crying myself to sleep night after night. The throb in my jaw from clenching it all day to keep the tears from falling.

It did none of those things.

"You've got dark circles under your eyes," Wes points out. "You sleeping okay?"

"Nope. I'm more exhausted than I've ever felt."

Lena touches my arm. "How are you tolerating the injectable anticoagulants?"

I switched blood thinners a few days after Jake and I broke up. My rationale was simple: I'm already spending a fortune on the car service that transports me to my internship, so I didn't want to shell out more cash for a ride to the lab. I certainly wasn't about to bug Lena to drive me there. Since these meds have weight-based dosing, there's less need for monitoring. It's a win-win. "The injections are a bitch, but I can handle it." I lift my shirt to show them the tiny bruises on my stomach.

Wes scowls and rubs at his surgical scar.

"How's your joint pain?" Lena asks.

"That pain's no worse than usual, but I've been getting a lot more headaches."

My lupus flare is half the battle. It's my empty hopes and raw regrets that make me a shadow of myself. I'm lonely and fucking sad. The world is devoid of color. Everything is flat, gray, and transparent.

I cried when Jesse detailed the extent of Jake's compulsions. I guess I really didn't understand how deeply rooted and all-consuming his illness is when he's unmedicated. That night, I sent Jesse home with some frozen dinners and made him promise to force-feed Jake. I allowed myself a glimmer of hope.

But it was false hope. Jake hasn't contacted me at all.

At least Jesse keeps me in the loop with his daily updates via text. Jake is thankfully back on his meds. Friday was his second appointment with his psychiatrist. It relieves me to know he's getting the help he needs, but God, I miss him.

Each morning, I meet my driver outside without so much as a glance across the street. I know I'll break down if I see Jake.

But it doesn't matter. My universe is full of reminders.

Last week, I had a meltdown in the produce section of the grocery store when one of his songs came on. I literally sobbed on the baby carrots. I'm not safe at home either. I can't watch TV without seeing a trailer for his upcoming Valentine's show.

The hardest part is how Jake haunts me with his thoughtful gestures— little acts of kindness that hurt as much as they soothe.

I woke up this morning to the scrape of a shovel outside. Last night's snowstorm delivered at least six inches of heavy white stuff. Jake shoveled *my* steps and footpath before doing his own. A few hours later, he scattered rock salt to melt the ice in front of my door. On Tuesday, he dragged my rubbish bins to the curb so the garbos could empty them.

None of it makes sense to me. Why bother doing all that if he doesn't want to be with me? Why put in the effort if he thinks I've moved on?

I broke you in for him.

The knife his words stabbed through my chest is still wedged in there. Every so often it twists. It will be a *long* time before I forget the disgust in his eyes when he looked at me.

If ever.

"So, what else is new?" Wes's voice breaks into my thoughts.

I shrug. "Not much."

"How's Bennett?"

I knew the question was coming, which is a huge part of why I've been avoiding Wes. I swore Lena to secrecy about my fallout with Jake.

I plop a clump of gingerbread dough on the counter. "You'd have to ask him that."

"Not speaking to him at the moment," he mutters.

"Well, that makes two of us."

"What?" His brows pop upward. "I thought you were star-crossed lovers?"

"Yeah. So did I." I clench my jaw. "But I guess I was wrong. He doesn't love me the way I hoped he would."

He frowns. "What makes you say that?"

"Um, maybe because he broke things off after the new year?"

He turns to Lena. "I assume you knew about this?" She avoids making eye contact with him, so he throws his hands in the air. "How come nobody told me? Why am I always the one left in the fucking dark?"

"I told Lena the next morning but asked her to keep her mouth shut. I didn't need you rubbing salt in my wounds." I narrow my eyes. "Or should I say, *glass* in my back?"

He sighs heavily. "Again, I'm sorry for how I reacted."

Lena grips his wrist. "Like I mentioned when we had our fight, I'll keep you informed on a need-to-know basis. Their fallout wasn't any of your business."

"I get it." Wes shakes his head. "But now I'm a little lost."

I meet his gaze. "I'm more than a little lost. I'm fucking devastated. I can't figure out where I went wrong."

The tears I've been fighting since the moment Wes said Jake's name spill over. Unable to face my brother, I hand Lena the rolling pin and pour drinks for them.

"What happened?"

I didn't plan to talk about it, but my brother's concern seems genuine. Besides, the dam's already been broken.

"It's like a switch flipped inside him. I know his anxiety is to blame, but it fucking hurts. The warm, loving man I've known my whole life became cold and distant and . . . cruel."

"That doesn't sound like Bennett."

"No shit. Like I said, something shifted for him. I'm talking a Jekyll and Hyde transformation, but I can't figure out the catalyst. It goes deeper than his anxiety. Something triggered him. He went from professing his love to pushing me away in the span of a few hours."

"When did that start?" Wes asks.

I narrow my eyes on his face. "Why do you care? You gonna gloat?"

"Why would I gloat?"

"Maybe my memory of Christmas differs from the one in your noggin, but if I recall, you said you'd never accept us being together."

He straightens. "Yeah, I said that—and I meant it then—but I've had time to think about the situation. Just because I'm not happy about it, doesn't mean I wanna see you upset. You're my baby sister. I still love you, Imp," he meets my gaze, "even if you hate my guts."

I roll my eyes. "I don't hate you, Wes. I'm angry."

"When Bennett confronted me, he mentioned that you cried all day on Christmas. I'm sorry I ruined your holiday. It was a dick move on my part."

"Wait, what do you mean when he confronted you? I thought you haven't spoken since Christmas?"

"We haven't. I'm talking about when he showed up at Garrett's later that night and got in my face."

Lena sets down the rolling pin. "Hold up. *What?* Where was I?"

Wes smirks. "Need-to-know basis, sunshine." She arches an eyebrow, and he sighs. "You were upstairs in a snit. This was *after* ya threw the bag of glass at me."

"Funny, Garrett never mentioned it."

"I asked him not to." Wes glowers at her. "I can keep secrets too."

I stare at him in disbelief. "Jake never told me you talked—"

"We had quite the row over it. Guess you could say he laid his cards on the table. He sure put me in my place—almost thought he was gonna hit me."

"How did he put you in your place?" I ask, bewildered by the newfound knowledge of their confrontation.

"He told me he's loved you since you kissed him on the beach. That he kept his distance out of respect for me, but he was done pushing you away. He apologized for crossing the line but refused to apologize for loving you. Basically, he made it clear you were his and there was nothing I could do about it." He rubs his jaw. "Anyway, for what it's worth, I apologized for throwing the hammer."

Lena cocks her head. "I'm confused."

"You're confused?" I sputter, gripping the countertop. "I'm fucking bewildered. If Jake said all of that to Wes on Christmas, why'd he immediately change his tune with me? I woke up from a nap and he was moody as fuck."

Wes shrugs. "Dunno, Imp. He gets moody sometimes."

I rub my temples. "He was acting so strange before we broke up. Talking in riddles, spewing nonsense. He kept using weird analogies—"

"Like what?" Wes asks.

Lena touches my shoulder. "Isla, you said he was pissed you never told him about the self-defense classes. He's jealous of Connor, obviously."

"Insanely jealous. In fact, he concocted some narrative about me being Wes's pawn. He called himself a stepping-stone on my path to Connor."

"That's utterly ridiculous." Wes scoffs.

"Try telling Jake that. According to him, our stories don't connect, but Connor and I are part of the same book," I say with air quotes.

"Is that what you mean about the analogies?" he asks.

"Yeah. Jake said he's only a stop along the way—not my final destination. Then some bullshit about horizons and illusions."

Wes stiffens on his stool.

"The part that hurt me most was when he insinuated that I'm gonna run into Connor's arms." Tears stream down my cheeks. "He said he broke me in for him. I'm ready to ride with the big dogs now."

Lena curls her lip. "I'm still so fucking pissed at him for saying that. It was a low blow."

I nod. "It really was. Makes me cry every time I think about it. I don't want Connor. I'm in love with Jake, even though he was mean to me. I saved myself—" *Fuck.* "Anyway, I hope you two are hungry."

Wes grips my wrist. "Are you saying Jake was your first?"

I flush and look at my hands. "Yes."

"Are you *serious*? What about all your boyfriends?"

"I never let them touch me."

"Seriously?"

I narrow my eyes. "I take it you heard the rumors too?"

He looks away instead of answering.

"Yeah. I kinda figured. Just so you know, they were *all* lies. I don't feel like getting into it right now. Ask Reed if you want the whole story." I crack my aching knuckles. "Anyway, after Lucas pulled his stunt, as soon as a guy pressured me for a fuck, I kicked him to the curb. Like I explained to Reed, that's why there were so many of them. They all wanted to fuck." I wipe my cheeks. "I held out for the only one I've ever wanted. I've loved Jake since I was a little girl. I knew he'd be mine five years ago when I finally had the courage to do something about it. He still needed some convincing. I took this internship over a similar one back home because I wanted to be close to him. I love him, Wes. He's the only man I've ever loved."

Wes clenches his jaw. "Does Jake know that?"

"He knows." I brush tears away. "And before you go all caveman on him, he did not pressure me for sex."

"Isla, this is my fault," Wes whispers. "I said something to Jake that night . . . something that clearly fucked with his head."

"What're you talking about?"

He rubs both hands over his face. "I told him those things. I put those ideas in his head."

I wave him off. "Don't blame yourself—"

"He used *my* fucking words, Isla. He told me he'd love you till the day he died, and you know what I said to him?"

"What?" I whisper, my heart sinking.

"I said, 'You're a temporary fix, a stop along the way. You're ready to settle, start new chapters in life, but she's not there yet—you're not her final destination.'" He holds his face in his hands, massaging circles on his temples. "I told him you two are opposites—like earth and sky. Then he said something about them meeting on the horizon, and I told him the horizon's an illusion."

"Jesus Christ," Lena mutters. "No wonder he freaked out. He's probably been obsessing over every little word."

Wes meets my gaze. "I'm so fucking sorry, Isla. This is absolutely my fault. I scared him, so he pushed you away. I didn't know you loved him. I didn't know you saved yourself for him. I assumed he was your crush of the moment. I figured you'd be done with him soon enough, then drop him and move on like you did with all the other blokes. *I* warned him away from you. I told him you'd move back home after your internship and forget all about him. I was worried you'd destroy him . . . not the other way around."

"What the fuck is wrong with you?" My voice breaks on a sob. "How could you do that to me?"

"I didn't want to see him get hurt."

"You threw a fucking hammer at him!" I shriek.

"We went over this. I thought you were being raped, for fuck's sake. I didn't see Bennett's face until after I threw the hammer. I'm sorry, but I reacted on instinct when I found you that way. I didn't expect to see—" He swallows tightly. "You two having sex."

"Well, it wouldn't have happened if you didn't pop in unannounced."

"Trust me, it won't happen again. Lesson learned. I'm sorry for blowing up at you guys on Christmas. All I could think about was you as a little kid and I wanted to beat the shit out of him for touching you. When we talked, he made it clear he felt nothing sexual toward you until after you were eighteen. And I'm sorry for what I said to Jake that night. I didn't want you two together because I was afraid you'd break his heart. You're so young. You have your whole life ahead of you. With everything you've been through, I didn't think you'd wanna be tied down. I was an asshole for assuming I knew what you wanted." Wes squeezes his eyes shut. "I caused this. I told him you'd wreck him. He made it happen."

"What about *my* heart, Wes?" I whisper. "All this time, I thought you were different from Reed. Turns out, you thought I was a slut too. Pity on the Emerson boys with that slutty little sister of theirs. God forbid she tarnish their reputations."

Wes grips my shoulders. "That's not true."

"But you bought into the stories about me—just like Reed—and you assumed I wasn't capable of a serious relationship. You projected your beliefs onto Jake, and he believed your stories. Looks like I'm not worthy of faith from the men in my life. I wonder what Dad thinks of me. Should I ring all our uncles?"

"Isla, I'm sorr—"

"I gave Jake all of me and he pushed me away. He wrecked me." Tears stream down my cheeks in rivers. "He broke my heart."

Wes's eyes water. "I'll talk to Bennett and fix this for you."

"No." I hold up my hand. "You've done enough. Jake needs to be the one who fixes our relationship. I can't be treated like shit every time his anxiety spirals out of control. More importantly, he needs to fix *himself*, instead of being so fucking self-destructive. He's not well, Wes."

"Whaddya mean?"

"He stopped his meds and shut everyone out—me, his mum, his doctor. Everyone except Jesse."

"I didn't know it was that bad." Wes drops his gaze to his feet.

"Jesse said Jake wasn't eating or sleeping, and he was all strung out on caffeine. His hands are a chapped, bloody mess. He's too busy being ashamed of his mental illness to get the help he needs. I told him I'd be there for him, but he didn't believe in my love enough to let me. Instead, he allowed your words to feed his anxiety, then used his pain as a weapon against me."

"I'm so sorry," he whispers.

"I deserve someone who has faith in *me*, who believes in my words and actions. Someone who won't hurt me because he's scared and hurting. Someone who gives me their all because they know I'm worth the risk. What good is having wings when nobody thinks you can fly?" I point my finger at Wes. "I won't be caged by the lies people tell themselves about me. I know my truth—if others can't be bothered to figure it out, that's their loss. All this time I've been waiting for a place to land, but I've never even left the ground. Maybe I don't have wings after all."

Lena takes my hand in hers and squeezes tightly. "Isla, I hear everything you're saying, and I respect your right to vent, but there's something you need to keep in mind. Jake has a mental illness. He needs a *medical* intervention. Namely, therapy and meds. I know his behavior hurt you, but you have to remember the clinical part of all this."

"Whaddya mean?"

"I'll give you a nursing analogy. Suppose he'd gotten into a car accident and—God forbid—suffered a brain injury. Depending on the trauma's location, it could have behavioral effects. It's common for these patients to not act like themselves. They might even be mean or combative. As nurses, we can't hold them responsible for things they say or how they behave, because we know there's a root cause. Same goes for Jake. Yes, he hurt you, but it isn't entirely his fault. Just like he's adapted to you having lupus, you need to make accommodations for his illness."

"She's right." Wes wraps his arm around Lena. "You can't hold him accountable for something he can't control."

"I know."

"Bennett loves you, Isla. I'm sorry my interference put doubts in his head." He tips my chin up to meet his gaze. "But I'd be willing to bet my life there are no doubts in his heart."

CHAPTER 53

Jake

Mood: "My December" by Linkin Park

"Too bright." I burrow beneath the blankets when Jesse flicks on my bedroom light. "Make it stop."

It's my fourth migraine this week.

Totally self-induced. I know my triggers, and I pulled them all at once. At least I haven't puked during this one. Yet.

"Sorry." He turns off the light. "Someone's here to see you."

My heart leaps. "Who?"

"I'll give you a hint. Meddlesome as fuck and doesn't take 'no' for an answer."

"Don't wanna see him."

Jesse sighs heavily. "Did you miss the second half of my hint?"

"No. I heard you. Tell him to fuck off."

"Just wanna talk, mate."

Oh great, he's in my fucking room.

"Got a migraine. Leave me the fuck alone." The mattress dips by my feet. "Get off my bed."

Wes's sigh and the telltale click of my nightstand lamp reach my ears. "I'm sorry."

I wedge my head beneath my pillows. "Great. Now leave."

"Not until you hear me out."

"Emerson, I feel like someone's beating my skull with a fucking sledge-hammer. I've got an ice pick in my eyeballs. The last thing I need is to add your voice to the mix."

"Then I'll make it quick."

"You're unbelievable," I mutter into my mattress.

"Good. I want you to *unbelieve* everything I said to you on Christmas. All of it. I was wrong, Jake. I talked to Isla. She'd kill me if she knew I was here, but I don't care—I need to fix the mess I created."

"Not fixable."

"I was operating under false assumptions, mate. Everything I said was a crock of shit."

"Most of what leaves your mouth is."

He clamps a giant paw on my ankle. "Listen to me. I didn't know, okay? I didn't know she loved you—I thought you were her crush of the moment. Nothing I said on Christmas applies. I was wrong. She told me she saved herself for you. Now she's heartbroken because you bought into stupid shit I said in the heat of anger. I know how you operate, Jake. You let it seep into your brain and fester."

I give him a thumbs-up and burrow deeper into my bed. "You can leave now. Hit the light on the way out."

Wes releases my ankle and stands. "I'll say it again—I was wrong and I'm really fucking sorry. Don't let my ignorance cause you both pain. You can continue to hate me if that's whatcha feel like doing, but don't break my sister's heart. Isla deserves better than that. She felt you were worth waiting for, so I suggest you live up to it."

I pace my living room. It's Tuesday night, which means Isla is at her self-de-fense class with Lena. *And Connor.* I beat back the jealousy and rehash what I plan to say when Lena drops her off.

Jesse dozes on the couch beneath the blue blanket Isla made him—no doubt exhausted from listening to me all day. He's the best friend a man could ever have. I don't know where I'd be without him.

Probably dead on a bathroom floor from chemical asphyxiation.

The rust is still there.

Jesse told me he'd give me a dollar for every day I let it linger. I'm seventeen dollars richer. I don't want or need his money, but it's helpful to get visual reinforcement. My goal is to make it a month. I honestly don't know if I can do it. Every day is a struggle. I'm proud I made it this far.

He took all my cleaning stuff and locked it in the guest room. The bastard is holding my vacuum hostage. And the steam mop. My Swiffer. All the Magic Erasers. He's got a fucking janitor's closet up there. Little does he know I hid the almond-scented floor cleaner I found at Target. He's not getting that.

I'm losing my fucking mind. I don't understand where the dust comes from. I purposely don't have carpets. Earlier, he caught me cleaning smudges off the fridge and literally snatched the cloth from my hand. Without my go-to coping mechanism, I've turned to pacing.

But at least I stopped counting my steps.

The twice-weekly appointments with Dr. Ortiz have helped. As does the Xanax, but I don't want to become dependent on it. Without cleaning to occupy me, I need something better than a chemical coping mechanism when the obsessive thoughts kick in. I've written a few songs, so I guess that's productive.

A car pulls up outside, and I discreetly peek through the blinds. Isla emerges from the passenger side of an unfamiliar vehicle and heads for her front door. It's not Lena's car. Squinting, I try to make out the driver. Suddenly, the door pops open, and a man climbs out.

Connor.

My heart lands at my feet as the voices add their two cents.

He's at her house. They're together now.

He's going inside.

He'll put his hands on her. Kiss her. Fuck her.

My stomach bottoms out. Bile rises in my throat.

Connor says something to Isla, which stops her in her tracks. He opens the car's back door, pulls out a bag, and jogs up the front stoop. He hands it over, and they talk for a few minutes before he leaves.

Down the street, his taillights slowly fade from view. I release the breath I've been holding.

"Why are you still standing there?" Jesse's voice makes me jump.

I turn to face him. "Oh, I dunno. Maybe because Connor is the one who left her on the doorstep?"

"And your point is . . .?" He's standing by the couch with his arms crossed over his chest. "Think about everything Dr. Ortiz said in your session today. Did you even try to use any of the techniques?"

"Don't you see it, dude? She went running to him."

Jesse marches over. "*You* pushed her into his arms."

"She was already headed there," I mutter.

He punches me.

Hard.

"What the hell was that for?" I sputter, holding my throbbing shoulder. He's never once hit me during our almost thirty years of friendship.

"Wake the fuck up!" he bellows. "You did this to yourself! Wes planted the seed, but you fucking watered it. You allowed yourself to believe the stories. *You* made it a self-fulfilling prophecy. He told you she'd leave, so you took the fucking initiative and made it happen. I get that you're sick, but own up to your actions, man. You've gotta be stronger than the voices in your head. Use the tools Ortiz has given you. Fucking fight them." He grips my shoulders and roughly shakes me. "Isla is the best thing that ever happened to you. She brought you to life and made you a better man. You broke her heart in return." He shoves me toward the front door. "Now go over there and fix it."

She'll never let you back in.

"I dunno if I can. Or if she'll let me."

"Well, you'd better fucking try." Jesse advances on me, blinking rapidly. "Listen to me right now, Jake. Listen and fucking hear me. I lost Hannah. Cancer took her from me, and I will never get her back. She was the love of my life. My best friend. My wife and partner. She was my *everything*."

"I know, man."

Tears spill from his eyes. "Losing her wasn't my choice. I will never recover from this pain. Isla is your Hannah. Your once in a lifetime. Except, you *chose* to push her away. And you're choosing to surrender to your anxiety." He swipes at his cheeks. "I'm angry because I'll never get my wife back, and I watched you throw away the woman you love."

"I didn't throw—"

"Your carelessness infuriates me." He grips the front of my shirt. "Whether or not you deserve it, you get to try again. I don't because Hannah is gone."

"Jess, I—"

"Isla is still here. Don't you fucking *dare* let her slip away."

CHAPTER 54

Isla

Internal playlist: "Monsters in Your Head" by Kari Kimmel

There's nothing like a good workout to end the day. Yawning, I hang my coat in the closet and remove my sneakers. Tonight's class was awesome. I accidentally punched Connor in the jaw, but he said my technique was perfect. I've noticed an improvement in my upper body strength and overall energy level.

There's a knock on my door.

Chuckling, I glance at my gym bag. Even after getting hit in the face, Connor thinks more clearly than me.

I pull the door open. "Now, what did I forget—"

Jake leans against the frame. "Can we talk?"

"Sure." I step aside and allow him to enter.

He wipes his feet on the mat. "How was your class?"

"Great."

He nods. "I noticed it wasn't Lena who dropped you off."

"She got stuck at work and missed tonight's class."

"So, he made a special trip to Brooklyn?"

"He was meeting up with Garrett and offered to drive me. You know, since Garrett lives a few blocks away." *Wait, why am I explaining myself?* I cock my head. "Why do you care who drops me off?"

He shrugs. "Maybe I'm jealous?"

"That's *your* issue."

"No kidding. All our issues stem from me."

I cross my arms over my chest. "Won't argue with you on that one, Jacob."

"I miss you," he whispers. "My life is dark without you in it."

"I don't have the energy for your mind games."

"I'm not playing games."

Shaking my head, I make my way into the kitchen. He follows and settles on a stool. I pour a glass of water for myself and point to him. "Never said you could sit."

He doesn't move, just stares at me. "Isla, I'm sorry."

I give him a curt nod. "Thank you."

"I fucked up and hurt you."

I slam my glass on the counter. "No, Jake. You *wrecked* me."

"I'm sorry."

"I gave myself to you. Mind, body, heart, and soul. You took *all* of me and made me believe we had a future. Did you ever really envision me at The Phoenix or was it lip service to get in my pants?"

"Isla—"

"Let me finish," I snap, marching over to him. "You asked me to love you. Made me promise not to walk away. You asked me to be there for you when it mattered. But you wouldn't let me. You shut me out and pushed me away like I'm a diseased cling-on, incapable of supporting you."

His eyes flash fire. "Don't—"

"I'm not done. Interrupt me again and I'll send you out the door. In case you misunderstood me when I said this the first time, let me make myself clear. I have *zero* interest in Connor. Yes, I agreed to the classes to appease Wes, but I am not his pawn. I didn't mention them to you right away because I didn't want to put a damper on our special night. You know, when we had sex for the first time after I'd saved myself for you." I glare at him and watch his throat bob on a swallow.

"I planned to tell you the following morning and explain my reasons, but Jesse called. You were devastated by the news of Hannah's passing. The last thing I wanted was to add to your plate, so I kept my mouth shut."

Jake nods slowly.

"I forgot about the fucking classes until the day before they started. Lena reminded me at lunch and my stomach turned when I realized I never mentioned them to you. I tried to back out, but the look on her face broke my heart. I missed Wes and figured maybe things between us would improve if I kept my word and extended the olive branch. Can you at least understand my line of thinking?"

"Yes. Your reasons make sense. At the time, I thought you purposely didn't tell me." He raises a brow. "Not for nothing, but you have a tendency to withhold necessary details, am I right?"

Shrugging, I sip my water. "That was different. And if you recall, the night before we broke up, I asked you to come over to talk. I planned to tell you about the classes. But more than that, I wanted you to explain why you were acting so cold and distant. You barely even hugged me after Christmas. Then you shut me down when I tried to be intimate. On New Year's Eve, you literally turned your back on me in bed." My lip starts to quiver as my eyes well with tears. "Do you have any idea how much that hurt me?"

"I should've never done that to you, sweetheart."

"Instead of giving me an explanation, you got moody. You kept spewing riddles and nonsense, talking crazy shit about the future." Jake opens his mouth, but I hold up a hand to silence him. "My brother told me about your confrontation, so I get it—you thought I planned to pack up and move home. Leave you in the dust or some bullshit."

"Wes asked me what would happen after your internship ended, and I couldn't give him an answer." Jake squeezes his eyes shut. "He told me how it would play out and I believed him. I panicked and fucked everything up."

"Even though *I* told you it would be a dream to work at The Phoenix? That spending my future with you was everything I've ever wanted?"

"The voices in my head are really fucking loud sometimes. Wes's words made sense to them and, therefore, me."

"He's a fucking idiot. I nearly strangled him when he told me what he said to you. For the record, I I didn't cross the ocean on a whim, and I had no plans to make it a temporary move."

"He showed up on my doorstep Sunday night." He rakes a hand through his waves. "To 'fix things' between you and me."

I roll my eyes. "Meddling prick."

He sighs. "Don't be mad. In his own fucked-up way, he was trying to help."

"He's the one who caused the problem in the first place."

Jake shakes his head. "No. *I* caused it. Wes planted the seed in my mind, but I let myself water it. Instead of coming to you for reassurance—listening to *your* voice—I let his words feed my insecurities. *I* stopped my meds. *I* avoided my psychiatrist. *I* skipped meals and stayed up all night. That was all me. The monster in my head took over, and *I* fed it. *I* pushed you away. *I* hurt you. And I will do whatever it takes to redeem myself."

"I don't know if you can," I whisper.

"Are you saying our ship has sailed?"

"I don't know if I can be what you need. When I told you I wanted to be with you, I said it with certainty. We were soulmates. Twin flames. I loved you for most of my life, so there was never a question in my mind. But now . . . that certainty has been replaced with doubt. I came to New York so we could be together, but I'm starting to think my compass was broken. Maybe my voice isn't loud enough. Going forward, I'm not sure I can trust myself to distinguish between fantasy and reality."

"What do you mean?"

"Well, I breathed life into my girlhood crush for years, but it turns out you're undeserving of the pedestal I placed you on. And yes, I realize you can't control your illness, so my expectations are on me, but what if I can't handle your reality? Maybe I'm asking for too much from you."

"You're not."

"How can you be so sure? I mean, look at us. The warm fuzzies of our sandcastle days are gone, Jake. You hurt me. Deeper than anyone else."

"Honey, I'm so sorr—"

"What if I held out for something that didn't stand a chance? Maybe I put my heart and soul into a ship that couldn't weather the storm. Now that I've felt what it's like to be shut out and lose you, I just—" My voice trembles. "I'm terrified you won't hear me over the voices in your head. So maybe I'm the one who can't weather the storm."

"I don't understand."

"I'm starting to wonder if I'm capable of holding my own with you. Maybe I don't have what it takes to handle your illness. I mean, look at me—I barely have a grasp on my own. I was so desperate to throw myself into your arms—finally be your woman—I forgot to test out my legs. I love you, Jake, but I may not be strong enough for you."

"You're the strongest woman I know." A tear rolls down Jake's cheek. "I will fix this, Isla. I promise you."

"No offense, but your promises don't hold much weight for me anymore. It would take a helluva lot more than pretty words to convince me."

He takes both of my hands in his. "I will do whatever it takes to show you we're still intact. I'll use pretty words because I can't help it. This time, I'll solidify them with actions."

"Until the next iceberg," I mutter.

"The icebergs are out there, Isla. We can't prevent stormy seas from rocking our ship, but I swear to you, I won't let anything sink us. Please don't let go of me, honey." Eyes swimming with unshed tears, he kisses the knuckles of both of my hands. "Please, let me try."

"I'll let you try to course-correct us," I squeeze his hands, "but I'm not making it easy for you." Releasing him, I cross my arms over my chest. "You've got a lotta work to do if you think you're gonna win me back."

"I'll do whatever it takes."

"We need to set some ground rules. I want to accommodate your illness, but you have to help me."

"Tell me what you need, and I'll make it happen."

"I won't hold you accountable for what you can't control, but I *will* draw the line at self-sabotage. No more skipped appointments. No stopping your meds."

He presses a hand to his chest. "Won't happen again."

"You'll work on your eating and sleeping patterns too."

"I'll try."

"Most of all, you can't shut me out. You've gotta let me in your head, so I understand where you're coming from when you start spiraling. I'm not trying to run your life, but I have a right to know if you're keeping your appointments and taking your meds. Don't keep me in the dark. It isn't fair."

"I'll link you to my Google calendar so you can see my appointments. I'll have the pharmacy add your cell number to my profile for refill text notifications. Would that help?"

"Yes. Thank you."

He rubs his jaw. "If you're open to the idea, maybe you can come to one of my therapy sessions? Or several?"

"Of course I'm open to the idea. I want to be there for you."

"I'll schedule a joint session with Dr. Ortiz. She wants to meet you." He peers into my eyes. "I won't shut you out again, honey."

He leans in for a kiss, but I stop him with a hand on his chest. "You need to earn back my kisses. We aren't there yet."

A smirk tugs at the corners of his lips. "I'll earn them. What are you doing on Valentine's Day? Come to my show."

"I've got a date."

His face falls. "With whom?"

"Not that it's any of your business, but I'll be spending Valentine's Day with Lena."

He cocks his head. "Won't she have plans with Wes?"

"If you two weren't being pigheaded arseholes and ignoring each other, you'd know that he starts filming his new movie next week. He'll be in Chicago for a few months. Lena's bummed he's leaving, so I'm gonna cook us a nice dinner. Then we'll watch rom-coms and eat chocolate."

He smiles a true Jake smile, and the warmth reaches his eyes. "Will you consider watching the show on TV? I'd love for you to hear the new songs I worked on with Austin."

I shrug. "Maybe."

"Would you make it a 'yes' if I told you I wrote one about you?"

"I already know you wrote songs for me."

Jake strokes the side of my face. "It's a new one."

I smirk. "Yeah, I'll consider it. I'll consider acknowledging your birthday sometime in the future as well."

"You watching my performance is the only gift I need."

CHAPTER 55

Jake

Valentine's Day

Mood: "Without Fear" by Dermot Kennedy

I've never been this nervous before a show—or for anything—in my whole life. I need everything to go as planned since I know Isla will be watching my performance.

Austin raises a brow at me. "Would you please stop pacin' and sit? You're makin' me nervous."

"Sorry, Memphis." I chug a bottle of water.

"You better quit drinkin' before you gotta piss again."

I twist the cap back on. "Right. Good call."

"You need to relax. We know these songs like the backs of our hands, and we've been rehearsin' your special finale for three days."

When I told Austin my plans to win Isla back, he was all in. Supportive and enthusiastic like always.

"I know, but she's watching it tonight."

Austin grins. "I guess it's a good thing she won't be sittin' in the front row, makin' you all nervous and shit."

He's right. I'd probably forget how to play the piano if I looked out and saw those big, blue eyes staring back at me.

I clap his shoulder. "Good point. I'd be fucked."

"How have things been?" He tightens a guitar string. "You win her back yet?"

"Getting there. She actually let me hug her when I dropped off flowers yesterday."

Purple roses, lilacs, and plum-colored calla lilies. I had the florist put them in a special vase I'd purchased from the woman who will be teaching pottery classes at The Phoenix.

Austin runs a hand through his sandy-colored pompadour. "You make it sound like she's rationing her affection."

"She is." I pace some more, counting my steps in my head. "She told me straight up I had to earn her kisses."

He chuckles, his baby blues flashing with approval. "She's a tough cookie."

"Isla said she wouldn't make it easy on me and she hasn't. Told me I didn't appreciate her affection when it was freely given, so now I have to earn it back." I meet his gaze. "After the way I treated her, I'm okay with that. I *should* have to prove myself."

He plucks a few strings. "I'm proud of you, man."

I snort. "Maybe wait to say that until after our finale. You know, in case I chicken out."

"You won't." He rubs his jaw and stares across the room for a moment. "There's too much at stake."

Something about his tone gives me pause. I know he mentioned Kate being upset about next year's possible tour, so maybe he's got some guilt about being here tonight.

"How's Kate feeling?"

"Uncomfortable. Crampy and swollen."

"Are you guys getting excited about the baby? Not long now."

"Yeah."

It's not like Austin to not elaborate, so I probe, "What's on your mind, Memphis?"

He meets my gaze. "Is there such a thing as prepartum depression?"

"Yeah, but I think it's called prenatal depression. Why? Is Kate okay?"

"I dunno, man. I'm sure some of the crying jags are normal, but this is all the time. She's not sleeping, and she's hardly gained any weight. I thought it would get better after the first trimester." He shakes his head slowly. "It didn't. Now she's startin' the third trimester and I'm honestly a little scared."

"Have you talked to her about it?" I ask, freshly armed with my own life lessons.

"I've tried. She can't explain why she's sad. She said she feels empty. The anxiety is insane. She keeps worryin' that she won't be a good enough mother. I know I'm preachin' to the choir here, but she worries about every little thing. Like future shit."

"What do you mean?"

"Who's going to get our daughter off the school bus? What if she doesn't make friends? What if she struggles in school? I keep tellin' her we've got plenty of time to figure it out." He rubs the back of his neck. "But it's the irritability that's killin' me. I can't do *anything* right, Jake. She's always mad about somethin'. When I try to get her to explain, she cries again. I don't know what to do anymore."

"This sounds serious, Memphis. She needs to keep her doctor in the loop." I squeeze his shoulder. "Maybe you should go with Kate to her next appointment. She may need medication."

"Yeah. I'll do that." His eyes water. He blinks a few times and clenches his jaw. "I'm tired of feelin' like an outsider in my own home. I want my old Katie back."

"I know you do. But this isn't about you, man. You've gotta be strong for Kate and get her the help she needs."

Nodding, he wipes his eyes. "Enough about me. Tonight is your night. Let's go win your lady back."

CHAPTER 56

Isla

Internal playlist: "I Won't Give Up" by Jason Mraz

Lena hands me another chocolate as we stare at the television screen, mesmerized. Jake and Austin are two of the most talented men on the planet. Austin's guitar, Jake's piano, and their phenomenal voices hold me captive.

Lena gestures to the screen. "Jake looks sexy in a suit."

"He's mine." The words leave my lips before I can stop them.

She snorts. "I see we're ready to claim him again?"

"Yeah, we're getting there. He's making the effort."

"Good. He should. You're a goddess. Mental illness aside, he needs to prove he's worthy of you," she declares with a sip of her champagne.

In the short time I've known her, Lena has become like a sister to me. After years of being forgotten by my mates back home, it's nice to have someone who "gets" me. She never isolates me when my limitations ruin our plans. Instead, she's happy to pop by with takeaway and spend time with me.

Wes needs to get his shit together and put a ring on it.

Lena squeezes my knee. "Oh, by the way, he called me today."

"Who, Jake?"

"Uh-huh." She flashes a wicked grin but doesn't elaborate.

"And?"

"They're nearing the show's finale, so you may wanna watch closely," she singsongs.

"What does that mean?"

Lena grins again. "You'll see."

I turn my attention to the screen. Jake looks gorgeous in an inky-black suit. He chose a red shirt and tie in honor of Valentine's Day, and I've decided it's my new favorite color on him. He styled his tousled chestnut waves to perfection. His decadent voice fills my ears, making me swoon.

The song ends and Austin turns to face the crowd. "As we all know, it's Valentine's Day. What better occasion to raise money for the Heart Foundation, am I right?"

The audience cheers.

"Jake and I wanna thank everyone for comin' out tonight to support this wonderful cause. To the folks at home, thank you for the donations pourin' in." He wraps his arm around Jake's shoulders. "For those of you who don't know, today is Jake's thirty-fourth birthday. Let's show him some love! We've got one more song for you, but first, I'm gonna turn it over to Jake."

Jake motions to the enthusiastic audience. "Thank you, everyone. Like Austin said, we appreciate your generosity and for spending this Valentine's Day—and my birthday—with us. As I'm sure you've noticed, the theme for tonight's show is love. We spent a lot of time in my studio working on the set list because we wanted to cover the full spectrum—love in its entirety. We sang about first loves, forever loves, forbidden loves, the first meeting, first kiss, you name it. Right?"

"But we left somethin' out. Didn't we, Jake?" Austin chimes in.

"Yeah, man. But before I get into that, I wanna see a show of hands. Who in the audience has ever been in love?"

The cameras pan through the cheering people.

"Wow, that's a lotta people," Austin exclaims. "Got another question. Since this is a special about hearts, who has ever had their heart broken?" He scans the audience. "Damn, y'all have been *wronged*. Look at all those hands in the air." Austin walks to the edge of the stage. "Okay, now here's the kicker. Is anyone in this room guilty of breaking someone's heart? C'mon now, fess up."

Jake steps forward. "I'm guilty."

Lena's head jerks in my direction. Snatching the remote, she cranks the volume.

"Jake Bennett, the King of Ballads, you mean to tell me that *you* broke somebody's heart?" Austin shakes a finger at him.

"Yes." Jake addresses the audience. "Have you ever messed up? I'm not talking about a little misstep. I mean, completely and utterly effed something up. Who's done it?" He scans the room. "I see a few of you out there who have been in my shoes. Anyway, I did exactly that. I pushed someone away when I should've pulled her closer. I took things at face value when I should've dug deeper. I made up the answers instead of asking questions. I was so damn stupid. I didn't know how wrong I was until I lost her."

"Hindsight's twenty-twenty," Austin points out.

"It really is. Anyway, I wrote this next song for her and I'm a little nervous because I know she's watching. But before I start, the producers of this show gave me some special birthday boy permission." Jake points to the screens hanging in the concert hall. "Up here, and for the people at home, on the bottom of your screen, there will be a URL for a new division of the Jake Bennett Foundation. I've partnered with the Lupus Association to raise money for medical research. It's a terrible disease that affects millions of people around the world—and the woman I love most on this planet. Please consider opening your hearts and wallets for this cause. At the end of the month, I will match every dollar raised and write them a big, fat check."

"Oh my God," I whisper, tears streaming down my cheeks.

Lena wipes her eyes. "I told you."

Jake holds up his hand. "Wait a minute, I can do better. Do you think you guys can help me? I won't match your donation, I'll *double* it."

A sob escapes my chest. Lena wraps her arm around me.

"This is a song about winning back the love of your life after you royally effed up and broke her heart." The audience erupts in cheers and Jake looks directly at the cameras. "It's called 'Place to Land.' This one's for you, Sprite." He makes his way to the piano and takes a seat on the bench. His fingertips float over the keys, producing a haunting melody. Then he starts to sing.

Never knew I was flying, until I fell.
Didn't know I had heaven, 'til I got hell.

So terrified to cage you, I pushed you away.
Desperate to keep you, but I didn't stay.

Now I am falling, but I can't see the ground.
Don't know when I'll get there, but I'm coming down.

What if I told you I'm sorry? What if I begged you to stay?
So, please, will you listen, my darling, when I tell you it'll all be okay?

If I reach out, will you give me your hand?
When I fall, will you catch me, be my place to land?

You're burning brighter, flying higher each day.
You lighten my darkness, keep my demons at bay.

You're everything I've wished for; on your wings I can fly.
You lift me from shadows, your colors paint my sky.

Now I am flying because you're around.
Not sure where we're heading, but I know I've been found.
What's on the horizon? No one can say.
But as long as I'm with you, we'll find our way.

What if I told you I love you?
That my feelings grow deeper each day.
What if I need you to guide me?
Would you show me the way?
If I touch down will you be there?
For the rest of our days?

I'll be yours if you let me, just take my hand.
All I ask in return, is for you to be my place to land.

I wanna give you forever, my dove. Please understand.
Let's fold our wings together, my love. Make our own place to land.

Jake finishes the song, rises from the piano, and takes a bow. The audience gives him a standing ovation.

Austin walks over and wraps his arm around Jake's shoulders. "How did y'all like that one? Made me a li'l teary-eyed. Let's give it up for Jake's new single, 'Place to Land.'"

"Thank you." Jake faces the cameras and holds a hand over his heart. "Sprite, I love you. Rest your wings with me, honey." He turns back to the audience. "Thank you for giving me the opportunity to play that one for you, but if you don't mind, I'm going to use this platform a little bit longer. That all right?"

The audience cheers.

"What's he doing?" I ask Lena.

"Pay attention," she murmurs, wiping her eyes.

Jake walks to the front of the stage. "They say that in order to fix something, you need to be willing to admit there's a problem in the first place. This is something I've struggled with . . . pretty much my whole life." Jake looks at the cameras once more. "I, uh . . ." He clears his throat. "I want to talk about mental health."

"Oh my God." I clutch Lena's arm.

"I've spent years hiding beneath a blanket of shame. As a man—and an entertainer—I've tried to portray a certain image of myself. The problem is, not only is that exhausting, but the façade you see doesn't mirror who I really am. Tonight, I want to come clean about something that's wreaked havoc on my life and the lives of those who love me. I want to give you a glimpse of the real Jake Bennett. Spoiler alert—he's not the same guy you see on stage."

He takes a deep breath. "I suffer from crippling anxiety and depression. Specifically, a form of anxiety known as obsessive-compulsive disorder." He sips his water and continues, "I'm sure you've heard of OCD. You may even be familiar with some common OCD manifestations like cleaning, arranging, hand washing, counting, and list making. Checking and rechecking the locks. Driving back home to make sure the stove is off, even though you know it is. I mean, of *course*, it's off—you haven't cooked in days. Why? Because you're afraid to cook. What if you leave the stove on and burn down your house? Wait a minute, you live in a brownstone. What happens if your neighbor's house catches fire too—and their dog dies—because you forgot to turn off your appliances? Cue the mental barrage of disturbing images of your neighbor's charred poodle. Wait, are you absolutely *sure* the stove is off? No. You're not sure, so you drive back home to check a second time. Guess what? Now you're late for your own concert." He stares into the cameras for a few moments. "*This* is what I deal with.

"People often joke about OCD or self-diagnose it, because they like things neat or consider themselves super organized. But I'm here to tell you it goes much deeper than that. You can't imagine the time and energy consumed by obsessive thoughts and compulsive behaviors. Unless you have personal experience with OCD, or love someone who has it, you may not understand how exhausting it is to have—and hide—this illness.

"The ones closest to you will know. Anyone can see evidence of the compulsions—be it pacing, counting, chapped hands from washing. I could go on, but I'm sure you can think of many easy-to-witness ritualistic tendencies. Personally, I'm a cleaner/organizer. My home is immaculate. My walk-in closet is meticulously arranged by color, style, and sleeve length. I see some of you chuckling, and I totally get it. You're probably thinking, 'What's the harm in being neat?' Neatness and organization, by themselves, aren't bad things. But it's the stuff up here," he points to his head, "that's harder to understand. By that, I mean the obsessive thoughts. The irrational associations we make that reinforce our behaviors.

"Let me give you an example." He rubs his chin. "Suppose Goldilocks were to break into my house like she did with the three bears. Maybe she'd raid my fridge, rearrange my closet, put shirts where the pants should go, mess with my shoes, and whatnot. If I stumbled upon the scene, panic would grip me, triggering a cascade of reorganizing, cleaning, straightening—anything to regain some control. Restore my sense of normalcy. There'd be no walking away from it. The mess would eat at me, consume me, until I made it go away. It would hijack my brain to the point where I couldn't accomplish *anything* else until my stuff was back in order. Somehow, I'd convince myself that unless I put the charcoal-colored dress shirts to the left of the light gray ones, I'd be doomed."

"Jesus Christ," Lena whispers. "I had no idea it was that bad for him."

"I did. I've seen his closet."

Jake continues, "When I say doomed, I mean it to varying degrees. My brain conjures different fears or consequences depending on the day. If I don't fix my shirts, maybe I'll hit a squirrel with my car on the way to my studio. Perhaps I'll get a stomach bug and make other people sick. Even better, maybe I'll forget how to read music. Is any of this rational? Nope." He crosses his arms over his chest. "My illness doesn't care what's rational or not—or whether I recognize it as irrational. I *know* my wardrobe arrangement has no bearing on whether a squirrel runs in front of my tire. But unless I fix those shirts, I can't stop thinking about it. What if I'm so determined not to hit that squirrel while driving, that I don't see an old woman in the crosswalk? What if I hit her with my car and injure or kill her?"

The audience is silent.

"People don't really talk about the monster that grows in your mind. Believe me when I tell you, it's all-consuming," he pauses for a few beats, "and it's a monster that's easy to feed. Sometimes, it's an endless loop of fears and worries." He makes a circular motion in the air with his hand. "As I've said, it's stuff that you *know* is ridiculous and far-fetched or just plain stupid. But you can't stop thinking about it, over and over and over again. Almost like there's an army of voices carving it into stone. The anxiety hijacks your mind and derails you." He gestures to himself. "This is what happens to me. A worry or doubt pops into my head. But instead of acknowledging it and letting it drift past me, I latch on to it. I breathe life into that little worry and obsess over it until I make it a bigger monster."

Jake stares at the cameras. "*That* is how I nearly lost the love of my life. I was so terrified to lose her that I obsessed over my fears and doubts. What if she figures out I'm not worth her energy? What if someone less complicated comes along? What if I can't make her happy? What if something terrible happens to her? What if I *cause* something bad to happen to her? Don't even get me started on the images that flashed through my mind when she didn't call to tell me her flight had landed safely the last time she traveled."

"Fuck. I should've called the moment I landed. I had no idea I made him freak out."

Lena squeezes my hand. "Don't beat yourself up, chicky."

Jake points to his head. "Actually, no. I'm here, so let's talk about the imagery. Many people aren't familiar with this aspect of OCD. These visuals are graphic. Disturbing as hell. And I can't make them go away. It's like a video montage featuring my deepest, darkest fears. I'd claw my eyes out, if only that would make it stop. But it won't. The only thing that helps is keeping myself distracted. So, I clean. I arrange and rearrange. I pace my living room and count my steps, making sure I don't step on that one blue stripe on my carpet because something bad could happen if I do." He forces a dark laugh. "Ever hear that saying, 'Don't step on a crack, you'll break your mother's back'? Guess who obsessively watches his footing when he walks." He raises his hand. "Yep. That'd be me."

"Jesus, fuck," Lena whispers.

Jake crosses his arms. "So, while this is happening, I try to talk myself out of it. Rationalize what I'm feeling and focus on the stuff that makes sense. Back to my example. Okay, so, the plane landed. I know because I checked twice. Then where is she? I'll tell you the real answer—she was exhausted and jetlagged. Calling me slipped her mind, and since she has lupus, she desperately needed her rest. Makes total sense, right? Meanwhile, anxiety painted an entirely different picture. What if there was an accident? Suddenly I could see her trapped in a mangled vehicle. What if she was kidnapped? Was she tied up in a warehouse somewhere? My brain conjured images of her bound and gagged, covered in blood." He squeezes his eyes shut. "What if she needs me and I can't help her? What if? What if? What if?"

He shakes his head and stares out at the audience for a moment before speaking. "Once I knew she was safe, I felt like a fool for my anxiety—like someone draped that thick blanket of shame over my shoulders again. That someone was me. Because I knew I was irrational. Yet I couldn't stop. Meanwhile, my love had no idea about the extent of my battle. She didn't hear the what-ifs or see the sick slideshow in my head. Why? Because I didn't tell her. I hid behind my shame and allowed myself to spiral out of control. This happened over and over again, until the situation came to a head. I made the fear of losing her a self-fulfilling prophecy. I fed my monster and used it as a weapon."

I squeeze Lena's arm tighter and swipe at the tears running down my cheeks.

"Instead of asking for help, I retreated within myself. I pushed away the people who love me. I stopped taking my antidepressants and anti-anxiety medicine, avoided my psychiatrist, and developed unhealthy eating and sleep patterns. Why? Because I'm so used to feeding my monster that it's become second nature. I'm so used to hiding what I deal with, out of fear of being judged, that I let it fester." He thumps a hand on his chest. "I'm done with that shit. I'm so damn tired of letting my anxiety win. It's time to starve the monster."

People climb to their feet as the audience cheers loudly.

"The mental health stigma needs to stop and it's up to all of us to stop it. For the next thirty days, with every download of 'Place to Land,' I'll donate one hundred percent of the proceeds to the American Mental Health Foundation. Follow the hashtag #starveyourmonster on social media for more information on how you can help support those suffering from mental illness. Let's unite, build each other up, and fight this."

He holds his hand over his heart. "For anyone out there who's suffering, know that you are not alone. Let me say it louder for the people in the back. You are *not* alone. I see you. I feel you. Don't make my mistakes. Don't be a prisoner of your own thoughts. Learn from me and get help. Don't stop your meds. Pull the people you love closer. Most of all, don't feed your monster. Grab it by the throat and starve that bastard with everything you've got."

Jake holds both hands over his heart as the audience gives him a five-minute standing ovation. When the applause winds down, he thanks them and bows. The credits start to roll as he and Austin disappear backstage.

I can feel Lena's eyes glued to my face. I meet her gaze. We both have tears, snot, and smiles that stretch from ear to ear.

She wraps her arms around me, squeezing me tightly. "I'm so proud of him."

"Me too, and I'm going to marry him as soon as fucking possible," I declare on a sob. "Lena, I love him so much."

"I know, sweetie. He loves you too." She wipes her cheeks, shaking her head in wonder. "Look at him go. He got up there, professed his love, and came clean about his struggles in front of the whole friggin world. If that's not bravery, I don't know what is."

"He's an inspiration," I whisper.

"You know what this means, right?"

"What?" I ask, blowing my nose.

Lena shimmies her hips in a seated mini-salsa dance. "Girl, you're gonna have some superhot, Valentine's, birthday, make-up sex." She flutters her wet lashes. "Trust me, Valentine's sex is hot, but birthday sex is even better than make-up sex, and you're getting it served as a trifecta fuckery combination platter."

Flushing, I erupt into a fit of laughter. "How about I let him kiss me first?"

"Kiss first," she wags her brows, "then copious hot sex."

"Is make-up sex *really* all it's cracked up to be?"

Lena grins. "Why do you think I pick so many fights with Wes?"

"Brother donger." I plug my ears. "Say no more."

She loves to tease me about Wes. Thankfully, she doesn't divulge anything too dirty, or I'd totally barf. There's a reason I don't watch my brother's movies. Last thing I need is the image of his arse cheeks burned into my brain. Lena filters out the sexy parts of her stories, substituting "and then we . . . *you know* . . ." for all things sex related. I, on the other hand, tell her everything. Like Cora, she's my soul friend. I can't believe how fortunate I am to have women like them in my life.

She eyes me. "Hey, I meant to ask this the other day. Did you ever get your period?"

"Yeah, it came, but it was oddly light. More like spotting, which was strange for me. Honestly, between the lupus flare and being heartbroken, my whole body's been in turmoil."

"Did you mention it to Jake? I know he was concerned after your sexalicious studio symphony session."

Lena has a thing for alliterations. Frenzied forest fuckery is probably my favorite of hers—even though it's in relation to my brother.

"I sent him a text when it came."

"I bet he was relieved."

I shrug. "He never replied, so who knows."

"Well, I'm glad you're seeing Dr. Beer next week for the IUD consultation. Trust me, it's way more convenient than having to remember to take pills or use a condom. This way you two can romp around whenever you want and not have to worry." She glances at the clock and stands. "I'm gonna head home so you can pounce when Jake gets here."

I peer through the blinds and frown. No sign of Jake's car. I glance at the clock. His show ended three hours ago—he should be home by now. Deciding to wait for him at his place, I slip my snow boots on and trudge across the street.

Jesse opens the front door before I can knock. "I was just coming to get you. Did Jake call?"

"No. Why?" I check my pockets. "Shit. I left my phone at home. Is he all right?"

"He's fine, but his mom had a heart attack."

My hand flies up to cover my mouth. "Oh my God! When?"

"A few hours ago. He sent me a weird text, then all my calls went to voicemail. I finally got ahold of him five minutes ago. He said he was calling you."

"Where is he?"

"On a plane to Myrtle Beach."

"Is his mum okay?"

Jesse shakes his head. "Donna's in the intensive care unit . . . She might not make it through the night. Jake's a mess. I'm going down there." He eyes me intently. "You coming?"

"Yes."

"Good. I'll book our flight. Run home and pack a bag. Don't forget your medicine."

CHAPTER 57

Jake

Myrtle Beach, South Carolina

Mood: "Unsteady" by X Ambassadors

Seven thousand, six hundred and ninety-four. That's when I stopped counting the beeps. The ventilator's whoosh echoes in my brain. While I'm grateful to the machines keeping my mother alive, I may actually go insane.

Seated in a chair at her bedside, I hold one of her hands, praying she'll squeeze it back.

Myocardial infarction.

Happy fucking birthday to me. The irony of Mom having a heart attack on Valentine's Day turns my stomach. Even worse, it happened while I performed at a benefit concert for the Heart Foundation. What are the odds? The producers didn't tell me until I went backstage after the show.

I can't lose my mom—she's the only family I have left. My eyes fill with tears again. I'm not a crier, but it feels like I've cried for a month straight. When I think about it, I have.

"Honey, I'm home." The familiar voice from the doorway makes me turn my head.

Jesse.

Standing, I blink a few times to make sure I'm not hallucinating. "Jess, what are you doing here?"

"I missed you." He walks over and wraps me in a hug. "C'mon, man, you honestly thought I'd let you go through this alone?"

"Thank you for being here," I whisper, dampening his shirt with my tears. "I love you, man."

"Love you too." Jesse releases me and claps my back. "Hope you don't mind, but I brought a stowaway."

"Huh?"

"Hello, Jacob." To my utter shock, Isla enters the room carrying a tray of coffees and a paper bag. Dressed in jeans and my Brooklyn sweatshirt, she's like a walking version of home. She tied her golden-brown waves in a loose bun, but wind and travel released wispy face-framing tendrils. Makeup free, her dewy, porcelain skin reminds me of the sun peeking over the horizon. She's a new dawn.

A fresh start.

Her vivid cobalt eyes shine with love, and she's never been more beautiful.

She smiles, and my heart jumps into my throat. "They didn't have turkey, so I gotcha a roast beef sandwich."

"You came," I choke the words out.

"Of course I came." She sets the bag, our coffees, and her purse on a tray table and wraps her arms around me. "I love you, Jacob."

"Oh, Isla . . ." Embracing her, I bury my face in her neck. I can't breathe through the wave of emotion that slams me. "I love you so much."

Isla softly strokes my hair. "I promised to be there when it matters, didn't I?"

I tighten my arms around her. "Yes."

"Look at me, Jacob." She tips my chin to face her. "I'm ready to fold my wings and land with you." Interlacing our hands, she lifts them to her lips and kisses each of my knuckles. "I'm here and I'm not going anywhere. Not today, not ever. You are my final stop. My destination. Your song blew my mind, and I am so fucking proud of you for baring your soul like that. I've never loved you more than I do right now."

Pulling our entwined hands to my lips, I kiss Isla's knuckles like she did to mine. "Sweetheart, you're my once in a lifetime. I promise I'll be the man worth waiting for."

CHAPTER 58

Jake

Mood: "Play Me" by Josh Groban

Isla nudges me awake. Groggy and stiff from sleeping in a chair, I rub a fist over my stubbled face. It's my second day sitting vigil in the hospital. I'm in desperate need of a shower and a shave.

"Jacob Warren Bennett, please tell me you aren't growing a goatee." My mother's strained voice reaches my ears.

I jump to my feet and rush to her bedside. "Mom! You're awake! Are you all right? How long was I asleep?"

They removed her ventilator yesterday, but she still hadn't come to. I've been torn between clinging to a shred of hope and preparing myself for the worst-case scenario of a lifelong coma.

"She's been awake for a couple of hours. Her throat's a bit sore, which is why she sounds hoarse," Isla explains, appearing at my side. "I told your mum I'd be her spokeswoman."

"How come no one woke me?"

"We wanted to letcha sleep," she murmurs. "I'm surprised you didn't hear us chatting. Jesse went to get brekkie."

Fresh tears spring to my eyes. "Mom, I love you so much. I can't tell you how relieved I am."

"I know, sweetie. Me too. It was really freaking scary. Thankfully, my friend Wanda was with me when I collapsed. She called an ambulance. The doctors think I'm gonna be okay. They'll keep me here for a while, but they expect a full recovery after I go through cardiac rehab. I fractured my hip when I fell. It's a bad one, so I'll need a total hip replacement too."

"I want you to come to New York for that. Come stay with me, Mom. I'll take you to all your doctor appointments or wherever you want to go."

"We'll talk more about it later, honey." She squeezes my hand. "You already have enough going on without having me in your hair."

"Yeah, but I can't have you this far away and be worried all the time. My brain can't handle it."

A sad expression crosses her features. As my mother, she's witnessed more than her share of my darkness. "I wish you wouldn't worry so much."

"We both know that's a lost cause. Not for nothing, but I wasn't happy with you moving south in the first place. Now, this happened. You belong in New York. Please come stay with me for a while."

"I'll think about it."

Jesse enters the room and hands me a sausage, egg, and cheese croissant, then gives Isla a to-go cup. "Here's your smoothie, my dear." He smiles at me. "Bet you were surprised when you woke up."

"I'm shocked. The doctors told me it didn't look good."

Mom gives a raspy chuckle. "Jacob, how many times do I have to tell you not to believe everything you hear? I'm not checking out of this life until I've checked everything off my bucket list. There's still *a lot* on there. And I'm sure as shit not being taken out on my baby's birthday. Not for nothing, but Satan can stuff it. Jesse and Isla, thank you for being here for my son. He thinks the world of you both."

"We love him, Mrs. Bennett," Isla says.

"Please call me Donna from here on out." The fondness in Mom's gaze tells me Isla won her over the moment they met. "We're family."

"All right, will do." Isla's phone chimes with a text. She reads it, then straightens and clears her throat. "Jacob, I need to ask you something."

"Sure. What is it, Sprite?"

She points to the chairs behind us. "Sit."

I settle and raise a brow at her. "Is everything all right?"

"More than all right, actually." Isla smiles and gestures to Mom and Jesse. "We discussed some things while you were sleeping. Anyway, I ran an idea past them, and they were both on board, so I figured I'd mention it to you."

I glance at the smiling faces in the room. "Okay . . ."

Jesse pulls out his phone as she takes my hand. "You know I love you, right?"

"Yes, but you're making me nervous. What do you need to ask me?" I sip my water and raise an eyebrow at her.

Isla sinks to one knee in front of me. "Marry me, Jacob."

My mouth drops open, ice water trickling down my chin and soaking my shirt. "Wait, are you *proposing* to me?"

Isla laughs and turns to my mom. "Has he always been this quick on the uptake?"

"No, honey. He's dense on occasion."

"You can't propose," I sputter, opening and closing my mouth like a fucking loose-lipped flounder. "I'm supposed to ask you."

Jesse chuckles. "Looks like she just did, dude." He's still holding his phone, likely getting video of my reaction.

"I planned to ask you this summer." I rake my fingers through my hair. "I don't even have a ring—"

Isla grabs my hands. "I don't want a ring or a big wedding. I don't give a damn about white dresses either. I want *you*, Jake. I want you to be my husband. My forever."

"I *am* yours, honey. I always will be. Of course I want to marry you, but before I give you an official answer, I need to talk to some people first." I pull her into the chair beside me.

"My parents love you."

"Not referring to your parents, Sprite." I stroke her cheek. "But I will speak to them too."

"You're worried about my brothers?"

"Not both of them, but yeah. If we're going to do this, we're doing it right. I won't fuck this up. You're too important to me. I'm going to get you a ring and ask you properly. Before all that, I need to talk to your parents and brothers. Make my intentions clear and whatnot."

Isla grins. "How about you start the process right now? You can come in, ya big brute."

"G'day, everyone." Wes appears in the doorway, and I nearly pass the fuck out. "I heard from a small imp that Donna was in the hospital, so I put my filming on hold for a couple days and flew in." He approaches Mom's bedside and kisses her on the cheek. "How're ya holding up? You gave us quite the scare."

Mom smiles. "Scared me too. I've got a long road to recovery, but I'm doing better. Thank you for coming, Wes."

"Of course. Memphis is on his way too." He pins me with his gaze. "Wouldn't let our best mate go at this alone." He gestures to Isla. "Well? Are ya gonna answer her?"

I slowly rise from the chair. "Huh?"

"Pretty sure I eavesdropped a marriage proposal."

I open and close my mouth. If you could bottle stupefaction, it's pouring off me right now. Someone should open a goddamn distillery.

Wes steps closer to me. "Would it help if I gave you my blessing?"

I search his face. "What are you saying?"

"Duh, mate. I'm givin' ya my blessing." With that, he wraps me in a rib-crushing hug. "I miss you. So fucking much."

"I miss you too, man." I hug him back, never so happy to hug another man in my life. "But wait, are you *serious*?" I motion to myself and Isla.

"Does a bear shit in the woods? Yeah, I'm serious. After plenty of time to sort it out in my thick noggin, I finally realized I was being a dick. Jake, I'm so fucking sorry for the way I reacted. You two are perfect together, and I couldn't imagine a better man for my baby sister. I can't tell you how much your performance at the benefit moved me."

"Oh, wow. You watched?"

"Are you kidding me? Of course, I watched! The song was *phenomenal*. Beautifully written like everything you do. Not gonna lie—I shed a couple tears. Then I completely lost it and dissolved into a blubbering mess when you opened up about your illness. Donating to two causes and baring your soul like that took balls. Big ones. I'm sure you haven't been following social media, but #starveyourmonster tops the list in trending. Celebrities from all over the world are coming out about their mental health struggles." He hugs me again, then meets my gaze, his eyes watering. "I love you and I am so fucking proud of you, mate. I donated a million to the Mental Health Foundation in your name."

"Thank you. That means a lot to me."

Wes points to Isla. "Well? She asked you a question. Don't leave her hanging."

I turn toward his beautiful, radiant sister, and take her hand. "Isla Rose Emerson, my answer is *yes*."

Squealing, she leaps from her chair and throws her arms around my neck. "You're officially mine, Jacob Bennett."

"I've always been yours." I grip her chin. "But we are *un*officially engaged. It doesn't become official until I ask you. Let me give you the proposal you deserve . . ." I flash her a wink. "One worth waiting for."

She gives me a pouty lip. "How long do I need to wait for that?"

"I promise I won't make you wait another five years, sweetheart." I kiss her, half expecting Wes to punch me, but he doesn't.

Instead, he wraps his arm over my shoulder. "Welcome to the family, Bennett."

I release Isla and hug him once more. "Thank you for being here when it matters. Means the world to me."

"Always will be, mate." He flashes a huge grin. "You're an Emerson now."

"Unofficially," I correct him with a smirk.

Isla nudges him. "I think whatcha mean is *I'm* gonna be a Bennett."

He laughs. "It's one in the same at this point."

"You're right about that." She eyes me, a smile lighting up her face. "I'd be lying if I said I haven't been scrawling Isla Rose Bennett in my notebooks since I was thirteen."

Her confession warms me. "Really?"

"Oh, absolutely. I've already perfected my new signature. Isla Rose Bennett," she repeats, interlacing her fingers with mine. "Mrs. Isla Bennett."

I touch her cheek. "I love the sound of it."

"Me too, actually." Wes squeezes my shoulder. "You've always been a brother to me, Jake. I just haven't been the same for you. I'm gonna change that. Starting now."

Isla hugs Wes. "Thanks for finally seeing what I've always known."

"I'm sorry I didn't see it sooner, Imp. Congratulations on your unofficial engagement."

She turns to me and cups my face. "I am *officially* the happiest woman in the world. I've loved you since you let me decorate our sandcastles with seaweed, Jacob. You're my twin flame, and I burn brighter with you by my side. I promise to fly and land with you."

"I love you, Sprite. Thanks for being my unofficial future wifey."

Isla smiles up at me, her cheeks flushed and glowing. "Does an April wedding work for you?"

"Before we go setting any dates, we need to make our engagement official."

"You may wanna get on that, love. My patience is wearing thin." She bats her lashes. "Your thoughts on April?"

I chuckle and turn to Wes. "Told you she's persistent."

"Christ, mate. I guess you weren't kidding."

Isla flicks his earlobe. "Where do ya think I learned it from?"

He snorts. "Good luck, Bennett. You're gonna have your hands full."

She tilts my face to look into her eyes. "Answer my question."

Grinning, I kiss the tip of her nose. "Yeah, honey, that works. We can do next April."

She shakes her head. "No, *this* April. As in, a month and a half from now."

"Why the rush, Imp?" Wes asks with a chuckle. "I need time to write my speech." He nudges me. "Sorry, but I'm not singing any songs for ya. That's all Memphis. Jesse can be your best man, and I'll stand up there with you and try to behave."

Mom laughs. "You can escort me down the aisle, Wes. That can be your job. Hopefully, I'll be able to walk by then."

"You got it, Donna. If not, I'll just carry ya."

"Wait." Jesse holds up his hand. "Can I wear a garter too?"

Everyone laughs.

Isla wraps her arm around him. "You can wear whatever you want. As long as it doesn't clash with my dress." She glances at me. "Would it be all right if I wear purple?"

"Sweetheart, you can wear whatever color you want. We'll do whatever makes you happy. April is too soon, given Mom's condition, but I promise it will happen this year."

"I suppose I can live with that." She presses a kiss to my lips. "As long as you agree not to wear a gray tux."

"Like I said, whatever makes you happy."

Wes hugs me again. "Thanks for being the perfect man for my sister."

"I'm far from perfect, but I promise to always take care of her."

"Speaking of weddings," Mom eyes Wes, "when are *you* gonna put a ring on it? Not for nothing, but you oughtta get a move-on. Don't miss your chance."

Oh, Mom. Ye of little filter.

My mother is hardcore Team Lena. She fell in love with her spirit the moment they met at the airport after our return from Alaska. Mom's been asking about Lena ever since, so I feed her tidbits here and there. She was so relieved when Wes got his shit together after the gala.

Wes flashes a devious grin and meets my gaze. "Bennett, I need your help with something. It's a top-secret mission of sorts. Like a field trip, but better."

Isla gasps. "Are you gonna propose?"

"You'll have to wait and see." Mischief glitters in his gaze. "Got a lotta tricks up my sleeve."

"Oh my God!" she squeals, jumping up and down. "You'd better not be messing with me." She rushes over and grips his face. "Wesley James Emerson, if you don't marry Lena, I'll kick your arse. Better yet, Jake and I will marry her and start a commune. I need that woman in my life because she's fucking amazing. You know damn well she's the best thing that ever happened to you."

"You'd be right." Wes's smile stretches from ear to ear. "Well, Imp, it looks like we've *both* got big things on the horizon."

THE END

PLAYLIST FOR HORIZON

1) "Waiting in Vain" by Annie Lennox
2) "Speechless" by Dan + Shay
3) "Waving Through a Window" by Ben Platt
4) "Sledgehammer" by Fifth Harmony
5) "Changing Colours" by Josh Groban
6) "I Want You" by Third Eye Blind
7) "Adore You" by Miley Cyrus
8) "Wicked Game" by Chris Isaak
9) "Power Over Me" by Dermot Kennedy
10) "Sledgehammer" by Peter Gabriel
11) "Turning Tables" by Adele
12) "Let Her Go" by Passenger
13) "In My Blood" by Shawn Mendes
14) "Water Under the Bridge" by Adele
15) "Paradise" by MEDUZA & Dermot Kennedy
16) "Blow" by Ed Sheeran
17) "Follow Me" by Craig David
18) "God is a Woman" by Ariana Grande
19) "Lights On" by Shawn Mendes
20) "Lick It" by Chris Watts
21) "Feelin' Love" by Paula Cole
22) "Your Body is a Wonderland" by John Mayer
23) "Like a Virgin" by Madonna
24) "If You Could Only See" by Tonic
25) "Versions of Violence" by Alanis Morissette
26) "Demons" by Imagine Dragons
27) "Bad Reputation" by Shawn Mendes
28) "Heavy" by Linkin Park
29) "Remedy" by Adele
30) "Find Me" by Boyce Avenue
31) "The First Taste" by Fiona Apple
32) "Lost" by Dermot Kennedy
33) "Happy" by Leona Lewis

34) "First Time" by Lifehouse
35) "I Got You (I Feel Good)" by Jessie J
36) "Desert Rose" by Sting
37) "A.D.I.D.A.S. (All Day I)" by Ro James
38) "Lips On You" by Maroon 5
39) "Our First Time" by Bruno Mars
40) "Sweet Love" by 112
41) "Make It Rain" by Ed Sheeran
42) "Spectrum" by Florence + The Machine
43) "Let It Be Me" by Ray LaMontagne
44) "You Say" by Lauren Daigle
45) "Tonight" by John Legend
46) "Sweat" by Zayn
47) "Sex On Fire" by Kings of Leon
48) "Utopia" by Alanis Morissette
49) "We Can Make Love" by SoMo
50) "Closer" by Nine Inch Nails
51) "Heavy In Your Arms" by Florence + The Machine
52) "I'm A Mess" by Ed Sheeran
53) "Hear Me" by Kelly Clarkson
54) "An Evening I Will Not Forget" by Dermot Kennedy
55) "I'm Like a Bird" by Nelly Furtado
56) "Tapes" by Alanis Morissette
57) "Control" by Halsey
58) "Unwell" by Matchbox 20
59) "Rome" by Dermot Kennedy
60) "Seven Devils" by Florence + The Machine
61) "Light On" by Maggie Rogers
62) "Linger" by The Cranberries
63) "My December" by Linkin Park
64) "Monsters In Your Head" by Kari Kimmel
65) "Little Do You Know" by Alex & Sierra
66) "Without Fear" by Dermot Kennedy
67) "Unsteady" by X Ambassadors
68) "I Won't Give Up" by Jason Mraz
69) "Play Me" by Josh Groban

Thanks so much for reading my words! It means the world to me. If you enjoyed *Horizon*, please leave me a review.

Stay tuned for *Symphony*, book 4 in the Compass Series! (Coming 2023)

In the meantime, check out Garrett's story in book 1
of the Prodigy Series!
Masquerade is available now!

Please subscribe to my newsletter for updates and new releases!

Website: www.ariawyatt.com

Facebook: www.facebook.com/AriaWyattAuthor

Join my readers' group on Facebook: Aria Wyatt's Speakeasy at www. facebook.com/groups/ariawyattsspeakeasy

Instagram: www.instagram.com/ariawyatt_author

TikTok: www.tiktok.com/@ariawyattauthor

Twitter: www.twitter.com/AriaWyattAuthor

OTHER BOOKS

Compass Series:
True North
North Star
Horizon
Symphony (forthcoming)
Title TBD (forthcoming)

Busy Bean Standalone:
Afterglow

Prodigy Series
Masquerade
Prodigy (forthcoming)
Supernova (forthcoming)

Devil in the Details

Masquerade

PRODIGY SERIES

As a photojournalist, my comfort zone is behind the lens. A disengaged observer. That goes out the window when I'm forced to work with a man who makes my haven feel like a cage.

Garrett Casey is the intoxicating lead of the provocative, new Broadway production I've been assigned to cover. As a recovering alcoholic who battles demons even darker than mine, his intensity is a danger to the shell I've built around the empty woman inside me. I vow to keep the brutally gorgeous actor at arm's length, but he immediately pulls me into his orbit. I see myself every time I look into his haunted eyes. **The pain he tries so hard to hide draws me closer, making me crave the surrender I shouldn't want.**

Garrett takes a wrecking ball to my fortress, and I lack the power—or the will—to stop him. As my walls crumble around me, I realize he just might be the only man strong enough to put me back together.

When my past threatens to shatter everything we've built, the smoke and mirrors I've hidden behind are what could finally break me. A lie of omission is still a lie. **It will take more than the truth to prove our love is not a masquerade.**

Masquerade is available now!

ABOUT THE AUTHOR

Aria Wyatt is a pharmacist mom who spends the inhumane predawn hours with a cup of coffee and her laptop, gleefully indulging in her passion for romance. Her novels range in heat from steamy to scorching, and she doesn't shy away from writing flawed characters with real life issues.

She resides with her husband and two children in New York's picturesque Hudson Valley, near the Catskills and iconic Woodstock. The avid reader balances marriage, motherhood, her pharmacist career, and her romance author dream. When not writing, she dabbles in photography, using the natural beauty of the region to her advantage. She's a self-proclaimed cat lady who cannot live without coffee, chocolate, music, and books.

Author of True North and the Compass Series, Aria has a soft spot for those who are searching, yearning, and ultimately, finding. Whether on a mission to find themselves, find love, find forgiveness or solace, she believes the answer is out there somewhere.

"Journey to Love."

ACKNOWLEDGEMENTS

This book was a labor of love, and there are many folks who helped make it happen.

First and foremost, **Melissa Y.** and **Cassandra N.**, I dedicated this book to you for a reason. Lupus is a cruel bitch and I admire your strength. Thank you for helping me make Isla's character authentic. Your guidance and feedback were invaluable, and I couldn't have written *Horizon* without you.

Kristel Storm, you may not have realized this, but your daughter was also inspiration for Isla. Leah's tenacity is astounding, and it's been a joy to watch her grow. I have tremendous respect for all the kidney moms out there—especially you.

To my sister: Isla's name was set in stone long before your daughter was a twinkle in her father's eye. (I kept my mouth shut when you were naming her because it's an awesome name—a perfect fit for the cherub you birthed.) I hope this doesn't make things awkward.

A huge thanks to **Amanda Pederick** and **Rebecca Allman** at **The Picky Bitch Editing**. You two kept my Aussie authentic, and I love you for it! Your comments in my manuscript made me snort-laugh on more than one occasion.

To my editors, **Silvia Curry** and **Eve Arroyo**, thank you for everything you do. Silvia, your help with the developmental stage was amazing. Eve, as always, thanks for your eagle eye.

To my proofreaders, **Marla Esposito** at **Proofingstyle, Inc.**, **Rosa Sharon** at **My Brother's Editor**, and my dear friend and fellow author, **Alexa Gregory**, thanks for catching the small stuff.

To my beta-readers, **Amanda Madsen**, **Jennifer Liese**, **Melissa Young**, **Liz Schille**, **Aria Peyton**, **Becca L'Amour**, **Cassandra Cripps**, and **Wren Murphy**, words cannot express my appreciation. You ladies kick ass!!!

To **Stacey Blake** of **Champagne Book Design**, thank you for giving me the perfect book innards.

Wander Aguiar, as always, your photography is fabulous. **Andrew Biernat**, thanks for letting me use your handsome mug on my cover.

A huge shout-out to my publicist, **Linda Russell** of **Foreword PR & Marketing**, for being my mama bear in this industry. Your support, encouragement, and virtual handholding give me the confidence to keep going. Thank you for everything you do! Love you buckets!

To the bloggers and bookish peeps of Romancelandia, thank you for your support! Self-promo is not my jam, so your help is much appreciated. Especially those who've gone out of their way to spread the word. I see you, **Krystal Dixon**.

To my author bestie, **Kristie Wolf**, I adore you. We've got this. We're real authors.

To **Dana Fisher, Dana Kragh-Swingle, Karen Harris, Jen Liese, Krista Villielm**, and everyone else in my inner circle (y'all know who you are), thank you for believing in me.

J.G., thanks for the inspiration. Keep being you.

To my husband and children, you're everything to me.

And to my readers, thank you for connecting with my characters. I couldn't do this without you.

Much love,

www.ingramcontent.com/pod-product-compliance
Lightning Source LLC
Chambersburg PA
CBHW051528100726
47898CB00005B/1620